Also by Patrick Cave:

Blown Away

SHARP NORTH

SHARP NORTH

PATRICK CAVE

SIMON AND SCHUSTER

First published in Great Britain by Simon and Schuster UK Ltd, 2004

A CBS COMPANY

This paperback edition published in 2005 by
Simon & Schuster UK Ltd.

3 5 7 9 10 8 6 4 2

Simon & Schuster UK Ltd
Africa House
64–78 Kingsway
London WC2B 6AH

A CIP catalogue record for this book is
available from the British Library

ISBN-13: 978-0-6898-7277-8
ISBN-10: 0-6898-7277-1

Typeset by Rowland Phototypesetting Ltd
Bury St Edmunds, Suffolk
Printed and bound in Great Britain by
Cox & Wyman Ltd, Reading, Berks

ACKNOWLEDGEMENTS

This book is for my beautiful wife, who told me it was one to stick with and cried in all the right places.

I would also like to thank Caradoc King and Vicky Longley at A. P. Watt for a steep and rewarding learning curve and for their amazing support.

Finally, thanks to Venetia and Hilary, my editors, for clear, insightful guidance on how to improve things.

PART ONE

PART ONE

ONE

The girl nearly didn't find out who she was.

What she was.

The house was dim, moist, heavy with a night's breathing and the ghost of the evening meal. Mira was impatient to be out. Her ivory-pale fingers tied the laces in quick, sure movements, so that the fabric cradled her feet tightly. Somewhere in the darkness Cobb was just up, shuffling about the cooking space, making a drink for Old Sarah.

Mira paused an instant inside the door, closed her eyes, felt the warmth, the breath in her body. Then she was out, with her heart lifting. The cold met her body heat and caressed it. Clean fresh snow and rich sappy pine filled her nostrils: she could almost taste them. The clearing was as empty as she could wish. First light lay behind the eastern parade of mountains, picking out their scarred, worn outlines. Soon she would be up in that light, running the ridges, breaking the new snow.

She walked softly to one of the trees and lifted her foot to its branch, disturbing a powder of white. The muscles along the back of her thigh pulled tight and she pushed gradually down. A strand or two of hair escaped from her hat and fell across her face. She turned her head sharply to move it aside. And her eyes met other eyes.

A woman, standing amongst the tree shadows across the clearing, watching her.

The woman was not young, but held her body with

grace and confidence. Maybe she was a dream from the shadows and the pines and the snow. She didn't look right for a raider.

Then the woman was running towards her and suddenly there was sound. Two large shapes were moving fast through the trees. Mira heard the slap of snow-heavy branches on fabric and deep, urgent male voices. She took her foot lightly down from the branch and drew in breath to call out.

Best to be sure.

But she saw Gil was there too and let the breath go. Even as the woman ran to her and the shapes came from the trees – huge men in light grey that blended with the snow – Mira saw him come out from his house and move forward to intercept the strangers. He looked unworried. He would know if they should call, or fight.

The woman was almost with her. Her hair was short, but the colour of Mira's own; deep-red chestnut. Her movements were tired. She was putting out a hand, starting to speak. And then she pitched forward, rolling untidily across the snow. Behind her one of the grey giants let something fall to his side. The two came on, heavy-footed but strong. They ran past Gil and he didn't stop them, just stood watching.

Mira couldn't understand.

The woman was rolling awkwardly back to her feet, clumsy with pain, the grace gone. Mira went to help her, but the two were there first and struck the woman down again. Mira let out a shout and flung herself on a grey shape, taking him sideways and down with her slight body weight hanging on his neck.

It was hopeless. She felt a blow between her shoulder blades and all air was pushed from her body.

Now Gil *was* there. She heard his voice speaking

sharply, and a grey man was flung backwards. Gil helped her up. He looked shaken now.

The snow was red and the woman who had watched her from the trees a minute or two ago lay unmoving, slung over a grey shoulder like the carcass of a deer. Mira had the idea that Gil was speaking quietly to one of the intruders. Then they were gone, back into the tree shadows, the red-chestnut head bumping gently against a pale-grey back.

She turned to Gil. He was his normal self again.

'Did you know them? Why didn't we help the woman? Why did you let them . . .?' She felt tears of shock and anger on her face.

His eyes were gentle, concerned. 'You know about police. I have told you.'

'They were *police*, those . . .?' Mira used a word she had heard Gil himself use. A bad word.

'Yes. The woman: she was running from them. She was an offender, I am thinking.'

'But you spoke to them.'

He touched her shoulder, smiled faintly. 'I would not have them hurt you, fool Mira.'

She looked round the clearing. The snow and the almost-dawn still gave the air that other, *singing* quality. Nobody else had stirred from the houses. Nobody had heard.

'I will run now.'

Gil was not pleased. 'If you must go,' he said tightly, 'then do not go the same way as those others.' She went back to her tree and warmed the muscles once again, then set off lightly, up through the forest to the higher slopes. When the sun did appear over the low peaks she was, as she had wished, close to the first ridge. She squashed her thick fleece down into her belt pouch, and stood in her vest with the sweat tickling between her shoulder blades, looking at the community in its clearing, the long humped line of snow-covered generators following the streamway off the mountains and into the colourless sea beyond.

When she had run herself to contentment, tested her body so that the muscles trembled, she went steadily, carefully, down again, feeling the air become thicker, resin-filled. In the clearing, all seven children were out, playing a sledging game with rope and plastic sacks. Mira joined them for a few minutes, straining at the head of a rope, laughing with them as they went wrong and fell headlong, arms and legs jumbled together.

It was here, she thought, that the woman was caught and hurt.

She left the game and cast around, but the red was gone. Maybe Gil had covered it. She dug a little with her hands, wondering again about dreams. Had that woman really been over there, silently watching amongst the red trunks?

Gil was not to be seen.

She went to the stretching tree and looked across at where the stranger had stood. She imagined again the abrupt flight into the open, the hand stretched out. The lips moving.

Pat Cassidy came up to her, hung on her sleeve, and said: 'Play some more! Aye, Mira?'

She didn't answer. On the surface of the snow, down in the slight hollow near the tree roots, was the tiniest thing. A ball of paper. She bent quickly and picked it up.

'Mira?' the boy repeated.

'Aye, later Pat,' she said vaguely, turning towards her house.

TWO

For sure she could read. Better, much better than Cobb: almost as well as Gil. The words on the paper were clear to her. The meaning was not.

Except that her name was there, like a sharp blow to her stomach, and Gil's name too. The calm of the mountain fled from her in shock. The paper had come from the woman, the *offender*, a person hunted and hurt by *police*. A person she did not know, who carried Mira's name on a paper: more than her name, for her birth date was there too, and the name of the village, and Gil's name.

Four names the paper held on the one side, the left. Hers was the third, and she saw that she was also third in years. Before her came Annie Tallis, a person with forty-two years of life, then Siân Latimer, twenty-eight. After her came one that must be a baby, Adeline Beguin, almost three.

Siân Latimer's name had been covered by a line of Xs. After the names and ages came places – three strange to her – and then, on the right, the word 'watcher' and one more name.

Gil was the 'watcher' on her line.

She took the paper to the shower room with her and locked the door. For a long time, she let the water pour over her, easing the muscles, making her skin glow and sing. The sweet steam wrapped around her body and soothed her, and she hummed softly while she cleaned the sweat away. In some way the world had just moved on its axis: she should be still inside and try to see the change clearly.

She stood naked before the mirror. 'What do I know then, from this paper?' she asked the faint pink form in the steam. 'Only that Gil is *watcher*. Only that.'

But even as she stood there, newly cleansed, other shadowy possibilities crowded into her mind. A name for the woman in the trees. A meaning to the terrible Xs. And a weight of questions that held no answer.

'Och, look at you,' she said scornfully to her image. 'As well as any day, and panicking over a thing that will be explained, without doubt, when it need be.'

After all, she could ask Gil, her friend. What could be easier than that?

Old Sarah was wrapped tight in quilts and covers, ready for the first free broadcast of the day. There were oatcakes and scraps of smoked fish on a plate close by, to keep her fed and content for the whole two hours.

She nodded a disapproving, tight-lipped greeting to Mira.

'Is there anything you're needing, Sarah?'

'No, dear, nothing.'

There was a tiny warning there, a baring of teeth: Don't spoil the first moments of the broadcast. Mira shrugged. It was long indeed since her mother had been able to hurt her. She went out and across the clearing to the generator path, enjoying as ever the prickle of cold on her face. Yet the shadows and mystery were lost for this day. Yellow light spilled over the peaks and picked out strong colours; the glossy, rich clouds of green needles that shifted their snow and steamed slightly, making the forest seem restless: papery red trunks and orange lichens.

Which world was real? The sun only showed some things and hid the others. What was the thing that had happened this morning, in the singing air, her world? What would it change?

Cobb was high up the line of generators. He'd cleared the snow from the dull black casing and was balanced on the cradleway between this machine and the next, trying to free frozen bolts. Ice water roared underneath. Mira was careful to approach from a way he could see: it would not do to surprise the old man, for he scorned the safety cable with all of his thirty years' experience on these machines. Only at night or in the worst weather could he be persuaded to use it.

When he knew she was there, he edged carefully to the bank and took out his flask. They shared a drink and a bite, and, as they chewed, Cobb laid a hand on her arm. 'I am thinking that you have come up here for a reason,' he said: 'Or perhaps to be with your da, just?'

'Certainly that.' Mira smiled and took a careful bite, chewed, swallowed: 'But also to ask how I came to be with you and Old Sarah.'

Cobb's faded blue eyes met hers, questioning. He ran a squat, calloused thumb across his lips, brushing crumbs aside. 'Mira, for sure ye know the answer to this, then.'

She recited carefully: 'You wished a child, but could not. There was not the money for medicine to change this . . . and so you asked for an adoption. Me. You were surprised to have such luck.'

'Aye. That's it.' The man scooped up some snow to clean his knife.

'Why surprised?' she asked.

'Och. The place, girl: look at it! And we were poor. And you were bonny.'

Mira considered this. Being poor, did that matter to

a baby? And, anyway, Cobb was made manager of the generator station soon after her arrival.

She asked: 'Where did I come from, then, before? What sort of place?'

'Away to the South,' said the old man, with a chuckle. 'And that might be anywhere.' He waved an arm vaguely. 'Ye're not told, when ye adopt.'

With a butterfly in her tummy, she said: 'There was nothing about *police*? In the adoption.'

Cobb looked at her strangely and stood up, wiping his hands on his overalls. He went to the cradleway and started to edge back over the rushing black water.

'Police?' he called. 'What d'ye ken of police then, Mira?'

She too had to raise her voice: 'Only what Gil says. Nothing. I just was wondering about them.'

'Nay then,' he called, 'there was nothing about police.'

And he turned his attention once more to the ice-locked bolts.

Pat got his wish: there were more games, and then lessons. Mira did these with Hannah, alone with her baby since her man had carelessly fallen in the streamway, six months since. Mira sometimes wondered, but without jealousy, if Gil might not choose Hannah over her when he took a woman. There was no proof for that, just unformed instinct, and the woman's secret, soft look when Gil was there.

The lessons were her own idea. No one minded. They used the toolhouse, clearing away some half-dismantled kit, sliding and shuffling out splintery plywood crates of generator spares for seats and tables. The dim shed was cold and Mira put the lights and heaters on full. Let the audit inspector complain when he came; she wouldn't teach human blocks of ice, not when the power hummed freely from the streamway. Hannah took the three littlest ones on one side, helping them to make their numbers with her right hand, cradling her feeding baby close to her warmth with the left. For the other four, Mira told them things she had found in her ancient Encyclopaedia, which she had used to learn her reading. It was the only book in their house. In any house.

Today she'd chosen insects. (There was so much to know about everything!) 'All insects have their bones on the outside,' she told them. Pat Cassidy started clowning, pretending to be a walking skeleton. 'That's right, Pat: it's like having a hard bony skin with all the soft bits inside.' She drew a rough picture of a beetle that could make a fearsome clicking noise by mashing its still more fearsome mouthpieces together.

'Beetles are the biggest group of insects. They even have bony bits that fit over their wings to keep them safe. "Wingcases".'

Wee Joan, her eyes on the dusty window, murmured 'Like the skidoo garage.'

Then Mira had them all following Pat's lead, trying to walk or crawl like beetles. 'What does it feel like?' she asked them. 'What can you see down there on the ground? What things are you afraid of? What makes your insect-self happy?'

Eventually the lumbering beetle-children invaded the other class a few metres away, making the little ones howl with their stiff crawls and clicking mouthpieces, and lessons were abandoned. This was often the way of it.

'Is it proper teaching, do you think?' Mira asked, wrestling a crate back to the wall. And Hannah said sharply, as usual: 'How would I be knowing that? Aye, proper enough, I doubt. Ask Gil, if ye've a mind.'

But Gil teased her about giving the classes, even though he had been the one to tell her of school to start with. And now she did not think that she could ask his help again. Not until her brain had teased some sense out of that word *watcher*.

She did notice that his house was dark and empty through all the day, and that late that night, long after Sarah's last broadcast had finished, when she stood peacefully alone in the clearing under the stars, watching the tendrils of mist form amongst the trees, it was still so.

He would be working high up the line or down at the tidal barrier. He did not keep usual hours, any more than Mira herself. All was as it should be.

She cursed herself for the unwanted clenching in her stomach and went to her bed.

THREE

Raiders had come again to the mountains. The rumours were the talk of the cookhouse. Raymie had seen something – *someone* – while checking his traps.

When Mira quietly let herself in, a squabbling, gleeful debate was going on about what exactly Raymie had seen, how close the raiders were camped, how real the danger was.

'. . . tracks in the snow; fifteen men at least . . .'

'. . . an attack today or tomorrow . . .'

'. . . Raymie spoke to them, offered them supplies, told them we'd nothing else . . .'

'. . . a trap sprung but no animal there . . .'

'. . . a camp of the brutes in the next valley but one . . .'

'. . . murdered while we sleep, right enough . . .'

'. . . smoke from their cooking fires . . .'

'. . . great monsters in grey . . .'

'. . . that's how Hannah's Martin went, I tell you: och, he never fell in any stream . . .'

The women's eyes shone with delight and terror, but Evelyn, smallest of all of them, fiery, banged her great stirring spoon on the worktop and said: 'Enough!'

Her sharp gaze went round them scornfully.

'So!' The glare softened. 'Today the daymeal is to be broth and tatties and cheese. And I am thinking now that ye all know these solid, good things better than Raymie could pick out a raider in an empty room, drunk or sober.' (Smiles all around at that.) 'So, let us do what we are here to do before we talk such rubbish.'

Mira, smiling with the others, took an apron from the shelf, then went to the dim, dusty storeroom for potatoes, wrinkled and shrunken and past their best, but sweet and smoky when baked on the charcoal. She doubted any raider would be a match for Evelyn, and it was true that Raymie drank thrice as much any other man, disappearing for days at a time to see to his traps . . .

. . . but then, for once, perhaps he had truly seen something? So. She would talk to him, if she could find him sober. Maybe at the daymeal.

For now, though, best to forget if she could. Best just to work.

Monsters in grey.

She pushed the thought aside and went to scrub her armful of tatties.

At daymeal, the children arrived first, bursting in with Hannah, snow in their hair and gloves, noses dripping. Somehow, baby on hip, Hannah got them sorted out and sitting properly at their side table, where they tossed hot potatoes from hand to hand. The men came in more sombrely, in ones and twos, stamping their boots, talking of work; which of the elderly units were due to fail, how long it might be before new parts came. They sat at the large table, leaving space for the women, reaching for the jugs of beer. Soon the low wooden room was steamed up, full of talk.

Raymie was there, right enough, but for this day the time for Mira to ask any question of him had passed. Not that there was a need: he was in full flow, his watery eyes passing unsteadily round the table.

'Round shelters made of *cloth*, I tell ye; white and dappled so as you couldn't see 'em easily . . . unless you's used to seeing things, unless you's got tracker's eyes.'

'Oh, he's used to seeing things, nae fear. Ain't you, Raymie boy?'

Amidst the laughter, Raymie banged down his cup and pointed with a shaky finger: 'That's right, Pete. That's right. An' my fine deer, that I brought down from just by there, under their wee noses, an' that's going to end up in your belly; I s'pose that's not imagined then?'

Mira stood in the doorway to the cookhouse, eating a piece of sour and salty goat's cheese, watching. At fifteen, she could perch on a bench with the men and women, in between her fetching and carrying. A place was there for her today next to Gil. Cobb was talking across the space, leaning over to say something to Gil, whose head was bent to listen. Neither man seemed to be paying the slightest heed to Raymie's performance, and Gil was nodding in reply to some question from the older man.

And yet as he talked and listened, it seemed to Mira, his eyes did not leave the drunk.

As if he could hear her thoughts, he nodded once more to Cobb and then suddenly his gaze was on her, his teasing, fond smile in place; and he was getting up and coming over to the kitchen doorway.

'Will you not join us then, Mira?'

She shook her head: 'I cannot. I must have an eye to the syrup.' She stepped back so he could see the sweet mixture, warming on the stove. But he stepped after her and standing close, murmured: 'But you'll have a dance with me at wee Joan's birthday? Aye, Mira?'

Blushing, she pushed him away, aware of Hannah's eyes on them. 'Aye. All right then. All right. But now, the syrup . . .'

He gave a little nod, satisfied, and retreated.

From her silent place in the corner, Old Sarah picked potato skin from her teeth and sent Mira a glance far less readable than Hannah's, except that it was as sour as the cheese.

Five times in five nights Mira saw the face of the woman under the trees, saw the red stain spread through the snow, and awoke sweat-soaked, frightened and angry. Furious as she didn't know was possible, didn't know was in her. It grew, instead of fading, and was directed at herself. Why had she simply watched until it was too late? Why had she not made Gil do more to help the woman?

Gil. Her *watcher*. Watching for what?

How sweet it might be simply to forget. To sweat it out on the mountain. To share a dance with Gil at wee Joan's birthday. Indeed, what else was there to do? Raymie might know something, but he was gone again. Running down from the mountain, she stopped on impulse at his little house and found it cold and empty; an uninviting, musty shambles of unwashed bed linen, bits of animal skin that he'd kept for some unguessable purpose, dead ashes spilling from the stove. She even looked inside his little coldhouse, but found only the hanging, dull-eyed carcass of his trapped deer. No doubt he was loaded up with more whisky and off to his traps and his ghosts again, not even bothering to lock and shutter his door as he left; not even wishing to taste the deer, when they should use it.

No attack had come and the cookhouse talk had quickly returned to earthier subjects. On the matter of the raiders, Cobb had said at the start: 'If they're there, lass, and wanting anything with us, they'd have come by now.' But Gil himself had looked thoughtful and said: 'Best to be careful. Best to leave off your running a while, I'm thinking.'

She did not leave off her running.

After all, raiders only ever went for what was stored in the warehouse, or at worst for the skidoo too. There was no intention for real bloodshed, unless it came in the taking of these things; not like that awful, animal hunt for the woman, with its stark, violent end: that lolling head as lifeless as the hanging deer . . . and she had accepted that because he – Gil – had said so.

Gil with his arm warm around her or flashing a quick, brilliant smile. Gil who knew everything and was now not the same person.

The temptation was to forget, but she didn't, wouldn't: *could not*. Someone had put her name on that paper: someone from the South perhaps, where her birth had been. From that small thing doubt was settling over everything she knew, as thick as snow, layer on layer. Without wishing it, she was starting to feel an outsider in her own home: a strange, new Mira who was careful, secretive and untrusting.

The change was there even on the second day following *that* day. Gil had seen her while he was out about his business. He'd called her over: 'And how does this bonny morning find Mira? No idiots stamping about disturbing our peace, aye?' Then a tender smile. 'Seriously, are you quite well now? It was a nasty thing; you should not have witnessed it.'

His words held nothing but concern. What could be more natural than to speak then about the paper and hear the soothing and sensible reason for it?

But she could not. The words would not come. For he was *watcher* and had never told her of it. And the woman who knew something of these mysteries had been shot. Not one thing in Mira's universe could change or lessen that terrible fact.

*

Today, a week and a lifetime since the scrap of paper had come to her, she knew from instinct that the sky and the frozen mist would remain one unending sea of opaque white until dark. A good day for the secretive and untrusting.

The path down to the tidal barrier was empty, but Mira trod carefully and strained to see ahead through the white, ready to slip into the trees. She wished a ship was in and that she was coming noisily, crazily, with all the children strung out along the path, to help with the supplies. Last time – months ago now – it had been a different vessel; smaller, with a sharper prow and new, pine-green paint. The young man calling orders for the unloading had had tight, dark curls and big, red hands. He'd winked and called her *darlin*, a word she didn't know. Ship nights were nights to celebrate.

But no other ship would come for weeks more, and now the way was blank and still . . . and her heart jumped as it should not with every soft shifting of the snow.

The charcoal sea, when she got there, was unusually tame, sucking listlessly against the great tidal barrier, which made electricity from the movement of the waves as the streamway generators did from the meltwater running off the mountain. After all, making electricity was why they were here; fifteen adults, seven children and herself, caught between frozen mountain and icy sea . . . allowed one means of contacting whoever there was, away to the South, to make sure the ships brought the right things.

Mira walked past the end of the tidal barrier and the empty jetty and came to the dark, stone warehouse building, where the things from the ships would be stored until needed.

She had Cobb's flat, heavy key to open the warehouse door and, when she had felt her way through the dark to the power switches, another tiny one to open the cover to the computer link. In the community hall, half an hour's walk from here, another noisy daymeal would be taking place. She had slipped away when the meal was cooked, pleading the aches of her monthly cycle to sharp-eyed Evelyn.

Still, should anyone enter and find her, she had a list of parts and materials needed: a list taken, along with the keys, from Cobb, who would be sure to defend her and agree he had asked her to do this, though he had not.

Mira's fingers moved in slow exploration over the keyboard, despite knowing from seeing it many times what one must do to talk to the strange machine. Start-up; select 'communicate-Saintlink'; key in the com-code . . .

This link is authorised for the acquisition of materials to Generating Station Q17. Do you wish to acquire materials?

She typed *yes* and the screen blossomed a welcome. She started to type in the codes for what was needed, so that the machine should be satisfied she had a right to be there, hesitantly, in case it could notice such things. It took twenty slow minutes to work through the list: daymeal would be ended now. The computer asked: *End request?* And Mira typed *No.*

This link is authorised for the acquisition of materials to Generating Station Q17. Do you wish to acquire materials?

No.

A new box unfolded in the screen corner.

Enter keywords for new request.

She considered, bit her nail, then typed: *Annie Tallis.*

Unknown request. Please enter new authorisation code for Saintsearch.

Fumbling for the right keys, she re-entered the

community's com-code and pressed the key to send . . .
but stabbed at the shut-down button, so that the
machine's light blinked off. Sitting back, away from the
screen, she drew in large calming lungfuls of air and
looked at her fingers, which were trembling.

Fathers! If she were to look for her own answers, insist
upon this unreasoned, untrusting path, she must learn
some control.

This time she went headlong through the mist, deliberately running out her fear and confusion, feet kissing the
snow, hair flying free. The water droplets ran like ice on
her face. At a bend in the track, a dark shape appeared
just in front of her, so that she almost collided with it.
Strong arms came up to fend her off.

'You'll have a man down, missie, have a care!' The man
grinned at her, unconcerned, and trudged on. Finlay,
Pat's merry, red-haired da, on his way to the tidal barrier
for something. Not grey-clad *police*. Not Gil.

FOUR

With wee Joan's birthday to be celebrated, Mira sent the children out to play early. She locked up the toolhouse and went home.

Old Sarah was cocooned in shaggy splendour on the couch, watching the last few minutes of the free broadcast, gnawing what looked like a mutton bone. She grunted acknowledgement of Mira's presence without taking her eyes from the screen.

'And now,' a strange, gushing voice said from the receiving set, 'Gabby is here again to give you some great tips on using make-up – or perhaps the lightest touch of surgery, ladies? – to shed ten years.'

For once, Mira perched herself on a stool and looked at the dusty screen. Old Sarah's dull gaze turned her way in faint surprise and annoyance. It was many years since the girl had cuddled close to the bulky old woman and watched the otherworld pictures with her. Now, for a long time, everything about this room – their main room – made Mira feel faintly claustrophobic: it should be aired and swept out if Sarah would allow it. But then, the girl had found it cosy enough as a bairn, warm against her mother's flank, gathered up by her great fleshy arm.

'I guess you all know by now, *everyone* knows,' the woman Gabby tittered brightly, 'those basic key steps to facial beauty. Enhanced lips, wider mouth, raised cheekbones, larger eyes . . .'

Was this the world into which she had been born? Mira

wondered idly. The broadcasts seemed to have nothing to do with what *she* knew or felt.

'Well, I'm here to give you a ten-step programme that will truly make you a Vision.' Tinny, tinkling laughter from Gabby. 'And here's Kate, who's going to model for us today.'

Frustrated, Mira rose from her stool and went back behind the curtain, to the cooking space. Somebody had better get the bread and cheese ready for their day-meal; Cobb would be in soon, and hungry. But when she had set the table, it was Sarah who first appeared, shuffling in in slippers, trailing a grubby corner of her blanket.

The ghost of a familiar numb yearning touched Mira. She gestured at the things she had set out. 'Beer, Mam? Shall I cut you some bread?'

But Sarah shuffled closer to her and reached out a puffy hand to grip the arm that was reaching for the loaf. And her face was set hard and grim. She said: 'You're thinking I'm soft in the head? You're laughing at me, girl, is that it?'

Mira looked at her wonderingly.

'Och, I know your thoughts, my daughter. No need to make me an answer. Sad Old Sarah, lying in that musty room for hours. Living in make-believe.' The woman's grip bit harder into her forearm. 'Maybe you want to be better than us. Maybe you hope you *are* better; settin' yeself up as *teacher*, askin' your da again about how we had you, pokin' around . . .'

'Nae, Mother, of course not . . .' Mira was shocked by the outburst. She kept her gaze on the floor and her face slack and dull. It would help her mother's anger to pass.

'Well,' the old woman's face snarled, leaning close to her own, spitting out the words; 'you are *not* better. No

prince will come for you. No one cares. Not even bonny
Gil, who you hope is yours, with all your blushes . . . Och,
I know about you. I *know*, do ye see? The pictures there;
they told me, years ago . . . Soft Old Sarah, who has eyes
to see and a brain to think. I know you. Too good for us
by half, aye? That's what ye are.'

Mira's thoughts tumbled uselessly. Was there some
secret that all shared save her?

'*What?*' she whispered. '*What* is it? *What* do you know?
What is it that I have done? Please tell me so that I may
put it right. If you have never told me before, then tell
me now, Mam. Please.'

But the woman seemed not to hear. Her eyes were
turned inward now, the squall past as quickly as it had
come. She moaned softly, an animal gurgling in the back
of her throat, and whispered hoarsely; 'A bairn. A wee,
dandling thing for us to bring up. Just like any other.
That's all I wanted . . . And the fool comes in and tells
me: we've been chosen!' Sarah's grip loosened. Her arm
fell useless and heavy to her side. 'And I was *that* happy,
so I was.'

They stood in silence a minute or more, the old woman
lost in her dreams, the girl trying to see the meaning
of what had been said, grasping for the right question. And a third figure was there too, when she looked
round, though whether newly arrived she could not have
said.

'Aye then,' Cobb said sternly. 'If that is all finished, we
will eat.'

Mira cut more bread, and in silence they began their
meal. But at the end, when Cobb put back on his boots
and left to his work, she ran out after him a few paces,
and he did not show surprise.

'Well then, my daughter?'

'Da. Forgive me. I must ask again. Where did I come from? What do you know?'

And he looked at her straight with eyes that to her knowledge had never lied to her. 'Truly, I do not know. And I care not. Be content with that, lass.'

He turned to go, and she said wildly: 'I had your keys, Da. For the warehouse. I went to type the lists . . . and . . . and to look in the machine there.'

She had thought to call it a favour for him, a chore that he need not now be bothered with: but then, she had taken the things without his knowing or agreeing, and what reason could she give for that?

He studied her and asked gently: 'You wished to ask the machine about your birth?'

'Aye. But it told me that it was only for the parts and supplies and such. And I turned it off. I became afeared and ran home.'

He sighed: 'Then we may hope that nae harm has been done by it.'

'Harm?' She spoke more sharply than she intended; '*Harm?* What harm might there be in me knowing these things, Da? Why should I *not* know?'

He shook his head, shrugged. 'The ways and the reasons they have away down there are not to be understood, Mira. It is best only to let them be and hope that they will let us be, here. Don't go chasing trouble, now.'

Still she pressed him. 'What is it that Mam believes about me? Why is she angry?'

'Och, Sarah!' He smiled sadly; 'Who can say what she imagines, lass?'

He turned once more and she said: 'Da . . . you willna tell anyone . . . about the warehouse?'

'And who would I be telling?' he called back.

Back in the house, the dishes were waiting and Sarah

was snoring on her couch, mouth lolling open. Mira pulled the covers tighter round the old woman.

By the time the music began — fiddle, guitar and drum — wee Joan was already sleepy.

She stood holding Evelyn's hands, shuffling her feet over the plank floor, while the older children hared round and under tables and the adults watched from the sides. Mira and Hannah watched the youngest ones. The young widow wore a dress, cobwebby and black, that went almost to the floor. Her eyes kept sliding over to Gil's back, where he talked with some others, perched on a trestle, jiggling a foot idly to the music. Mira felt restless, impatient with all of them.

She said: 'I will watch the bairns if you wish to go to him.'

Hannah flushed but said: 'Aye. Perhaps I will then.'

'But bring me a glass of something?'

Hannah brought the drink immediately: beer, a large mug. She said, tauntingly: 'Careful though, Mira. It is strong tonight: don't be addling your brains, now.'

She had meant a glass of warm, spicy punch, or even water. Hannah deliberately brought her beer.

Mira watched her come up to Gil's elbow and murmur something and his head come round with its quick grin, his hand touch her shoulder lightly. At the same moment his eyes flicked across to Mira's own. She looked away, made her gaze carry on round the room. Then Hannah's baby, Rory, started to howl, so she took him and the other two young ones to settle them in a quiet corner of the cookhouse.

After that, there was food to bring out. Baked fish rolled in oats, parsnips and a large, flat tray of seedcake, with Joan's nine candles on top. Remembering, Mira said to Muriel, who was arranging the candles: 'What of Raymie's deer? I had thought we would eat venison tonight.' But the woman looked at her strangely and said, 'Deer? Raymie gave us no deer. Doubtless he thought he had one but had not. Och, you know the man! Daft as a pine cone.'

Mira murmured: 'Aye, I know him . . .' and thought of the solid carcass hanging in Raymie's little coldroom.

They spread the food on the trestles and took in more jugs of beer. They tidied and washed up in the cookhouse, looked at the sleeping babies. By the time Mira got back into the main room, the dancing was at full strength. The noise and movement and warm, ripe air washed over her, bringing more thirst. With her head swimming very slightly she went to find another drink.

'Here lass.' Evelyn's smiling, flushed face appeared and a new glass was pressed into her hand. 'Have a wee taste, eh? After all your work. Our Joan's had a bonny time, has she not?'

And Mira found yet more beer in her hand.

The unaccustomed drink made her feel more apart than ever. Her senses reeled, her head span as she joined the breathless dances, and she chattered to those around her, but somewhere inside her a tiny ice-cold thing was watching from behind thick glass, seeing life here as something suddenly become strange.

Watching Hannah as she went up to sing a song or two in her sweet, reedy soprano, her dark eyes fastened on Gil throughout.

Watching Cobb, grizzled head bent, eyes on the floor as he concentrated on his drumbeat.

Watching Finlay laughing with Gil during a break in the music, and gesturing towards her, making some joke.

Watching Pat's animated, young-old face in front of her as he talked: 'Are you OK, Mira? You's awful quiet tonight, so you are.'

Gil came over and claimed the promised dance and she took his hand to spin around the floor, aware despite herself of the smell of him and the hardened skin of his hands. And he said the same thing as Pat: 'Mira, where are your thoughts these days? You seem not the same person. Finlay says you nearly bowled him over, a day or two ago, running like a mad thing in the fog.'

The breath caught in her throat. Were they all 'watching' her now? Did they help Gil with the task? The room turned around her. Gil's kind, mocking face was close to her own. Nausea threatened to bubble up inside, but she fought it down. Just let the music end, she thought, so I can get away from him and think.

As the last notes of the reel died, she made her excuses and headed for the door. Outside, the world was clean white, ice-cold, sobering, all as it should be. Mira wandered to the edge of the clearing, away from the muffled noises of the party. There she put her back to one of the pines and sank slowly down onto the snow.

She had such thoughts. Such fears. Tiny worms of doubt wriggling through her mind, soiling all they touched.

Gil and the watchers, police and Raymie's raiders: they danced through her thoughts waking and sleeping. Where was Raymie now, to answer her questions? Why hadn't he given them the deer before he left again? What did Old Sarah know, or Cobb, or any of them?

If Gil was her watcher, who had been watcher before him? Roy? Not Roy, who had been kind to her, told her stories of the mountain spirits and the great, ancient heroes of her land when she was tiny. Please not him.

How did you get trust back, when it was gone? Where could you look for it?

Numbing cold was seeping into her, unnoticed. For almost an hour the girl sat unmoving under the tree, eyes unseeing, pale hands resting limply on the snow. One or two others – the oldest and the youngest – left the party to go to their beds, but did not notice her in the shadows of the forest edge.

The houses sat quietly around the clearing, Gil's little place as dark as the others.

And whether it was the beer or the need to move and get warm, or simply desperation, at the end of the hour Mira rose to her feet, walked to that house, and let herself in through the unlocked door.

She knew the place well enough. She knew how Gil kept it, where his work boots would sit, where his tools were, his cribbage set, his ice axe. She knew that he hung a torch inside the door to take when he must work at night, and she felt for this now, lifted it down and slid the switch forward.

She shivered. She was mad, beyond doubt, but at least she was doing something to root out the fears. And if Gil was – despite everything – her true friend, he might still forgive her. They might still laugh over it.

She played the beam around the room. All was exactly as she knew it and Gil's smell was faintly in the air, comforting and now also frightening. She started her search in the cooking space. Pan by fork, by flour bag, by beer mug, she went through the things, trying to see them with new eyes, waiting for them to yield up any secret they might hold. There was the pretty cup she drank from when she visited, there was Gil's battered coffee pot, sitting in its knitted cover, there was his little bag of herbs nestled in the corner of the shelf, for the thick spicy stew that he made in the largest iron tin.

Then to the tiny sleeping alcove, and Mira felt doubly an intruder as she examined the hard plank bed, reached underneath it, looked through the chest of man's clothes, with nothing to show except her blush in the dark.

Almost, now, she lost her nerve. What a fool she'd been to imagine that Gil might laugh if he found her like this, deep in his private things. Her breath came too fast and too loud. How long had she been? No more than fifteen or twenty minutes, she thought, surely. Faintly, the noise of the party drifted across from the hall, unchanged. Mira thought too late of the telltale beer fumes she was breathing into this unbeery room.

The main room took longer. Shelf by shelf, she went along the walls, lifting each object and replacing it softly. Then she felt under the rugs and all around the chairs, and rifled through the work tools in their cupboard, each gleaming and clean in its place. Spanners, screwdrivers, tool-belt, hammer, a tray of bits of splicing cable, plastic ties, nuts and bolts, a clasp knife, welding goggles.

The kit could have been Cobb's or any man's.

Finally she was done, and there was nothing. Nothing that screamed to her of the South or strangers or *watching*. Nothing she had not seen a thousand times. With relief and frustration she left the heavy light on its hook and stepped back into the night.

When she walked back over to the wooden hall and slipped inside, she saw at once that Gil and Hannah were both gone. The music had stopped – when had that been? She'd heard it so clearly from Gil's house – and there was just a murmur of quiet talk, and the clatter of plates and glasses as one or two of the women cleared away.

In the back of the cookhouse, baby Rory was still

sleeping peacefully, but alone now as the other two had been reclaimed and taken home. Carefully scooping up the sweet-smelling child, Mira whispered to Muriel, back on kitchen duties, 'If Hannah should ask, I've taken wee Rory safe back with me for the night.'

'Aye, OK. Sleep tight then, lass.'

And Muriel, watching her go, thought: There's a strange one, no mistake. But with a kind heart, right enough.

FIVE

Two mornings later, sucking in the sweet, icy air on the mountain's great shoulder and with her mind at rest, it came to her. The thing that was important from Gil's house.

Even as the light climbed over the peaks that marched away to the south and east, a quiet little image stole into her thoughts, stopping the breath in her throat, locking every limb tight in shock.

A knife.

A hunter's clasp knife. Most of the men had them. Handled in wood or horn, and worn black by use. Gil would have one too; she was almost sure he did. She had seen him with it.

And yet it seemed to her now that the hand that she had last seen holding that particular knife that lay in Gil's kit was the grimy hand of a drunk, a babbling hunter, using the point on his nails. Perhaps a year ago or more, sat on his wooden step in the midday sun.

'And a good morning it is to ye, my pretty thing,' he'd called as she passed, flashing his whisky-stained teeth.

Was it enough? Was it sure, a memory she might trust?

Why did the man's cabin lie empty now, the deer unclaimed?

She made herself breathe again, looked out towards the rising sun and thought finally, and with something like relief, that it *was* enough.

Without even replacing her fleece, she came down

from the mountain more swiftly than she had ever done, deliberately crashing and skidding through the powder where she would usually run silent, thinking of what she must now do.

SIX

Three nights she had to wait and be patient. She had no choice, for they were three nights of mist so thick that even she would be lost on the mountain. Between them were three days when she must seem unchanged ... and no more so than to Gil. To that end she sought him out, mentioned his absence with Hannah after the dance and played the jealous girl. Perhaps the jealousy was even half true.

'Nae then,' she said, with her face turned deliberately away from him; 'what man would wait for a girl barely grown when such a woman turns her large, dark eyes to him. Ye need not fret. It's better that the choice is made.'

And Gil looked first furious, then perplexed: 'Mira. You don't know what you're saying. You don't understand . . .'

'Och, I think I do then. I think I understand better than you would wish.'

There were others, too, to deceive. Before Old Sarah's sour glances she humbled herself, staring at the floor like an idiot. Most difficult of all, when Cobb cast questioning eyes on her, she met his gaze boldly and said: 'Do not worry, Da. I will do no other foolish thing. As you said, why should it matter what I once was or where I was brought into the world?' A tightness in her throat almost choked the words.

On the fourth night, though, the moon shone out clear, the mist had not come down and she stood alone in the scented tree shadows. From here she looked at her little life: the scattered wooden dwellings, the toolhouse, the skidoo garage, the three lone trees that marched away from the shadowy fringe of pines; all alive and standing sharp in the milky-blue light. This was all she knew. This place. This handful of people. Always it had been enough. She had never imagined being anywhere but here.

She drew in a calming breath, went once more through what she had rehearsed, and then ran the thirty metres from the treeline to Gil's door.

Deliberately she raised a hand and tapped lightly on the planks. Gil must still have been up, despite the hour. He appeared almost immediately. As the door swung back she made herself breathe quickly and heavily and gasped out: 'Cobb needs you. Up the line. Number 61.'

The sweat on her and the colour in her face was real. She'd made sure of that, had already been up to that generator, and beyond. Gil barely gave her a glance before he was taking down his thick jacket and his tool-belt, precise and quick in his movements, seeing that speed counted.

'What is wrong at 61?'

'An animal. A deer caught in the stream. The machinery is damaged and still blocked. Even the sluice at the side. Cobb fears for the generator, with such a weight of water.'

She allowed her breathing to come more steadily, walking along beside him to the path up the mountain, as he buttoned the jacket and pulled on gloves. Their two plumes of breath melted together as they went.

'Go to your bed then, Mira. I will go to help. All will be well.'

'Nae,' she replied: 'I might help too. If I am to live my days in a generating station, I should learn the work.'

He shot half a grin at her, crunching along in his heavy

boots. 'Stubborn as ever. And I thought you were angry with me! Let us go fast then.'

And they broke into a jogging run, in and out of the tree shadows, up the steepening way, him heavy-footed and solid and tireless; her light and lithe, picturing in her thoughts what must come next.

The generator numbered 61 was on a slight bend in the streamway, at a place where a hump of solid rock on the outside of the bend held the water into too narrow a channel. Good for making electricity, but bad for a break-down: any blockage here would store up water at twice the rate. The scene was picked out for them when they stepped from the forest onto the bank. A yellow tool-belt such as the one Gil wore, lay next to the cradleway, spilling its tools in a heap as Cobb had rushed to get at what he needed. The hooded generator covers folded up and back into a narrow black triangle pointing skywards. The roaring water – dangerously high – cascading down through the machine. And the shapeless matted corpse of a young doe, pulled half onto the bank but with its hind legs still buffeted by the water.

'Oh fathers!' Gil said, bleakly; 'Stay here Mira, don't come closer.'

She let out a sob as she saw what he had seen: Cobb's safety line, plunging down taut into the torrent and under the spinning, gleaming turbines. Ignoring his command, she ran to the water's edge and helped him prepare a second line, hooked it onto his belt for him with awkward, frightened hands.

'Please, Gil! Please hurry!'

'Mira, he won't be . . . he couldn't be . . .' Leaving it unfinished but obvious, Gil shrugged off his jacket and started to edge out onto the cradleway, peering down, centimetre by careful centimetre on the slippery wet steel. About a third of the way across he shone the white beam of his service light down into the torrent. Mira could see flecks of foam or sweat on his narrow, handsome face. As he went on, reaching out for the taut safety line that jumped and twisted in the middle of the current, played by the weight at its end, Mira helped Gil's own line coil neatly back onto the smooth sprung drum on the platform where she stood.

In theory the line should have held Cobb safe. When the engineer arrived to work on this or that generator, the line was always waiting. It ran from its sprung drum out to the centre, through a pulley and back to a hook on the bank. The worker had just to unhook the end and fix it to the centre back of his belt. Then, as he went across the cradleway, the slack was wound in by the drum: if more slack were required, the drum would only deliver it slowly; any sudden jerk – a body tumbling into the stream, for example – would lock the drum solid and keep the man safe.

Gil had reached the centre now, where the second line bent down as it should not. Bracing himself with one boot on the generator frame, he started to haul the nylon-covered wire in, hand over hand, the sinews on his neck standing out with the exertion. From the bank, Mira silently saluted his determination and courage. Also his strength, to bring the thing in at all, against the rush of water.

Nevertheless, she did what she must do. Near the doe lay a length of sodden branch, which she took in her left hand, while her right felt inside her belt pouch for the heavy wirecutters, taken from the toolhouse many hours before. Part of her brain asked if she had not lost all reason, but another, strange, newly woken part watched in satisfaction and interest as she reached out with steady hand to place the jaws of the cutters over Gil's line. From where her friend laboured they would be hard to discern in the shadow of her hand.

He had the thing now. With a cry audible even above the thundering stream, he heaved it free of the water and brought it to balance on the cradleway. In the moonlight it was clearly not a man, but a gleaming length of pine log, deeply scored by the turbine blades and the rocks in the stream bed.

Gil looked at it a second, his chest heaving, then his head snapped round. His eyes bored into Mira's own with their question: *What is this? What is your purpose here?*

It was time. Mira stood up hard against the end of the cradleway with her branch raised and cried: 'What is a *watcher*, Gil?'

His eyes flicked over her, the branch, the spool holding the line. His face showed confusion. He called out, puzzled: 'Mira . . .'

She cried again, as if he hadn't spoken: 'What is a *watcher*, Gil? You are my watcher, so tell me, what does that mean?'

He started to edge back towards her. His face was incredulous. 'I do not understand,' he called back: 'I do not know what you ask. Who tied that log to the line? You, Mira? For what reason?'

Charming, clever Gil. He had come up here trustingly, to help her and her da.

She watched his approach and called yet again: 'Who is Annie Tallis? Adeline Beguin? Siân Latimer? What is a watcher? Who am I, Gil? Who are you? Are you police?'

The sweat was coursing down her back, but still the hand with the cutters was steady. He was a bare three metres away now, the sprung line feeding out smoothly from the drum as he approached the bank.

'Police?' His face cleared a little. 'This is about the woman who we saw arrested? That is all this is?'

The beginning of a smile touched his face, a look of relief that the misunderstanding was all so silly, so easy to clear up. Still Mira did not move. The branch was lowered, blocking his further progress.

'You spoke to the police that day. What did you say? What did you tell them? I have the paper that she carried, Gil. Do not lie. I know that you are *watcher*.' He was near enough for her not to need to shout, near enough for both faces to be seen clearly.

The smile on his face stayed uncertain. He stopped trying to advance. He looked upset, hurt. His gentle voice carried that hurt. 'I do not know of any paper, fool Mira. What did I say to that animal of a policeman? I told him that if he touched you again I would make a complaint, to have him excluded from police service. And that if he hurt you he would have me to answer to.'

He looked into her eyes, searching, not trying to move further, just answering her questions . . . and so they stayed, facing each other above the icy water, each trying to read the other familiar face. And at the end of that time Mira thought, shakily: Aye. It is enough. I have been a fool. And she lowered the branch, stepped back for him to pass.

What must I do, she thought wearily, to get his trust after this?

But in that second, as he moved on again almost to the edge of the cradleway and they looked at each other, she saw a new thing in those green-flecked charmer's eyes. A tiny moment of triumph, of contempt, something . . .

And without any conscious thought the muscles in her right forearm drew taut and she felt the razor teeth of the wirecutters dig into the safety line, then snap shut as they parted. And in the same instant, she brought the branch up and swept it hard in an arc at Gil's feet.

For the blink of an eye he stood swaying on the wet metal in surprise, then he was gone, the useless piece of safety line snaking through its pulley and into the torrent after him.

With the thing that she had most feared done, she was very nearly lost.

New, powerful waves of doubt swept over her, and all the carefully collected evidence for her suspicion shrank to a puny wisp of girlish imagining. What am I? she thought, swaying and giddy, staggering back from the stream edge. Have I done this terrible thing just for some writing on a paper?

It was madness. It was too big an answer, whatever the question. It was murder. It was her friend, sent down the merciless turbines. Her insides lurched at that. She thought of the scoring on the log and bent to retch her supper onto the snow. The roaring of the blood in her ears and the roaring of the black torrent became one, overwhelming her, so that she sank unknowing onto the frozen metal platform. In a moment, when strength returned, she thought hazily, she would go down to the house, to Cobb, and tell him what she had done. Then the grey-clad *police* could be sent for.

Unbidden, the image surfaced through the tumbling thoughts: the image of the woman – Annie Tallis? – crashing forward into the snow, and a man behind lowering his weapon . . .

. . . and Gil standing looking on, with nothing at all showing in his face. Nothing at all.

A detached voice spoke in her head, calmly, reasonably:

the voice of the strange new her. There is more to do. This is just the starting of it.

Thus the black moment passed. Mira stood and felt strength return. Half an hour had been lost since Gil fell into the stream. Precious time wasted in weakness, self-pity, useless tears.

Slowly at first, then moving with more purpose, she sorted through the tools on the bank to find what was needed. Then she started to edge out, as Gil had done, towards the centre of the cradleway. There were only two safety lines per generator – the black water and spinning blades might claim her too, – but that would only be justice of a kind. At the centre she first detached the loop of wire from the heavy length of pine that had doubled for Cobb's body and let the wood fall back into the current, where it bobbed clumsily a moment before being sucked back down under the machine. Its passage brought a scream of protest from the generator parts: this unit would soon need to be serviced or replaced. All the more reason to be thorough tonight.

Then, with the free line clipped reassuringly onto her belt, Mira reached up and forwards, straining with numb, cold fingers for the edge of the generator cover. With this folded down into place, there were eight heavy bolts to secure, equally spaced along the bottom rim of the machine. By the time the eighth was locked tight, she was warm again.

Back on the bank there were more tasks: the stolen doe's body to add to the debris that had gone through Number 61, then the tools to tidy together. Nearly, very nearly, Mira pitched the rewrapped tool-belt after the deer ... but then, she thought, when Gil's body was found (as it must be, sooner or later), there would already be a belt on his waist, if it had not been sliced off by the blades. A second one discovered would not fit. She also decided against the time-consuming reattaching of a karabiner to the cut end of Gil's safety line, for when they found the line on him they would search for the drum with a piece missing. Instead, she tried to fray out the ends, to look more like a break or the cut of a turbine blade as the body went under. Hopefully the savage current would do the same to Gil's piece of wire.

Gil's jacket posed the biggest puzzle of all, for if they found that in the water – separate from the body – it would seem unnatural, but if she left it here on the bank then someone would certainly see it on their way up the line in the morning and they would start looking for the missing man sooner than she would wish. Eventually, she wrapped the heavy garment tight, with the tools inside, and carried it with her, leaving Number 61 generator behind with relief, heading further up the service track. Instinct would have had her going deep into the trees, away from the thundering water, but from here on the path stayed just at the forest edge, and to leave it would be to disturb unbroken snow. Already she would have to trust that all evidence of activity around 61 – not least the snow-cleared generator cover – would go unremarked. Just another unit that had had attention recently.

What Cobb might guess was something different. Age had not dimmed his steady perception. He would be sure to remember her questions of late, the taking of the warehouse key . . . And besides, she owed him all her life until now, and much more. For this reason, she had left a short message only for him: *When I can, if I can, I will try to explain what I have done. Your M.*

It was tucked into his cap rim: inside, where he would

feel it when he put the cap on. What he decided to do about it was up to him.

She climbed on and up. When she had picked up the things hidden earlier near the topmost generator – a simple pack, provisions, other, stronger shoes – and struggled on to the highest ridge, her limbs were trembling. Three times she had been up the mountain today.

As she turned and looked back one last time, the slopes below her seemed almost daylit. The scattered buildings of the community were together no larger than her fingernail, but sharp against the white, so that she could have named each and who slept within. She picked out Gil's house, a little apart from the others and empty now. Inside, she thought, his things would have lost their meaning. Clothes that he would not wear again that still had his scent on them, the dirty pans from whatever he had eaten tonight before coming up the mountain to die: air that would not stir with his passing or vibrate to his voice.

She made her gaze follow the forest downwards and along the warehouse path to the tidal barrier. By the time it got there it was blurred by silent heavy tears of shock and grief, impossible to stem; so that those buildings and the sea beyond, which should have been splendid and shining and swaying softly in the moonlight, were indistinct.

Time to move, the inner voice said.

But when she stood and prepared to leave her world behind, she looked anew at the remote shoreline. Tears? No, even through the tears her vision had told her true. There was an indistinctness, a blanket greyness coming slowly across the sea and onto the land, obscuring, centimetre by centimetre, all that she had known.

This was fortune indeed. A blessing from the mountain.

Turning south, Mira started down into the new valley, further than she had ever been. Gravity coaxed her heavy limbs into a jog, and despite all that had passed in these last days – in this long, difficult night – she felt her heart lifting and thrilling as it did when she stepped out alone into the singing pre-dawn.

She was strong. The life was strong within her, and not made for despair. And indeed the luck was with her, for even before she reached the treeline of the new valley the first heavy, floating, otherworldly flakes of the fresh snow were falling. Feeling them on her face, Mira threw the awkward jacket and tools aside to be covered in blessed white, along with her tracks, the casing of generator Number 61, and all else that she would wish hidden.

Such weather would remove any tiny chance that at home, in the morning, they would decide to burn precious skidoo fuel to look for her.

Without the extra weight she went more quickly, diving down through the cloud pines, breathing in their familiar resin, weaving between trunks. The snow came thick and fast, whirled into her face, stuck to her hair and clothes.

She gloried in it and knew that she was Mira again, for all her days of doubt.

SEVEN

The new snow fell thick and unending for three days, keeping the temperatures up, blinding any that might follow, and blinding Mira too.

She knew for sure that she had begun by heading roughly south, but with no sun or stars or coastline to guide her, she could only hope that her course remained true. Often she stopped and held her breath to listen for any sound of pursuit, but she might as well have been alone on the face of the earth, except for the few animals she startled in the blizzard: mostly silent deer and scampering orange squirrels. Either of those could mean food, but the beasts were too shy, too quick: and even with no sign of followers, she felt an urgent need to keep moving.

Indeed, when she had to slow or stop for a meal or a rest, she could easily imagine that the blizzard hid a multitude of enemies. Pursuers from the village, grey-clad policemen; even Gil himself, risen from his death in the stream and bent on terrible revenge. On the second afternoon, while she squatted resting against a trunk and watching the dim light fail, a sudden succession of deep, throaty noises came from the trees nearby, so that she was sure many men were there, closing in, coming through the forest as they had come for Annie Tallis. She dropped the food she was chewing and ran on . . . almost colliding with her 'pursuers', who were no more than a line of boar, passing swiftly, snout-to-tail through the blanket white. The heavy male at the front lurched shortsightedly at her and rumbled his warning, but without conviction, and then the beasts were gone.

Mira stilled her heart and mourned the truth that her own perfect world was no longer fully hers, nor fully safe. There was no way to take back what had been lost.

For those three days she drove herself onwards, sleeping as little as possible, seizing every minute of what poor daylight there was, using a stolen service light – and trusting to luck – to avoid the drops and crevasses by night. Mountain followed mountain, valley followed valley, so that the way went from forest to bare ascent, choked with impossible drifts of the thick, fresh white, and back down into forest again. Except that the third time she found the bowl of the valley, below the pines, filled with a long white oval, very flat, stretching further than she could see in the snowfall. Clearing a small piece of ground at the edge she came, half a metre down, upon black ice. Like a tiny frozen sea, she thought.

Not sure if she could trust the snow-covered crust she trekked round the edge, using valuable energy and time. But then in the next valley it was the same. And the next. And the next, each descent ending in the expanse of snow-covered frozen water.

When she stopped to sleep for the third time, wriggling down into her sno-bag – part of the equipment kept for emergency night-work up the line in case the weather should come down hard – she was starting to doubt that she would arrive anywhere. Except to a lonely death from exhaustion and hunger. She had no idea of how far the mountains ran and her food would last no more than a week. Her clothing – between sweat and snow – never quite dried out. Her feet and body ached from the effort she asked of them.

Worse, when she did fall into damp, cold sleep she

saw, not Annie Tallis pitching over in the snow, but Gil tumbling again into the swollen streamway . . . and woke, breathing hard, fists clutched tight. Whatever wild fantasies she had allowed herself about Raymie and Martin and Roy seemed absurd in the darkness, mocking her. Total madness, that had driven her away from her home and Cobb and Pat and the others. And yet, in the first ghostly glow of morning, cocooned in the soft white, she could fumble inside her pack with numb hands and take out the sodden scrap of paper and see Gil's name there again, next to her own.

The new Mira helped her, soothed her, whispered her clear truths. She had *not* imagined the savage hunting of the woman that had brought this paper to her. She was *not* conjuring the unknown danger, or the secrets that Gil had kept until his death, from the empty air. She was *not* mad.

It was enough to drive her on. Even to lonely, frozen death, if that was all that awaited her.

That fourth day when she awoke, she could not move or feel her left arm. Somehow it had wormed out from the sleeping sack and sprawled onto the ground, where snow had covered it without even waking her in her exhaustion. Then the blizzard must have died and the temperature fallen – she felt much colder air on her face and could smell even before opening her eyes that the skies were clearing – so that now the arm lay like a dead thing. Panicking, horrified, she wormed free of the sack and started frantically rubbing the cold flesh, cradling the useless limb against her. For twenty minutes she rubbed, and danced about and willed the hand to open and close, and then for the same time again she sobbed with the pain as finally the blood started to move there and the arm became hers again.

The peril was clear known to all in her village. The plummeting of temperature with the ending of the blizzard. Now she would really have to press herself if she were to keep her tired body from freezing; and to arrive somewhere before the end came. At least, as the air cleared, she would see further and might be able to steer a truer course across, or around, the peaks.

With this in mind, she chewed a scrap of salt fish for her breakfast, and chose the higher of the two climbs that stood ahead, jogging lightly through the unbroken powder to make her muscles warm and fluid, then slowing to a walk as the way steepened and a fresh, biting wind blew up from her right side, making her eyes water, cramming the topmost powder into any small space between clothing and skin. Three-quarters of the way up, huddling into the lea of a bare, overhanging slab of rock, she turned to see the way she had followed.

As far as she could see, north and east, the view was unbroken by any movement, path or building. Only one lone eagle, a speck in the sky, hung above, hoping for a bold rabbit to stray from the protective forest cover. Mira realised as she looked, that the peaks climbed higher towards the north and the community. When she had stood on the bulk of *her* mountain, she had been able to see only the next great, snow-clad wedge of ancient granite. Now, she could see chain after chain of mountains running, it seemed, roughly south-west to north-east, each topping the last.

Perhaps, she thought, with a surge of hope, this is the last. Once across this peak I may find the South. She knew from Gil and the broadcasts that the South did not look like her world. The snow was much less or often not there at all – how strange that must be! – and there were great areas where unfrozen water flooded the land.

There were no mountains in the South, Gil had said, but instead the thousands of people who stayed together in *cities* made high, square buildings to live and work in. Perhaps, she thought, I shall pass over this mountain and the snow will end and there will be a city.

But instead, as she came down over the mountain shoulder, there was more forest and then a great, long band of white, which she knew by now would be the frozen water, winding up the next valley for miles . . . and after that, only more mountains.

The sheer length of the new barrier sapped her tired spirit; and now that she could see clearly, the temptation to try a crossing of the ice lake was far greater. But was that sense, or desperation? Scrambling down the southern face of the mountain, Mira knew that the sea must lie somewhere to her right, but how far she had no idea. She might have struck far inland in her snowblind journey. And yet if she turned west and tried to circle the ice strip that way, she risked finding only an open mouth to the sea, with no crossing possible. But then, the way east – left – was visible for much further as the valley ran straight that way; and there was no ending in view to the frozen lake. Also, turning left would take her in the wrong direction, north as well as east. With so little food left, going north would be madness.

In truth, she had to admit that she knew nothing of this land: its size or nature or where she might find a friendly face and a meal. Her ignorance shocked her. Her only thought from the start had been to learn whatever it was that was hidden to her: most of all, whatever Annie Tallis' paper should mean. Now she had only instinct to guide her.

Accepting this, she found a stout length of red pine, and started, carefully, to edge out onto the snow-capped ice, prodding a step or two in front of her to test for weakness. If the ice can hold the weight of snow, surely it will hold me too, she thought. But she discovered with dread that this much greater lake did not have the half-metre covering of the others already passed: more like a bare ten centimetres.

A third of the way across Mira had her answer. With a small but sickening noise, the probing end of the pine rod disappeared abruptly into a neat hole, a hole from which a fine cobweb of lines raced out and through which water started to lap with frightening speed. At the same time the surface below her feet seemed to shift and bend. Fighting down the desire to pound for the shore, forcing herself to move as slowly as a mountain cat on the hunt, she lowered her body to the ice, spreading her weight on the fragile surface, *thinking* herself light. Her knees and feet and hands were lapped by the freezing water, but the ice skin held her and she dared to take a breath. Staying on all fours, sweating with concentration, she crept back to the shoreline and finally lay trembling in the snow.

Aye, fine then, she thought shakily; west it will be.

But perhaps the spirits were with her in this, for a scant hour later, jogging softly along the lakeside in the fading light, she found a thing that sent her pulse hammering once more. A thing that brought back vividly all those days of doubt before she had lured Gil up the mountain. A series of large, compacted circles in the snow, five of them, arranged around an area where many feet had passed back and forth; and a deep hollow filled with ash and blackened fragments of wood.

She stood alone on the bank of the frozen lake, looking at where the people had been, and Raymie's whisky-sodden, tracker's voice spoke in her head: 'Round shelters made of cloth, I tell ye.'

She said carefully to the voice: 'But you said unseen; shelters that were hidden by their colour. These people cannot be the same as those you saw: they have made a fire. They did not care if they were seen.'

The reply was scathing: 'Think, lassie! If they had stayed here in the bad weather, what risk then from their fire? No eyes to see the smoke in that blizzard, I'm thinking.'

The voice spoke truth. Raymie's raiders could have sheltered here through the blizzard. After all, the signs of their stay would have been covered if they had moved much before the snow stopped falling. Which meant that they were no more than a day ahead of her.

Casting about, Mira found faint tracks in the snow taking the same direction that she had been following – south-west – but these went only fifty metres and then stopped by the lakeside.

What now? Had fresh snow covered the rest? Had someone just walked away a little to relieve themselves in the night? Her tired, frustrated brain gave her the answer in Raymie's voice: 'Sleep, warmth, a bite and a dram . . . The morning is cleverer than the evening, lass.'

She knew that she was near exhaustion: finding these signs of a camp had drained the last of her energy. It was to be wished and also to be feared. Tottering back to the site of their camp, Mira tried to see their faces. Giants in grey? Careless, callous raiders? Police? She could imagine the heat from their great fire and the way the light played over the dappled cloth shelters and the shadowed faces. The snowflakes must have danced and hissed in the flames.

A few paces into the forest, stacked against a thick trunk, there were roughly cut branches and broken sticks that had not yet been used. With a last effort, Mira dragged these down to the fire pit and – not caring tonight who might see – started her own blaze. When it was burning fiercely, she stripped down to her underwear, hung her clothing and shoes on sticks to dry out, and then melted a little snow to wash herself.

The warm water was delicious on her skin.

Ten minutes later she was asleep, curled deep in her steaming sno-bag, face peaceful in the light of the flames.

Again the voice had been right.

In the new light of another bright, bonny, freezing day Mira saw at once the thin glinting wire that had been stretched high over the lake. On this side it had been attached somewhere in the treetops and although it dipped down towards the centre, she doubted that she could have put her fingers to it even there. How the men had used it to cross – if they had – was not clear.

No matter. With the sunlight starting to spill over the peaks on to the metre or two of mist that lay flat and silver over the ice, with dry clothes and a trail to follow, Mira did not mind the puzzle. Even if she should fail – find no one, perhaps – what then? For the first time since the ugly thing that was the shooting down of a woman, she felt *right* again, part of this land, able to hear its song.

She would find a way – or not. But she would not stay fearful.

While the porridge water heated on the remains of her fire, she sought out the tree that held the northerly end of the cable and considered it. Someone had climbed as high as they could to attach the thing, and she supposed that they had done the same at the other end, across the lake. So even if she could move this end and reattach it low enough to hold as she stepped on to the ice, it would still rise high above her head before she reached safety on the other side. And with the natural sag, much of the wire would simply lie slack across the frozen lake and offer no support.

She considered hanging from the wire, going hand over hand, but dismissed the idea: this looked like the cable used for the generator safety lines: strong and hard and merciless on the hands, slight enough to cut gradually into flesh. Mira imagined letting go, dropping down through the ice crust from ten metres up, and shivered. With other rope to loop over the wire on to her wrists or under her arms, it might perhaps be done, but she had none.

Finally, over the pan of porridge, the solution came. If only the wire could be undone . . .

With her fast well broken, and with new hope, she struggled slowly up to the canopy to investigate, crossing two-thirds of the way up from another tree whose branches started much closer to the ground; and found there just a simple loop around the pine trunk, with a clip holding the loop shut. The weight of the wire stretching out across the lake – and the weight of those who had used it to pass, however they had done it – had made the steel bite deep into the soft, sappy wood; but using her knife, balanced on a lower branch, Mira managed eventually to prise the thing free and spring the clip. She wasn't ready, however, for the way the freed wire would tug sharply away and down like a live thing, and so she seared her palm through the glove trying to stop it. But when she had climbed painfully down she saw with satisfaction that the end had come to rest only a few steps out onto the ice.

Now, right enough, there was the need for much care.

Unrolling her sno-bag, with its plastic base, across the first little section of lake, Mira lay flat on her back on the bag, spreading her weight, hardly daring to breathe. Her pack was hooked under her knees, and the hood of the bag was up over her head to allow the 'front' of her improvised sledge to move without catching, like the skidoo runners. Pat would approve, she thought. Reaching over her head, along the ice, her fingers brushed the wire. Then, digging deep inside for the courage, once more *thinking* herself light enough for the frozen layer to bear her, she took the steel in her hand and pulled gently.

Movement.

She pulled again. And again.

Hand over hand, centimetre by centimetre, Mira tugged herself out onto the white crust. The morning was almost past: the sky above her eyes was clear. Sweat started to resoak her clothing.

She thought: If the ice does not hold me, I will still have a chance, if only I can keep my grip on the wire.

Was that truth or foolishness?

A third of the way over now: perhaps even half. With her head slightly angled up by the hood, she could see the sun-drenched shoulders of the peak she had crossed the day before. To keep her mind from thoughts of ice water, Mira tried to seek out the way that she must have taken. She could not see where she had come out by the water without lifting her head further and turning it to the right, but surely *there* was the blunt spur of rock just above the forest line that she had skirted on her way down; and – tracing upwards with her eye – *that* must be the place, a short horizontal on the silhouette of the shoulder, directly under the almost-sheer climb to the summit, where she had first looked over into the new valley, hoping like a fool to see a *city*. Yes, that was the place, looking as if a giant had knocked a piece clean away from the mountain top.

And then her hands, and her heart, stopped.

Oh fathers . . .

Just for an instant, up there where she had stood, there had seemed to be a tiny flash of light. And now, here was another.

Mira lay flat on the treacherous ice, ignoring the need to keep moving before her body heat melted the crust, and waited for more; but there was nothing. Her eyes locked onto that place, bored into it until they swam; and saw nothing.

A piece of ice, she thought; perhaps a stalactite of ice catching the sun. Or the reflection from a wet sheet of rock. No pursuit from the community could have tracked her this far and fast through the fresh snow: that was sure.

Nevertheless, her hands pulled a little faster for the rest of her ice crossing. And when she did finally half-roll, half-crawl onto the solid shore, hauling pack and bag after her, trembling from the effort, she saw clearly across the lake a pencil line of blue smoke that must be the remains of her fire, that she had thought dead.

No more fires, she promised herself. I must not believe in luck. I must make my own luck.

Hand over hand, she started to pull the slack wire in from the ice. Whoever might wish to follow, they would have now at least to skirt the end of the lake to pass.

EIGHT

It was never sure how long the snow would stay away, but for now the trail left by those who had strung their wire over the lake was fresh and easy to read. Better than this, they also seemed to know the land as well as Mira knew her own mountain.

Setting off lightly in pursuit, she was expecting more puzzles and obstacles, yet found none. The path the men had taken avoided both the highest ground and the lowest, preferring to skirt around the peaks where possible, seeking out saddles of land and narrow passes where Mira's eyes might have seen nothing except possible danger, and often keeping just above or within the topmost fringes of forest. A hiding place when needed, perhaps.

Even when the trail dipped down to cross the successive valley, there was nothing like the long lake with the wire. Her quarry either chose ways that went around the ends of the ice strips, or simply crossed them on foot, presumably knowing that with these smaller areas the ice would be thick enough to bear their weight. Mira, in her turn, trusted *their* knowledge and went as they did. It would be foolish, she thought, to lose this chance through fear of breaking ice.

And if – or when – she should draw close to the men, what then? She could not yet answer. The men ahead might or might not know what she sought, they might or might not be those that had come to her own home: but they were at least *there*, other human beings in the wilderness, eating, sleeping, surviving, showing her the way south.

The route was many miles longer than any that she would have taken, and (she had to admit) many times faster. Yet she saw no one, either ahead or behind. Perhaps, after all, these men did not sleep when the good weather came . . .

For two days the girl pressed on, alone but focused, even content. She felt with pleasure the new hardness in her body, the ease with which her muscles carried her across the snow-packed land. But her ribs were also beginning to stick out hard, and she knew that she must have a fresh supply of food soon. The last scrap of oatmeal was chewed for breakfast on the second day following the trail: if necessary she would have to stop and try to trap something edible; bird or fish or deer.

At mid-afternoon on the same day, as she had dreaded, the sky started to pale into white and the air grew still and quiet. This changed everything once more. By morning the track she followed would most likely be gone. Thinking on this grim possibility, wondering whether to press herself doubly hard along the trail in one final effort, Mira did not see what lay ahead until, emerging from a stand of snow-heavy spruce, her feet were almost upon it.

A bridge. A real metal bridge, made by human hands, spanning a short steep drop where unseen water roared and fell under layers of ice, far beneath. She stood breathing deep, resting her hands on the metal rails at the start of the bridge; and for a minute forgot those she was tracking and thought weakly of hot food, a proper bed, talk, laughter . . .

Perhaps this small thing, this bridge, was the start of the South. Where the *cities* were. In the next valley, or the next after that. The men she followed might be going there: not raiders from the wilderness after all, but men sent out from a city on some task.

Mira stepped out onto the bridge, sliding her hands along the rails like a child, disturbing a powder of white which fell silently below. She would follow the trail until new snowfall had hidden it, she decided, and then look for friendly shelter if necessary. If somebody had seen the need for a bridge, there must be *some* people. Yet, under its heavy paint, this bridge was bubbled and cracked with rust. Her fingers felt it. As if it had been made long, long ago. Perhaps . . .

And then, as if a hand had slapped her, she came out of her dream, stopped her humming mid-bar. Ahead of her, at the other end of the bridge, was a bulky figure; a man with a beard, wearing a heavy white parka, unsmiling.

Instinctively she turned, ready to run back the way she had come, to dive into the forest. But a second figure stood there, cutting off all escape.

It said: 'Evan sends his greetings and asks you to come and make his acquaintance, little miss.'

The man's accent was strange, the vowels drawn out long and flat with no life in them and the polite words were a mockery, for they bound Mira's wrists behind her and made her walk between them. She didn't manage even a single blow in her defence.

'Impressive. I won't lie to you: it's very, very impressive. I reckon you been covering twenty-odd mile a day. And over some nasty terrain, too. *These* great animals don't manage *much* more . . . do you, animals?'

A few sniggers broke out from the pack around her.

'Now. There *is* something. I'd particularly like to ask

you about the loch. The large one. How did you manage there, eh?'

Evan seemed to go deep into thought, resting a finger on his forehead, looking down at Mira's feet. Then his face lit up and the smirk was back.

'*I* know. You took *down* our sodding wire and pulled yourself across on your sodding sleeping bag. *Am* I close? *Am* I?'

It was hard to hide her surprise, but already Mira had learned that it was best simply to stay silent. Let this Evan have his performance alone and he would grow bored. It happened now. He gazed at her a while, waiting for a reaction, and Mira silently returned his gaze, watching the white flakes stick to his face and instantly melt. And suddenly the smirk was gone and Evan was giving orders.

'Three minutes, then, gentlemen. Perky and Green: you're flanks. Hopkins: point. Randy, you follow after thirty. I want ten more mile tonight, see if we can't reach that nice spot in those woods. Leave the big water for tomorrow, eh mates?'

Whatever all those words meant – *flanks, point* and the rest – the white-clad men, understanding, got to their feet, put out cigarettes and started shouldering their packs. Mira avoided their eyes. She felt fear of what she saw there. Beyond doubt, these men were raiders. They were used to taking, not asking.

As if reading her thoughts, Evan said: 'And you, mystery lady? Who's to look after you?' Again the charade of thinking and then he said: 'Well, I think it had better be me. Mmm?'

Three men had disappeared off into the trees ahead and to the sides, another waited behind – that must be the one called Randy: it was he who spoke on the bridge, she thought – and although there were seven or eight others, they all walked far apart, glimpsed only now and then through the trees. That didn't seem right, but she didn't want – didn't dare – to ask any question.

Instead, she walked numbly beside Evan, cursing her foolishness, trying not to think of what would happen next; trying to keep control of herself and not beg or sob or question or run off a few paces just to be brought down again, like a naughty bairn. Well, Gil had taught her a little already, hadn't he? Hide your thoughts. Watch and listen.

And fight down your fear.

At least the pace was easy. Her things had been rooted through and then thrown aside by the pack of men, all except the sno-bag, which Evan had tied to the top of his own pack, so that there was nothing for her to carry. Even with hands bound, Mira had no trouble keeping up. It heartened her that the brutes moved so slowly. If the time and opportunity came to escape, she'd only need a few minutes' start . . .

It was dark now, still snowing, but not the heavy, swirling fall of a few days before: more a silent dusting of tiny new flakes. Mira felt her stomach groan and wondered if they would feed her. So far there had only been cold water from a flask. If they had kept her sno-bag then surely they intended to look after her, which meant there would have to be food, too. But then, why keep her at all? Why set the trap on the bridge to catch her? And *how* did they know about her crossing of the lake? (The *loch*, they'd called it.)

One thing was heartening above all others. These men wore white, not grey, and she would swear that none of them were those who had shot the woman down in front of her. Besides, if they'd meant her harm, they need not have taken her with them. The silent drop from the bridge would have been enough.

Presently, the man called Evan broke the silence. 'Very impressive,' he said quietly, as if there had been no gap in the one-sided conversation from earlier; 'Young lady knows how to handle herself, don't she? Must have a head brimming with questions and be frightened half to sodding death too. But keeps her cool; handles herself OK.' He glanced sideways at her. 'But then she *would*, wouldn't she?'

They were out of earshot of the others. Evan seemed to keep his acting and clowning for his men: the play-acted mockery from before had faded to simple shrewdness.

Mira raised her chin: 'Aye? Why would I, then? "Handle myself OK"? And what is your purpose with me? Maybe I'm no who you think? Maybe you've made a mistake.'

The man chuckled and shook his head. 'Not time, Princess. Your questions'll have to wait. Pretty accent, though, and a pretty face to go with it. I think that deserves something. Tell you what . . .' Mira saw the glint of a knife and felt the cord around her wrists suddenly parted . . . 'How's that for starters?'

'Aye. It's good,' she said, rubbing the skin where the rope had been. 'Thank you.'

'That's OK, Princess.' He held the knife up meaning-fully. 'But please try to remember. Those idiots can move much faster than this, specially with something sweet and tasty to chase. Best you stay close as you can to Evan. Day and night, eh?'

They walked on in silence.

Waking, Mira could smell meat. Smell and taste and hear. A piece of meat, sizzling in a pan, invading all her senses.

Fathers, her stomach felt like it had shrunk to nothing.

Without looking, she could feel that it was *her* time, the singing pre-dawn, the night spirits soon to make way for the day; yet someone was cooking meat. Snow hare it smelled like. She shifted onto her side, stiff from the cold ground, and opened her eyes.

Ten metres away, there was a giant of a man wearing white, bent over a pan. The flame underneath it was pure blue and came surprisingly out of a shiny silver cylinder, no bigger than a fist. Around him were others with the same clothes, some standing with steaming plastic mugs, one or two squatting or sitting to rub their boots with oil, working away with the blackened end of a rag.

Evan's men, she remembered. And she a prisoner.

Something, someone's boot, prodded her back and a voice said: 'I 'spect you'll be wanting some of that, won't you, Princess?' Evan himself stood there, eating noisily, gesturing at the pan with his knife.

'Yes. Please. I am very hungry.'

'Thought you might be. Can't have you starving, can we? Lucky my boys are so handy with the old crossbow, eh?'

Crossbow. She could remember that from her book. A very old weapon, she thought. And nothing like the weapon the man in grey had used. Again, the little difference reassured her.

Evan said: 'Lovely and quiet, the crossbow.' And then, calling; 'Here, *Gatt*! Bung a bit over here for our young lady. The man with the pan silently came over and dropped something into her hands; a piece of flesh and gristle, half burnt, half raw and bloody, and too hot to be held without juggling it.

'That's it. Long way today, Princess.'

Mira said, her mouth already full: 'Why do you call me that?' but Evan was gone again, wandering away, talking to his men. She had hardly swallowed down the food when she heard his voice, like yesterday: 'Five minutes, gentlemen.'

She pulled on her shoes and went to find him: 'I need to pee.'

He broke off what he was saying to another man – Hopkins? Perky? . . . she wasn't sure – and looked at her with irritation. 'Bed roll tidied away?'

'What?'

'Is – your – bed – roll – tidied – AWAY?'

'Oh . . . nae.'

'Tidy it. Then you may pee. If we're feeding you, you can make a sodding effort.'

How he seemed to change from friendly to angry to joking and back, without warning. Blushing, she went back to roll up the sno-bag. When it was done and tied tight, she went to ask again, aware of the ugly leers that followed her.

'Well?'

'I've rolled the bag. I need to pee. Please.'

'So, pee!'

She looked around at the eyes on her, returned to Evan's cold gaze. 'Well?' he said; 'You don't need me to pull your sodding pants down for you, do you?'

Abruptly the mood around her seemed very different, very tense. Mira thought that the men behind might have come a little closer, but didn't want to look to find out. There were murmurs and growls and chuckles from the tree shadows, as if they were wild beasts. Yet the boar in the blizzard had meant her no harm. These were not shy beasts, but savage men.

Evan, too, seemed to notice the change. She saw his

gaze flick round: and then without warning he was bursting out laughing, wiping tears from his eyes.

'Your blooming face, Princess! Please, sir, I need to pee, sir! Sodding priceless. *There*: use those little trees over there, past where you slept. Don't try anything, though: you've got one minute.' And then, as she went, head down: 'And YOU, you ugly lot of skivers . . . Now you know the proper way to ask for a pee, I'll expect the best sodding manners from you all.'

She heard the laughter, felt the release, and suddenly understood. In Evan, neither the anger nor the laughter were real. She shivered to imagine what the others would be like without him there to harness them. Perhaps he had simply been showing her that. He wanted her frightened, obedient.

I will be as he expects, she thought. I will play the game, as I did with Gil. Poor, dead Gil. How she would prefer him to these pigs, with their rough, strange manner of speech. *Blooming* and *sodding* and *skivers* and *flanks*. If Gil had truly had any business with them, he had bitten off something harder and more sour than he could chew, right enough.

Evan called: 'Right. Move out. We'll take usual positions after the big *loch*.'

Mira's hope that a city might be close was unfounded, or so she guessed. Nothing was said to her directly, but she felt from the mood of the men in white that there was still a long way left to go in their journey. They seemed intent on their purpose, efficient, determined: there were no celebrations of an imminent arrival. She would not ask, though. Some questions, perhaps, but nothing that told them how little she knew, how ignorant of the world and the South she was.

The 'big loch', when they came to it, was like the others, running north-east to south-west directly across their path, but was three or four times bigger even than the one Mira had crossed on her back: a massive, majestic open space, with its flat table of white flanked by mountains that she was sure were again diminishing in size, although the low, trailing snow clouds hid the peaks.

She and all twelve men stood silently in the fringes of the pines, well above the level of the ice, whilst Evan took binoculars from his pack and scanned the other shore. Behind them was the end to a steel wire, slightly thicker than the last one, and this time bolted fast into a solid piece of snow-covered granite, protruding out from an angle in the slope amongst the trees. Again, Mira had had nothing to carry so far today and her hands had stayed united. The piece of snow hare in her belly had brought the strength flooding back into her, although she had taken care not to walk differently or show it in other ways.

Evan lowered his binoculars and said quietly: 'OK. Let's move.'

The men started taking things from their packs. White straps made of some material or perhaps nylon, short steel wires and small chunks of metal that seemed to hold a tiny gleaming wheel and a handle.

'Gatt: you're first.'

The bear who had scorched the meat stepped forward. He was wearing his straps now, round his waist and thighs, and they were connected to the steel wire, with the metal chunk at the end. Reaching up to the suspended cable, he hooked that piece over it and clicked something shut. Bending his knees, he tested his weight on it, swinging free on the wire.

Evan winked at her, without humour. 'If it won't hold Gatt, we try another way, see?'

Then the man Gatt reached above his head and started to wind the handle. Silently, easily, he floated off out of the trees and towards the great *loch*. Evan watched his progress with the binoculars. Even with her naked eyes and the snow as white as his clothing, Mira could just make out his bulk, swaying slowly over the ice. Eventually Evan said: 'Man over. And he signals all well. Perky, up you get: you're on.' And again a man floated away in silence. One by one the men went through the same procedure and disappeared across the frozen valley floor.

'What about me?' Mira dared ask. 'You don't have one of those . . . *hangers* for me, I'm thinking?'

'No, Princess, we don't. No room for spares on these trips. So you go with me. We'll clip you on tight.' He saw her expression. 'Unless you'd rather choose one of the others? No skin off my thingummy-jig. Up to you.'

He laughs at me, at everybody, Mira thought; he is too sure.

Surprising herself, she enjoyed the slow trip across the wire, strapped though she was to Evan with his rank breath and sharp eyes. It was a beautiful place from which to see the valley and the great *loch* stretching away and gently around the curves at the base of the mountains. It felt like floating on an island of soft white cloud.

When they were halfway over, Evan murmured: 'Now if I wanted to have a bit of fun with you, this would be the place, eh, Princess?'

Her moment's peace stolen, Mira looked him in the eye and said: 'If you . . . *touch* me, I will unclip us both and we shall fall through the ice.' Inside her fleece her heart thudded and her muscles grew taut. She hoped he would not see that she was afraid of what he said.

Evan appeared to consider: 'Well, in that case, another time perhaps?'

On the new shore, as before, three men went a little ahead and one stayed behind, to follow on later. The others walked in their fanned-out group, first along the loch side for a mile or so and then, turning south again, started to climb the flank of the next mountain. 'Keep sharp eyes for those forester idiots,' Evan had said to his men; and now Mira realised as they plunged back up into the woods that the trees here grew in a pattern of rough diagonal lines. The *forester idiots* must be people. Maybe people who had planted these trees, like her own people made electricity. *Foresters*. It was cheering to think that they might be close, whoever they were.

Should I try to become free? the girl wondered. When they have given me more meat, perhaps? Or when I can take some, in secret? Reluctantly, she could see that there were fine reasons not to run off, or not yet. For now these men were taking her towards the South, by paths that she would not have found alone. It seemed that they would feed her and keep her safe, after a fashion. And the pace was easy, allowing the rest her body needed. It would do her no good to run, if she could not find the strength to stay free.

She remembered Evan's threat: 'Those idiots can move much faster than this . . .'

Also, there was still the hope, more than the hope, that they knew something of Annie Tallis, or Adeline Beguin . . . or her. Even if they were not the *police*, or Raymie's raiders, even if they had not after all been anywhere near her home, Evan acted in a way that seemed to suggest he knew her, or *about* her.

And with that impression came new courage, for if it was truly so, then it was the first solid thing since the scrap of paper to show Mira that she had not plunged into madness these last weeks. She might discount Old Sarah's vague accusations, she might even have been mistaken over Raymie's knife, but there was no mistaking the fact that she had been trapped and made prisoner by strangers who knew something of her, and even knew how she had followed them.

Coming abruptly out of her thoughts and seeing that they had climbed once more, high above the lochs, she realised that he – Evan – had said something to her.

She glanced across. 'Sorry?'

'I said: "Penny for them".'

'I don't understand. What is a penny?'

Evan sighed. 'And I thought you had the intellect of a sodding Einstein. A *penny* was a sort of money, once.' And, seeing that that wasn't enough: ' "Penny for your thoughts" means "What are you thinking about?" Get it now?'

She said: 'Och. Yes. I'm sorry. I wasnae really thinking at all, right enough.'

'Right: and there's a flying pig. Tell you what, why don't you ask me all those juicy questions that you can hardly keep inside of you? Then *that* will be out of the way, won't it?'

His tone was light, but his eyes stayed small and hard and probing.

And if I did, then? she thought: It must be nothing that will show him what I do not know about the world. Nor anything that will show my purpose in being here.

'Aye, all right. Will you tell me then, do you not have round shelters for the nights?'

He shot her a glance: 'What else?'

'Who puts the wires across the lakes . . . the *lochs*?'

'What else?'

'Why would you want to keep me prisoner? I am nothing to you. What is it that you want?'

'What else?' He asked it like a threat now.

'Nothing else.'

'Huh.'

They walked on, and Mira began to doubt that Evan had ever intended to tell her anything, but then he said: 'OK then, the answer to the first is yes. We have *round shelters*. For the worst weather, when we don't move.' He chuckled. 'Except our shelters are *magic* and can *fly*, see?'

She did not see, but asked; 'What do they look like? Are they of metal . . . or plastic?'

'Cloth. Silk. White and grey. How did you know about the "shelters" then? Fair's fair, eh?'

'I saw the circles on the ground, where you had camped.'

'Smart girl.'

'And the wires?' She did not want him to lose the desire to talk.

He said: 'The wires? Why don't you guess, for them? Just how did we get those wires there, eh?'

Play the game. 'On your way to the North. You left one end attached and then someone went over the ice, or around perhaps.'

'Both wrong: you're not thinking.' He was scornful. 'Just imagine how much bloomin' cable you'd need to walk it round the edge. Bloody miles of it. And this is the first time we've been this way for an age, anyway.'

Somewhere up ahead a bird was singing. Just a low two-note song, repeated half-heartedly. The first she had heard for days.

Evan paused in mid-stride, hissed; 'Lie down! Quiet like!' and pointed to the base of a tree.

Mira whispered back: 'But you've no answered my

third question.' Immediately his hand was on the back of her neck like iron, forcing her to bend down to the ground, pushing her face roughly into the snow. Slipping off his pack, he lay next to her and she felt the edge of a blade on the soft skin of her throat.

Wild thoughts of rape span through her mind, but Evan made no further move, just lay there watching the way ahead through the trees. In a moment she understood. There were voices coming, and then three men in big, bright red jackets, one holding a wide, folded paper full of bold lines and colours. When they spoke, their voices were like her own people; not like Evan's group.

One was saying: 'This whole area, man. 23J to 18J. It'd be nae bother to take it down before Michaelmas. Not on such an easy gradient. An' think o' the bonus!'

'Aye,' said a second, wryly: 'If we do that and nothing else, mind. Aye, it's possible. Though my Meg might not be so keen.'

They drew level with Evan and Mira, bent over their paper as they walked, and the girl felt the blade press deep. Then they were past, and disappearing down the slope towards the loch.

After what might have been a few minutes or an hour, Evan silently rose, putting his finger fiercely to his lips, and went a little way after the strangers, taking his binoculars. When he came back, he puckered his lips and whistled: the same as the bird Mira had heard up ahead, but a three-note song. Soon, silent white figures were filtering through the trees.

Mira climbed stiffly to her feet. The fingers she touched to her neck came away red with blood; she felt faint and sick. One man started to speak quickly, nervously: 'It weren't me, Evan. It were Green. They came in from the left, from the trees. There's no way *I* could've covered 'em. First thing I knew they was be'ind me.' He broke off, looking worried.

Evan stayed silent, making them wait, running his eyes over them.

Eventually he said, silkily: 'First things first.' And without warning his hand flashed out and slapped Mira full across her face, so that she fell back against the tree and then to the ground where they had lain unmoving before. 'When I say jump, you *jump*. Immediately. Is that clear?' His face was pinched and deadly: humourless. Mira nodded dumbly from where she had fallen, her head pounding. With relief she saw his attention switch to the man who had spoken too fast.

'As for you, Hopkins, you prattling worm: you're *supposed* to be the best. That's why you get these nice jobs. So your cock-up'll cost you fifteen days' pay and a horrible poxy comment on your field report. Same for you, Green.'

There was a clamour of voices. Grateful that they were arguing between themselves, still dazed from the blow, Mira found that she was sprawled across Evan's pack, still on the ground from before. A huge, metal-framed bag, white like the men's clothing, and covered in zips. Hard objects inside stuck uncomfortably into her belly. Mira could taste blood in her mouth and hazily saw the scarlet drops staining the white material. Shifting away from the bulges, her hand brushed a zip tag. On sudden impulse, trusting that the voices she could still hear vaguely above her meant that Evan was occupied, she let her fingertips tug at the tag, teasing it down, keeping it hidden by her body.

Evan was speaking again, casting his judgement after some argument: 'Punishment stands, gentlemen. You put us *all* in danger by your sloppiness. But if you want to sort out between you who's to blame, private like, you can do that tonight when we camp.'

Jeers and catcalls and harsh laughter. Mira's fingers wormed into the hole and pulled at the first thing they found. Just an edge, a scrap that came out into the light. Pale grey cloth.

'Come on, Princess. Stop sulking and bleeding on my bag. Up you get! We need to move.'

She hadn't heard him approach. Praying that he'd seen nothing, she tucked the corner of cloth back in as she rose, and made a show of straightening her clothes. *Play the game.*

'I am ready,' she said, eyes looking down at the white beneath her feet: a suitably chastened prisoner.

'No hard feelings then,' Evan said, cheerfully.

And so they were off again.

NINE

Evan did not invite Mira to ask her questions again, and nor did she try. The scrap of pale grey was enough: enough to pour every ounce of effort into making herself seem ignorant, lost, helpless with these men.

Of course, helplessness had its own dangers too, right enough.

When Hopkins and Green, the two who were blamed for the foresters coming so close to the group undetected, faced each other to 'settle it', Green, who had dull, unkind eyes in a wide, sallow face, said: 'How about we fight for *her*, then Evan? Forget the other thing.'

'*Her?* Why, she'd have you for sodding breakfast, Green, old son. Hard as nails this one is, whatever she looks like. No, nobody touches her unless *I* say.' Again, Evan was able to make the men laugh, but he did not see the sour, spiteful, hungry look that Green gave Mira while they jeered at him, and she shivered. There was a real enemy that Evan had made for her.

When the fight was started by the leader chopping his hand sharply down through the air ('Twenty minutes, gents, and *I* will name the winner. Not too much noise now, if you please'), Green lowered his head and charged viciously at Hopkins, growling his anger. Hopkins, who was smaller and sharp-faced, stepped nimbly aside and sent the larger man sprawling with a kick behind the knee. But while he was still looking smug, Green rolled to his feet and in the same movement flicked out a meaty fist, which glanced off the side of the other's face, opening a deep cut under the eye.

Despite herself, Mira was drawn to watch. Balance, she saw, was crucial: and fitness, flexibility . . . And yet still these were nothing compared to the ability and will to do damage without flinching.

Sickened, she thought: I could never do that. Nobody I have ever known is like that. Not even Gil. Especially not Gil. But those who had shot down Annie Tallis had been like that; cold, murdering brutes without restraint or respect for life. And in truth had she not herself killed a man?

The two blood-streaked men grunted and growled and lashed out and rolled in the snow while their fellows looked on, grinning and smoking, and then suddenly Hopkins managed to punch Green up under his ribcage and it was over. The larger man stayed down, gasping, clutching his stomach.

'We have a winner,' Evan announced neutrally; 'Green; looks like *you* were to blame for not keeping a sharper watch earlier. However, punishment for the both still stands, as I said it would.'

To add to his humiliation, Green was given the first camp watch – two or three others were further out in the trees somewhere – and Mira could feel his eyes on her as she lay unmoving in her sno-bag, near the deep-breathing Evan. When Green lit a cigarette, she hastily shut her own eyelids, for fear that he should see by the flame that she was awake and come over.

Perhaps, the tiny, dispassionate voice at the back of her head whispered; perhaps Green could be the one to help, when the time comes to run.

She shuddered at the thought of what that might

involve and made her mind turn to the grey material, though that was worse.

If these truly are the men that hunted Annie Tallis, then where are the two I saw come from the trees? Were they sent off ahead to lay the wires used to cross ice? Or to take their victim somewhere? Or . . . so that I did not see their faces?

The last possibility would mean that they really did know who she was, and even *why* she had run from the community. That didn't seem possible. How *could* they know so much? Had someone been watching her all the way? She would swear not, especially in the blizzard.

But there had been that momentary flash from the mountain top; and now something else that troubled her: the tracks she had followed from that *loch* had all been bunched together, a churning up of the snow that was impossible to miss, but whenever the group had moved since she had been their prisoner, the men were spread wide, leaving as little mark as possible for the snowfall to cover. This seemed to be second nature to them, their usual way of travelling.

So why did they leave the heavy tracks before?

There seemed no room for doubt: they had allowed her to follow. They had intended to trap her.

A few metres away, Green's dead eyes reflected the glowing tip of his cigarette as he drew in the smoke.

Perhaps Mira was successful in hiding her new fears, for the routine continued as before for three days, with Evan becoming almost friendly as they walked together. Almost. She constantly reminded herself how quickly he could change and how subtly he could control people. Of them all, she feared him most.

'Cat got your tongue?' he joked from time to time

as they walked through the frozen forest and over the passes, the endless tiny white flakes drifting around them; but better her tongue given to the cat than to have it run away with itself.

At least there was more meat. One of the men managed to hunt a boar with his crossbow: a lean, sinewy young tusker that they cut into strips and salted, to be cooked over the magical silver cylinders when needed. The crossbows were light metal frames that could be collapsed quite small to fit in a side pocket of a pack. But when they were clicked together – it took only seconds – and the short length of cord that fired the bolt grew as taut and hard as steel, the weapon was deadly. The hunter's bolt had plunged completely through the neck of the boar and showed its bloody tip on the other side. Without emotion, the man dug it out with his knife, cleaned it of blood and sinew, and put it back with its fellows for the next time.

'*I* can cook,' Mira said to Evan, thinking of the magical burning cylinders: 'If you need someone. I helped cook for the men at home.'

But he looked at her with his flitting, teasing, unkind grin and said: 'Gatt will do just fine.'

'Do you no trust me? You're afraid I'll poison you? That Gatt scorches the food: I can make it tender and sweet.'

'Gatt is our cook. Just be thankful I let you keep your hands free, Princess.'

She sensed, though, that they were drawing closer to somewhere significant. The men were becoming more restless and the pace quickened. The mountains had diminished to half their former size, and from time to time they came upon places where the forest had been cut down in a great swathe.

At night she noticed that Evan sometimes left the camp for ten minutes or more. In a rare moment when no other eyes were on her, she tried asking the big bear, Gatt: 'Where does he go, then?' but the giant just looked at her as if he didn't understand her question, and walked away to see to some task. The next morning, the cords around her wrists were back, without explanation given or asked for. By the end of the day's travel her arms were aching from being drawn back into the unnatural position and she saw with dismay that Evan meant her to stay tied all night.

'I have given you no cause to bind me like this,' she said, bitterly.

'Maybe. Maybe not,' Evan replied; 'But bound you must be, Princess. We must have our package safe on arrival, mustn't we, eh? Otherwise certain parties will be more than a little pissed off with old Evan.'

'*Who?* Who is it that is making you do this?' She couldn't help it: the question came out.

Evan reached out and gave her cheek a little, irritating punch. 'Time enough at Lomond, eh? For all your questions. Be good now, won't you?'

Lomond. A place? Their destination? Somewhere in the South?

One thing was as clear as the water from the stream-way: even if her white-clad captors had done her no real harm, whoever waited in the place called Lomond could not be relied upon to be so gentle. She must escape *before* Lomond, if it could be done. She had learned all she could from these men. Which was little enough.

But it seemed now that she had tarried too long, missed her chance. Even when she was untied to relieve herself, someone kept a close eye on whichever tree she hid behind. And then, on the fourth night since the fight, she saw two of the men laughing together, nodding in her direction. One said: 'At least tomorrow we'll get a drink.'

As if some inevitable game were being played out, Mira listened without surprise when Evan chose the first watchmen of the night and Green was sent a few hundred metres ahead of their camp, up to a higher piece of land, a ridge that they would be skirting on the morrow.

'The wind's getting up,' Green said sulkily; 'It'll bloody whistle right through me up there.' Even as he said it, a teasing little gust blew through their camp, lifting the topmost snow.

'Nothing could whistle through a lump like you,' Evan replied evenly; 'Up you go now. Eyes and ears sharp.'

Mira thought dully: So it is to be tonight . . . and it is to be Green. There was no avoiding it: somehow she had to get her hands free of the biting cords if she was to stand the slightest chance. From the cocoon of her sno-bag, she watched the men moving around the camp, talking, smoking and eventually lying down to sleep. All the while, the wind that Green had moaned about freshened and became more urgent, and Mira realised, gazing up past the treetops, that the clouds overhead were moving swiftly, starting to break up, revealing fragments of deep liquid black, glinting with stars. Perhaps more clear weather was on the way, although she would not wish it now: better another blizzard.

Lying stiffly in the dark she thought of Cobb and the others, and of her own low bed, set next to the window below the roof at home. How have I come to this moment? she wondered. How has my life been swept away in only . . . How long was it? A month? A little more? It was hard to remember what her days had been like *before*.

There were always four awake and eight asleep (plus Mira herself) for the nights with Evan's group. The four

awake were the three further out and the one who sat
in camp. Twice during the night, they would change,
although Evan always took the last camp watch of the
night. That gave each man a watch of about two and
a half hours, Mira reckoned. Two and a half hours for
Hopkins – the man in camp – to need a pee or to take a
walk to stretch his legs.

When it happened, Mira almost missed it, having
grown drowsy in the warmth of her bag, even with her
hands tied stiffly behind and the savage wind across her
face. Perhaps she had slept a while, yet something in
her must have been watching, though, for suddenly she
was fully awake and realised with panic that Hopkins was
not in sight. How long he'd been gone she could not
know, nor what time it was, but soon the men would
change and Green would come down from the ridge.
It had to be now. Hopkins could not be counted upon to
disappear twice.

Worming silently, savagely, up out of the bag, she bent
over and used her teeth to take her jacket and force it into
the space she'd left, pressing it home with the side of her
face, holding down a corner of the bag with her knee. Not
a perfect imitation of a sleeping person, but all she could
manage. She stole a quick look over to where Evan lay
facing her, two metres away, with eyes closed, and then
she pushed her feet into unlaced shoes and crept away
between the tall dark trunks.

Not that there was much cause to be silent, with the
wind buffeting the pine tops. More important that
Hopkins hadn't wandered up this way for his pee – there
seemed no sign of him – and more important that she
managed to fit her feet into whatever marks Green had
left and pray that it was enough, in the dark, to fool Evan
and the rest.

She did not yet think of the thing that lay ahead. She did not even properly have a plan for *that*, just a vague notion that she might convince Green to slash the cords . . . The temptation simply to try and skirt around the man ahead – to run as she was, laces trailing and arms forced numbly back, with neither jacket nor supplies, nor sno-bag – flowered up in her throat, almost bringing a blind, stumbling panic: but she angrily pushed it down again. She had only this one chance. The freedom would not be worth the having if she could not keep it. With hands tied she would not even be able to balance as she ran and would most likely end up dead at the foot of a slope of icy scree or in a crevasse.

Please let him be easy to persuade.

Please . . .

She was free of the trees now, and the gusting wind nudged her sideways. The speeding clouds meant that the light kept changing. One moment would be fully dark, the next, a sliver of moon gave a faint glow to the white slope. In those lighter instants, the ridge just ahead was a sharp line.

Where is he? Mira thought, fighting for her balance as the last section of slope steepened. Is he asleep? Oh let him be asleep. Hopkins would surely be back from his pee: every moment she expected the sound of heavy running feet behind her, and Evan's knife at her throat.

Then, suddenly, Green was there.

Coming from nowhere he stepped silently in front of her so that she almost collided with him, and grabbed her upper arm. Those dead, soulless eyes regarded her silently. She heard a sobbing, choking noise and realised that it had slipped from her own throat. No good. If this was to work, Green must *not* see her real fear.

'On your way somewhere?'

'Aye,' she made herself say, 'just a walk, up to the ridge.'

His eyes raked over her. 'A walk,' he repeated.

'Aye, a walk.'

'And nobody saw you go?'

'I couldna say.'

He looked past her, at the forest edge, and then un-clipped binoculars from his belt to look again, although how he could see through them in the night she did not know.

'Well . . . well. Evan must be slipping.'

'It's OK, though, isn't it? I'll go straight back down. He needn't know? He . . . scares me.'

'He should scare you.'

'He needn't know, though?' she said, making sure the idea was planted in the brute's head.

For perhaps a full minute, they stood like that, with his fingers biting into her arm whilst he looked at her face, then looked again at the forest, then back at her face. Maybe she had misjudged him, she thought in panic; maybe he would take her back to Evan. If he did, there would be no more chances. That was sure.

Worst of all – a black pit in her thoughts – he might simply take her, tied up as she was.

And yet, Evan had said that nobody should touch her. If he forced himself upon her, he'd need to go further still to keep her quiet, and even then he risked discovery. He, too, feared Evan, if only he would remember it. If only. Who could say what a man such as this thought or felt?

Green, too, seemed to be thinking over the possibilities of finding Mira the captive here, alone. His slow, lizard's eyes kept passing over her and she thought his hand on her arm trembled: but more likely that was her.

'Green?' she said coaxingly, speaking loud above the wind. 'I can return silently and wake no one.'

Slowly he brought his second hand up and placed it on her cheek. It was cold and clammy, but Mira stopped herself from flinching.

He said, slowly: 'That depends. It must be worth a kiss, before you go down. If no one is to know of your "walk".'

'Aye,' she made herself say; 'A kiss then. And I'll slip back before they miss me.'

His mouth on hers was slack, sour, wet. She felt sick. Then he drew back and looked her over again. She'd known he would, like a sickly, predictable boy, more of a child than she was.

'A kiss and a cuddle,' he said, with his face shining moist even in the cold wind, as the clouds flitted away from the fingernail moon.

This is the time when I must be perfect, she thought. Almost she could wish that Evan *did* come from the trees. Perhaps he would still hear if she shouted? Aye, she would try that if all else failed. Her pulse hammered as she said, casually: 'Free my wrists for a minute, then. But only a cuddle. Then I must go back before we are discovered.'

His dull eyes held hers, and she returned his look. 'You don't need your hands for a cuddle,' he said, leering.

'For a proper cuddle I do. Unless you're afraid of me, Green, like Evan said.'

She had gone too far there: a moment of anger crossed his face. His anger would lead to the other thing, too, she thought: the thing she feared above all. Then he said, roughly: 'Turn around.' And turning, she felt the cords undone, so that the blood screamed back into her numb hands.

Immediately his great fleshy paws were on her, groping

around, suffocating. 'This had better be good,' he grunted.

For an instant she felt weak, overwhelmed, nauseous. She could sense his strength and malevolance. But still she opened her arms and drew him in closer. Then brought her knee up hard between his legs, so that he groaned and fell.

'Pig,' she whispered.

With hands to balance, she was up at the height of the ridge in seconds, coming suddenly into a wind that pierced her clothing and whipped her loose hair across her eyes. How long would Green take to recover? She had that long to find his pack. *All* the men on watch took their packs, and she had seen Green leave with his earlier. It must be close; but if she could not find it, she was dead or worse. She ran a few paces along the ridge, straining to see *that* ghostly white lump against all the other white.

She heard Green roar, and saw his bulk scrambling up the slope after her.

Oh fathers! The pack was nowhere to be seen. Think! Surely it could not be far, as Green had come upon her so quickly to begin with. He must have been watching from somewhere nearby. He must have.

Green himself was up at her level now, maybe twenty paces away, close enough to see his snarling, screwed-up face and hear his panting and cursing. He would surely kill her now, or whatever he wished: the time when he would remember his fear of Evan was past. She had pushed him too far. With her laces still undone she might not even be able to outrun him . . . and every muscle in her body seemed to be collapsing, impervious to the signals from her brain.

And then she saw it. Sitting just below the lip of the ridge on the northern side. Green's rectangular white pack, just a few paces away, outlined a moment by a tear in the ragged cloud. Gasping, she threw herself at it and ran her hands over the material, searching for the right pocket, sobbing in her haste. Her back was to Green now: he would reach her at any second, she could hear the muffled thuds of his footfall on the packed snow. But she had it! Her fingers found the right shapes and tugged the zip open. Out came the cold, light, deadly metal frame. Green was three steps away, two, one . . . Her mind remembered: *somehow* her mind remembered what she had seen, and she felt the struts in her hand lock rigid. There were always two bolts clipped to the handle; she knew. She found one, ripping her palm on the point, and slotted it into place.

'*You little bitch.*'

Snarling, Green grabbed a handful of her hair and yanked her up to her feet and round to face him, grunting in surprise as the crossbow pressed into his stomach. Now, her mind screamed, shoot now. Yet her fingers did not listen.

'Bitch!' Green screamed again, his spittle flecking her face. 'You haven't got the guts!' Then his open hand rammed hard across her cheekbone, as Evan's had done, but much much harder, and with her senses exploding Mira felt herself slip and tumble back down the steep slope towards the trees where the other men slept. Rolling to a stop she hardly knew where she was.

Think!

But the thoughts wouldn't come, her mind was drifting. Above her there was a noise. A great unnatural noise. She held onto it and tried to remember what it was. It was *important* that she remembered . . . *so* important. A man shouting, running down towards her. She could even make out his shape through half-closed eyelids. Green. It was Green. Coming down to finish the job. Coming down to kill her. That was it.

Only she had *something*: this thing clutched tight in her hands, cold and smooth. Blearily, she looked down at the crossbow, squinting through the blood. No good. No good! The bolt was gone. Fallen. Lost.

The second one, the cold voice chided her. Use the second one.

Green came down on her like thunder and her fingers found and unclipped the second bolt. He had seen what she was doing: he ran the last ten metres at a sprint, all his bulk coming to destroy her. His finger was raised, pointing at the weapon in her hands. His mouth was twisted into a smirk. His eyes were feverish.

At two paces, the bolt jumped noiselessly into his belly and, equally silently, his legs buckled and he pitched face down onto the snow and moved no more.

Mira was crying.

The men would come any moment. It was certain. All the noise . . .

Yet they did not come.

Eventually, like a stranger in her own body, she stumbled to her feet, tied her laces tight, heaved the body over in case there was yet some life there, needing breath. At the top of the slope the pack was where she remembered. In it she found many more bolts, a thicker fleece, big enough to hang to her knees. Somewhere there would probably be food and other useful things, if only she could think what they might be. But she couldn't think, didn't want to.

Tying the fleece round her shoulders, she smeared the blood away from her eyes, crammed a handful of snow into her parched mouth, and picked up the crossbow and bolts.

And then she crested the ridge once more, and headed south.

TEN

How many hours she ran, she did not know. She would not choose that time again. But first light she was looking on a wonder. A thing wholly new to her.

An expanse of partly frozen water that seemed big enough to be the sea, though a low, flat bridge went out across it, disappearing into the distance amongst a vague suggestion of other pieces of land, no more than shadowy smudges.

A few figures were moving on the bridge, some with cargoes pulled by animals, and there were two ships beyond, steering through black pathways in the ice. And along the shoreline, at the place where the bridge met land at this northern end, the place also where a group of other ships – seven or eight of them – nestled unmoving in their berths, there was a settlement. A town: a *city* . . . she did not know. A place surely big enough for a hundred (a thousand? More?) people to live, though it did not seem to tower up like the cities she knew of from the free broadcasts and from Gil. No matter: the buildings were massive and made of stone and metal and even glass, clustering in a half circle round the ships and the bridge, overlooked by the last of the northern mountains.

Hardly knowing who and what she was, hair and lips crusted with dried blood, legs trembling from her flight, one ankle swollen and black where she had turned it on a hidden branch, Mira limped forward.

Staying at the water's edge, and walking into an icy

wind that came steadily from the west, she drew gradually level with the buildings and the mouth of the
bridge, and tottered on, towards the ships. It was easier
now. Her feet were on a hard, black surface, cleared of
its snow. Somehow she needed to find a place to rest,
medicine perhaps, food. She might find a warehouse,
with stores.

Hazily, she realised now that here, next to the ships,
there were some people around, and that they were
breaking off from their tasks, staring at her. No good, she
thought; I am too easy to see. They will tell Evan, when
he comes. That Evan and the others *would* come was
not in doubt. It was just a matter of time, though she
had run like the hunted beast she was to outdistance
them.

On she went, stumbling on the bad foot, seeing no
place of refuge but unwilling to stop and draw further
stares. And the place was not perhaps so huge, for already
she was almost at the end of the quay. Beyond lay only
empty shoreline, curving back round the last mountain
and towards the north again. No warehouses lay next
to the ships; if she wanted supplies she would have to
turn back up into the city and ask for them: and a hiding-
place too.

She stopped walking, turned round and stood, swaying
slightly, trying to summon energy to head back up
towards the great, dark, fearsome assembly of buildings.
Absently her eyes wandered to the ship that lay here, the
last of the line. A bonny little vessel in green. There was
a man leaning on the rail and watching her intently as
those others had watched her. Bitterly she wondered
why these people couldn't just ignore her, or offer help,
or *something*: she was sure a stranger to her own home
would be welcomed and well fed.

The man on the ship was young, handsome, capable-looking. She noticed his big, weather-hardened hands resting on the rail, and then he spoke. 'Are you wanting to shoot someone down with that thing, or is it bloody murder that you've done already and are fleeing from?'

His accent was not like hers, yet not unlike either. Confused, she looked down and realised that she was still holding the crossbow, locked tight between her fingers. No wonder the people had stared, with that and her bloody face! She made to toss it away, but the man quickly put up a finger: 'Nae lass. Not where they'll find it.'

'Who?' Mira asked; 'Not where *who* will find it?'

'Those that would harm you,' he said neutrally.

In silence they regarded each other for a moment, then Mira said: 'I know you, so I do. You are the one who brought us supplies in your ship, the last time.'

'And you are the pretty lass who led that pack of young hooligans that kept getting in our way for the unloading.' He grinned suddenly. 'Come on board and you may wash and eat. You've time for that: they won't come yet.'

How did he know she was pursued? Even as she asked herself the question she pushed it aside. The man did not seem like an Evan or a Green, and now he offered her help, the first to do so. And she needed help: she was finished. With relief Mira went to the ship's metal side and started up the ladder there, handing the crossbow over the rail to the man, and accepting his hand on her arm as she dropped down to the deck herself, wincing.

Down below, in the rooms inside the vessel, he showed her to hot water and soap, and then left her, to 'cook up some fish and porridge'.

'What about the other men?' she asked. And he replied:

'My crew? Och, they're up to no good in the town there. We sail at midday: it's their last chance. They'll come skulking back before too long.'

The porridge was hot and impossibly sweet, making her shiver. But the man – Sean – stood looking on and grinned no more.

'And so to what we are to do with you. To save you from your hounds: for they *will* be here soon, lass.'

In the warm belly of the ship, her eyes closing from fatigue, it was hard for Mira to imagine Evan finding her *here*. She felt safe, drowsy, light-headed even. To sleep in a real bed after the cold, hard snow for so many nights . . . Anyway, the answer was obvious. She said: 'I will sail with you in your ship at midday. If you will allow it.'

Sean frowned. 'Nae. That will not serve. Doubtless you were seen coming aboard this morning. You must no think yourself hidden here. Some of those others would sell their mothers for a credit or two. And you made quite a show: one they will not forget.'

Mira laughed at him: 'But if we are away, on the water? My hunters cannot run over the waves, I think.'

'No. If they know you to be on my ship, they will take you, at sea or on land. It makes no difference to them.'

She put down her spoon with a clatter, suddenly irritated with the man. And below that, the fear returning, taking away her appetite.

'How do *you* know all this?'

He gestured at a dull metal box in the corner, lit in three or four places with delicate little green lights. 'I have listened in to your hunters.'

She did not understand. 'You know them? You know what they want with me?'

'No. They say little enough that might be heard. But I know enough of them to understand that my boat is no sanctuary. And, lass, my boat and my men must come first, do you understand?'

She stayed silent, head bowed. Eventually she said: 'Then I should no hae tarried here.'

He came and sat down opposite her at the table. He spoke softly: 'I do not agree. You needed food and rest for a while. And . . . I did *not* say that I would not help: just that we cannot sail away in the daylight with all the town knowing you are aboard. No matter. If I can do it, without risking ship or crew, I would gladly rob those men of their prize.'

'And so? What should I do?'

Almost guiltily he looked at her, looked long in her eyes as if to see what lay inside. 'And so,' he said gently, 'you must run a little more, if you can.'

Dull, she asked: 'Aye? Run where?'

'Out along the stiltway, over the ice and water. Out where every soul can see you and point the others to your trail when they come.'

'Like a snow hare on open ground with a hawk above,' she said, bitter once more.

'Yes, exactly like that. But as swift as the hare, too, to keep ahead of that hawk until the stiltway turns east again the flanks of the next hills. Fifteen miles from here, perhaps.'

'Fifteen miles. And then?'

'And then, lass, you will see the open sea very close and I will send a boat across the shallows to find you. *If* you have stayed ahead of the hawk, it will be near dark by then and you will be hidden by those hills, even from their nightsights. They will think only that you are further down the way than they had guessed.'

Mira felt her ankle throbbing and the stiff ache in her calves and thighs. 'Fifteen miles?'

'Yes,' he said. 'Can you do it? Have you the strength?'

She doubted that, but shrugged. 'I will try. If there is no other way . . .'

'There is no other way. Trust me.'

Trust, she thought bleakly. Trust was something that she would have to learn again. Given time.

She took the crossbow with her, when she went, in case it should come to that. Retracing her steps past the other ships, she was again stared at and even whistled at and called after, but she refused to heed these people who would betray her to Evan if they could. The bridge – the *stiltway* she must call it – was as empty as before, with only two or three souls to be seen, braving the biting west wind. Before she stepped onto it, she raised her feet as if it were the singing morning and she about to run the mountain path. As if all was well: her old life given back. Behind her the buildings of this *town* – not a city, after all, it seemed – lay stacked up, filled in her imagination with eyes watching for her to depart.

Do not fret, she said silently to the watchers, you will see me go. There will be no doubt in you when you are asked. And then she was off, coaxing one more effort from exhausted limbs, feeling the swollen foot stab at her despite the soothing medicine Sean had rubbed into the joint.

This journey was worse than anything since the night she had seen Gil fall. Quickly it became a nightmare, an endless stumbling, shuffling run along a straight, jarringly hard way that seemed almost to float on the ice and water, with no place or time for rest. Real or imagined, she heard the pursuit behind her, echoing her own footfall although, turning, she could see nothing. Soon, even the town was hidden by the distance and the mountain behind it became no more than a pale shadow of itself.

The dim light grew then quickly waned once more. As the day failed, she had no idea how far she had come. It could have been four miles or forty. All she knew, with a dull, hopeless certainty, was that no boat would be waiting for her and that Evan's men would catch her. There was no other possibility: she only ran at all because she would *not* sit and wait for the inevitable like a weak child. And when they *did* catch her, she would make the crossbow sing a few more times, perhaps . . .

Thus she passed into a fever, shivering and sweating while she ran, twice stopping to be sick, hanging tight on the rail while her guts came up and the world turned to cold, swirling grey. She could no longer feel the bad foot banging down on the cruel, unnatural surface; or anything that troubled her, except exhaustion and despair.

Let it be soon that they come, let it be soon, let it be soon, let it be soon . . .

The mantra went through her head. Or perhaps she was mumbling it aloud? 'Let it be soon.'

And her wish was answered, for she realised that they *had* come, without her even having the strength to fire off one bolt. Feebly she reached for the bow, finding vaguely that she was lying on the snow-clad surface of the stiltway, although with no memory of falling.

Too late. It was all too late. Someone held her arm, stopping it slotting in the bolt.

Sean said: 'Easy. Easy lass. We're no the ones to hurt you. You've done just fine. Lie still now.'

And she felt herself lifted. And then she was in a boat and the tears were pouring down her cheeks. And then . . . nothing.

*

Not long afterwards, on the stiltway, a small group of men stood silently in the darkness, smoking and taking a bite. Two of them stood apart, against the rail.

One man said: 'We'd have sodding got her if we hadn't waited for *you*. Anyway, we'll get her in an hour or two, or tomorrow at the worst.'

The other gazed silently down the dark way. 'I wonder. She should not have got so far. Not injured, if those fools told us right.'

'Oh, our little princess is a right one for leading a chase and making grown men cry, you'd better sodding believe it. Ask Green. Oh no, can't do that now, can you?'

Evan's companion looked at him with distaste. 'Perhaps you are right,' he said; 'But why confine herself to the stiltway? Answer that.'

'Exhaustion. The blind desire to stay ahead. Like an animal . . .'

'Perhaps.'

In the hot, light, noisy room below deck in the bonny green ship, Mira passed from nightmare to nightmare and soaked and resoaked the clean, white blankets they rolled her in. Somewhere in the nightmares she saw that the men here had a receiver for the free broadcasts: its luminous glow lit the strange faces around her. More surprisingly she saw for an instant on the screen the face of the woman who had been shot down in her community.

'Tilly Saint,' the receiver voice said, 'recently back from the World Ski Cup in Canada.'

No, she thought; That's wrong. They mean Annie Tallis.

And she spiralled down again into fever-ridden sleep.

PART TWO

Blessed children,
You are given this sleeping serpent;
Stretched across the years,
Its strong, bright coils buried deep
In the marshes and the flood waters;
Its mouth closed on its tail.

And when the serpent wakes,
And it is full grown and nourished,
And the beautiful, sleek, knowing head is lifted up,
And the two eyes open, one brown, one green;
Then, blessed children, you may ride its back
To freedom and love.

For this serpent is no tempter:
She is your truest friend.

(From 'Truthsong' or 'Dreams, # 7')

ELEVEN

Kay was lost.

He stood encircled by the dark pads. Dreamlike, he saw his hands flitting across them like restless birds. Swelling up from some hidden place in the floor, there were tones and rhythms that multiplied, wove together, built palaces and oceans of sound. The sound touched him where he was alive. He was high on it, swaying in the stifling, sweat-soaked atmosphere. His long fingers moved effortlessly to their destinations.

Below and around him a crush of bodies writhed to the same urgent, sensual sound. Some were in trance state; some – pale and white as ghosts – had used drugs to get where the music took you. But all were locked together, connected. There was no fear here: only music. Only celebration. The fear was left outside.

As the sound built to crescendo, wave breaking on wave, player interacting with player – nearly there, *nearly* . . . – Kay opened his eyes a moment, wanting to drink in the scene, share it with the other players and the dancers, commune together for the bittersweet last few moments.

And he saw instantly an ugliness, a thorn, a drag . . . Hedge, his bodyguard, standing there motionless amongst the motion, arms folded, face impassive. Kay felt his hands falter. Damn the man for being here, for seeing his private pleasure, for clinging like a black shadow; drinking the joy from his life. Damn his family for sending him. He would have to find a new place. Would have to evade Hedge more carefully next time.

Whatever.

Anyway, he knew he wasn't going to be nannied back tonight, even if he'd been found. Any moment now the last deep bass tones would burst out and die in a hundred fizzing spirals of melody; and the dim, swirling glowlights would die with them for a time, until the music should begin again. That must be his moment . . .

Five minutes later Kay was out on the street, huddling anonymously into his jacket against the roaring wind and sleet. Hardly anyone was to be seen. It must be late, only an hour or so until the night people took to the slushy streets to drag themselves home. For now he had the solitude he wanted, and the heat in his belly left by the music. Hedge and Tomas and Tilly could all wait. If he chose, he could probably even get Hedge replaced, for losing his charge again, right outside the Saint Building.

Anyway, he thought vaguely, anyone who wanted to jump him now, in *this*, probably deserved anything they could get. A handful of credits would be about it, unless they wanted the jacket too.

Not that he was unarmed.

Kay smiled inwardly, untouchable in this mood, and turned to skirt the docks, surprised at how far he'd come in those few seconds since the music. Below him was the glint and suck of the water. He liked this way. The clumsy, heavy shape of the ships – hundreds of them, bobbing and grinding together in the wind – reminded him that escape was possible, one day. Even right now, tonight! He had only to choose his time, find some crummy, rusty tub going further than just up the coast. Anything was possible for a Saint.

For now he made do with the possibility, not the deed, and a little further along – before the wild fires and the knives of the derelict old docks – turned back towards his real purpose in coming this way. The road led up sharply past the Port Controller's towers and the customs and immigration buildings, and then at the top of its climb, blossomed out into a market complex, set around a series of squares. Here there *was* some action, making Kay shiver happily in his coat. Hot food shops, spilling out dim yellow light, ready to tempt the all-nighters when they left their clubs: and around them, a straggle of pedlars, prostitutes, beggars, jivers, lovers, losers of all sorts. Hedge would have a fit.

This was Portable Road, so-called because it was gone by daybreak. Scroats and addicts and misfits and the insane huddled together, hoping for a snack or a smoke or a score from the clubbers. Or failing that, hoping simply to keep off the weather with their patchwork of membrane and resin and polythene.

Kay drifted across the square, the ice water dripping off his nose, and into the nearest of the arteries. It felt like home. He exchanged words when they were offered, handed out a few food credits, stopped a moment to listen to a half-naked Floodite, and knew enough to steer subtly away from the *really* mental ones who came lurching towards him, babbling nonsense laced with good cheer and the threat of sudden terrible violence. None of them knew him; not who he was. He'd be torn to pieces. But then, he wasn't *that* beautiful. Not a guaranteed Vision. Imperfect enough to be left alive.

Annoyingly, his head started to ache and he thought of how far he still had to walk to be in his bed, already forgetful of how pleased he had been to come here. He should do what he came for and go.

He took a new turning, into an even narrower way. From inside the jacket hood, his gaze skated over the

old-young faces, the dull eyes, the outstretched hands, the
sniffling, pitiful kids. He was careful not to look too long,
but somewhere, somewhere . . . Yes, *there* she was, the
real reason for this trawling, strange, longer way home on
a miserable night: a girl who fitted in well enough with
the others, sheltering alone beneath a sheet of corrugated
resin. Her eyes were vacant, her hair twisted into crude
scarlet spikes, her face white with the eyes bordered in
heavy black. Next to her a woman was tunelessly singing
the new song, about a snake. He came level with the girl
and slowed, almost stopped. Her jagged-edged sheet of
resin banged up and down on her knees in the wind, her
eyes crawled lethargically to his face and, like the others,
a hand came out unenthusiastically and without hope for
whatever he wanted to give.

Again his mood changed track – that was the way of
it when he was tripping – and he was gripped as he
had been before, the first few times. He smiled at her
and she did nothing. He didn't mind. He wondered what
she would say or do if he just sat down next to her in
the wet filth.

Swiftly, before all the rest of the no-hopers could see
and come crawling and wheedling down here, hanging
onto his clothes, Kay unzipped his jacket and slipped
out a small pack. In the same movement he tossed it to
land just over the lip of the resin, where it could be
hidden at once on the girl's lap; but the wind flapped the
sheet violently at the crucial moment – or perhaps it
was a poor throw – and the pack bounced off the outside
and slid to the ground in full view.

Immediately the clamour began.

'Mister, mister, mister, mister, mister . . .'

'Give, please give, please give, *please* . . .'

'Just a smoke, some food . . .'

'*She's* not pretty, *I'm* pretty . . . I can do it for you, whatever it is. I'm very good. Take *me*.'

The singing woman stopped her song to pull two tiny shapes from under a wet, tattered mess of polythene: 'My children!' she said. 'My poor children. Look at them. Look at *this* one. *That* bitch has no children.'

Deliberately Kay turned back into the sudden scrappy tide. How had he felt that this was a home, a minute ago? All this pain and ignorance. He took out the last of his credits and tried to give them out evenly, fumbling in his haste, hoping that the girl had managed to get hold of the pack and pull it under the resin sheet. She didn't look as if she had the intelligence *or* the strength, but if she could only manage that simple task, she'd find food, cream for the sores round her mouth, vitamins, shoes even.

'No, that's it! That's all I have now. Leave me alone.'

His voice sounded strange to him, pitched too high. A few of the uglier ones were bearing down on him now. Pimps maybe, thinking his interest in the girl was physical, or vultures with hidden claws. In disgust and fear, Kay turned about again, sidestepped a shape who had crawled out from the shadows and was reaching for his leg, mumbling and spitting, and walked quickly away. He did manage not to run, just, and he managed not to reach for his sidearm in panic, which would be fatal. Of the pack he'd brought there was now no sign, but the girl showed no recognition either, when he passed. Maybe the singing woman had indeed grabbed the things for her babies. He'd just have to hope . . .

How he wished he could stay and reassure her. Keep her safe.

In five minutes he was deep in the blustery dark of the finance sector, amongst the heartless steel-and-glass monstrosities that he could see from his own apartments.

Already he was thinking of Portable Road fondly again. It was probably more dangerous *here* than there, despite the cameras. But he didn't much look like anyone's prey; could even be a Scroat up to no good himself. Hedge was more likely to get done than he was, with his gleaming rings and perfect, symmetrical face.

Except it would take three or four of them to do Hedge, even if the attackers were lucky and had the edge of surprise.

How his thoughts swam. He thought of the girl again and smiled, danced a few steps, waving his arms, skidding in the slush. There: now the cameras would *know* he was just mindless Scroat scum not going anywhere special.

Another long, steep climb, and then Kay was at the top of the city. The top of the capital. Of Briton. The place where his family lived, like Roman emperors, overlooking the misery of the rest. Thankfully no bodyguard stood fretfully outside to end a good night with hassles and explanations, and Kay was able to thumb-print his way in and up through all the security doors to his rooms, high in the south-east corner. His fortress within the fortress.

'Lock,' he said to Jane, and she murmured back. 'Locked, Kay.'

Immediately he felt exhausted.

He kicked off his soaking boots and went to lie in the tub, shivering up his spine with the heat as he lowered himself in and closed his eyes. Behind the lids, the image of the girl danced between other images, looking blankly up at him from the filthy, slushy ground, hand outstretched. If only some sort of life could flicker in those eyes. She was so pretty, so familiar. The strong feelings somersaulted about inside him making him giddy, and he let them, without trying to work it all out.

But after the soak, maybe he'd see what he could find

in the family database. Not with Jane; with a keyboard –
the old-fashioned way.

Sliding further down into the water, so that it tickled
up over his lips, he thought of the club. Only the music
mattered, and the joy, and the place inside, where his
family couldn't reach.

Outside the Saint Building, a little down the hill towards the finance sector, the girl with the scarlet spikes
stood unmoving at the corner of somebody's expensive
residence. Her head was tilted back and her eyes fixed on
the lights that had appeared high up when Kay had
opened his personal door. She stayed there for a long
time: an hour, two hours . . . The weather worsened but
she didn't feel it too badly, and her feet were dry in their
new shoes. In her stomach was food and vitamin pills.
Sweet of him.

After a while Hedge came striding easily up the hill,
moving like a big, predatory cat, but she pulled back
further into shadow and he went by without seeing her.
At the Saint entrance, as Kay had done but more aggressively than the boy, he offered his thumb-print to the
machine outside and was admitted.

Eventually, with a dawn of sorts about to try and break
through the never-ending storm, she turned and went
back down the hill, on to Portable Road, where the action
was all done now, and the first daytime traders were
brushing the rainwater and the filth into the drains, and
finally, a mile or two up the waterside to the cellar –
stinking of fish from the docks, and damp from seeping
silty water – where she slept.

'Here,' she said to the old couple already there, a
double lump on two carpet-covered pallets, and gave
them what was left of Kay's food.

On her own pallet she lay silently and thought about Kay.

He could be what I need, she thought. But I'll leave it a while yet.

'If I can beat Jan next month, I'll be the first girl to top the league. Did you know that, big brother? The only girl ever, I expect.'

'Good. Fine. Whatever.' How his sister prattled on. Kay looked at what was out on the table and gestured to Hedge, who came over. 'Can I have some toast, please, Hedge?'

The bodyguard's dark eyes also raked over the dishes set out down the table: meat, fish, out-of-season salads and vegetables from France or beyond, rice even. 'Toast,' he repeated, growling.

'Yes, please.'

Silently the man turned and left the room.

'Why do you *do* it, Kay?' Clarissa was looking at him with her chiding expression, copied from their mother. I love you despite your many weaknesses, it seemed to say, but do try to better yourself.

'Do what?'

'Wind that man up like that. Surely you want him on your side, just in case . . .'

'But he's *not* on "my side", is he? He's on Tomas' side. I didn't ask for him.' Even to his own ears he sounded petulant.

'Oh grow up, big bro.' Clarissa smiled at him sweetly and reached for more green beans. They couldn't be together without needling. It never stopped.

Presently, their grandfather came in with Copper, his own bodyguard. At eighty-three Tomas moved easily enough, and had most of his own hair, flattened into silver wings down the sides of his head. He came to the table and steered his paunch comfortably onto a chair with a sigh. Copper, deceptively short and cheerful-looking, went to stand near the doorway, where Hedge, and Clarissa's guard, Sebestova, were usually positioned. With all three of them there, Kay always thought, it looked like a comedy act from one of the old video reels.

Tomas rubbed his hands, as he always did, and said: 'Well, this all looks splendid. *Splendid*. They've done us proud. What will you take, Kay? A little salad?'

Clarissa said, with her mouth full: 'Kay's having toast. He sent Hedge to get it.'

'Ah. Toast. Hmmm. What's wrong, my boy? Stomach a little delicate, is it? Now why's that, I wonder?'

There was no reply to that, so Kay kept silent. Maybe when Hedge came with the toast, Kay would send him back for something else. The tail fins of a puffer fish, perhaps, marinated in wine from Australia. Something to teach him not to be such a sneaking killjoy.

If the man had told his grandfather how he ran off, he'd be bound to get an earful from Tomas soon.

But he wouldn't play their games. Remember, he said to himself, you're the only normal one here. The rest of them can't help it, after all. And it wouldn't be for much longer. Soon enough, he'd find his ship and go. But for Tilly's unusual and old-fashioned whim, he wouldn't be here at all.

All the old resentment came churning up, giving him a pain in his belly. Not for the first time, he wondered who his father was. Not somebody like that awful Greek that she was seeing at the moment, he hoped.

Clarissa had gone back to talking about her stupid Slam competition. 'I'll be the first girl to do it, if I beat Jan,' she said again. '*When* I bet him!'

Tomas said: 'Ah, yes! That would be something, eh? Good-looking young man that Jan, too, isn't he, my dear?'

Clarissa blushed.

Kay murmured sourly, to nobody in particular: 'But will he still be, when Sis has finished with him?'

'Well, we'll all turn out to see it, on the big day. Won't we, my boy? And win or lose, I'm sure it will be quite something! Your mother will be proud.'

As soon as he'd had his toast, Kay excused himself and went back to his own apartments, sighing with relief as Jane locked the doors, sinking down onto the floor, his back against the entrance. He felt ragged. The night was catching up with him now: he shouldn't have bothered getting up, except that Tomas hassled him when he missed meals. The long, dull hours until the next nightfall were lined up in front of him like tombstones. Inside his jacket, the little silver tube beckoned, but he was no fool. He must be sparing with that. You couldn't live your life in freefall.

Instead of the tube, he thought of the girl. He hadn't had any luck this last night with his network search, but that didn't mean that it wasn't there to find. It had to be done gently, delicately, like making music, or old Tomas would find what he was about and make a fuss. Well, 'fuss' wasn't exactly the right word. The kindly old grandfather routine might fool Clarissa, but it didn't fool him. It wasn't as if they were really a family, after all.

He found that he had risen and that his steps had led not back to the computer keyboard, but to the calm and emptiness of the music room. His one truly safe place. A better kind of freefall than the other. On the other side of the large oval of plexi-glass, winds battered the capital, for once carrying neither rain nor sleet. Inside, there was complete silence. *Complete*. Nowhere else in the city could be so quiet. Only the faint whisper of hidden lights, reflected here and there from the shining sprawl of drums and tone-pads. Absently, Kay pulled the thick door shut behind him, picked up a drum stick and gently bounced the squashed-pea end on the skin of a snare.

Tchuk. The living sound jumped round the room.

He picked up another stick and slid round onto the stool. The two squashed peas, as if separate from him, ran in a fast cascade from left to right, over each taut disc, and he reached out to adjust the position of the third cymbal.

Already he was lost again. *This* was worth being a Saint for. This tiny sound-proofed paradise. These beautiful antiques.

At the push of a button, a swirling, distant melody stole sweetly round the room. Kay sat a moment, considering, and then allowed his hands to join with it, lightly at first, but soon growing more urgent, more dynamic. If anyone had been able to enter the room twenty minutes later, they would have been almost deafened by the tide of sound in that quiet place, as ecstatic, sweat-soaked Kay – eyes shut – poured out layer upon layer of animal rhythm.

But then, no one *could* enter this room. He'd seen to that. Not even Jane had eyes in here. And outside the door . . . only the usual background hum of the building's systems.

He might be the only living thing on earth.

TWELVE

How quickly you got used to it, Mira thought. The hunger, the squalor, the *ugliness* of the place that they called a capital. Already she ached for her mountain: the cloud pines, the floating, singing *otherness* before the day broke. If they'd ever had that *otherness* here, it had long ago been driven out. Things were hard, loud, tangible, obvious. Only the clearly seen existed for these people. It seemed to the girl that they were only half alive.

'What d'ya expect?' Beebop asked her, half teasing, half needling as usual. 'Ya want *spirits*, an' *heaven*, an' aren't we all *beautiful* then . . . Well, go an' listen to the "Snakies" then. Or even better, get yer face done. Be a Vision. Be a Saint. Who else 'as time for all that crap?'

'Oh yeah, sure. And where'd I get the credits for *that*?' she asked him back, in the same accent, the same bitter tone. It came without thinking now.

'Never mind, Spark. Yer cute enough fer us. And who'd want all their bones scalpelled and jiggled about and that anyway?'

They were outside the back entrance of the eating house called Crimson, moving from bin to bin, picking over the leavings of exotic foods; a mess of congealing creamy lemon and coconut sauces, half-gnawed bones, bits of wild rice, great flat leaves of some herb that had gone black overnight, the claw of a crab . . . It was barely day: they were the first. One by one, they filled the oddments of plastic boxes from Beebop's bag with the food waste.

Mira almost liked Beebop. He was certainly funny, full of mad energy when it suited him, kind to those he thought of as his own. But then he was also bitter, resentful, scathing. His thin, earnest face could change from grin to sneer in the bat of an eyelid. Sometimes he seemed angry that he was even alive.

'Right. That's it, then. Let's clear off,' he said, tucking the last box away in his shirt. '*Pedestal! Yo, Pedestal!*' The pup appeared back from its own scavenge hunt and fell into step beside them. Beebop spat on the door of the restaurant as he passed it, despising the source of their food, but Mira thought that it was he himself who had poisoned the world he saw with those challenging eyes, not the hated Visions, or the accident of the wrong sperm meeting the wrong egg.

Together they headed down wide, low avenues. Vision territory though the winds didn't discriminate. From time to time a passing line of orange Caplink wagons would stop to let people descend, stepping from the warm, silent interior into the restless, gusting wind. Mostly Visions of course, but a few Scroats too, on their way to work up here somewhere: in shop storerooms or restaurant kitchens, perhaps. Mostly these workers gave Mira and Beebop scornful or disgusted glances, looking away again quickly. The Scroats were worst of all, ashamed to be what they were.

'*Yes*, mate? What's yer problem?' Beebop said aggressively to one or two of them. '*You* ain't got so much to smirk about.'

Reaching the edge of the richer district and the start of the descent towards the water and poverty, Mira saw a police transport stopped up ahead and felt her heart rate increase a little. There were four of the burly figures in grey, sipping from beakers of hot drink, idly watching one of the street screens with its Level One nonsense. A ten-minute freeview present from the Saints: quite common. Later, at the time when Old Sarah was shuffling to her sofa, the screens here would also have the free broadcasts.

Mira couldn't see *police* without thinking of Green and Evan.

'Don't wind them up, eh, Bee?' she murmured to the boy; 'Let's get back with the food. Martha'll be waiting for it.' And he replied: 'So long as they treat us with *respect*. That's all it takes. A little respect.'

There was no good crossing over to the other side of the avenue, or doubling back to take a different way. That would only get them noticed. The best thing was to be dim and direct and not worth the policemen's effort. Sure enough, as Mira and Beebop drew level with the four, they gathered round, blocking off the walkway with their bulk, sensing the chance of fun.

'Oho. A fine pair out walking their dog. Good morning, miss, morning, sir. Who might you two be, then?'

'Good *mornin'*, officer,' Beebop said with a grin and an edge in his voice, which Mira knew the policeman would not miss. 'I'm Beebop, this is Sparkle. Who are you?'

'Nice names. Very . . . suitable.' The man, a sergeant, lifted a finger to one of the others, who went over to the transport, spoke into a com set. 'Now, then, *you*. Sparkle. Can you tell me a proper name? And what you're doing all the way up here this morning?'

Beebop said: 'Sparkle *is* a proper name. She don't need to tell you *nothing*. Why don't yer ask those other idiots, eh, mate? In the Caplink and that. Or are they too flippin' good to be harassed?'

With no surprise Mira watched two of the policemen take Bee off, pushing him through the open side doors of the transport, and start to search him, slinging questions and insults in equal measure to see if they could get an arrest to take them back to the warmth of the police building. Bee was squirming around, half obstructing them, swearing loudly at them. Inevitably, the few other people out so early weren't looking away now: they were staring, enjoying it, wondering what crime the no-hoper Scroats had committed *this* time. The sergeant, left with her, said: 'If you could just answer my questions, miss. Your name for a start.'

With dull, stupid eyes, but not the empty drug stare of Portable Road and the old docks, she let her gaze fix on his face and said; 'You want my other name? What my mum calls me?'

The man rolled his eyes at his mate in the transport: 'Yes. That's the one. What does your mummy call you?'

She appeared to consider and then said: 'Lizzie. Lizzie Hepton.'

'OK then. That's much better. Now, Lizzie Hepton, it's very early to be out in this wind. What were you and your friend doing, I wonder?'

'We wanted food,' Mira said, fidgeting about, looking down at her feet. On the ground someone had sprayed the shape of a green snake, half fading away. You saw them everywhere. 'From the bins. 'Cause my mum's ill now, isn't she?'

Keep it near the truth, simple, believable. Be no threat.

The sergeant looked at her, at her scraps of clothing and plastic held together with old cord; at her dirty, tired face and lifeless eyes, and she thought; It will be OK. This man has children himself, perhaps.

'Which bins? Do you know which bins, Lizzie?'

Thinking of the spit on the door of Crimson – could they know about that already? The cameras had not caught it, but anything was possible – she shook her head, and then said: 'It's all orange and green and white at the front, isn't it?' as if he should know where they'd been.

'Ah. You mean Dolce Vita I expect. Was that it, Lizzie?'

She shrugged, then nodded once like an imbecile, still studying her feet. At the edge of her vision she could see that in the transport the others had finished searching Beebop. His mouth continued to run away, unchecked, but they might still be OK.

'Just boxes of puky old leftovers, Sarge,' said one of the searchers in disgust.

'All right,' said the sergeant; 'Thumb-print him to be certain, and . . . check this one's name. Lizzie Hepton.'

Mira felt her muscles relax. The name check would be OK, she thought. A thumb-print might not be. She really didn't know. They probably wouldn't have anything on Lizzie, but she couldn't be sure. If they'd wanted to print her too, she'd have had to run.

Beebop didn't take the same view. 'Why d'ya *do* that, Sparkle?' he asked angrily, tight-faced and disapproving, as they went on, freed by the coffee-drinking police. 'All that speakin' like you was five years old, an' mumblin', an' looking at yer feet. Where's yer *pride*? Is that how you *want* them to think of us?'

She said, 'I don't want them to think of me at all. I just wanted to get on home, Bee.'

'*Home!* Is that all that matters to you, then, is it? Bein' all warm an' cosy and not in trouble with the nice policeman? Thought you 'ad more bottle than that. You *did* to start with, the day you come. What 'appened to it all? Where's it gone? Sod it, you even gave Lizzie's name. What's *that* all about?'

Mira almost laughed at him. Warm and cosy! Nae, she hadn't been that in a good long while. But she said only: 'Lizzie won't mind. But yeah, I 'spect you're right. It's not good for me to act like that. But still, it was *me* that fooled *him*, wasn't it?'

It was a mistake to argue the toss, even gently. Bee deliberately wouldn't see her point and went on at her all the way across the city and down to the water, making her head ache. With the boy's clothing and face and tone, she felt like she was being pecked continuously by a sharp, bony bird, fluttering along beside her. But then, typically, his bad mood spent itself without warning, and he grinned suddenly at her and said: 'Ow about if you go up to Martha's an' start to cook this stuff up and I'll see who's about an' hungry?'

'Fine,' she said, returning his smile.

Bee wasn't bad. At least he could think and had some life to him. Many times more human than the ones she had to meet in the night.

Kay woke with a start, still grasping a single drum stick and with the image of the girl fresh in his mind. He was stiff, knotted up, one leg had gone to sleep under him. His brain could make no sense of things. He tried to focus, wondering where on earth he was, and saw the instruments around him, familiar shapes. Oh God yes, he'd sat down against the wall of the drum room after playing. He'd only shut his eyes for a moment, exhausted by the music. And by the night, of course.

Hot water was needed. And a drink. Unsteadily he got to his feet and saw through the oval that night had already returned to the city. He must have slept for hours.

As soon as he'd released the door seal, Jane welcomed him in her quiet way and informed him that: 'Mathilda Saint has come to your rooms three times during the afternoon. Tobias Hedge came with her the third time to attempt to open the music-room door, but did not

succeed. I told him that he would not. There are messages
here from Tomas Saint, Mathilda Saint and Clarissa Saint.
Should I play them to you?'

'No. Run me a bath.'

Undressing, he imagined Hedge trying to get into the
music room, getting hot and angry and losing face in front
of his mother. It was a nice thought. There was some
justice. After all, they must have overridden the external
door locks even to be in the apartment.

He slipped into the water and said 'Screen, please' to
Jane, who switched it on and asked: 'Do you require
computer or broadcast functions?'

'Broadcast. Level One,' he said.

Level One showed an old comedy. A rich, beautiful
married couple and their two fine sons, always having
arguments and getting into scrapes with the neighbours,
but falling on their feet in the end, finding out that they
did somehow fit together as a family after all. A cathartic
message for the masses. Something to aim for.

'Level Two.'

Wildlife. A whole highway of ants, carrying little
sections of leaf across the forest floor and back to their
nest. Into the real credits here: only a few Scroats could
afford this stuff.

'Level Three.'

Sport. A Slam contest somewhere in the Americas.
'Oooh and that's *nasty*,' the commentator said gleefully;
'he's going to need attention for that.'

'Four.'

Information. The Scorch Belt of North Africa and how
it might be made fertile again, given the almost infinite
sum of money mentioned by the programme makers
and a long, long time. Pie in the sky. Feel-good crap for
the Visions.

Kay smacked his palm irritably on the surface of the steaming water. 'Level Five.'

News. 'Thirteen "Wreckers" were arrested today,' said the woman, 'following an attempt to enter and vandalise the Stoneywall Fertility Centre in Wales. A security spokesman said that no motive had been identified and that damage had been slight. The thirteen are due to appear before the Justice Panel tomorrow.'

No motive. That was a good one. Up to the usual Saint standard.

Kay carried on up the Levels, into the realms where no Scroat could possibly be watching, under normal circumstances, and only the richest Visions. At Level Ten there was news of a series of rearrangements in Pax, the security service. 'Shareholders are to vote today on whether to endorse the board's choice of Jan Barbieri as the Junior Executive Lieutenant in waiting. Mr Barbieri, seventeen next month, has passed out of the Pax Academy with unprecedented grades and is widely tipped to be accepted as the youngest lieutenant ever in a landslide vote. Executive power has rested with a rotating committee of leading shareholders and board members since the death of Mr Barbieri's parents, four and a half years ago, at the hands of the "Wrecker" group calling itself Evolution.'

There was a picture of Jan's rubbery face, barely smiling, looking unexcited about all the fuss, wearing the light grey Pax cadet uniform with ease and elegance. Frustratedly, Kay flicked soap bubbles up at the hateful, waxy features, and Jane's unhurried voice came immediately: 'Kay, I recommend that moisture is not brought into contact with the screen.' And then, without pause, 'Mathilda Saint is outside. I have told her you are in your bath. She asks admittance.'

Can't they leave me alone, just for an hour or two? Kay thought. Can't I even bathe? But at once he was guilty. He always felt guilty when his mother was around. Somehow she was less easy to hate than the rest.

'Yes,' he said. 'Admit her. Ask her to wait in the living quarters. I'll join her there.'

He stayed in the hot water another few minutes, letting the muscles unknot, then went to face her.

'*Kay*, my treasure,' Tilly said, sweeping him into a soft, perfumed embrace as soon as he entered. 'Can you have been avoiding me, I wonder? It's not nice, you know, to shut us all out like this.'

The whole room had taken on her fresh, heady smell in the few minutes he'd made her wait.

'It's only when I'm playing,' he said, trying to wriggle free, 'you know that. I'm not shutting anyone out. Anyway, Jane says you came in when the locks were on. What about my privacy? I wouldn't break into *your* rooms, would I?'

Again he heard himself sounding like a petulant child.

'Oh darling,' she tutted. '*Break in* is a little melodramatic isn't it? I simply wanted to spend some *time* with you, having been away so much recently . . . You don't think a few little locks will keep me away, do you?'

'Oh no! You're good, Mother. Very good. I wouldn't expect locks to stop *you*, not unless you had some feeling for privacy.'

Briefly she looked hurt and he felt her pain. Typically, she was as beautiful as ever, even while her mouth twisted to show the negative emotion. What was real, Kay wondered? How much did those large knowing eyes know of themselves?

'Don't let's argue,' she said. 'Tell me what you've been up to. I hear you've been running off from poor Hedge again, getting up to all kinds of no good . . .' – and then, when he didn't reply – 'Well, I can't say I blame you and wouldn't do exactly the same thing in your place. What is it? The music?'

Reluctantly, he nodded, surprised at her understanding, wondering also why old Tomas had said nothing about him running off. Was it possible that Hedge had informed only his mother?

'Yes. With me it's skiing and the mountains and my trips . . .' (And your men, Kay thought.) '. . . with you it's music. We both make pretty poor Saints, don't we, darling? Your sister seems *much* more in the mould. No inclination to escape at all, bless her.'

Was that true, he wondered. Were he and his mother alike? There was no reason for them to be so: *he* was the odd one out in this house, not her. She always made him feel so muddled. He said bitterly: 'Why not take me with you, then? When you go off again?'

'Oh, but darling. You know I can't do that. Not yet. Not in the middle of your training. Tomas would blow a fuse. He's coming to rely on your electronic wizardry. He foresees great things for you.'

Kay went and started rummaging in a container for clean clothes. 'How could he?' he asked, with his back to her. 'How could he foresee great things? When I'm . . .?'

'When you're what, darling?'

He turned, ran a hand over his face. 'Well, look at me, Mother. I'm *not* from the mould, am I?'

She said, chidingly: 'I really don't know what you're talking about. I expect your hormones are going a bit haywire at the moment; that's all. Don't worry darling, it'll pass.'

How he wanted to believe her. How plausible she sounded. He could just return her embrace and call her

'Mummy' and work hard to reach the end of his training so that they could spend more time together; the two Saints who liked to escape.

'Shall I get some food sent up?' he asked. 'It must be suppertime by now.' Even before she answered he knew what she would say.

'Oh. Kay. I really would love to, but Christo is expecting me. I'm late already, in fact. I only stayed to be able to see *you*. We have a show to attend with the ambassador from the Chinese Broadcast Agency. It wouldn't do to insult the poor man. You see, even *this* Saint has to make an effort! Our time is never really our own. You should make the most of your private nights out in the city while you have them.'

She laughed her pretty, peal-of-bells laugh and Kay said: 'Does he have "Wreckers" too? This Chinese ambassador? Is he as hated as we are?'

She gave him a quick, sharp glance, out of character with the laugh. 'Really, Kay! Don't be a pain. He's a perfectly charming man. I must go.'

What was real? What could he hold onto?

'There are further messages from Tomas Saint,' Jane said, in her soothing, relaxed way, as soon as the door had shut. 'Shall I play them?'

'Yes, OK, play them. And lock the door again, please.'

'Door locked. Message from Tomas Saint, timed 7.42 pm today.' 'Are you there now? I hear from Systems that you're more than thirty hours down on your training.' (There was a pause while the old man cleared his throat noisily.) 'Thirty-one hours and twenty-two minutes, if you want the figures. Now, come on, my boy. Don't let me down. I expect you to make up the shortfall over the next ten days. And I expect to see you at at least one meal a day to tell me how it's going. You *can't* afford to relax now, of all times. I have a post for you in Systems Design next year, if you can show me you're worth it.'

Oh God.

'Jane. Please contact Terry in Systems and say I'll call in tonight for three hours' tuition.'

'Of course, Kay.'

Miserably he got dressed, made himself a snack and left the building, picking up the inevitable shadow before the front entrance had closed behind him. Hard pellets of hail were rattling and spitting over the dark ground.

A post in Design? It didn't seem likely. Far too much power for such a misfit. As he walked the short distance down the hill to the Systems complex, the hail stinging his face, it even crossed his mind that it might not be coincidence, his visit from Tilly at the same time as that message. Were she and the old man just playing with him, using all their tricks? He remembered vividly just how much he had longed to believe in his mother this evening and squirmed at the memory.

At least he had something that was real. Something that had nothing to do with being a Saint. Something that there could be no doubts about . . .

'All right, are we, Hedge?' he called back angrily over his shoulder, although he couldn't see the man. It was against procedure to call out to your shadow and Hedge would not reply.

Later, after the three hours with Terry, he would find a new club, somewhere way across town. And after that, he would pass through Portable Road again and see the girl.

Poor Hedge. He really wasn't going to be pleased. Kay grinned to himself, his good mood returning. He couldn't help it if he wasn't in the mould, could he?

THIRTEEN

'I don't know your real name and I don't want to know,' Sean had said. 'But you should be for choosing a new one. To use in the city.'

'What kind of name?' she'd asked in surprise.

'Och, you'll find that most of the Scroats down by the docks have names they picked from pure fancy, lass. Meat Pie or Sunrise or Seashell or Vomit. Anything. There's that many coming in that don't want to be known, whatever their reason. And the waters still rise.'

She'd giggled. 'I'd rather be Seashell than Vomit, right enough.'

'Aye. You're no Vomit. But *you* pick something. Something you feel comfortable with. And get used to it with us here on the boat. Then if they ask you, you won't forget yourself and give your real name.'

And so she'd become Sparkle. Chosen on the one day that a sliver of sun broke through and set the surprising, infinite waters shimmering. Called so by all the crew, when they took notice of her at all, which was near to never.

'Only mind now,' Sean had warned, 'the new name is not enough. You must change how you look – that is very important – and how you talk. And even then, they have ways to know who you are. They can scan your thumb-print, your DNA, and the Lord knows what, if they really want to know.'

'Who are *they*?'

'Those that hunted you.'

'Aye. But *who* are they?'

He sighed. He was turned away from her, checking the boat's course against his instruments. 'I cannot say, for sure.'

'Then why are you helping me?'

'I have nae love for them, lass, whoever they are. Leave it at that.'

He knows, she'd thought. He knows full well who they are but will not say.

It seemed almost as if, despite all his kindness, despite robbing the hunters of their prize, *he* was unable to trust *her*. He'd sat with a closed face, and listened patiently and sympathetically to her story. Even the parts to do with Gil and Green, which made her a murderess twice over. And at the end, nothing. No condemnation, no comment from himself. No advice for her when she would reach the capital, except for that concerning her name, her look, her accent . . .

'It seems that you are a survivor,' he'd said, with a wink and a brief, tight smile, 'and no doubt you will find your own way when you are there. Everything you need is surely inside you. As with all of us.'

She didn't understand. Perhaps he hadn't believed her tale at all and was mocking her, regretful now that he had allowed a mad, runaway girl aboard his ship.

She said: 'Tell me this then, at least. Who is that woman I saw on your screen?'

'What woman is that, lass?'

'When you carried me on board, or sometime afterwards, there was a woman on the screen. Smiling. Happy. They said Tilly Saint.'

He'd bowed his head a moment in silence and then said: 'She is one of the Saint family. Those that run the broadcasts; and the computers, of course. The Saint

Network, d'ye ken? Though you don't often see *them* on the Levels we can afford to watch, mind. Just that one, Tilly, from time to time.' And then, with a wry grin, 'As bonny a face as any for the poor Scroats to see and look up to.'

That was all he knew or would say about Tilly Saint.

'Tell me again about Scroats, then,' she'd persisted. 'Are *you* a Scroat, Sean?'

He'd laughed freely at that, no inhibitions, and said: 'Aye, no doubt that's what I am, bless my dear old ma for it! She left it all to the good Lord's chance and got me.' But no more information was offered, except for the day they'd finally nudged into their berth on the wind-battered waterfront of the capital, one of hundreds of boats it seemed, swarming at the side of such a dark mass of buildings and people, stretching up as far as she could see, that now she faced the reality of it, Mira would have stayed for ever on the bonny green ship rather than enter this city. But that the ship was exchanging loads and leaving again before nightfall.

'You'll do fine,' Sean had said to her gently, joining her at the rail. 'Only remember what I told you. Change everything about yourself. Tell nothing. Or if you are asked, give a false story. You've run from a father that beat you. You come from a mountain farm where the sheep hae finally frozen. Anything. *And think on this*: the questions you ask may also say too much. Go carefully, lass.'

'Sparkle.'

'Aye, Sparkle.'

She'd stayed on the windy deck for those two hours, delaying the inevitable, watching rough planks of wood and baskets of fish come out of the hold and machine parts and grain go back. The men worked quickly, with hardly a word, anxious to be out at sea again, she would have said. When the last sack was aboard she stepped down onto the quay with her few things and saw her one friend pilot his boat away, shouting his sharp commands through the open wheelhouse door.

On another boat, somewhere out in the melee of craft on the restless water, a woman's thin voice was raised in song.

> See the serpent wake,
> Its eyes are holding you,
> Blessed children:
> It is love.

'Shut that daft rubbish up and get a life!' another voice shouted angrily.

Tomas Saint sat alone as he so often did, at his worktable; a bare teak surface rippled through with the wood's grain. A glass of dark, syrupy brandy stood within reach of his right hand, but the old man sat unmoving, eyes half closed.

A miniature bank of screens flickered in front of and above him, angled down, suspended from the ceiling. Behind them, the city fell away down to the docks, battered as ever by gales and filthy rain. A hateful place, full of the ungrateful, who did not know the burdens he must carry. On the screens, various members of his staff moved around the building: preparing meals, performing security functions, working on materials for the broadcasts. The building was massive, a hive of activity, twenty storeys above ground level, eight below.

On one of the tiny screens, Clarissa entered a large, empty room and began a training session for her Slam competition. Tomas was immediately aware of her and murmured: 'Enhance twenty-three'. Silently, the image grew larger. Tomas did not like his room systems to talk unless absolutely necessary.

Clarissa went through a warm-up, then plunged into simulated training, wearing a headset, spinning and striking at opponents that only she could see, dropping suddenly with her arms tucked in to evade a hold, flipping backwards onto her feet to deliver a sudden blow, never losing balance and grace . . . She moved easily, lithe and strong, totally focused on the combat. A good match for the Barbieri boy, in more ways than one, he thought. And yet . . .

Tomas brooded quietly on all the possibilities, different paths of cause and effect. Despite himself, he could feel the weariness in his body.

On screen twenty-three, Clarissa, breathing hard, finished her session and ripped off her headset, casting it aside. She looked at her right hand, fingers splayed out, and then turned to face the miniature camera.

'Did you see that, Grandfather? Are you impressed?' She giggled, and then in a mercurial change, said crossly, 'But I've broken a nail.' She waved the hand up at the monitor so that he could see.

'Reduce twenty-three,' Tomas said, sighing. He lifted the brandy to his lips, and closed his eyes completely to savour the taste.

'You a new one then, are you?'

It was a girl about Mira's age, perhaps a year younger, who'd been standing a little further down the quay when she left the boat, looking puzzled, as if she was trying to remember something. A girl wearing a too-big jacket made of joined-together scraps of material, and black spidery things on her thin legs. Her face was smeared with grime and grease and her eyes looked empty.

Mira had simply nodded, mindful of what Sean had said about the way people spoke. She could hardly deny she was new: the girl had seen her step from the ship.

'You 'ungry? I know someone who can give you food an' stuff. An' somewhere to sleep, outta the wind.'

Mira nodded again, wondering what was wrong with the girl's eyes.

'Don't say much, do you?' the girl intoned, dully. 'Come on, then. Ed'll sort you out.'

Meekly, Mira had tagged along behind her. The accent was quite like Evan's, she thought. Maybe her guess had been right, and the raiders had really come from a city. Still, she'd heard enough of Evan. With a little practice, she might be able to sound like that.

'What's yer name, new one?' the girl had asked without interest, picking her way across a double set of metal bars sunk partly into the ground.

'Sparkle,' she'd answered, trying an Evan-from-memory voice, not quite saying the 'k' properly, not rolling the 'r' as she would at home, deepening her voice a little.

There was a sudden high shrieking and a sleek line of metal boxes on wheels came fast along the metal bars, making Mira jump to one side. The greasy girl laughed – a high, unreal-sounding noise in her throat – and said: 'I wouldn't stand on the rails, Sparkle. Come on.'

A minute later, they'd turned down, away from the water, into a narrow way between two large warehouses. A sharp-eyed, sharp-faced boy with short spiky yellow hair, sitting on a bollard, had watched them and slowly shaken his head from side to side.

'I wouldn't,' he'd called. At his feet, a small shaggy shape had barked, as if in agreement.

Ed, who would 'sort her out', had turned out to be a

huge, hard-breathing tower of fat with a baby's face. The tiny, open, lopsided building he sat in, no bigger than the skidoo garage, leaned against the side of one of the warehouses, and the dim passage on either side had a scattering of other girls – and boys too – like the one leading Mira: lolling around on the ground, sleeping under plastic sheets, standing silently with eyes closed. It was like a sickness had taken them.

'Sorry,' she'd said to Ed as he wheezed and struggled up from his chair. 'I think I made a mistake. Thank you anyway.' And she'd turned to go.

But Ed had picked up a little handbell from the tiny table – dwarfed by his pale hand – and rung it, and two large shadows appeared a little behind Mira. 'Just a moment, love. Don't rush away from us when you only just come,' he'd said. Then, turning to the girl who had brought her, who stood vaguely nearby looking at the ground: 'New one, is she?'

'Yes, Ed,' she murmured, without interest.

'Speak up and buck up! What's 'er name?'

'Calls 'erself Sparkle,' she said, a little more certainly.

'What ship she come off?'

'One down from the North, Ed. The *Helicon*.'

'Still in port is it?'

'No, Ed. Reloaded and sailed.'

'Hmm. She's a pretty piece, ain't she? Lovely bit of clothes, too. Proper fleeces an' all. She could pass for a Vision, eh, Lizzie?'

The fat man raised stubby fingers to Mira's hair, held up a lock and let it fall, grunting appreciatively. She took a step away from his reach and said, as calmly as she could: 'Please don't touch me.'

'All right, girl, don't go getting all steamed up. No disrespect intended. Now, what can we do for you, I wonder?

There must be all *sorts* of things you'll be needing. Information. Lodging. Work. *Identity*.' He shot her a quick, shrewd look. 'Identity's always a popular one, with you incomers. We can do you the best on the waterfront, right 'ere, price negotiable. 'Oo knows, for a bit extra, we might even bang you out as a bona fide Vision. Screening pedigree an' all. It's been done before. Not often, but it 'as, and you got the face for it. What d'ya say to *that*, eh? Only,' and his tone changed, 'first things first: what you got to pay with, love?'

She said, imagining the words coming from Evan: 'I don't 'ave *nothing* to pay with, and I ain't *asked* for nothing. I got to go. Really I 'ave. I reckon Lizzie there made a mistake about me, or something.'

The other girl's head jerked up at that. For the first time she showed emotion: fear. 'I *never*, Ed,' she babbled. 'Promise. I seen 'er come off the ship, an' asked 'er if she was new an' if she 'ad somewhere an' all that, jus' like you tell us. It's 'er that's lying.'

White-faced, she started to sob quietly.

'Shut it, Lizzie,' Ed said dismissively, 'I'll tell you when the waterworks is required, girl.' And then, to Mira; 'Well now, you got a bit o' spunk about you. Think quickly an' that. I *like* that. But remember *you* come to *me*, didn't you? An' I already given you valuable time an' effort. Trying to sort you out for your life in the big city, eh? I reckon you already owe me for that, at least. So why don't we waive the fee so far – 'cause I like you, see? – and jus' sort out a nice little identity for you? You won' regret it.'

'I told you. I don't 'ave nothing.'

The tiny eyes glittered in their folds of skin. 'Well, luckily for you, my dear, we got ways round that. Which is that you do a little *work* for me, until the current debt is cleared, see? And *after* that, we can fix a price for the other. You see, I'm a fair man.' He had taken a step closer once more. One of the stubby fingers jabbed at her waist pouch. 'First, though, let's take a little look at what you *'ave* got. You never know, girl, it might be enough.'

The look on his face seemed to contradict that. Mira was starting to imagine just what life was like for the boys and girls unfortunate enough to 'owe' something to Ed. She could feel the two silent giants behind her breathing down her neck. In the shadows, the girl called Lizzie was looking down again, shutting out the world. Mira could not imagine any help coming from her, or any of them.

'Don't be shy,' Ed said, greedily.

Mira unzipped the pouch and showed him.

'What's that then, when it's at 'ome?' the fat man wheezed, disappointed. 'Bits of old metal, is it?'

'It goes together like this. See.'

She'd practised on the ship, many, many times, sat on deck, gazing out at the grey seas, washed by the spray. Her hands could do it in their sleep now. Less than two seconds to fit the struts together, in light or darkness.

'Now then,' said Ed. 'Let's not all lose our senses 'ere, shall we? I'm sure we can sort it out, love, with no 'ard feelings.'

'Please ask those two to go down there,' she said, gesturing at the shadows behind her. 'And then you walk up to the end with me. And then I'll be off. No 'ard feelings, like you said.'

For the second time the girl, Lizzie, came to life and showed her fear. She was watching with round eyes and open mouth: 'Oh don't 'urt him, Sparkle, he'll kill me! Or them others will. For bringing you 'ere an' that.'

'You leave too, then, if you want.'

The suggestion seemed to throw the girl into confusion. 'But I can't. *I can't.*'

Mira had left her repeating the words, swaying from foot to foot with her face buried in her hands, as she and Ed walked up to the mouth of the alley, he in front and propelled by the nose of the crossbow.

'Now then,' Ed wheezed again, speaking uneasily over his shoulder, 'easy on that trigger. No need for no blood spilling.'

At the end, the angular, yellow-haired boy watched them emerge with his sharp eyes and a sudden flash of a grin, showing crooked teeth. The loose tattered ends of his clothing were splayed out, fluttering round him in the wind, looking like the feathers of a scrawny bird.

Mira said to her prisoner: 'OK. Turn around. Walk back down there to your place. Don't look back.' And Ed, grumbling, had obeyed.

The boy had unfolded his long, ungainly body and come over, the dog trotting at his heels: 'Time to get away sharpish, new one. Ed won't 'ave enjoyed that. An' you don't wanna make too much excitement down 'ere, when you just arrived. You'll learn.'

As he spoke, a roar of anger and a shriek of fear had come from the alleyway, and the girl Lizzie had come stumbling out into the grey afternoon light, blinking, looking back over her shoulder. The noise of heavy running feet echoed up behind her.

'Right. Come on then, you'll 'ave to move it!' the bird boy said, decisively: 'Grab 'er hand, new one – she won't make it otherwise – and *run*!'

He himself had taken Lizzie's other hand and set off fast in a long bony stride along the quay, and then, turning left, up the hill through narrow, steep streets towards the heart of the dark sprawl. The dog ran playfully alongside them, barking and jumping up at his master. When they'd finally stopped, sweating in the sharp wind, standing on a way thronged with people, the boy had coughed painfully three or four times, his pale face screwed up, and spat messily on the pavement.

'I'm Beebop,' he said. 'And you've made a bad start, ain't you?'

The dog barked its agreement. The girl Lizzie said nothing, sunk back in her pale dreamworld.

FOURTEEN

So far, Kay's search for information on the girl had been fruitless. He didn't mind, though: he could be patient. There was precious little else to do in the long hours until night.

Obviously there would be no file, no black and white account to be accessed by anybody with the right pass codes. That would be madness. So the trick was not to look for the thing itself, but to look for the ripples it left in the Network. Exceptional movement of credits, employment records for the tiny satellite communities dotted around what was left of the flooded countryside, unusual licences from the Fertility Board.

It was a huge task, but Kay was good at this. He could lose himself in the circuitry. He hummed softly as he worked, at peace for once, anticipating what would come later. In the new club, the music was waiting for him. The place was smaller than the last, shabbier, further to get to – it nestled under the western floodwalls – but the people loved their sounds no less. And while you were there, the music was all that mattered, whether you were Scroat or Vision. It writhed through the hard-pumping hearts of the dancers like a giant snake.

Then, afterwards, he'd see the girl. It was the same routine each time. He'd re-cross the city, keeping away from the cameras. The dirty weather would cradle him, hide him. Mostly she was there, in her same spot, under the flapping, useless piece of resin, rain matting down her scarlet spikes and running over her white face. Mostly he managed to get his gifts to her without the others seeing and swamping him as they'd done before. But *she* never showed anything. Not the tiniest sign of recognition or gratitude.

'What's your name?' he tried, speaking softly. 'Do you know how old you are? Were you born in the city?'

But she would just look at him blankly, and by the time he saw her in these dark, dreamy hours, the questions didn't seem so important, even to him.

'Don't worry,' he murmured, as the columns of data scrolled down before him: 'I'll find you. You're in here somewhere.' These extra hours in Systems were proving useful after all. By chance it had been the same night that Tomas had bollocked Kay for getting behind in his studies that Terry had said with a twinkle: 'Tonight, young master, we move on to pure art. How to pass inside this old heap of components' (he patted the mainframe casing fondly) 'like . . . a . . . *whisper*.' He even whispered the word. 'Traceless. Invisible.'

It was far in advance of what had gone before and Kay was surprised at the level of trust. Maybe nobody had told his teacher that he wasn't the genuine article, a proper Saint. Still, he wasn't going to miss out, if the goodies were being offered, especially now that he had such a use for them. It was unlikely that *nobody* would be able to tell that Kay had been digging through the system – he was getting better, but not yet perfect – but with luck the shadowy footprint he left would not betray what he had sought. In vain, so far.

As for that crap about a post in Design, well he wasn't going to fall for that. The old man was playing with him, trying to keep him out of trouble, trying to keep him away from Scroats. Even the *word* Scroat was forbidden at home. There were no Scroats or Visions. Just good citizens and a few, a very few, 'Wreckers'.

Sometimes he vented his feelings to his mother. 'So why do they put up with it?' he'd ask.

'Why do *who* put up with *what*, darling?' she'd say distractedly, holding up evening suits in front of her wall of mirrors.

'The people. Our people. The people who live in this city and the other four. The *British* people. Why do they put up with things going on and not changing? You know what I mean.' Even to her he couldn't use the words everyone in the city used daily.

She glanced at him, sighing as if he was a slow learner that she wouldn't give up on. 'This is a democracy Kay. You know that. The people have the chance to change things in the normal way if they're not happy. The systems are all in place: the rules and procedures are there. Perhaps one day they will.' She gave a sudden smile and came across to kiss his hair. 'I hope they do. Really.' For that moment she seemed quite different – younger, gentler – and he believed her. Then, later, he thought that she, too, had played with him.

To change things in the normal way.

Nothing changed! You needed information to change things, didn't you? Real information, the sort kept for the Families themselves and the richer Visions, able to perpetuate themselves indefinitely with the expensive Fertility Board 'enhancement' licences. Vision numbers in proportion to the Scroats were slowly rising: 'second child' permits were also out of the reach of the poor. After all, Tomas would argue with a chuckle, Briton must keep to the ICSA convention on population management, just as any other country. And so, gradually, the numbers of people who might want to *change* anything were dwindling.

Of course there was no shortage of Scroat 'trouble-makers'. Floodites, protesters, Snake preachers, Wreckers; the lower levels of the city was heaving with them. Yet all they had was word of mouth, the power to shout for a few minutes from some upturned box, before they got moved on. Who, after all, would pass *their* ideas for broadcast? The occasional Wrecker even made it past the sea gates or over the marsh walls to bring messages of support from other cities, other countries, stirring up hatred that bubbled into protests and perhaps violence. But Pax was always there, infinitely strong, waiting to deal swiftly and unpleasantly with such types and their followers. Even the pathetic raggedy preachers and mystics that came to the city, worming their way in somehow, ranting on about messiahs or the end of the world; even they were locked up or thrown out if people got too interested in their stories and songs.

'To change things in the normal way,' his mother said. But who could say where power really lay now? Pax and the Fertility Board and the Saint Network . . . all of them were contracted by the state to provide an essential service. They answered to their (happy) shareholders. Where in all this was the state hiding? The contracts were centuries old. They were monopolies. There was no state left to issue new ones.

Sometimes, especially with the drugs, Kay could see all of this clearly, the whole city set out below his window like a drama, layer upon layer. He could see the bonds that kept life as it was. He could see the tensions, the misery. But what could he do, being no more than a Scroat himself?

Which was also why the post in Systems Design made no sense at all.

There was a young man picking his way through the lunchtime crush on the edge of the new docks who would probably have agreed with Kay about the corruption and hopelessness of the city. Not that it bothered him one jot.

The man – Moore, he called himself – had often walked the streets as a boy, seeing both the contented and the discontented. There was no part of the capital that he did not know. He went easily where he chose and offended no one. He was unrecognised, forgettable, nothing. A few scars, perhaps, but these were mostly out of sight, under his faded clothes. There was a faint smile on his lips as he slipped between the teams of ham-handed dock workers, trudging heavily and noisily to where they could get their breaktime bite or drink or smoke. The dockers would have enjoyed a man in their way to knock aside, but Moore would not be that man. Moore was a problem solver, an intelligence gatherer, an adviser, a protector, a hunter, a killer at need. He was the product of the most extensive and costly pre-fertilisation screening that the Fertility Board could provide. He would not have disagreed with Master Kay if asked about the city, but he would not have cared much, either. Caring was not what he was employed for, except in special cases. They could all rot, for all he cared.

The coffee house where he entered and sat unremarkably in a corner was heaving, smoky, full of the crews just in, dockyard scum, pushers and addicts, pimps, other nothings. The city's throbbing heart was here, near the water, near the sea gates; and so was the city's misery and anger and tension. A silent, strained Scroat woman of eighteen or so, with the dead eyes that were so common, brought him his drink, took his payment and his message. Moments later, a fat, sweating man squeezed with

difficulty through a corner door, peered round the room
and elbowed his way across to Moore, widening the small
path the girl had opened between the tables and sinking
heavily into a seat.

'Moore,' he said, hoarsely, with a small nod.

'Business is good,' the slighter man remarked neutrally,
indicating the wide expanse of drinkers with a finger
lifted from the table top.

The other screwed up his face with nervous pleasure.
'Isn't it, though?'

'You have something for me?'

'Per'aps.'

Moore waited, still smiling, hands unthreateningly at
rest in front of him. The fat man knew that there were no
bargains to be struck. That was not how it worked.

Eventually, with a clearing of throat, more came. 'I
'eard that there was a girl. From the North. One someone
might want to meet.'

'Oh yes? Where did you hear such a thing, I wonder?'

The question was pleasant enough, but the fat man
squirmed. He *knew* Moore, by reputation at least. 'There
was a rumour. That's all. *You* know 'ow these things pass
down the waterfront.'

A pause.

'A rumour. I see. Let's leave that then, for now. What
of this girl? Have you seen her?'

'Yeah,' the fat man said with relief, 'one of my own
brought someone like that to me. A while back, mind.'

'And you lost her?'

'Well . . .'

Moore smiled lazily: 'Careless.'

'There was *circumstances*, wasn't there? An' I didn't
know then that you and your lot wanted 'er, did I?' A
sheen of moisture clung to the baby face. 'But I can give

you 'er name. Sparkle. *An'* the name of the ship what brought 'er. The *Helicon*.'

'Is that all then? Truly all?'

Ed had his hand half out to Moore, an entreaty. '*An'* the ones she went off with, after. A boy. A no-good toerag, stirring up trouble. Beebop, 'e calls 'imself. Hangs about like a ghost. The other's one she took from *me*, little bitch. Lizzie 'Epton. A sweet thing. Earned me good money. That's all, Moore. Really.'

Moore rose to leave, brought his mouth close to Ed's ear as he passed. 'You must have looked yourself? Especially if you lost the new one *and* this Lizzie Hepton?'

The fat man nodded, swallowed. '*Nothing*,' he croaked. 'Leastways, I seen the boy about, but not the others. He dosses down somewhere above the old eastern dock, I think. That's all. Really it is.'

Moore rested a hand on his shoulder. 'I've enjoyed our chat, Ed. Keep me informed. You'll find me if you need to tell me something more.' He didn't make it clear if this last was a command or a prediction. A moment later he was gone, a slight, unmemorable man.

Ed took a few deep breaths to slow the thudding of his heart and then bellowed hoarsely at the serving girl: '*Stellaaa!* Get your lazy arse over 'ere!' A drink would help. That Moore and his kind should be done, he thought shakily, left in the flood water, face down, to rot.

Moore wouldn't have been surprised, and wouldn't have cared about these wild and violent wishes in his informant. Any more than he would have cared about Kay's views of the city. He *did* care, very much, about the interesting information scrolling down the screen of his handset as he stood in a broken doorway a few blocks from Ed's coffee house. Lizzie Hepton. Apparently stopped and questioned routinely, quite recently. In company with one Marcel Allen, known vagrant, and incomer from a flooded farming area, now calling himself Beebop. Possible Wrecker leanings but no serious violations to date.

Good. He could set his snares now: it shouldn't take long.

But at his own terminal, Kay was slumped over, breathing evenly and deeply, the keys pressing into his cheek. The elusive information would have to wait another day or two. You couldn't rush it. The nights were hard on him.

He didn't know about Moore of course, not even that he existed, although he knew his kind.

If he *had* known, he might not have succumbed to sleep.

FIFTEEN

Dawn over the city generally broke chill and damp and bleak for the homeless. On this morning, Marcel Allen, alias Beebop, was coughing his guts up. He coughed a lot these days, couldn't seem to shake it off. The three rusted cooking braziers in Martha's strip of yard dispersed a thin, blue film of smoke that caught in the throat, but Beebop's cough was worse than that. His meal lay only half finished. His bony face was white and contorted with pain.

Out in the alley, someone was wailing and beating on the iron door. The row had been going on almost since sunrise. 'For the love of the serpent,' a voice sobbed. 'Open the door to me. They're coming . . . they're coming!'

Another voice outside the walls laughed aloud, and then was abruptly quiet. Something – a piece of timber perhaps – was scraped slowly along the brickwork. The few men, women and children still to leave the yard sat or stood quietly, ignoring the noises and the shouting, trusting their sanctuary. Some spooned down the stew, swilling each mouthful around slowly over their tongues to draw out the goodness; some had their eyes closed or their faces in their hands; three of the youngest ones chased here and there, kicking a fragment of brick amongst the weeds, reminding Mira of Pat and Joan and the others at home.

Martha, squatting solidly over a pail of water, scrubbing away at a cooking pot with a knot of sharp wire, said mildly: 'We must get a medic to that cough, Bee. It should have cleared up by now. Weeks, it's been.'

The boy said sharply: 'No. No medic. Can't trust 'em.'

Martha looked up as if she was going to argue the toss, but then shrugged and went back to scrubbing. She knew how stubborn Beebop could get.

At this time of day, the yard was almost empty. Martha insisted that people either ate or slept or both while they were there. Apart from that they were expected to go out. What they did out there in the city was up to them, no questions asked, provided they didn't bring it back with them. That was the golden rule. She knew from experience that if she let people waste away their days and nights behind her walls there would be an end to her no-drugs policy and that before long the yard would be noticed, either by the authorities or by the waterside scum, vultures like Ed, hungry to use and corrupt and take a percentage from the vulnerable homeless and incomers.

Bee was different. An exception. She'd looked after him a long time. He was family, of a sort. She could stretch the rules a little for him.

Presently a man called gruffly: 'Going out here, Martha. Three of us.'

'OK, Root. Three of you to go out.' She rose, wiping her hands on her thick skirts, and went to the door, where the banging continued unabated. There she silently took down a long, curved tube that hung on a hook and lifted it so that the end breasted the top wall. Swivelling it first one way, then the other, she peered into the bottom. Then, just as quietly, she replaced the instrument and, nodding to the three who waited, lifted out the metre-long iron rod that served as the main bolt. This she hefted easily by its end. The man Root eased back the smaller

bolt and in a single movement Martha swung wide
the door and passed into the alley with a shout – 'Stand
back, there. Behave yourselves, if you know what's good
for you.'

From inside the yard, Mira heard the sound of running
feet in the alley, Martha's angry growl, the voice that
had called to be let in, calling now in fear; 'Don't beat me,
I beg you! They said the serpent would be angry. They
said they would report me!'

At the same time, with much scrabbling and scraping
and grunting, a face appeared at the top of the wall furthest from the door, a grinning, weaselly face, and then
a hand which groped up and landed squarely on the
glass strewn over the wall top, making the mouth in the
face open to swear violently. The groping hand angrily
swept the glass aside and more of the man appeared.
He levered himself over, dropping untidily to the ground
near the three younger ones playing their game. A
moment later, his space on the wall was reoccupied by
a second, more gormless set of features, loosely arranged,
which said plaintively: 'Wait for me, Nasher. I'm coming,
but I ain't got nobody to bunk me up.'

Martha was coming back in through the yard door, still
bristling from clearing the alley. She saw the newcomer
and roared: 'Don't you dare!', but it was too late: the man
Nasher had grabbed one of the children.

There were angry murmurings at this from the handful
of inmates. Some, finally stirred to action, got to their feet
and advanced angrily on the intruder. Bee was there before any of them. He said, 'Go on, get lost, yer not wanted
'ere. Can't you see that?' He squared up to the second
man as he dropped down, chin sticking out aggressively,
and was swept aside as if he were a mosquito.

'Nasher, they don't want us. Why don't nobody want

us? It's not fair.' The man danced from foot to foot, eyes rolling nervously as if he needed to pee.

Nasher snarled over his shoulder: 'Belt up, Fish. It's not us who 'as to go, it's all of them.' He turned back to the little crowd facing him. 'Hear that? My mate and I fancy a nice spot of that soup, and then a bit of kip. In fact, we fancy moving in here, permanent like. Change of management, you might say. So get moving! I'll throw the kid out last.'

Martha was there facing him now, bulky and formidable, but they could all see the pellet gun he held loosely against the child: homemade and inaccurate, the weapon of the waterside gangs, but quite deadly enough at that distance.

Silently, Mira went to a brazier and ladled more steaming food into her bowl. Then she came uncertainly over, making her eyes large and shy and her steps unthreatening.

'Here's some soup,' she said. 'Please don't hurt us. It's good soup. I helped make it.'

She reached out timidly with the bowl and the man, looking hungrily at it, grunted: 'Put it down there, then, and get more for my mate. And you others, push off, I said. Go on!' He waved the weapon wildly round at them and Mira emptied the boiling stew over the waving hand, pulling the child back and away from the man.

The rest she left to Martha, and it was finished swiftly. First Nasher and then his large, childlike companion were seized in an iron grip and marched quickly to the door, to be thrown into the alley, where they were treated to a few of the hostess' choicest thoughts on manners and behaviour towards children. The weapon was given a single contemptuous blow with her metal bar, shattering it into harmless pieces, thrown out after the intruders.

'And stay away!' Martha yelled. 'I won't be so forgiving next time.'

In a few minutes the door was re-bolted and all was quiet once more, except for Bee's coughing.

As if nothing had happened, Martha returned to squat by her pans and said: 'I know a medic. One you can trust. We could go up there today, before dark.'

'Can't,' Beebop shook his head, concentrating on not coughing, examining a scrape on his pointed elbow from where he'd been pushed over. 'Got a meeting, ain't I?' He shot her a sly glance.

'Beebop!' she said sternly. 'Stop right there. I don't want to know.'

That was another rule. No politics here. No protests. No scheming. No religion, either. These would be even easier ways to get noticed and lose the yard. After all, it didn't *belong* to Martha. It was just a derelict piece of wasteland near the old docks, a weed-filled concrete rectangle behind high walls, open to the elements except for the tin roof Martha had wedged up on bits of upended rail at one end. She'd also put in the heavy, bolted door, spread nails and glass along the wall tops, cleared away the worst debris, made the rules. Now it was Martha's yard . . . but she didn't own it. She ruled her space through energy, force of personality and mutual consent from the 'inmates'. They needed the haven she'd provided. They knew her rules made sense. Anyone who crossed her would be turfed out pretty sharpish, either by Martha herself or by the others. Not that she needed protection. She'd done her years on the boats and was as strong as any man, despite the grey in her hair.

Lizzie Hepton had sat silent during the excitement, hiding her face, but now she put down her tin bowl with a clatter and said quietly to the empty air, 'I'm off then. Out.' She nodded jerkily to herself to confirm this decision. She was not the same girl that Martha had met that first day on the docks, not vacant and vague and frightened: now she was twitchy and irritable and scowling. She still wouldn't meet your eye. She brought nothing to put in the pot, never bothered with making friends, except with one or two of the men. Mira could almost believe that she *blamed* them for taking her away from Ed. She'd filled out, though, and had some colour in her cheeks. That was something.

Martha gestured dismissively with her head, not liking Lizzie much. 'Let her out, would you, Sparkle? Should be quiet out there now, for a while.'

Mira said: 'I'll go too. Thanks for breakfast.'

'Thank you for the oddments you brought, pet. It all helps. And for your help with that bum. Off you go then: Bee will lock up after you.'

The two girls stepped into the alley together, but Lizzie made no farewell to Mira, and nor did she even glance at her. Instead she put her head down and hurried quickly off towards the heart of the city on some business of her own, without looking back. Mira followed more slowly and more warily, aware of the dangers of these smaller, broken-down ways. Yet she was no further than the end of the alley when she heard Beebop's unmistakable flapping run and felt his hand on her arm.

'I thought that maybe . . . you could come too. To the meeting and that,' he said awkwardly.

'No. I'm dead tired, Bee.'

He drew back a little and looked at her in challenge. The righteous anger was never far from the surface. 'There's more to bleedin' life than goin' through the bins together, ya know. You can 'andle yourself, OK, we all know that.

So don' you want to *do* something, *show* the bastards?'

'Do what? Show 'em what?'

It was a mistake to ask the simple question. She regretted it at once. It got him more stoked up, not less.

'Sod it, girl! Show 'em that we *know* what they're doin'! Show 'em that *we're* as good as they are and won't *never* be quiet, like they want!'

His eyes flashed and his thin face looked harsh and fierce, as it always did when he talked of these things. But Bee's explanations usually seemed muddled and muddied to her. Who, then, should they 'show'? The ones they called Visions? The ones who sat like toads on the wealth of the city and primly crossed the road if you went near them. Who kept themselves clean and busy and beautiful and went to their guilt-free dreamless sleeps early each night. For all the hatred, it seemed to Mira that half the Scroats she met wanted (in secret, at least) to join the Vision ranks anyway. And that made little sense to her, for they – the Visions – were more lacking in *otherness* than anyone in this city. They seemed as locked in their world as Old Sarah was at home. Bee himself was worth ten of them.

Then again, maybe it was the ones at the top, the Great Families, that they would 'show'? A fine idea, but Mira knew well enough that the Families were never there to be 'shown' anything. They passed their lives in their bleak towers, behind guards and steel doors, or flitting across this vast city in transports that burned the energy of ten skidoos, even then hidden by the metal and blackened glass. In weeks of careful searching for her answers, she had found only one person, one single boy from the ranks of the precious Families, who would show himself and move amongst the people. And what was he? An addict, deep in self-pity, playing at being something he was not, stealing back to his hiding hole and his guards when he wanted rest.

She went on up the alley and his voice called after her, desperately: 'Sparkle. It's not just protests an' that. Something *big* is gonna happen. Something *important*. Things are really going to change.'

'Tomorrow,' she called back.

He watched her go, moving easily, head up and alert, very different from Lizzie's secretive scuttle along the street. There was something that didn't fit about Sparkle. Something he was almost frightened of. He couldn't put his finger on it, but he knew it was there. Dead pretty, though, under all that muck she put on her face. Irritably he stalked back up the alley and banged on the iron door for admittance. Martha was sweeping out the open sleeping space, her beaded hair clicking with the regular movements.

'Is it love then?' she teased, glancing up.

'Hardly,' he replied, sourly.

Out in the city, hungry for some precious time alone, Mira relived the threat to the child in the yard and felt deeply shaken. It was something she could not get used to; the casual violence of this place. She didn't know how she managed to become part of it all, day after day, hiding her real feelings until she was sick with it. What price did she pay? she wondered.

Wearily, she made herself go through the self-imposed routine for getting to her sanctuary. She took a different route each time: never the tempting direct approach along the line of the water: more often than not, a climb up into the busy central districts of the city before finding one of the narrow, half-empty descents to a quarter which had been given up to the floods years ago.

Today, not paying much attention where she went, she avoided the shopping streets and coffee shops, but skirted through areas of housing that were wholly Vision. Solid, three- or four-storey blocks, laid out in a drab grid of streets, well served by Caplink and police patrols, by Vision skill-centres and sports parks. A different city from the colourful, cluttered lower areas, where old, blackened stonework sagged metre by metre into the water and people promised you the saviour was coming, even while they stole all you had. She pulled her hood up to pass through the Vision districts and wiped any expression from her face, keeping her eyes down. But she was not the only Scroat: beggars and scavengers were always combing the richer parts of the capital, and here and there maintenance or building teams were at work, under Vision guidance. It was safe enough.

When you were down by the water, it was easy to believe that Bee was right. Something big was happening, something important. The floods were creeping higher, the hopeless refugees continued to worm their way in, needing food, a place to sleep, someone to hear their story. The tensions were growing. People said the city would end, that the Families would be devoured by a serpent, that scientists in the East had found a way to make humans re-evolve to live in water: there were a hundred different horror stories and predictions. Hunger and protest and violence were swelling.

Up here, away from all that, it didn't seem that anything would ever change.

Mira heard young voices laughing and saw that she was at one of the places where Vision children were taught. They were between their lessons, crowded into a high-fenced play area, twenty or thirty of them, chattering away. She stood at the fence a moment to watch and saw that even to these sharp, young eyes she was invisible. Each child was intent on its game or talk: what was beyond the fences was unimportant. Like adult, like child.

But no, that wasn't true. One boy was peering at her through the mesh, staring silently, his little fingers holding the wire. She smiled at him, but he did not return the smile. He simply stared. And then he said: 'I seen you.'

She laughed at his intent little face: 'And I seen you too.'

'No!' he sounded scornfully. 'Not here, silly. I mean I *seen* you. In your nice proper clothes. You know: on the viewer, with Mummy and Daddy.' He gazed seriously at her with the confidence of childhood, taking one hand from the fence to pick his nose, then replacing it.

She said: 'Oh, whoever you saw, I don't think it was me. Just someone a bit like me, I expect.'

He said stubbornly: 'I know what I seen.' And then: 'Watch out!'

Mira felt someone grab her wrist and wrench her arm painfully up behind her back, so that the muscles strained.

'Remember me?' a voice breathed in her ear.

Yes, she remembered him. Nasher. She must be more tired than she'd thought. She was angry with herself. He might have been *police*.

He said: 'What you doing up 'ere then, eh? What you up to, Martha's girl? Old Nasher's been watching you since you left the yard. You're not after grub, you're not thieving an' that, so what you up to here?'

Even now, nobody but the little boy paid any attention. *He* looked on with interest. Mira said: 'I'm just walking.'

'Well, ain't that nice?' Nasher pushed her arm up higher. 'And now, Martha's girl, you can "just walk" with me a while.'

A whistle blew and immediately the children started to file into the building, play time over. The boy who had talked to Mira peeled himself away from the fence without a word and joined the quiet procession inside. Two adults counted the children in, and then disappeared themselves, sliding the heavy doors firmly shut.

'Where are we going?' Mira asked in her little girl's voice, as she was turned away from the fence and propelled back the way she'd come.

'That would be telling. We got a little score to settle, ain't we? Only this time, don't try nothing. I'll break yer arm.'

She said, testing the water: 'I'll scream. I'll bring the police.'

But he laughed at that: 'Go on, then. How many times you seen the pigs helping the likes of you, eh, Martha's girl? How many Scroats you seen rescued from their own kind, or anyone else? No . . . you call out if you like, and I'll tell 'em you're my girl, what run off and I'm takin' home again.'

She sighed. It was true, right enough. The police were not there for Scroats. Nor would she get help from anyone else up here. And in truth, the less she were noticed, the better. She had to lose this Nasher quickly and without fuss. And take more care next time, tired or not.

She waited until they were walking past a flight of steps, leading down to the underground service floor of one of the grim housing blocks, then turned suddenly to bring Nasher's back towards the flight and, bending her knees, pushed hard backwards, cannoning into him, at the same time bringing her free elbow up into his stomach.

With a curse he staggered back down the steps, falling as he went, and she followed, landing as heavily on top of him as she could. His grip on her arm loosened on impact as she had hoped and she was able to twist round to wrench it free.

By the time that he had shaken himself and climbed back up the steps, rubbing the lump on the back of his head, Mira was well away, putting a maze of streets between her and her attacker.

It was only many hours later, waking fretfully in the dark and damp of the cellar, that she remembered the little Vision boy.

'I seen you.'

The simple words were hanging in her mind before she even knew she was awake.

Nobody knew where she slept. Not even Beebop or Martha or the others. It was the only place where she allowed herself to be Mira; to speak like Mira, in her true voice. To take to her pallet in utter relief and shut out the raw, numbing days spent in the capital. And compared with the things she must see, the people she must meet out in Portable Road, or watching the tower on the hill . . . compared with that, the gentle, wandering eyes of her landlord and lady were a comfort.

She would not leave. Not yet. Not without the answer she sought. Perhaps when she had it, she could take passage again on Sean's boat. The *Helicon* came often to the city, he had said, plying its coastal trade up and down. When she had the truth about Annie Tallis and Tilly Saint and the truth about Mira, she could perhaps sail with him back to her home, or to some place where no Evan would find her.

Yet for all her watching and listening, she'd done no more than make contact of a sort with the boy Kay, and that had been only because her first target – the woman on the broadcast on Sean's boat – had so far stayed invisible.

'Saints?' Bee had scoffed, when she'd asked idly about this Tilly. 'Ya don't want to go near *them*. Bleeding worst of the lot, they are, or almost. All those bleedin' screens on every corner, all those terminals, d'ya think that's a *gift*, do you? Enter-bleeding-*tain*ment for the unwashed? Well I'll tell you what it is. It's anaesthetic. It's pap. It's crap. It empties yer head and drains the blood from yer heart. Ten times worse than the poor old Floodites, and they're bad enough. It sends you to bleeding sleep.' Who had taught him to say this, Mira wondered then. It sounded rehearsed. A lesson well learnt. 'No, don't go near those poncy, so-called Great Families. Worse than the Visions, they are. Oh yes, you saw that Tilly on the broadcasts. We all do, don't we? Looking bloody lovely, no doubt swanning about the place. Well, don't be fooled, Sparkle, don't be fooled.'

But when she'd gone to the great, glass-clad edifice on the hill, slipping close to watch from the shadows of other buildings, she'd seen not Tilly or the old man Tomas, that Bee had told her of, but the boy, Tilly's miserable son, plunging out into the night with the silent man – the big cat – following. Night after night he did this, and he was the only one of the family, it seemed, to show himself on the streets. She found out that he was a little older than her, the black sheep of the family. He had a smart sister that the grandfather doted on. *She* was rumoured to be going to marry somebody in Pax, and was supposed to be mean and hard. She never came out: only the boy, the black sheep, heading for oblivion.

Slipping from his keeper, he would go to the place where they played the strange music and half lost their minds. Sometimes she followed him there. Then, much later, he would walk aimlessly along near the ships, seeking out the places where the homeless and hopeless gathered, as if he felt that *his* home was there. When she'd learned his habits and saw that she would come close to no other from that family, she'd joined the throng at Portable Road, planning that he should see her enough times in that setting to make contact possible. The club might have been better, but sometimes the cat prowled there too, unseen by Kay, keeping an eye on things.

And then, beyond understanding, it had been the *boy* who'd noticed *her*, and stood and stared, and came to seek her out, and brought gifts. The first time, she'd thought his surprising attention could mean danger, but he'd spoken into no handset, produced no weapon, called no one to catch her. Gradually she'd relaxed into the part of vacant streetgirl, paying him scant regard, though to be found reliably in the same place, night after night. She had needed to do nothing, save play the part, wait for the odd bond to strengthen. He seemed even to prefer the fact that she was stupid and speechless.

There was more to his obsession with her than simple kindness, though. Like her he was searching for something: an identity. The joy shone out of him when he believed that he'd shaken off the cat and headed towards his secret music. By the time he had crossed the city and come to her with his gifts, he was at peace. This never changed.

And what did the cat do, while the boy visited her? Where did *he* go? For sure he was not watching, she'd been careful of that, yet he usually did not return to the glassy building until after Kay. Who, Mira wondered, did the man put on his act for when the boy ran off and he cursed and seemed thwarted? The cameras? She understood about those now, and the way a person might use them to show something that was not the whole truth.

More importantly, where did the cat go afterwards? Why did he leave his charge alone?

The questions circled round her head like predatory birds; they ran in tangled threads through her dreams, but there were no answers. Not yet. And then, on this waking, sweat-soaked and huddled tight, she thought of the Vision child saying 'I know what I seen', and of herself seeing the broadcast on Sean's boat. Annie Tallis' face, called by another name.

It filled her with dread. What did it mean?

SIXTEEN

While the singing pre-dawn wound its way between the cloud pines and over the crystal white slopes of Mira's old life; while the buffeting gale blew across the half-flooded croplands and windfarms and rotting, soon-to-be-submerged stiltways of the lower country to the south, growing imperceptibly warmer as the brief summer came into view; while the boy Beebop stood alone in a high place in the capital, on his way to his Wrecker meeting, letting the wind stretch out his shiny tatters of clothing so that he was like a thin, ruffled bird, but with tears coursing down his face for all he had already lost in seventeen years of life . . . while Mira was creeping to her cellar after eighteen hours awake, cursing the hardness of the *city*, a green ship called *Helicon* cut through the dangerous waters that lay offshore from the rocky Welsh coast.

Aboard there were crates for the fishing and weather station at Menai, then more for a line of windfarms around Preston. On the return journey there would be broken equipment needing repair, seafood, timber perhaps.

The ship was almost blind with the weather: thick, icy rain, beating hard on the glass of the wheelhouse, and a swollen, black sea that broke again and again over the deck and ran off in sheets through the gunwales. Unworried by the elements, Sean read his instruments and ran the wheel gently through his hands, feeling the ship respond sweetly. If he wished he could use the computer to guide the vessel unaided, but where was the skill in that? Where was the joy? The *Helicon* gave him freedom, and he'd be a fool to throw it away by surrendering his job to a machine. Scroat though he was, he had the skill, the deep memory in his genes, of how to meet and harness the dangers of this planet. Why leave that skill to rot?

His thoughts, though, were troubled. It seemed to him now that he might have done more for the brave, strange, beautiful girl who had ridden his ship out of danger in the North and had been set down in the midst of greater danger on the quaysides of the capital. That had been the trip before last. Like Martha, his rule was, 'Don't be noticed'. Don't be noticed in case they took your boat and your freedom; don't be noticed in case somebody visited your woman and the child the two of you had at last, Fertility Board or no Fertility Board. But for all that, his instinct to help the hunted girl at Lomond had been the right one. And he could surely have done more. Given her the knowledge she needed to survive in the city. Given her the names of people she might trust, some of the ones he'd carried to the city before, perhaps. Tight-lipped, watchful ones, sowing the seeds of revolution. He could at least have told her what he guessed about her.

Sean glanced again at his panel and frowned. Instinct, that deep gene-memory, told him that it was time to tack away from the coast. They must give a wide berth to submerged lands that jutted far out west, before the ship could make shorewards again to their next drop-off. The instruments, however, had not moved. Continue course unchanged, they advised.

'Mick,' he said over his shoulder, 'paper, man: and something to write if you would. And the chart. Quickly now.'

When he had the things, he handed over the wheel to
the man Mick – 'steady now, half speed, this course' –
and started to jot down speeds, bearings, estimated wind
factors. He arrived at an answer in just a few minutes, but
made himself check it, go through each calculation once
more. Again, there was the computer if he wanted,
designed to do just this, but . . . *but* . . .

'Mick. Hard a port. Steer into the wind for a time, due
west. Run her out to sea, man!'

With eyebrows raised in question, but obedient, the
mate swung the wheel and the little ship keeled over
sharply into its new course. Sean took weatherproofs
from a hook and binoculars, and slid back the hatch door
to go on deck.

Outside, in the gale, he clipped himself to the rail to use
both hands on the powerful glasses, swinging them
around from horizon to horizon. Yes, there it was, right
enough. The smudge of land – behind them now, on
the starboard side – that dipped down like a giant slipway
into the sea, waiting to catch the unwary. Sean growled
to himself, cursing his foolishness. He swung the glasses
out along the hidden danger to where the light should
be, relic of a more trusting past. Even in this weather,
the light should come out, clear and strong, in its three-
second pulses.

But there was nothing there.

His fingers were white on the binoculars now. He
murmured: 'Oh, my sainted mother! What kind of an
idiot am I, then?'

Feeling the pressure of fear in his chest, he hefted
the door to the wheelhouse back angrily, swung inside,
shedding the dripping weatherproofs onto their hooks.
One button killed the useless, jammed computer –
'We sail without instruments, until you hear different,

Mick lad' – another, on his own special, home-made box of tricks, sent swift pulses of sound fanning out, above and below the waterline and even far into the dark skies.

Sure enough, there was a blip. Another boat, only a mile or two behind.

'Skipper?' Mick was watching his face, looking for reassurance. The man was no fool.

'Aye. Trouble. Here, give me that and get the other lads up here, man. Armed.'

As Mick went below to rouse the sleepers, Sean hastily thought through his few options, the ports they might make for from here. The Irish capital was close enough, clinging to its upland, but they would hardly be safe there: probably would not even make it into port. Besides, they'd have to turn across the path of the pursuing boat. So where else? Mourne? Snaefell? *Snaefell!* He could think of nowhere safer, if they could only get there. It was not close. Sure, though, *if* they could make the run, they might even give their chasers a thing or two to think about. The dissident cell there owed him many favours. There would be friends on the seas around.

If.

He plotted their new course, an eye always on the blip of pursuit, swung the wheel, let the engines run up to full power, using precious fuel that he would not be allowed to replace, even if by some miracle he found a way to keep his licence or get another one forged.

The day was fully broken now, a wild, grey, hollow beast of a day. Sean thought of Rebekah and little Kitty, lingering over breakfast, having their stories together as they looked out on the tempest from his cliff-top house. The fear was gone again, as quickly as it had come. He felt calm. The boat ran like the wind over the hills of green water and, gradually but visibly, the blip closed with them.

SEVENTEEN

'Friends, shareholders, fellow officers of Pax, esteemed colleagues from the Fertility Board and the Great Families of our nation, I pledge my service to you in hard work, to continue the tradition of law and order, fairness with responsibility, that all of you have yourselves established over many years of labour. I am indeed honoured that you entrust me with such a post at my young age.'

Sitting at his family table, Kay let the bland, formulaic words drift past him, scowling faintly. Jan Barbieri's acceptance speech was like the boy himself. There was no originality, no individual life. Just a perfect, polished conformity. It made Kay sick. Jan wore a black formal tunic, trimmed with the Pax grey: blond hair immaculate, teeth white, eyes blue, intelligent and dangerous, skin waxily smooth. His bearing, addressing the room, was assured, easy. He was a high achiever, a flyer, a performer under pressure. Everything Kay was not. He – Jan – was also a turd.

'He's a turd, your Executive Lieutenant,' Kay whispered to his sister.

She giggled and whispered back: 'Yes, I suppose you're right. But a very handsome turd. Anyway, he's not *my* Executive Lieutenant.'

'Not yet. But he will be, won't he?'

She looked at him, serious a moment. 'Maybe. But only if I want. I haven't decided yet.'

Yes, only if she wants. All the choices are theirs, Jan's and hers. They were born to it.

Beyond Clarissa and his mother, Tomas raised a warning finger for them to be silent. The speech wound on relentlessly and Kay's thoughts turned yet again to the girl, *his* girl. He almost had her now. His finely woven electronic net was closing. He could already make a guess, perhaps, as to the places she had travelled from. He had dialled the library images up on his screen and marvelled at the wonder, the harshness. In his mind he was already placing the scarlet-haired girl in that landscape, though it seemed impossible that she should survive there when she struggled in the infinitely easier habitat of the capital. Her beauty would be right, though. *That* would go with such a place.

Uneasily, Kay glanced again at his sister, with her eyes turned in seeming concentration upon the droning blond figure, her shining hair dark and rich.

'. . . finally to acknowledge the support I have been lucky enough to receive from all of you since the death of my parents a little over four years ago at the hands of cowardly and malicious Wreckers: most of all from Magnus Stein and Pieter Budd, joint chairmen of the Fertility Board, who have somehow managed to give a little of their busy time over those four years. Ladies and gentlemen, I raise my glass now to these four: my loving parents, Matteus and Olive Barbieri, and my good friends, Magnus and Pieter.'

At the Board's table the two slight, silver-haired men stood and nodded briefly around the room like elderly dolls and then sat down once more. The applause rippled back and forth for a bare minute and then finally the speeches were over. At Tomas' signal, the four Saints rose from their places, picked up their glasses and began to circulate. Around the room, the other Great Families were doing the same, hurrying as ever to cement and re-cement the steel bonds of this paranoid ruling club. Along the octagonal glass walls, blocking out the impressive view of the city, the bodyguards stood in their lines, Hedge amongst them looking on impassively, aware always of where Kay was standing, who he was talking to.

'Quite a thing, isn't it? Young Barbieri taking office so young?'

That was the usual, bland comment.

Or: 'What can we expect from our young friend eh, Kay? I must say, he's impressed us all.'

Or: 'A star is born. Aha . . .' – with a wink – '. . . good at that, aren't we?'

'What about *you*, though, my boy?' one great walrus of a man from the Becker family (food technologies) asked. 'I hear great things are expected in Systems Design? Very important work, mmm?'

Another, a bored-looking woman he could not remember ever meeting before, commented: 'I say, your mother goes from strength to strength, doesn't she? She seems tireless. *Such* a boost to our image . . . out *there*.' She shuddered at the thought. 'And I see young Clarissa's grown up now, too?'

'Yes. Ah. Of course. Mmm.'

Kay varied his pleasant, non-committal responses to the stream of pointless, unanswerable questions and moved on. Again and again he made the right noises, laughed in the right places, made ambiguous, bland comments about his own shadowy future, passed politely to different hated faces, started once more. It was harder than usual. The Families seemed out of sorts, chillier than the last time he'd been at one of these functions. But perhaps that was his imagination. Perhaps the chill came from the snowbound landscape that lay at the back of his mind, the girl's landscape. He pictured her there and it thrilled him. He tried without success to add himself to the scene.

Didn't anyone notice that he was different? Out of place? Didn't they see that he despised them all?

In desperation he blundered into a toilet, took out the silver tube, warm with his body heat, and let a small amount of the powder dissolve on his tongue. Then he took the time to wash, tidy his clothes, drink a little water. There, that should do it. He'd cope now. It was just this once, though. He wouldn't do it again. He swore it to himself: an easy promise.

By rotten chance Kay left the bathroom and found himself face to face with Jan, just as Clarissa was also converging on them from another direction. They checked and stood formally apart, the three of them; the two boys serious, the girl smiling slightly at the situation, arms folded, expecting friction. All three had played together and been educated together, on and off, until Jan's parents had been killed. But it had been an uneasy companionship. From the nursery onwards, all three had argued endlessly. Three was a bad number. Gradually Clarissa had learned to play the diplomat, getting what she wished without force, making alliances as it suited her. The boys had stolen toys from each other, fought like tigers and competed to have Clarissa side with them. She had quickly seen the value of the coin she carried, and teased them both.

In all that time the boys had never found agreement or friendship. How could they, with such different futures?

'Executive Lieutenant.'

'Kay.'

'Quite a thing, isn't it?' Kay found himself saying,

hearing his words sound unaccustomedly muddled. 'What can we expect from our young friend, I wonder?'

The blue eyes flashed icily. 'Do you really want to know?'

'Now now, boys,' Clarissa murmured pleasantly, 'be good. Don't needle him, Kay.'

Ignoring his sister, he said belligerently: 'Yes, why not? Yes, I'd love to know.'

'Well, I think I can sum it up quite easily for you. In my opinion, we should move quickly to a new phase in our approach to security and overall stability. After all, if you go out – as I'm sure *you* do Kay, *often* – into our great capital, look around, walk the streets, visit the waterfront, you'll see that we have a positive tide of . . . flotsam . . . debris – call it what you will – choking up the system.'

Kay felt the anger flowing in him, knew he was being provoked and didn't care. 'You're talking about the Scroats. The homeless. The jobless. The ones coming in from the floods. The ones we don't look after. *People*, Jan.'

Beside him, Clarissa gasped a little at the use of the dangerous word, looking round to check they were not overheard, but Jan showed nothing. Moving marginally closer he said flatly: 'Call it what you will, as I said. The point is that the . . .' – the blond head inclined towards Kay's ear to breathe the word – '. . . *impurities* are not being removed quickly enough. Hence all the trouble we get these days, not that anybody here seems to care.' He gestured impatiently at his guests. 'Oh yes, fertility licences have helped – are still helping – of course, but we need to act. Push things along as they are going now, but faster. We can't spend forever in this halfway house. Take that appalling Portable Road. You'd have to admit that *that* is a wound that needs to be cleansed, cauterised.'

'*Impurities!*' Kay was aware that his voice had risen, that

Clarissa was shushing him; he saw that his hand had taken hold of the other boy's immaculate grey-and-black lapel; 'And me, Jan, look at me! *Look at my face!* Am I an *impurity* to be sponged away by your Pax arseholes? Am I? Where does it stop?'

Jan struck his hand away, hatred and scorn in his eyes. 'Perhaps, Kay. When you show so little control . . . It makes one wonder!' Then his gaze slipped over Kay's shoulder to someone behind and he visibly collected himself, bowed slightly, moved off across the room.

'Oh dear,' Tilly said, appearing with her easy, sweet-smelling fluidity, slipping an arm through Kay's, 'you seem to be making quite a scene, my darling. What do you think your grandfather will say?'

Kay's fists were clenched tight by his side, watching the hated grey back retreat. 'I don't care what he says. Jan Barbieri is an *animal*. Giving him power is idiotic.'

'I'm sure you're right, darling,' his mother murmured, soothingly, her party smile still fixed on her face as she sent little nods and acknowledgements to people in other parts of the room, healing the brief disturbance.

Kay looked at her searchingly, looked at both of them, mother and sister standing there, fresh and stunning and smiling away, unfazed by his outburst, charming all these powerful people. They were alike and incomprehensible to him: Clarissa hinting now at doubts about taking Jan as her partner; Tilly, out of the blue, apparently agreeing with his assessment of Jan's new post. Or was she just saying anything, calming him, manipulating as she always did? His head swam. He shouldn't have brought the tube after all. This wasn't the place for it.

Somehow, he held it together to get through forty more grim minutes of mingling and empty small talk. It wasn't often that all twelve Families assembled, with seven of them having to travel across the floods from other cities. But now they were together, it seemed pointless. Empty back slapping and reminiscing. None of them were fit to rule. Maybe Jan himself was the only other person present who could see what was happening out there in the streets – the discontentment, the restlessness – and Jan wished only to wipe it all clean.

Going home in the official family transport, surrounded by their silent guards, Kay brooded reassuringly again on his own secret: what he already knew and guessed about the girl, and what he should do with such knowledge. Across from him, in the corner seat, the old man watched him coldly, watery eyes glinting from the shadows.

After a while Tomas said: 'I expect you to show greater control in future. Have you learned so little of the art of politics? Have you been trained so poorly? There is always a wider context to consider. Unknown factors. Always. This is a delicate time for us. We must court our allies.'

'*Control!*' Kay wasn't going to take such a reprimand in front of his sister and mother. He'd only been at the rotten function for them. He leaned forward, trembling. 'Control! Do you know, Grandfather, that's just what Jan said. You're all obsessed with control, aren't you? All of you. I want to *live*. Is that all right with you? Is it?' Three pairs of Saint eyes gravely regarded him, and he knew he was trapped by his mood, cast unwillingly into the role of sulky child. It stung him into saying: 'So what about *your* control, Grandfather? Has that slipped up at all recently? Have you *lost* anything? Let anything go?'

The old man's reply, when it came, was icy: 'No Kay. I never *lose* anything. Merely discard what is worthless.'

The edge of threat was unmistakable. Kay instantly regretted his words, his sulky mood evaporating. What was he doing? He must be nuts, after all the hours of careful, painstaking research. A wrong word from him would have the girl found and destroyed. They were right, damn them. He needed to learn more control. Not their kind, maybe; not control of individuals, cities, nations. Just the ability to curb his temper and hide his feelings. Enough control to find a space to live in, unhassled. He just wanted to be alone, behind his thick doors. That's all.

Tilly's warm, motherly hand rested on his. 'I have an idea,' she said brightly. 'I'll tell Christo that I'm staying at home tonight, and when we get in we'll have a big jug of whipped chocolate sent up. We can all play a game. Tomas can get his mah jong set out and we can play together as we used to. Just us. Just the family. What do you think? Kay? Clarissa?'

Kay thought of the music he would miss. Thought of the girl, sitting waiting for his gifts.

'That would be lovely, Mummy,' he said, with great effort. 'I'm sorry for my outburst, Grandfather. I apologise to all of you.'

'*That would be lovely, Mummy,*' Clarissa parroted sourly from her opposite corner. But she did it under her breath and, even if they heard, nobody responded.

In his own official transport, barely a mile away, Jan Barbieri had already dismissed his acceptance speech and the tiresome evening that had followed. It was something he had to go through for now, brown-nosing to the walking fossils from the Great Families, endlessly smiling at their patronising delight in his progress, as if *they'd* had anything to do with it . . . But they didn't begin to dream the half of it.

He was the future. He could feel it in the tingling of his

fingertips. And *now* this news of Hunter's: a gift from the gods. He couldn't stop grinning, could barely sit still in the leather seat.

'So the old fool's lost a spare!' he said, drumming his palms on his knees.

Hunter, his personal bodyguard and strategist, said: 'So it seems. Not yet confirmed.'

'A spare who's actually *here*, in this city, and has so far eluded that idiot Copper, and whoever else they're using.'

Hunter frowned. 'Copper's no idiot, Jan. Besides, as I say, nothing is confirmed. These are only probabilities. I'll need to look over the records of Saint deployments and intelligence gathering to be sure. Maybe send a man up North, to the sleeper settlement.'

'It *is* true: I can feel it. And it fits what we do know. Face it, Hunter, they've lost their touch, the precious Saints. They're history. Who needs their piss-poor broadcasts; or *any* of the Network? Subliminal messages, non-information, drugs . . . It might have served once, during the ice, but not now, not in the present. This is *our* time, Hunter. Things are moving.'

The larger man stayed silent.

Jan appealed to Magnus and Pieter, who had shown no surprise at Hunter's announcement. But then, surprise was alien to those two. Any strong emotion was.

'It's a laugh, isn't it? The high and mighty Saints slipping up like that! Did you know already? You *did*, didn't you? Why didn't you tell me?'

Pieter inclined his head slightly, the cropped silver hair catching the light faintly. 'We . . . suspected.'

Gods above, couldn't they ever get excited? Jan felt a burst of irritation, turned his head sharply to look out into the night to hide the anger. They'd been so good to him, taught him so much. They believed as he believed, in a purer city, a nation of achievers. And now at last he had real power, as they did. What a combination! Between them, they'd find a way to set things right. They already had wonderful – truly *wonderful* – ideas! And here he was, fizzing with the future and energy and good humour. It was *his* night. All he wanted was to enjoy the harmless joke at the Saints' expense. It was not a big thing. Maybe they had just grown too old now, too cautious . . .

He turned back to them, said; 'Look. We needn't worry about the spare, if that's what you're thinking. Tomas will get her eventually, if she *is* here and any kind of threat. We can even offer to do the job for him, if you like.'

The two of them returned his gaze neutrally in the soft interior light. Both were ivory-skinned, slight to the point of being skeletal.

Magnus said slowly: 'It is true that the undesired presence of a spare in this city might have many implications for the Families, and for us. We could discuss this further another time. But you must excuse us if we seem subdued. There has been other news, besides this. News that you must hear and that will doubtless cause you some considerable grief.'

Abruptly, Jan felt the good humour and excitement drain out of him. His stomach contracted at the gentle, concerned look on their faces. With such a look, four long years ago, they had broken the news of his parents' death. 'An attack,' they had said sadly. 'A cowardly ambush on the transport returning them from their official visit to our own facility.' They had let him cry with his face buried against the thin prickly material of their tunics. The only time they had ever touched and the last time he could remember crying. And after the first dark months, they had helped him to become strong again, as he was now.

He gathered himself and tried to sound light-hearted:

'So what is this terrible news? There is no one else I could lose, no one I'd miss. All those I care about are here.' He gestured round at the three of them.

It was Magnus again who spoke: 'No doubt you have heard in the broadcasts and from your good and able Hunter here that there have been occasional, recent attacks on the Stoneywall research facility. Vandalism, eco-demonstrations, that kind of thing. Tiresome and pointless.'

'Yes. *And?*'

'Yes. Well, the last of these was more organised. Entirely different. Clever even.'

'And?'

'And they managed to penetrate security.' Magnus smiled apologetically, thin palms up: 'We don't have a great deal of security, as you know. Why would we? The location and nature of the building is enough to discourage most . . . potential ill-doers. But this time someone did get inside. With explosives. And somehow – I'm so sorry, Jan, we don't know yet *how* this was possible – they managed to access the vaults, *some* of the vaults, and destroy the material inside.'

Now Jan could see where this was going. He was sweating, trembling.

'The destroyed material included . . .'

'NO! NO! NO!'

Immediately, as if his shout had caused it, the vehicle lurched to a stop, and outside there came an angry cry and a heavy bump against the side of the transport. Then another. Some sort of old garbage, rotting eggs and fish slid over the window, heads loomed up, screaming, mouthing obscenities. A boy with yellow hair pressed his thin, bitter face against the glass briefly and looked at where Jan Barbieri was sitting, though he wouldn't be able to see through the darkened panel. He mouthed a single vicious, foul word and the face was gone again. Somebody else outside was beating a metal bar on the transport skin. Jan could see the swing of the arms and the sharp recoil as the bar bounced back. On the glass next to where the mild old men sat, the image of a serpent was appearing, being sprayed by a shadowy hand.

Withdrawing from the window as if it were death, Pieter muttered: 'Wreckers! What do we do? Are we safe?'

The boy looked at him pityingly. The old farts, quaking away at the least thing! Already the anger and grief of a few moments ago had added to the ball of fiery energy inside. It was *his* night after all: nothing could touch him. He said, coolly: 'Don't worry. You stay here and you'll be fine. Nothing can penetrate the skin of this thing. We'll get rid of those idiots, won't we, Hunter?'

He tapped a message to the security detachment in the next compartment, took down a weapon, activated his door, smashed aside a figure that appeared in front of the hole. Reluctantly, Hunter followed. He didn't know what the point was. As Jan had said, nobody and nothing could get into this vehicle, not without firepower that this lot obviously didn't have. Opening up was more dangerous, not less. The boy seemed to think with his anger, never his brain. And if anything, it seemed that those two old stick insects from the Board seemed to encourage this recklessness. Why couldn't Jan see how they played him? The old master, Matteus, he'd have kept well clear. Olive too. All that guff about poor security at Stoneywall! For two pins he'd let the harmless egg-and-fish throwers inside the transport.

Oh well, better just concentrate on the job in hand and

leave the ideas to others, he thought grimly. The boy with yellow hair whooped and screamed in front of him as he stepped into the night, and then ran laughing like a maniac down an alley. Just some poor Scroat. Run, you bastard, Hunter thought, half sympathetically; run before the poisonous new tide that is going to sweep your kind away for ever.

Next to him, the newly appointed Executive Lieutenant of Pax was striking left and right at the last few protesters, preferring his hands to his weapons. And he laughed while he struck.

EIGHTEEN

For the first time in many weeks, Lizzie Hepton was content.

There was a comforting, cosy warm glow to this day that had been absent too long. Edges to things were picked out in sepia yellow or soft mauve, as they should be. The storm winds were as remote and unimportant as the life in her belly that stirred and would *not* give up its spiteful, determined little hold.

She picked her way through a few bins, not noticing if she found anything, and instinctively wandered away from the smart district where her handsome new friend had taken her and back towards the east of the city. She was no Beebop coming, parentless at eleven, from the empty, sodden marshland and fields of another universe. No Sparkle, arriving from the North. The capital was all she knew or wished to know.

Both of them would probably be angry, furious with her. Playing the high and mighty. Martha too. And yet, even that did not matter. People were always getting angry, in her experience. Big deal. She had got some peace at last – surely even *she* was allowed that? – and had not had to do much to get it. Just talk a little, smile. She knew what they wanted. Or she thought she had known. Everything was so surprising. *That's* what they couldn't see, her precious friends, for all their cleverness. She was blessed. Everyone was blessed.

Thinking the nice word, she unconsciously hummed the new tune:

See the serpent wake,
Its eyes are holding you,
Blessed children:
It is love.

'Blessed children: It is love.' That was beautiful. *Somebody* understood how she felt. And now she was free of Ed there wasn't much to worry about. The little life? That strange, unwanted creature would not be allowed to her by the people that decided about those things, anyway, in their big white building. Or maybe it was just the application process that was too difficult; she couldn't remember. Whatever it was, the reason, the life would have to go, somehow. *That* sort of blessing was an uncomfortable, chafing one. She already had all she needed. She was no mother.

There were ways, even if she could get no money for the permit. Of course there were ways, when some Visions could only afford to screen the growing embryo. She'd only have to make friends with one of the nice porters at the dumping places. She was good at making friends.

Lizzie shivered. There was a little market here. Fish, grain, things like that. She was in the middle of it. People smiled at her and talked to her. Men mostly: rough ones, not like the nice one earlier, who'd rescued her from the boring policemen. He had talked too, but what about she hadn't the faintest idea. What did it matter when he gave such gifts and said such nice things. *Had* he said nice things? Perhaps he had bullied and threatened just like the rest. Or perhaps he'd only bullied the policemen, to let her free? Anyway she was sure about the gifts and about not doing anything to get them, except talk and smile. She always knew what they wanted.

She was blessed.

Vaguely, Lizzie opened her bag and put one or two things inside. Food, probably. A shrunken little man came, shaking his head, and took the things back and she watched. She moved on. The ways wound down – easy walking – and she felt a movement in her belly. How was that possible? How did it live? How was it so strong, to push up against her heart with its sharp little fingers? She was too young for a child. Her life had only just begun.

In the large walled yard with its sprouting mushrooms of rusted metal and broken crates, even flowers forcing their way up and dancing in the winds, Martha was already cooking the evening meal, for those that wanted it. The smell was sharp, salty, hot, making Lizzie's eyes sting.

Martha smiled at her when she came through the iron door and then did not smile. There was anger, as she'd known there would be. It wouldn't last. Anger never did. Soon she would eat the hot, salty food, sleep by the dancing flowers. Everything would be remote, comfortable, wonderful. Just her and the spiteful little life, curled up inside.

Martha was not alone with her anger. Other people were angry. Why was everyone in such a mood!? But then other, new people started to arrive, and *they* were angry too, shouting at *everyone*, very smart in their grey jackets with yellow edges. What had they to be so furious about? she wondered.

People started lying down. A few were running. Lizzie smiled. Life was certainly interesting. But now she wanted to eat and then sleep. Enough excitement. Enough. *Stop everyone!*

And then she was lying down too.

*

Beebop, as wired with nervous energy as a stray dog, knew without seeing a thing, that all was not well. He could almost smell it. The approach to the yard was never so empty, so quiet. In an instant, he'd dumped the rooted-for bin stuff he was carrying, veered off sharply before he got to the last alley, and lost himself expertly amongst cranes, junk, quay trucks. The pup Pedestal followed at his heels, wondering why they were not now going to the place where there was food. When he was far enough away, Bee stopped and picked up a piece of wood and splintered it on the rusting strut of a crane, angrily, bitterly, again and again. *Thwack.* Until there were just a few fragments left in his hands and splinters beneath the hard skin of his palms.

Let nothing happen to Martha, that's all. Or Sparkle.

He'd make the bastards pay if it did. He'd had enough. Those *bastards*.

Copper's man watched and did nothing, as instructed.

Tomas sat at his table and considered the two men before him.

'Well, gentlemen. So where have we got to in this interesting state of affairs? All is well, I trust?'

Copper was the spokesman, reporting the facts without emotion. 'As we guessed, the spare, Mira, is in the capital. She arrived on the ship *Helicon*, out of Lomond, more than two months ago. Since then she has used a different name and appearance. She has even been stopped routinely by security on one or two occasions, but allowed to move on, as there seemed to the officers concerned to be no ground for holding her. As might be expected, she has adapted very quickly to conditions here and for that reason has so far evaded efforts to locate and detain her.'

The taller man was smiling faintly, nodding. 'Aye,' he mimicked, 'as might be expected.'

Copper blinked once and continued in the same tone. 'Recently, however, Moore here received intelligence on her entry method, current friends, identity and so forth. As a result of this extra information, the *Helicon* has now been . . . shall we say, impounded indefinitely, and known associates of the girl Mira – mostly vagrants, but not of any known Wrecker faction, despite what the Pax contingent involved in the raid were allowed to believe – have been taken and questioned. Unfortunately, these actions have not as yet produced the girl.'

Copper paused, considered.

'We have, however, allowed one close associate to remain at liberty for the time being. A boy calling himself Beebop, an incomer from a flooded farm community. We are reasonably confident that he will lead us to the spare in time, especially now that his previous refuge has been taken from him. We have indications of the two being together on several occasions: it may perhaps be assumed that they are friends.'

Tomas gestured impatiently. 'Friends! And why would I care for her friendships? And with some incomer farmer's son! Come now. Tell me your thoughts. Will we have to eliminate her? Is she going to be too much trouble? Clearly she can lead us quite a dance when she chooses. We can't let her run wild indefinitely under our noses. And yet . . .' He gazed out of the window at the bank of grey cloud, musing, '. . . and yet, it would be a pity not to be able to use such a tool in some way.'

Copper said: 'I think we can pick her up soon, sir. Her death may not be necessary if you don't wish it. But there is also Master Kay to consider.'

'Oh yes. Master Kay. You mentioned something about him in your preliminary report?'

'Yes, sir. And those guesses are now confirmed. It has come to light that Master Kay has been using his privileged status within the network for research that seems to point to him knowing about the spare, although what contact they've had, if any, is not clear. His own guard claims none to his knowledge.'

'That fits,' growled Tomas, 'yes indeed, that fits very well, Copper. Kay knows of her, you can be sure. He almost told me as much, the hothead. What else?'

'There is also limited intelligence from our operatives within Pax to suggest that the girl's presence here may have been registered and be causing some interest with them, but for what reason the intelligence does not indicate. Obviously, Jan Barbieri's views and intentions are well known and command considerable support across much of Pax and the Board . . .'

'Fools!' murmured the old man.

'. . . but, again, we cannot say whether interest in the girl might be linked to these intentions, or not. Obviously they would wish to discomfort us in any way possible. They have made no move as yet, but we're watching for such a development. Best guess at the present time: they could see the spare as a lever to help persuade members of the Saint group to allow them a free hand. How this might work is unclear. Obviously, they could not make her existence known publicly. They stand to lose too much. Could they therefore be planning a move against a specific member of the family? Kay, perhaps, or his mother because of her perceived weakness for the boy, and his supposed origins?'

There was silence while the three of them considered this last possibility. 'Thank you, Copper. I will give these matters much thought. For the time being we let the girl live, and keep our options open. Let me know as soon as we have her. You may go.'

'Sir.'

The automatic door closed after the unremarkable back and Tomas allowed a broad smile to spread across his face.

'This is as you had planned?' the other man, Moore, asked, with a hint of disbelief: 'This is the way you expected things to move?'

The old man laughed briefly, without humour. 'No! Think, man! Nobody could plan all of this. What about Pax? What about my grandson ferreting around in his machines, keeping to a task for once? Could I have predicted that? And yet . . . given the right raw materials, one can certainly create *interesting* situations. Right now, I would still back the girl to become a great potential resource to us. At worst a weapon to use against Barbieri if that time should come. The bait for a trap perhaps, or an assassin . . . who knows? But at best – and this is only a vague hope, Moore – a match for him in marriage. The Saint genes with a clearer, tougher head on her shoulders than my granddaughter can offer. She'd have to be trained up, of course.'

'I see. And what is my role here now?'

'Your role, yes. A little extra insurance, my friend. Try not to tread on Copper's toes – I think the man resents you: this is *his* territory, after all, despite your unique knowledge of the subject – but make sure he finds her again for me, will you? And most especially, stop her getting into the wrong hands: better dead than that. If possible, do not harm her. Then we'll see. Of course in the end there is a chance that her death will be unavoidable. In some ways she is a remarkably unknown quantity. In extremis, I am happy to trust your judgement. But use your *own* security personnel for any pick-up, won't you? Put them in Pax uniforms. Unless you or Copper can see to it personally.'

A buzzer sounded and Clarissa's voice floated into the room. 'Grandfather? Are you coming down to lunch? It's only me at the moment, and it's very dull. I can't find anyone else.'

Tomas sighed and rose. 'I had hopes for that one, but I've spoilt her somewhat. She shows great vanity and now I think there is the first hint of rebelliousness too. A great trial for an old man! I'd better go. I will expect your report soon.'

The other man murmured: 'Aye. I will find her. She shall not hide from me. But what of Master Kay?'

Tomas guided Moore towards the door. 'I think,' he said thoughtfully, 'that we will let Kay play the scene out unhindered for now. Who knows; if the yokel incomer doesn't perform, he might be a more interesting lure to bring the spare to us. I wonder . . . what is he making of it all? Imagine, if he's actually made *contact*, he must be at sixes and sevens, to say the least. I mean, consider how . . .'

The last words were lost as the two men left the room. Tilly said: 'Stop play-back,' and the images on her hand-set blinked out, leaving her quarters calm and silent. By the ever-open window, rough strips of translucent silk danced in the cool air, pink and orange, soothing her. She lay flat on the rug, softly rubbing her temples, trying to see clearly where all this might lead, trying not to give way to anger.

The arrogance of that old man! Playing casual deity with the life of the girl Mira . . . and with her son and Clarissa too. And yet, Tilly wondered in shame, was she any better? It had been her alone who had pressed for Kay being allowed to believe himself nothing more – or less – than her natural son, born from her body after the nine-month term. (She still glowed with pleasure at the memory of bearing that tiny life.) And now, despite all the love she could give him, the boy had grown bitter, inadequate, secretive. Her fault. Even his sister had suffered from Tilly's decision, it seemed. She who had never believed herself a true daughter had become jealous, desperate to please, to be acknowledged: to please her grandfather most of all. It was a mess.

Did it matter that Tilly had done what she had done for unselfish reasons? Perhaps not.

So – she brought her mind back to the present – what did Tomas hope for? To use this enterprising 'spare' (how Tilly hated that word!) to make the family strong again and counter the new strengths appearing elsewhere? To have this Mira step into Clarissa's intended role at the last minute and forge an alliance with the despicable Jan Barbieri?

If so, he was fooling himself. The girl was no politician. She was pure, untainted, subtle and strong. The best of them, better for having grown up half wild in the icy mountains. Tilly was pleased that she had helped Kay make his contact: the girl would do him good, whatever Tomas thought. And if the old man used Kay as a lure, as he had suggested to Moore, she could always intervene if and when it became necessary.

Tilly smiled, reassuring herself: all was yet well. With or without her, things were moving. Tomas had surely not grasped how *quickly* things were moving. Having played its part, the old order was shifting, disintegrating. Almost three centuries of the Great Families! It was enough. Across the five cities and beyond there were people ready for change, hungry for it, feeling their way like infants.

The serpent was waking. A larger design than her own was at work. Perhaps Mira's arrival at this time was no accident.

She rolled up to her feet, stretched, went to bathe and choose clothes for this evening's engagements. It occurred to her as she spread out the things that in her heart she was deeply excited. To see and feel the change coming, but not to know the outcome . . . to watch the spilling gene pool of humanity refresh and adapt itself . . . to see the tensions mount and resolve. It was beautiful, thrilling.

And dangerous.

The design was not her own – that was truth – but there was still much work to do. Tonight she must discuss these new reports with Christo. Possible sightings of unknown operatives in various sleeper settlements. Some kind of attack at Stoneywall, with no details given and a blank, unexplained silence from her own operative there. A series of low-key meetings between those repellent old stick insects from the Board and some of the other Families.

Whatever Tomas thought – and at least they had this in common, that they did not wish the young Barbieri to be the future – the time to hold onto the status quo was gone. She must activate more of the Wrecker and Floodite cells. She must have someone explain his thank-less, desperate task to the man Hedge. Most of all, she must speak to Marie and her team, check all was well there, make sure that the youngest of them was still kept beyond harm, in case . . .

Well, just in case.

As she had told herself, the design was not hers. Whose it was she did not know.

NINETEEN

Mira's eyes flicked open.

Something was wrong. She lay flat on her pallet, unmoving.

First there was the lurch of surprise and disorientation at her surroundings, the same as it was each time she awoke in her cold sanctuary. Then the soaring, numbing sorrow, almost too much to bear . . .

Usually she would try to hang onto the last few moments of sleep, to keep her eyes tight shut and imagine the soft snowfall outside, the spirits weaving through the trees, the scent of resin, the silence that was not a silence. But now was not the time for that. Something was happening that required her concentration.

She lay still until she was certain that the danger was not here, in this room. Then she rolled gently to her side and looked across at the old couple. Their eyes peeped shyly back at her from under the mats and rubbish that kept them warm. Mira smiled at them so they would not be frightened and then put a finger to her lips. They understood. They nodded. They knew about not being found.

She rose from the pallet and found her shoes, slipped them on. She had nothing to take, if the time to flee had once more arrived, except the clothes she wore and the crossbow, snug in her belt pouch.

As she was tying the laces, it came again. The thing that had woken her. Against the faraway, background noise of the city, the deep notes of the boat horns out on the water, and the nearer, endless whine of wind, there was a voice, quite close, calling her adopted name. Beebop's voice. She waited, and a minute or two later it came again, from slightly further away. And then, after a space, a third time, closer again. Bee must be walking all round this broken-down quarter in the hope that she would hear his call.

Mira relaxed. She had only to stay silent and hidden and he would lose interest and go. There were too many ruins to search, too many places to hide: he would do no more than call. Later she would meet him in one of their usual places and she would perhaps be angry with him for putting her at risk. Or perhaps not: for he did not know what he did, knew nothing of the danger that had followed her from the North. He thought she was simply paranoid, touchy, guarding the secret of where she slept. He teased her about it.

But, she thought sharply, *why* was he looking for her? Why was he here? The answer was inescapable. He would not spend this futile effort unless something had happened. Some bad thing. Bee was here for support, friendship, help . . . or to warn her, perhaps.

Ice crept up her spine. Oh, the fool!

If the bad thing – whatever it was – was because of her, then he might have brought *them* to her door, the men in grey. Even now, there might be transports full of them coming through the city to tear every broken door from its hinges, reduce every building to rubble, until they found her.

The peeping, shy, trusting eyes watched her.

'I will go,' she whispered. 'I will go and then you will be safe, right enough. Stay quite quiet now until all the noise has gone away.' They nodded again. An ancient, fragile hand, as small as a child's, came from under the mats. She took it, squeezed it, smiled.

Bee's voice came again, closer than ever: '*Spar-kle! Answer me! Where are you? Spar-kle!*'

Softly, Mira opened the door a crack, letting in the pale, late afternoon light, slipped through, wormed her way up the broken stairs to street level. At the top she lay flat and risked a glance out at the street. Beebop was visible standing at a junction two short blocks away, looking round him, calling, kicking angrily at the debris in the street. His yellow hair stood out round his scalp, wilder than ever. The streak of fur weaving excitedly through the rubble was Pedestal, sniffing for rats.

If there were followers, where would they be, she wondered. Up on the roofs? Hidden in other doorways? Somehow she would have to get as far as possible from the cellar steps before she was seen. And then . . . lead them away, far away from the couple hiding under their bits and pieces.

At the junction, Bee got fed up with immobility and started to walk away from her, peering into windows, pushing at doors, cursing, still calling now and then. Keeping as low as possible, hugging the darkness of the buildings on this southern side of the street, she stood up and ran softly in the opposite direction, back towards the dark heart of the city.

One block. Two. All seemed well. One or two icy drops of rain stung her cheek, but no more came for the moment: only the rattling wind.

Halfway down the third block, there was a shout and, turning, she saw a shape up on the roofs to the left of her. An answering call came from somewhere ahead and to the right, possibly in the next street. Then another, behind her. She was moving fast now, all secrecy abandoned in favour of life-saving speed, weaving through the rubble. In her hands the crossbow had blossomed. Deliberately she checked her stride to loose bolts at the men she could see. Not to hurt them, just to make sure of their attention, to bring them out from their cover so that Beebop would understand that he must run too, if he could see any of this. In the same breath, a piece of concrete at her feet cracked and splintered, the fragments skittering away. It had worked all too well. The men were returning her fire, coming out into the open, calling to one another, speaking into their communicators. She could hear Beebop's angry shouts behind her. She sent him a silent message: *Run, Beebop. Go! Make yourself small. Survive.* The adrenalin flooded through her and she sprinted for the jungle of the docks, wishing for trees and snow and ice and shadows instead of concrete and cameras.

Four of them, she thought, or possibly five. Enough. One emerged from a street on her left just as she ran past, lunged at her, tripped on the broken bricks, and fell heavily as she dodged. More shots rattled the stones around her. Five men, she thought, all speaking into their communicators, saying where she was, where she was headed, calling their friends. The water came into view, lapping up the street at the bottom of a gentle rubble-strewn slope and sure enough there were more grey shapes waiting there already. They had expected her to take this way. The docks were a dark, dangerous maze of alleyways where anything or anyone could be lost. They weren't going to let her hide there.

Without checking her stride, Mira changed her target, ran along a short way that went parallel to the waterfront, then back up steeply, climbing streets that would hopefully slow the heavy-footed hunters down more than her.

There was only one chance left, that she could think of. Hiding was impossible, with the nearest men only twenty or thirty metres behind her. Nor was she going to stay ahead for ever, not with the chattering communicators and their greater knowledge of the city. She emerged onto one of the larger east-west throughfares, a Caplink route, and looked round wildly, hoping to see the orange wagons.

There was nothing.

She swung round and loosed two more of her precious bolts, buying a little time, sending the pursuers diving for cover. Then they were up again, coming headlong. She ran on, following the Caplink rails – would they guess what she was trying to do? – hoping to hear the familiar hissing sound. Another bolt, another check. But now her heart sank: two other grey figures had appeared further down the way, blocking her off.

The chase was entering a more inhabited part of the city now, which meant more cameras, twisting silently on their stalks, tracking her progress. It was a poor but thriving area, mostly Scroat, a few Visions. Most would be eating in their homes, but there were a few people on the street. 'Help me!' she screamed at them, and watched the heads snap away, pretending not to have seen. People did not help each other here, in this godforsaken place. They were too frightened, too dead in their hearts.

She started to weave in between the people, making it impossible for the pursuers to use their weapons, but gradually the walkway cleared as the pedestrians stood back, not wanting to be shields, not wanting to risk the anger of the grey men. The first of the figures ahead was running back towards her now, moving to intercept her. This one was a woman. Mira slotted a bolt into the bow and she backed off, hovering close, ready for her quarry's concentration to slip. Deliberately, Mira ran straight at her, bow at the ready, and pushed the woman to the ground as she retreated.

There were just too many. She was tiring.

Glancing back she saw that there were perhaps ten of them at her heels now, not gaining as yet, but not losing much ground either. Soon, she thought, there would be transports, summoned by the communicators, catching her without effort. Even as she thought it, there were sirens in the distance. The remaining man ahead – close now, but wary – grinned nastily at her.

'Give up,' he called, 'save your strength, Scroat! There's nowhere to go.'

But there was. There *was* somewhere to go.

Behind the man, a line of orange carriages hissed smoothly into view, pulled up at a stop. On the other side of the wagons, doors were sliding open. Mira heard the gentle automated voice from inside, announcing what stop it was, reminding passengers that they had only thirty seconds to get on or off the service. She coaxed an extra ounce of speed from her legs, a little more effort from her bursting heart, and ran flat out for the orange safety, taking a path well wide of the man ahead.

'Oh no you don't!' The man closed with her. Again she raised the bow, but he came straight on and she didn't want to shoot: not unless there was no choice left. She'd had enough of bloodshed. On the Caplink service, the buzzer was sounding for closure of the doors, but she was almost there. Ten metres: no more. With a last effort she threw herself forward, planted her foot between the closing orange panels. 'Attention!' said the gentle, automated voice. 'This service is ready to depart. Passengers must stay clear of the doors.' The panels slid back invitingly, but as she made to enter, a heavy hand gripped her arm and pulled. The doors were already closing again: she could hear them as she struggled to get free of the man, and flung out a hand, got her fingers into the gap.

'Attention! This service is ready to depart. Deliberate obstruction of the doors will constitute a service violation. A fine may be incurred. Please stand clear.' Once more the panels slid back. The man was as strong as a boar. Mira could feel her own strength draining away as she fought him. Desperately, she swung the metal crossbow frame up at his face with her free hand, seeing a line of scarlet appear across his cheek.

The man roared in angry pain and for a quarter of a second his grip loosened. It was enough. With a cry, she wrenched herself free and pitched forward, full length, between the closing doors. As she fell hard onto the carriage floor, she was aware of sudden fire in her arm, singing white hot through the nerves to every part of her being.

Fathers!

Dimly, through the pain, she was aware of movement, a gradual increase in speed, the hissing of the motors. She looked down at her arm and saw blood. Around her, one or two passengers hovered, undecided what they should do.

'Stay back!' she warned, breathlessly, sobbing from the hurt: 'Stay away!'

She fought to bring the crossbow out from under her, struggled to her feet.

'But you've been shot! They shot you!' a woman said, looking pale.

Oh sweet spirits. Mira realised the woman was right. The blood, the pain . . .

She pulled herself up to her knees, looked out through the smoky glass. There were men running after the carriages, others just standing watching as they accelerated past, others talking once more into the little boxes. The wagons were going fast now, sizzling down the rails, but the next stop would be only a mile or so, maybe less. The little chattering boxes would bring others, ready to finish her when the Caplink doors opened once more.

Feverishly, she looked around the interior. The automated voice was saying: 'All passengers joining the service *must* submit to a thumb-print or retinal scan, or present their security card to the screens provided. Failure to do this represents a service violation. A fine may be incurred.' The screens, tiny rectangles, were dotted down the carriage. Apart from that, there was nothing. Just seats, handles for the passengers to grip, firmly closed access doors at either end. Nothing loose, no opening windows, no movement from the doors when she pushed at them. The whole thing was a sealed, secure unit, proof against attack from demonstrators and Wreckers. Not even a driver or Caplink representative to make sure that all was well.

'For your listening pleasure,' the voice said, 'we now return to our excerpts from Uttley's tone poem "The Great Melt".' A soft, shimmering, throbbing sound enveloped the interior of the carriage. Blood dripped from Mira's arm. The orange decor had started to spin. Still the woman, a Vision, hovered close by, looking on anxiously. 'We should do something!' she said, and then, louder: 'I said we should do something. This girl's been shot!' Nobody else took any notice.

No need, Mira thought fuzzily. No need to do anything. In a few seconds, it will all be done for you.

And then she saw the button. A lonely red button, placed behind a clear screen, with a neat label: *Emergency door release. Break the screen. Incorrect use constitutes a service violation.*

With a snarl she raised the bow and threw it hard at the plastic. The effect was magical. With a hiss, the carriage slowed dramatically, throwing the passengers forward, and stopped dead. As soon as all movement had ceased the doors on both sides of the carriage – and those on the other carriages further along the line – sprang sharply back. The automated voice, cutting off 'The Great Melt', said: 'Attention! Emergency procedures have been initiated. If you are able, please disembark from this Caplink service and wait. Assistance will be here shortly.'

In Mira's carriage, the passengers were angry. Now they did notice her. How dare she interrupt their journey in this way? Who was she, anyway? What had she done? They would see that the full force of justice was applied to her as soon as the police arrived.

'But the poor thing's hurt,' twittered the Vision woman, unheard.

Despite their outrage, nobody tried to interfere as Mira half fell, half stepped from the orange carriage, and ran clumsily off, into one of the connecting side ways. It was only when she was a mile or more away, huddled shivering and grey-faced in a doorway, with sirens all around, that she realised she had left the crossbow behind.

As for the twenty-three men and women who had hunted her across almost two miles of wasteland and into the fringes of the populated area, they had themselves melted away before the sirens came.

Copper wondered what Tomas would say. Perhaps he should have waited for Moore.

The heat in Jan Barbieri's recreation room was delicious, almost too much to bear. The pond of dark water lay unbroken. A little steam curled up from the surface and round the overhanging boughs of great sponge-leaved plants. Beyond the little oasis, there was nothing but pale yellow desert, even paler as it retreated, until it smudged into the white horizon and the baking, shimmering sky.

'It must be very clean,' Jan said lazily, gesturing into the distance with his drink. 'The desert. The sand.'

'Very clean. Very empty. Very dull.'

'Not empty. Things live there. They have adapted. There's a fine living to be had for those things!'

Clarissa sighed. 'Oh Jan, you're such a weirdo. Come for a swim.'

He watched as she ran to the brink of the water and in the same movement stretched out into a flat dive. Gods above, she was perfect. A graceful, lean shape, but becoming more of a woman every day. The water seemed to welcome her. With the flash of silver from her swimming suit she could be a fish, an eel. She went completely under, swimming silently, and only surfaced at the other side. She was laughing at him, waving her arms, bobbing up and down. Grimly he forced a smile, waved back.

He had to have her. He *would* have her, for she had been promised to him. It was part of the plan.

'Weirdo!' she called, giggling.

He went down to the water and dived in himself, proud of his physique, of the powerful, fast stroke that he could keep up for an hour or more. Drawing level with her he caught her hand and said: 'When I have beaten you in the final next week, you will learn to respect me.'

'When I've beaten *you*, you'll resent me for it and probably won't want to see me for days, weeks, months . . .'

He pulled her closer. His face was just centimetres from hers. The droplets of moisture ran from her dark hairline down across her pale skin. She looked at him questioningly from those large, bottomless eyes. Gently he placed a kiss on her mouth and her lips under his did nothing, stayed immobile, unmoved.

The anger flowed in him again. Little bitch.

He drew back to study her. 'Listen to me. We are to be together. There are things you don't understand. Things I can't tell you. Not yet at least. But it is certain that we *will* be together, Clarissa. And we will make a fine couple. A strong alliance. The people will adore us.'

'Your buzzer,' she said, puzzlingly.

'What?'

She splashed him with her free hand, straight in the eyes, making them smart. 'Your buzzer. Is sounding. On your towel.' She twisted his grip sharply so that he was forced to free her hand. 'Go on. Answer it like a good boy.'

She was no longer smiling at him.

He looked at her furiously, swam strongly back across the green water and climbed out. Sure enough, the tiny wristcom on his towel was signalling.

'Yes, Hunter?'

'Sorry to disturb your recreation, sir. There's been some kind of disturbance in G2. I think we should go there. I think it will concern you.'

'OK, Hunter. Five minutes.' It would be a relief, anyway, to get away from the little tease. For now.

'Check.'

He picked up his towel, said: 'End hologram.' It amused him to see Clarissa suddenly left in a bare pool in a bare room. He would leave her the heat.

'Stay as long as you wish,' he called politely; 'someone will come if you need anything. I'll make sure you're monitored.' There. That should take away any remaining pleasure she had in swimming by herself. She would learn in time not to cross him.

Down in the garage level Hunter was already in the transport. Jan slipped in beside him and the hatch door slid shut.

'Well?'

'There's been some kind of a manhunt. Over in G2, but spreading into E2 and E3. Not much surveillance over there of course, to catch the fun, except at the end. But the quarry took to a Caplink service. I thought we should see the unit concerned, and watch the tapes.'

'I see. Why?'

'Just a hunch.'

Jan let it go. Hunter's instincts were usually worth listening to.

At the empty line of orange wagons there was a security cordon. The men parted silently for Jan. His eyes raked over the blast damage on the set of doors Hunter indicated and the smears and spatters of drying blood inside. The dark mess could also be seen over the handle of the battered metal crossbow lying beneath the broken emergency panel.

Jan beckoned the sergeant of the security detail. 'DNA-print the gore. Find out who uses a bow like that, where they're made. Analyse the blast damage. I want exact, documented results within twenty-four hours.'

'Sir!' If the man resented being commanded by a seventeen-year-old, he was mindful enough of his own skin not to show it overtly. Already the Executive Lieutenant had a reputation.

'Now. The security tapes.'

Hunter was fiddling with his handset. 'They're just being patched through now, sir.'

The two of them stood side by side and watched Mira's attempts to throw off her assailant and gain the sanctuary of the wagon. They saw the figure in grey loose off a blast through the closing doors and the girl collapse, nursing her arm. They saw her rapid assimilation of the situation and eventual decision to activate the emergency system.

They saw her stumble from the Caplink, watched by the other passengers.

'Where are that lot now?' Jan asked, gesturing at the frozen picture.

'In there.' Hunter indicated the larger transport that had brought the sergeant's detachment.

'Good. Record and witness interview with each one, Hunter. Everything they saw. And when all the samples have been taken, I think we'll keep this wagon too for good measure.'

Hunter said: 'Aye, sir,' smartly, for the benefit of the grunts outside, but when they were alone once more, travelling back to the sombre Pax building, he raised his eyebrows questioningly. 'Why are we spending so much effort on this? It's the spare. There's no doubt about it, even with the change in appearance. And I suppose the ones after her must be Copper's lot.'

'Yes. Copper's "lot" wearing *our* uniforms, Hunter. Why should that be?'

That was surely obvious. 'They're embarrassed about one going AWOL. They found where she was hiding and went in to get her, but didn't want the world to see Saint uniforms cluttering up the streets. For them – and for all of us – it was best not to draw attention to what was happening.' Which was why it seemed mental to Hunter to be interviewing all the witnesses, fixing it all in their minds, making them relive contact with the spare. Not that he planned to say it.

Jan was smirking. 'But they still didn't get her.'

Hunter shrugged. 'She's wounded now. Tired. I expect Copper will pick her up soon. Then she'll disappear, poor lass.'

'Yes, I expect he would succeed, given time. She's just a fifteen-year-old girl, after all. How hard can it be? But . . .

get this, Hunter; I don't *want* her to disappear. I want her found *first*. I want her put in the spotlight. I want to tell *everyone*!'

'You can't be serious!' Hunter wondered in dismay if this new, cocky infant Barbieri *meant* to wreck everything. Could he be trusted with the power they'd given him? Or were other steps necessary?

The boy-man's eyes flashed dangerously. 'Yes, Hunter, I'm serious. No, I'm not mad. And no, you won't need to eliminate me, if that's what's going through your diseased mind. Listen to this. It has been decided to make contact with ICSA, invite a delegation. *When* we find her, we will use the spare to discredit the Saints and push them out of the power-sharing agreement.'

'Decided?' Hunter growled. '*Who* decided?' As if it wasn't obvious.

Jan ignored him. 'By then, steps will have been taken to ensure that we ourselves have *no* spares remaining, and nor will the Fertility Board council members or other Families, providing they side with us. It has been agreed. All records will be wiped. After all, our own banks of genetic material have been destroyed. You heard Magnus and Pieter. Don't you *see*? It's beautiful!' His boy's eyes shone with enthusiasm. He couldn't even imagine that Hunter might not agree with this. He thought the bigger man was just slow, not yet understanding the elegant plan.

'Listen, my friend,' he said, with exaggerated patience; 'It's true that the news of the attack on our vaults came hard at first. Of course it did. Do you think I didn't *feel* it, after what happened to my parents? I promised myself the *death* of the Wrecker bastards for that. More than that – well, you know as well as anyone – I'd thought one day to replace my parents. Clarissa and I would need children,

in time, do you see . . .' He swallowed. 'But then, later,
Pieter talked to me. He said they'd seen a way to turn this
thing to our advantage. Imagine. No other surviving
vaults. No spares, not for anyone. The only evidence
will be against old Tomas and his brood. They will be in
obvious contravention of the International Crisis Strategy
Agreement charter. They will be finished. The other
Families have almost all agreed to this. With most of their
own vaults destroyed, they can see the logic. And the
Saints' carelessness in letting this girl come here, to this
city, has further convinced them. She will be our trump
card for the inspectors.'

'It's for ICSA and the other Families, then, that we are
documenting evidence of today's events?'

'Yes. Of course.' At last the man understood.

Hunter gazed out of the window into the darkening afternoon. Fresh rain spat heavily against the glass.
The cub had only arrived at power this very month, and
already he wanted to turn ungratefully on many of the
people who had allowed him that power . . . 'So,' he said,
'You will use the spare, discredit the Saints. And then?'

'Ah, you think I'm throwing away the tools we
need to rule. I can read you so easily, man. But that's
all finished anyway, just like the broadcasts. Let's not
fool ourselves: we've barely kept our noses ahead of the
mass of Visions as it is . . . and the *Scroats*' – he said
the word with loathing – 'are the unpredictable scum
they've always been, ruining everything! What we need
is something new!'

'Something new. I see. Which is?'

'Which is a fresh screening process from the Board.
A *new* one. Not just an update. Not just making sure in a
vague way of intelligence, looks, all that, with a certain
degree of conformity and obedience. Not just weeding out

dud sperm, dud eggs. A *total* screening process, Hunter. Do you get it? *Exact* aptitudes in every skill area. *Exact* susceptibilities, weaknesses, strengths. *Exact* lifetime expectancy. Even ninety-eight per cent certainty for the opinions they'll form. *Everything*, Hunter. Nothing left to chance. Imagine that.'

Hunter imagined it. His head ached. Suddenly, he felt old.

'And the I C S A delegation? Will they OK this new technique, do you think?' he asked sarcastically.

The Executive Lieutenant smiled. 'Nobody knows about this yet. By the time they find out, it'll be halfway done. And we'll be a model society. Perfect. Everybody will want to be like us. Perfect rulers, perfect citizens. Equipped for whatever is to come as the waters rise and half the earth burns dry.'

The transport turned sharp left, approaching the Pax Building. On the corner they swept past a lone figure, out in the rain, dancing barefoot, unwatched, unheeded. The figure was wearing a crudely made snake's head, swaying and writhing like a lunatic. On the pavement he'd written a message in childish coloured chalks, quickly being washed away in a watery, rainbow stream – THE SAVIOUR COMES, PREPARE FOR OUR SALVATION.

Hunter said, wearily, hardly caring now for the answer: 'What about Kay Saint? He's a special case, isn't he? *He* won't be discredited by your plan.'

'Oh, yes, poor Kay! Well, he's not exactly a threat. Look at him, floating about with every kind of debris you can imagine, living in a dream. We'll think of something suitable for him. Nobody will even notice he's gone.'

'I see. And his sister?'

'The gorgeous Clarissa? She may be allowed a part in the new order. She's not all bad. I have hopes for her.

As long as she understands which way to jump. After all, Magnus and Pieter think it will help smooth things over with the other Families – and with the ICSA – if I take her as a partner: after the other Saints have been eliminated.'

Magnus and Pieter seemed to have an opinion about everything, Hunter thought grimly. Magnus and Pieter having this new screening technology all nicely set up and ready to go? That was perhaps just a little too good to be true. A coincidence too far. Not that the cub would listen. Not to him. He was their pet.

Perhaps it was time to look for a new job.

TWENTY

Kay had it all now, but it was too late. He must face facts: she was gone, and probably it was his fault. His childish taunting of Tomas was to blame. A word out of place, as he had feared.

'Lock doors.'

'Doors locked, Kay.'

'I'd like some tea, please.'

'Certainly, Kay.'

When he had the drink he took it wearily, sipping and burning his lips, into his sanctuary. This was the third time, the third consecutive night that she had not been there. His head pounded. He felt exhausted, disillusioned, alone. The thick oval of plexi-glass showed night over the city: the torrents of water ran in silent streams over the outside of the window; distant flashes spoke of the first summer thunder.

Inside, spread out over the precious drums and tone-pads, picked out by the tiny spotlights, there were pictures, lists of data, maps, Fertility Board records. Oh yes, he had it all now, painstakingly teased out from the network. Not only the girl, whose given name was Mira, but the others too. Four from the present generation – apart from his family, of course – and *lots* of others, stretching back into the past, almost to the twentieth century. Of the current four, two had definitely been eliminated. Which meant murdered. The images of the oldest, called Annie Tallis, made his heart miss a beat when he first printed them out.

How were you supposed to deal with a thing like that? How did you handle it?

Two dead, one still a tiny, ignorant child in some hole in France, and *his* one, Mira, who had disappeared, probably because of him. His first instinct was to go and see Tomas, to confront the old devil, to make him confess . . . but that wouldn't help, would it? Not much anyway, he thought ruefully.

He looked again at the large glossy stills of Mira, as a little child and now, at fifteen, but before coming south and losing her mind and maybe her life. He reached out and touched the beautiful strange-familiar face.

How did you handle it?

Arriving abruptly at a decision, he gathered up all the papers, the pictures, everything, and tucked them inside his jacket, smoothing the front so that Jane and other eyes in the complex would not see. 'Please tell my sister I'm coming down to see her,' he said, when he was outside the drum room.

'Your sister is sleeping, Kay. Do you still wish to proceed with this request?'

'Yes, I still wish to proceed with this request.'

'My counterpart in Clarissa Saint's quarters is waking her now.'

'Thank you. Lock all doors after me.'

'I understand.'

When she let him in, Clarissa was tousled, grumpy, confused. She wrapped herself in a duvet and sat on one of the sofas, squinting at him in the unwelcome light.

'Honestly, bro, couldn't it wait?'

'No, sorry, it couldn't.'

'So?'

There was no easy way. Having temporarily suspended her room system on the service board – to raised eyebrows from her – he silently laid the things out on the floor, and she bent over to look, still huddled in the bedclothes. He watched her reaction, heard the intake of breath at the image of the Tallis woman and saw her gaze freeze when it reached Mira. Mira before she had scarlet spikes and cold sores. There was no underlying surprise, he noted. But of course she would have known about all this, even if seeing it in full colour was a shock. She was *part* of it, after all.

He wondered what he would feel in her place. For once he did not envy her. Perhaps it was best after all *not* to belong. His sister looked up at him, stared him straight in the eyes, fully awake now. 'Are you trying to make me feel uncomfortable? Guilty?'

'Of course not, you loony.'

'What, then?'

'I just wanted . . . needed . . . to talk. To show someone what I'd found.'

'Great,' she said, sarcastically.

'Also . . .' he took a breath; 'she's here.'

'*Who's* here?'

'That one.' He pointed. 'Mira.'

She looked at him, open-mouthed. 'Where here? And how do you know?'

'Here in the city. I've seen her. Talked to her.'

'You've – *talked* – to – her?'

'Yes.'

'Why?'

'I wanted to help. I wanted to find out.'

Clarissa sighed, making him feel as if *he* was the younger of the two, as if she must explain everything slowly and carefully. Again it reminded him of their mother: where was the sulky, vain, funny, childish sister he thought he knew? But then there was nothing vain or childish about her when she stood in a Slam square. Then she was angry, cool, dangerous. 'Oh, Kay,' she said, as heavily as an adult. 'So what now?'

'I don't know. She's gone again. I think Tomas knows she's here too and arranged that. I wanted . . . I wanted to help her,' he said again, inadequately.

'Help her! Help her to do what? To get high? To stop using her brain, like you?'

He flushed, looked away from her without answering.

She said, studying his face: 'Oh shit, what a mess. I don't even think *you* know what you want. And I suppose you want me to keep quiet about this, bro?'

He looked up shyly. 'Yes. Of course.'

'I see. Well, I'll think about it. We can talk again in the morning.'

He silently started to gather up the things, but she pointed at the image of Mira. 'Can I keep that?'

Reluctantly he agreed. He could always print another. She had a right, he supposed.

As he was leaving she caught him by the arm and asked him again: 'Are you sure you didn't just want to shock me? Hurt me? Bring me down to earth? Because of . . . everything?'

He shook his head. 'I don't think so. I don't know.'

They looked at one another, brother and sister. 'It *is* shocking,' she said. 'Even if you're ready for it.'

While Kay went back to his rooms, and once more spread out the papers, wondering wretchedly how he might put things right, haunted by the girl's beauty – Hedge sat looking into bright, white light, waiting to be told his task.

He had come here immediately when the boy was safely in his club, lost in the music. It was the usual routine. The club was safe enough, and others would be watching out for Kay while Hedge was absent from his duties. That was the arrangement.

Tonight they had kept him waiting a long, long time. For more than four hours he had sat in the darkness, not that that bothered him. When the light snapped on, a voice spoke to him that was sweet, gentle, female. A voice like honey, one that he felt he might have known all his life.

Did they think that would make a difference, he wondered. Did they think he could be swayed by beauty or desire or persuasion? The path he took was his own, no one else's. He was here for his own reasons. Let them be grateful and efficient in their use of him and leave it at that. Let them not try insulting tricks to ensure his recruitment. He was a Saint bodyguard, top of the line from the screening process, not a drugged child.

'The time has come,' the voice murmured; 'We wish you to perform one single function, which we believe to be of paramount importance to our cause. Will you do that for us, Tobias Hedge?'

'Get on with it,' he said shortly, 'and let's have no names.' People only ever called him Hedge.

There was a silence.

'Very well,' the voice purred, finally; 'In one week from now there is to be a Slam contest. The final of the Junior City League. Unusually, two rising stars from the Great Families are to compete.'

Hedge nodded. 'Clarissa Saint and Jan Barbieri. What of it?'

'This competition represents a rare opportunity. The venue will be considered safe. The young Barbieri will be almost alone in an open space, well away from his many minders, for perhaps fifteen minutes.'

Hedge nodded again, his mouth suddenly dry.

'Your task,' said the silky, caressing voice, 'is to eliminate the boy.'

Gods above! 'Kill the boy. And then?'

'And then make whatever escape you can.'

Escape. That was a laugh. He'd be lucky still to be breathing two seconds after the boy went down. He concentrated for now on the practicalities. 'No side-arms are ever allowed there: you must know that. Copper makes good and sure.'

'You can't do it?' the voice said, sounding puzzled, disappointed.

'Sod you! Of course I can do it.' He blazed with anger at the hider behind the light, who so casually asked him to spend his life. 'Why don't *you* come out and try it?'

'We believed that you wished to help the cause. If the task is too great, you will be released from your obligations.'

Hedge was tempted. A way out: a way to carry on living. But then if he refused, he'd probably be dead anyway, now that he knew their target.

'Why Barbieri?' he asked, after a pause.

'First,' caressed the voice, 'because Jan Barbieri and those behind him wish a world with only Visions. He is the first to want this. The idea must not be allowed to gather momentum. Second, it is probable that he has become a tool for the Board in their quest for greater power. His death will restore balance.'

He'd known why, of course. He was no fool. He gazed into the light, trying to see through it. 'If I agree, you'll continue to look after the other boy? Kay Saint?'

'As far as we can, yes.'

Hedge closed his eyes a moment and sighed. 'It is done.'

When his lids flicked open again he was alone, in the darkness.

Mira lay far out in the marshes and sweated, her breath shallow and fast. It had been dangerous to leave the city. She understood now that on open land you could be seen, even at night, from very far away. They had machines to do many such impossible things, the ones that hunted her. But she had needed time away from the filth and the fear and the *people*. People everywhere, wherever you went, crowding you in, stealing your peace. A million, Bee had told her. It didn't seem possible. A million in each of the five cities.

She needed to be alone. She needed some peace.

Her arm, just above the elbow, was tight, swollen and black. She'd cleaned it as well as could be managed, bound it tight in a piece of fleece, but even now she could feel the fever mounting in her, spreading out from the wound, sapping strength and willpower. She knew she was light-headed. There was stolen food and drink in her pouch – stolen where she could not remember – but she had no appetite. For now she would sleep. Trust in the thorn bushes and the lapping waters and the sucking mud to keep her safe, and just sleep. She could feel it settling on her irresistibly, a heavy blanket, deadening all her limbs.

And she was dreaming.

In her dream she stood before the long white building they called the Fertility Records Office, exactly as she had stood there in her first week in the city. Even for a new one, an incomer like her, it had been easy to find and seemed friendly and welcoming. A contrast to the buildings around it. The white steps leading up to the neat row of glass doors were polished smooth. Helpful, uniformed men and women stood at the top of the steps to open the doors for you and direct you to the place you needed inside. There were no cameras visible. Many people passed up and down the steps: Vision or Scroat, she wasn't sure yet. Some looked bored, or rushed, some perfectly content, stopping to chat with the door openers: none of them seemed in the least frightened. At the foot of the steps there were rectangles of turned earth, where pretty things had been made to grow. A man was working there now, making little holes and putting in new plants whose thin fronds jumped and twisted wildly in the wind.

If her birth had been legal, they would know about it in there. Sean had told her this. She had only to climb the steps and ask. Every legal birth in Briton was remembered there, in their computers.

'And if it was not "legal"?' She hadn't really understood the word.

'If there was no licence, lass, they'll expel you from the city, or lock you up. Even the natural-born need a licence. And there'd be fines or worse for your parents, passing to you if they were dead.'

In real life, she'd passed the test. She'd resisted temptation and contented herself with a long look at the building. She'd remembered the computer in the warehouse at home, and her sudden instinctive panic. Nae, whatever secrets lay inside this place, she wouldn't make that mistake twice!

But now, helpless in her fevered dream, events took a different turn. She stood as before at the foot of the steps, and the figures at the top called out to her, beckoned; and she found herself climbing slowly up. They opened the doors for her and pointed and she passed through and into a long corridor. It started wide and light and airy,

with many others coming and going down the same
way, but gradually there seemed to be a narrowing and a
darkening of the path and her fellows grew fewer. To left
and right were many turnings and doors that she would
have liked to try, hoping to find lighter, more populated
areas of the building again, but each time she made to
turn aside, a uniformed attendant moved her on, pointing
further into the gloom.

Her feet trudged on and on as if they had their own
will.

Eventually, after much time, she saw she was alone
and there were no doors, no turnings, nothing to do but
go on. In the dimness, she reached out her fingers and
found the walls close on either side. She felt scared now
and longed to turn around and run back the way she'd
come: but she could not.

And then she came to a door. A last door, blocking off
the end of the corridor.

With numb fingers she reached for the handle and saw
that this and the door itself were the same as the door
at home, that led into her own bonny house. She might
even expect it to open and Cobb's honest old face to look
out at her. With a deep pang for her da, she pushed down
on the handle, stepped inside. *At last I shall know who
I am. The computers will tell me.* Yet she saw in dismay that
there were no computers, no people waiting to help. It
was nothing but a bare empty room. Only a mirror hung
on the wall.

Tears of disappointment sprang into her eyes and she
felt her last energy drain away. It was hopeless. She had
come this long way for nothing, and now she would never
be able to return. They had lied about this building, after
all. They had lied about everything. There were no secrets
here. She would never get away from this cursed city.

Through the tears, she caught sight of herself in the mirror. Dirty, injured, scared; barely recognisable. 'Who am I?' she asked the image. 'Tell me who I am.'

TWENTY-ONE

Beebop didn't care any more. Not about anything or anyone. He especially didn't care about the stiffening bruises those Pax bastards had given him when he'd done over the transport. That had been a laugh and a half. Worth a few aches.

He shivered though it was early summer and the winds were warm. A raggle-taggle of kids came out of holes and doorways, pulled at his tattered clothes, asking for food as he passed. They reminded him of his sister and brothers back near the Gloster floodlands: illegal of course, illegal little Scroats, bless them, with no birth permits. Maybe he should have stayed and helped his dad to find new, higher land to plough, fresh crops that might stand the winds and the short growing season. Little Jody would no longer be little: almost eleven, he reckoned. Not far off the age he had been when he'd made it, somehow, to the capital, and Martha had taken him under her wing. He didn't think about what might have happened to them since he left.

'I'll send money,' he'd said, 'and I'll come straight back if you need me, Dad.'

He'd thought he'd be helping them: one mouth less to feed, the chance to earn something in the city. But he knew now that they'd just been pushing him away to safety before the ship went down. There was no decent land left, the water kept rising, they were not a state-sponsored farm: his dad must have known the end was in sight. Why not give the oldest one a chance? He was the legal child, just about old enough to travel if the weather was kind and he didn't get lost. The only one that *could* be saved.

'I'll send money,' he'd said importantly in his high child's voice, standing in the doorway, and they'd said, 'Yes, of course. Off you go now. We'll let you know where we move. We'll give you a new address to send the money to.'

He shook the children off, gently, showing them his empty palms – 'Do I *look* like I have food for you?' – and headed back for some sleep, Pedestal skittering along at his heel.

The new place where he stayed was not like Martha's yard. It was a place for dossers, losers, old farts, thieves and pushers. A free-for-all. A great hollow concrete shell, an old warehouse stinking of piss, where you trusted nobody, told no secrets, kept every scrap for yourself. There were fights, stabbings: you had to keep your head down. He would find a new place soon, somewhere more like Martha's.

He found a space amongst the other scum, took the old blanket from his bag, lay looking up at the dark, noisy, turbulent sky where the roof should have been. Soon the tears came. He couldn't help it, he found himself crying often now. Maybe he was ill, losing his mind. Even in his sleep he cried, sometimes.

'All right, mate?'

There was someone coming to sleep on the bit of ground next to him, a young man with a ponytail. He couldn't see the face clearly but the man breathed heavily, wheezed a bit. The voice was true capital Scroat, as his own had become.

'All right, mate? All right if I doss down 'ere, is it? Not pinching nobody's bit o' space?'

'No,' he brushed away the wetness on his cheeks, hoping the darkness hid his features. 'No mate, you're all right. Ain't nobody there.'

The man unrolled his own blanket, settled himself. Beebop went back to his private thoughts, but the voice whispered again to him. 'Bit of a shit-'ole this, in' it?'

'Yeah.'

'Don' blame you fer 'aving a good cry. Could do wi' one meself.'

Bee stayed silent. The man should not have mentioned it, even if he'd seen.

'I come from further up west, me. 'Ad some friends an' that up there, like. Then they came and bloody took 'em. Jus' like that. When I was out doing the bins an' that. Bloody place ain't safe no more so I come down 'ere, found this shit-'ole.'

Despite himself, Bee asked: '*Who* came? Who took yer mates?'

'Who do yer bloody think? Bloody *Pax*, in' it? Bastards!'

Don't talk. Don't trust anybody. Keep your secrets to yourself.

Bee said: 'Yeah. That 'appened to me an' all. Only a few days back. Everyone decent I knew, all taken.'

'No! You an' all, eh? Poor young bastard.'

The man asked no more, shifting around trying to get comfortable, muttering to himself. Beebop, aware that he'd broken the key rule for survival, relaxed his guard. Nothing important had been said. The man was just another misfit, like him. Another victim of the Pax bastards. He only had to think of the word and the anger rose in his heart like a black beast, choking him. Those rotten *bastards*. What were they up to? Why arrest so many Scroats? he thought. Why, most of all, had they appeared like that when he was looking for Sparkle, and then chased her when she came out of her squat, tried to shoot her, even?

But then it was like she expected it too. She had that weapon, all ready, that she'd had out that first day, down at the water, but never since. And she *moved*. He grinned briefly into the darkness. God, he'd never dreamed she could move like that, their Sparkle. He'd almost forgotten to run himself, watching how she scorched away, weaving between the piles of crap.

Sparkle was a mystery all right, but he was no fool. Shamefully, he'd arrived at the conclusion that *he* must have brought the security scum with him when he went looking for her. Which meant that it was probably *her* they'd been looking for when they did Martha's place over. It made sense, now he thought about it. Ever since she'd stepped off the green ship she'd acted strangely. Scared to bloody death half the time, it had seemed, but not so scared that she couldn't deal with that toad Ed on her first day, or Nasher in the yard: or run like a hare, shooting away with that weird weapon, when Pax came after her. And what about her voice? She was pretty vague about where she'd come from, but it certainly wasn't the city: yet she arrived speaking almost like she'd been born here.

The only answer Bee could come up with was that she was one of *them*. One of the *real* Wreckers, like the ones he'd heard about, breaking in to Stoneywall and that, making life a misery for the Board. Not the paperweight protesters he hung around with, flinging their bloody eggs. Why else would the security bastards make such an effort to get her?

Please let her have got away, he thought, staring up through the broken roof. In his heart he doubted that she had. After all, there had been three of them, probably more out of sight, and none had gone after *him*. Why, he couldn't say: presumably he just wasn't important enough. But that was going to bloody change. If she *had* made it away from them, he'd find her and ask – demand! – to join the group. And if she hadn't, he'd search out his heroes anyway, even if he had to scour the rotten, flooded country to do it. He'd do it for poor Jody and the others! He'd do it for himself, too. It was time the bastards paid.

Next to Bee, shifting and muttering and coughing as convincingly as any of the loser Scroats here, the man with the ponytail thought: So. This one should lead me to her, given time.

Clarissa stood in the centre of the prepared Slam square and looked around with satisfaction. The floor of the Saint function room was real wood, pale as honey, polished to perfection for the occasion. The seats, set out between pillars for Barbieris, Saints and the rest, were red velvet, bordered in gold. Overhead, crystal chandeliers fluttered slightly in the draughts from the underfloor heating. Apart from the small stands erected for Network cameras – the match would go out live on the higher levels – she might have been looking at the distant past.

The Slam square itself was new and immaculate, no more than a felted green mat, marked out with starting positions, and a simple white rope lying around the edge, which they must not cross.

Clarissa slipped her feet from their shoes and felt the textured grip of the mat, very slightly yielding to her weight. Experimentally, she lowered herself into fighting stance and went through a few practice moves, spinning, ducking, parrying, countering, withdrawing again into crouching preparedness. She imagined how it would be, when all the seats were filled. Would she perform? Would she beat poor Jan?

Yes, it was beyond doubt.

A movement at the side entrance of the room caught her eye and she saw Hedge there, watching her. What a creep the man was. What did he think he was doing here?

'Hedge,' she said curtly.

'Miss Clarissa,' he acknowledged; 'Sorry to disturb your practice, miss. Just having a look round at the security arrangements.'

A likely story, she thought, sarcastically. The large man seemed uncomfortable for once. Maybe he was in trouble with Grandfather for losing Kay too often.

'I wouldn't worry about that,' she said to him, slipping her feet back into their shoes, 'Jan is bound to bring his own private army of security. You know what they're like.'

'Yes, miss. I know. Just thought I'd be sure.' He turned on his heel and left as silently and abruptly as he'd come.

They were well suited to each other, the prowling, oddball Hedge and her even odder bro, always worrying himself about things, never fully enjoying anything but his music. But now, she corrected herself, he *was* interested in something: this girl, Mira. No, not interested, more like obsessed. And what was she to make of *that*?! She shivered, half in disgust, half in envy. He steered clear of her, Clarissa, but felt he had some sort of mission to Mira, the spare. He'd made *contact* with her, for God's sake.

The trouble was that she was infected now, too. Just when she should be focused on the final, only two days away, she was forced to think about this other thing; the strange other-existence the girl had had, the way she had arrived here, the way she was hunted. What was happening to her *now*, this minute?

Too many questions.

But she knew that when she went back to her rooms, she'd look at the picture once more. How could she not?

The dreams were done.

Mira climbed slowly to her feet, leaning on the thorns, feeling as fragile and clumsy as a baby. She stretched her fingertips up towards the grey, blustery sky, easing her spine and shoulders, swinging her limbs awkwardly around to get the life back into them. The arm that had been grazed by the blast still throbbed, but the swelling was down and she didn't believe there would be any infection. For the first time in days she felt ravenously hungry. A good sign: the fever was leaving her.

Three or four miles away, across wide, dull stretches of water and thick black mud, across wind-flattened yellow grasses and reeds and trickling, gurgling streamlets, gradually rising towards rubble-strewn firmer ground, the fringes of the city began with a ring of banked-up flood defences. Mile upon mile, the concrete barriers rose, each one topped with thick steel plating, tilting outwards to contain and drive back the worst possibilities of the imagined future, whether water or refugee.

In her wounded flight, without seeing clearly the nature of the barriers, Mira had dropped heavily from the lip of one of these plates onto the soft, spongy ground. Getting back *in* would take much more effort: the wall-makers had known this. Either she must find a way to climb in like a fly, hanging upside down on bare metal, or circle the city until she found a bridge and gate where one of the stiltways entered – yet surely they would watch all such entrances? – or circle further still until she was on the southern, harbour side of the capital.

Yes, that was the best chance. The harbour was the loosest of the city's defences: it was no coincidence that the docks were haunted by those that had escaped the floods, without a permit to enter, and by those with their own private reason to leave. Yet even there, she knew from her entrance hidden aboard the *Helicon*, there was a moving sea barrier and lock through which the ships must pass. If she was to go back in, the moving sea barrier would offer the best chance, if only she could find strength enough to try it.

She thought wearily: Why should I go back in at all, now that I am outside, now that they have found my friends and my hiding places? I could leave this city behind me. Go home. Anything. There must be a place beyond Pax and Saints and all of them.

But it wasn't a choice. Not really. Her fate was still bound up here a while. With Beebop and Kay Saint and with his mother, who she'd seen only that once in her fever on the boat. 'Tilly Saint, back from skiing in Canada.' Not 'back from being hunted in the distant, icy North'.

She had begun to have the shadow of an idea now – one she didn't understand – but ideas were not enough. She had to *know* what mystery surrounded her birth. Only with such knowledge could she perhaps find a way to leave the unequal hunt behind, if such a way existed. Only with such knowledge could she find peace.

And the new life she had found, the city life? The new friends? It was true: she had changed. If she had her answers and found that longed-for place beyond Pax and the Saints, would she be able to go back to what she once had been?

She would know only when the time came.

Aye, she'd wait until night then, and find a way back inside. Find Kay Saint. He would be at Movies or Portable Road or somewhere. He came out of his prison often enough.

The risk was great after they had so nearly caught her, but she was used to being invisible, had learned quickly. The people on the street, Vision or Scroat, never looked at her, never met her eyes unless she had business with them. She would change her hair again, right enough, and her clothes. She must not even be stopped or questioned once now. But somehow she would be there for the Saint boy to visit after he had played his music. The time was as right as it ever would be. He knew something, and she would draw it from him, now while she had the strength.

For now, though, some food and then more sleep. Blissful, forgetful sleep under the thorn bushes for another few hours. She'd need it if she was to swim the torrent when the great sea barrier was lowered for a vessel to pass.

The ponytailed man had latched on to Bee. In the light, he probably wasn't much older than Bee himself. He had a limp and scars across one cheek, and said his name was Moore. He suggested they went scavenging together.

'Jus' fer a day or two, eh? So you can show me round a bit, where the best stuff is an' that? 'Cause I always stuck well over west, me, see?'

Beebop doubtfully agreed. He stayed unusually silent as they combed through the bins and rooted behind shops, but Moore rabbited on endlessly. If only it was Sparkle out with him again. He'd thought she was a bit soft, before. He'd given her a hard time, teased her for her strange ideas. Soft in the head, but sweet, he'd thought;

and a bit of a dreamer too. What a bloody idiot he'd been. He longed to have her back and tell her that he knew he'd been an idiot. Would she forgive him?

Please let her be OK. Please.

Moore's chatter drifted through his thoughts: 'O' course I come in from the Outside, original like, not that I remember much. Come up wi' me grandpa, see? From our farm down Kent way. All bloody flooded out now, I 'spect, isn't it? I were only eight an' all.'

I *must* find her again, Bee thought for the hundredth time: Someone's got to have heard something. Maybe she needs help. Maybe they didn't get her.

She'd always gone out of her way to avoid trouble, unlike Bee himself. He *liked* winding the police up and having a good go – mouthing off at the stinking Visions and – worse – all the Scroats who had all the proper papers and wouldn't even look at him. *They* were as much to blame as anybody, and it made him feel better to shout at them, see them scurry away like mice. It was the same when they – he and his mates – had bumped the Pax van around and tipped rubbish over it. *That* was worth a few bruises. Good harmless fun and it made you feel like you could do *something* to show how you felt and at least hold your head up.

Sparkle, though: she kept her head down. Well down. Meek as anything when they got stopped. Yes sir, no sir, three bags bloody full, sir. He'd thought she was plain scared.

What a fool he was.

Moore said: 'Me grandpa only lasted six months. Really cold winter that one was, see?'

'Right,' Bee replied vaguely. 'Downer.' An alarm bell sounded faintly within him. Had the man said something about coming from a farm, like Bee himself? That didn't seem right, somehow. He didn't seem the type. 'What winter was that, then?' he asked sharply: 'When yer grandpa died?'

Moore looked up at him from the bin he was sorting through and smiled slightly: 'Ten or eleven year back, I reckon. Hard to keep bleedin' track, in' it, in this shit-'ole? I were only a snotty kid.'

Beebop grunted and started packing findings away in his large flapping pockets. He couldn't remember *what* the winter had been like eleven years ago. There had been a more than usually cold one, one year. A throw-back to the ice. But exactly *when* it had been he couldn't remember. Moore was probably harmless enough, just a bloody big mouth, that's all, going on all the time. As soon as he could, he'd ditch him and start having a look round some of the likely spots again, to see if he could find Sparkle.

Someone would know something.

He'd make a good Wrecker, if they let him in. He'd bloody smash the whole lot, if they wanted.

Tomas read the incoming message while Tilly gazed coldly out of the window, fighting down her impatience. Then deliberate and unhurried he wiped it from the tiny screen at his side.

He looked up: 'Our operative has started to cultivate a fresh lead. I expect to have new information on the spare soon.' He did not mention Kay, the other string to his bow. Tilly had strange ideas of how she did and didn't want her son treated. Enough that he had informed her of the matter at all.

She did not even look round. The day was unusually clear. The ever-changing sprawl of shipping that clung to the lowest rim of the capital had a kind of sharp-edged

beauty. The orange Caplink worms danced their automated dance. Thousands of Visions sat in their homes
and offices and shops and restaurants and parks and
congratulated themselves on their unearned superiority.
In *their* homes and factories, thousands of Scroats congratulated themselves on how closely they mimicked
their Vision betters, sweating so that their only child or
their child's child might even be Vision themselves, bright
little fishes carefully caught by the Board's net.

Life did not change here. Yet it seemed to Tilly that
it was about to: that the shout from the darkest corners of
the city had got louder, wilder, brighter: that the Floodites
and mystics had tapped into some deep savagery or hope:
that the million souls in this place were poised on the
brink of . . . *something*.

'You disapprove,' the old man murmured.

She brought herself back to the present, back to the
ancient figure who was the past.

'Yes, I disapprove. For what that may be worth.'

He shrugged: 'I'm simply allowing – no, encouraging –
potential to shine through. And then we'll see what use it
may be to us.'

'The child had a life already. Maybe she didn't want
yours.'

'Maybe. And maybe if we sit here growing soft and old,
we'll find one day that power will have passed to worse
people than us.'

More silence. Should she warn him, show him the
real danger? No, he would not see it: Tomas was intent
only on his own designs and the part this Mira might play
in them. She would be wasting her breath. He saw no
further than the need to rein in the Barbieri boy and keep
the Saint glory alive.

After a moment, she said: 'Tomas: what if the girl

is killed? What if her potential doesn't shine brightly
enough?'

He looked at her evenly. 'Yes. That is always a risk,
isn't it?'

Kay felt like shit.

He stood in front of the mirror in his bathroom,
splashing hot water onto his face, trying to focus. He
could neither sleep nor eat. He couldn't get warm. He felt
restless, pent-up like a caged animal. He couldn't concentrate on anything, not even his drumming. Worst of
all, the solution was within easy reach. In his jacket, by
the door.

He ran trembling fingertips across his face. Just a day
or two more, he promised, and then he'd give himself
some relief. It would be pointless to give in before then.
Pointless. It would fuck up the one real decision he'd made
in his life. He'd never make it away from here with a
mind like soggy cardboard. He had to be sharp.

Of them all, I am the only one who's free. Free to
decide. Free to act.

He had to hang on to that thought to give himself
strength. Tomas, his mother, even Clarissa; they all had
lives that had been mapped out from the moment they
were born. Only he was different. Think of his poor
sister, destined to link up with that Jan, just so the public
could have a half-hearted cheer for their betters and the
self-satisfied Families could tie themselves ever closer.
What kind of life would she have, 'mother' to a brood of
Barbieri freaks? And think of her now, looking ceaselessly
at the picture he had left, sleepless as he was. There, that
was one reality that he wouldn't wish for, wouldn't swap
his own problems to have.

It was surprising when he thought about it. Clarissa

had always seemed so perfect, so able to cope, so much her mother's daughter. She had been born to live out her easy existence on the back of this half-drowned country. How he had envied her! How they had quarrelled and needled over their differences! But now, tentatively, he wondered if it were not in truth a *gift* that his mother had given him. To be different, to be excluded. He had thought it a curse, but it was not.

Why had he missed knowing this for so long? Was it being surrounded by those who were *not* free? Was it simple fear?

I will find her again, if I can; Mira, the spare. Take her away with me. But even if I can't, I will find another way to live. Another place. The voyage in the boats that I have always dreamed of.

Yes, a day or two more. He could be strong enough for that, couldn't he?

The Scroat face in the mirror grinned back at him uncertainly.

TWENTY-TWO

Blessed children,
You are given this sleeping serpent;
Stretched across the years,
Its strong, bright coils buried deep
In the marshes and the flood waters;
Its mouth closed on its tail.

And when the serpent wakes,
And it is full grown and nourished,
And the beautiful, sleek, knowing head is lifted up,
And the two eyes open, one brown, one green;
Then, blessed children, you may ride its back
To freedom and love.

For this serpent is no tempter:
She is your truest friend.

Mira rested her back against the stump of an old pillar and watched the boats, nibbling at the slab of hard bread she'd been given by some kind soul. She liked this place, right at the heart of the old docks. Despite the filth and the danger and the water lapping even to the base of the pillar, soon to claim it, there was peace, even a shred of *otherness* about the place. No wonder the strange preachers used it for their ranting. There was one now, a slender woman wrapped round with green cloth, making her shy way across the wasteland.

'Good eve to you, sister,' the woman murmured. 'I will speak from here to any that will listen, when my breath has come back to me. I hope I will not disturb your supper.'

Mira shook her head. 'No. I'll move.'

She still had many hours before she should look for the boy, so she found another place to sit, resting her back against an upturned rail wagon, and continued her munching. She watched to see how many the woman preacher would persuade to stop. The woman had said 'speak', but in fact when she began – abruptly raising her bowed head and looking straight before her – the words she used were in song. High and clear, rising and falling in soft curves of sound, the preacher sang words that Mira recognised at once, for they were the words cut into the pillar itself, words about a serpent. Bee had shown her the pillar on one of her first days in the city. He had pointed out the strange, rotted slip of green metal that wound round the thing like a snake itself, embedded in the stone, carrying the words the preacher now sang.

'It don't take much to get some of these crazies going,' Bee had scoffed, 'a few old words 'ere and there an' they go potty with it. Next year it'll be something else. You wait and see.'

The woman's music was sweet, soothing. When she got to the last line – '*She is your truest friend*' – she did not stop singing and start to speak, as Mira had expected, but went straight on with the song from the beginning once more. Again and again the words wound round the little patch of open ground. Nobody seemed to hear or care or stop – nobody was in sight – but the preacher carried on regardless and Mira herself, forced to listen or move, found the song at first haunting and beautiful, then disturbing and persistent, and finally nothing at all, for the exhausted girl had slipped back into healing sleep, the last crust of bread spilling from her open hand.

When she awoke in the full night the pillar was deserted, yet the strange music echoed in her head. She felt dreamy and heavy, yet refreshed. But other figures now prowled the wasteland. Thieves or worse. It would not do to stay here.

So, for the third night since swimming the sea gate, the girl picked her way through the city, uphill, away from the water and towards the Saint Building, keeping to the tiniest streets and to the deepest shadows, avoiding the never-sleeping cameras. For the third night she settled patiently to watch the great, smooth-sided building. And for the third night it seemed that the boy was not going to show himself. The darkest hours came and went, and she thought to herself: This will be the last time. If he does not come tonight I will seek another way to know the truth. Even the Records Building, if I must.

Perhaps Kay Saint was ill, or had lost interest in her. That didn't seem likely, yet she had seen the beginnings of the heavy drug trance about his eyes, and she had seen also how people changed when this happened, how they stopped caring about anything. You only had to think of Lizzie.

It was this city. This terrible place. She'd smelled the familiar stench of it as soon as she'd crawled from the water; the concrete and fear and unhappiness that filled this place. She'd almost turned to dive back in and get away.

Abruptly she snapped back to the present.

A figure had appeared from the shadow at the side of the Saint Building, where she hadn't expected one. Perhaps there was another entrance there. With a shiver she knew immediately that it was Kay. He was hooded, and without his guard, for once, but she could see it was him from the way he moved. There was a reluctant determination to it, as plain as a fingerprint.

She pulled well back against the dark wall and waited for him to head towards his music. Instead he took the road that would lead past her and directly down to Portable Road.

At their nearest, the boy was only a few metres away. She could easily call to him from the shadows, or follow him a little down the hill and intercept him at a better place, well away from the glass tower that was his strange home. She felt words form themselves in her throat. 'Kay. Kay Saint,' she would call softly: 'If you are looking for the girl with the red hair, she is here.' He would be amazed, after her weeks of dumbness and stupidity.

But the words didn't come, and she held back, immobile, while he passed. The habit of caution was too deep in her. Even now, she thought, she couldn't be entirely sure. Who was to say that *he* hadn't unleashed the grey hunters in some way? Or someone that watched him, or used him? No, it was better to meet as usual: to look at him in the light and bustle of Portable Road, where she could read his face and get away more easily, lose herself in the throng, if he was followed or if the blue eyes had deception in them.

The decision made, Mira turned quickly down a small way between the cold buildings and started to run, zigzagging through the streets, anxious to get there before the boy and to appear unchanged from what he would expect. As she ran, the never-distant rain began again, blowing in great wet gusts through the city, soaking through the old, torn fleece she wore, spattering the empty coaches of a Caplink service that passed smoothly and silently before her.

The wild weather was her friend. It reassured her. They couldn't shut it out; not even here in their city.

She reached the familiar maze of dimly lit walkways and jostling, writhing humanity. The savoury smells from all-night pie shops mixed as ever with the dirt and sweat and urine. People were pulling their bits of plastic sheeting into better positions, covering children, pushing up against the walls and doorways at their backs, protecting themselves against the rain. Or they were simply standing dull-eyed, vaguely smiling, shivering, not noticing or caring what the winds brought.

Coming into the throng, Mira slowed down to an aimless, meandering walk, put any trace of feeling or thought out of her own eyes, made her face go slack as if it wasn't a human thing at all. She wove towards her usual place, estimating that she had at most two or three minutes before the boy would appear.

She felt excited, fearful. If the spirits were willing, she would soon have what she sought, for better or worse. Would Kay Saint be the friend she hoped? Would he help? Her heart thudded and the voice inside sang: *soon away from here: soon away*.

She was so wrapped in her hunger for the moment to come, for knowledge to release her from any need to stay here, that she didn't even hear the first call.

'*Sparkle!*'

It came again, and now she heard it.

'*Sparkle. Wait!*'

A chill passed through her. Fathers! *Bee*. Again he had found her, when she did not wish to be found.

She turned about slowly to face the call, keeping the illusion of the dazed, the hopeless. The yellow-haired boy was hurrying towards her, the strips of clothing flapping like wet feathers. He had a swollen, many-coloured eye, she saw, and a cut at the side of his mouth. From the grey men? A beating to ensure his help in tracking her down? There was nothing she could do to avoid him: she would have to talk to him. And if he had brought the men to her once more? She shuddered. She couldn't lead another such chase. Not now. Not tonight. She just didn't have the strength. She knew now how Annie Tallis might have felt on that snowbound morning.

Beebop was grinning all over his tight, thin face, bustling up, saying: 'Sparkle, you're all right! I *knew* it was you!' And even as he said it she saw his expression change, heard him shout '*No! Mind out! You bastard!*' and felt a heavy thud between her shoulder blades, sending her crashing dizzily to the ground. Instinctively she rolled to one side, daggers of pain spreading out from the injured arm, making her gasp. As she rolled there were some grunts behind her, as if of a struggle and then a sob or a sigh. Then she was back on her feet, looking round for her attacker. In the wet walkway, close to her feet, lay Beebop, white-faced, unmoving. The wild feathers stuck to him, wet with rain and blood. He looked childlike and alone. A figure stood next to him, watching her, waiting.

The world span. Her breath caught in her throat.

'*You!*'

Oh sweet spirits.

Trembling, her eyes never leaving the other, she bent over Bee, laid her hand on his cheek, looked for some sign of life, and saw at once that there was none.

She rose again, full of wild, cold anger and stepped towards the murderer. He also stepped forward, as if welcoming her, mouth open to speak. But then without warning he grinned in his old familiar way, shrugged slightly as if in apology, turned about and set off away from her, running fast and easily.

For an instant she was caught between desire to stay and do what she could for poor Bee, spend a minute thinking on the spirit that had fled from him; and to pursue the figure and finish what she had begun. But a muttering, murmuring crowd was gathering, prodding and pawing at the pathetic body, some growling in anger as if *she* had done this thing. Then the first siren sounded and it was decided. She stooped and kissed the boy's cold face, smoothed back his wet hair, said his name once, then wormed out through the crowd and set off in pursuit of his killer.

Kay didn't have much hope. There was no reason why the spare – *his* spare – should suddenly reappear tonight after her absence. But he couldn't sleep anyway: his body was used to the night routine and he was going half mad, pacing about, looking at his photos, finding nothing that he could settle to. About eleven Hedge buzzed through to him, sounding unusually agitated himself: 'Are we off out then, sir?' and he replied; 'No. Not tonight Hedge. I think I'm getting a cold. I'm going to stay in again.' Hedge grunted his acknowledgement and signed off. He was nowhere in sight when Kay did actually slip out, though he should have been alerted by the automatic systems. The man was a mystery.

The gusting, slanting, warm rain was almost comfortable after the months of sleet and icy gales. As soon as he was out, the good resolutions fled and Kay was tempted after all to go and play for an hour or two, perhaps get a hit. Just one. One wouldn't hurt, would it? But no, tomorrow morning was the silly contest, his sister's big day. He'd be required to be there and rested and an asset to the family. Another round of pressing the flesh, grinning like a baboon, acting as if the Great Families were truly great. It would be the last time. One day soon, he'd find his promised ship and go.

If Mira is not there tonight, I'll know I've lost her and give up . . .

On the fringes of Portable Road he felt a stab of hunger, the first for two days, and lingered to buy himself food: a spicy wrap, spilling hot dark sauce. Eating it, he wandered down into the familiar alleys, running his gaze over the many wet faces in case the girl Mira had chosen a new place. It was as good as ever to be out, anonymous amongst his fellow Scroats. When he escaped, he would find a place without divisions.

On he wandered, savouring the sharp, scalding sauce on his tongue, the rain on his face. His senses were sharpened, since he'd left off with the joydust. Up ahead, where two narrow ways met, he saw that there was some sort of disturbance. Raised voices, figures struggling briefly. It wasn't unusual round here. One of the figures had fallen: it looked bad. With a rush of disappointment, he knew that if someone called for the security services he'd have to leave again quickly. Tomas would not forgive him if he was seen down here and recognised.

But then he saw that a third figure was there, facing the first across the fallen shadow on the ground. She had her back to him and a cloth tied over her hair. The cloth had come loose, letting a little bright colour slip out. She was saying something angrily to the man facing her; or perhaps she was just snarling, he couldn't be sure. She bent to the ground, stooping a moment, then straightened and stepped across the body, her intention plain.

Kay couldn't understand. What was she doing? Was it the drugs? Had the man before her knocked down some lover? Perhaps he was her pimp. He felt a flare of jealousy at the idea. Why should he feel like that? What was the

spare to him with her empty eyes? Half the girls here
would sell themselves for a hit or a little money.

He came closer, not knowing what he intended, his
hand fumbling clumsily for the small weapon that nestled
against his calf; and then the figure facing the girl saw
him, looked full at him, smiled broadly, turned and ran.

It made no sense. He had not known the man, although
he was no Scroat or vagrant, that was sure. What game
was being played here?

While he stood, he heard the sirens and saw that the
creatures of Portable Road were ringing the girl round. He
must leave. But what about Mira? Would she understand? Still half jealous, he moved forward. He would
take her hand. Lead her away. Find the truth. Make her
his. They would leave the past behind.

Still she did not see him. She had stooped down again.
What was she doing? Kissing the lover's face? Crying for
him with those empty eyes?

Now she was back on her feet. The sirens were close.
Obviously she knew enough to want to avoid them.
Without looking round she set off at a light run down the
way that led towards the water. Kay barged forward,
parting the small crowd and saw now that the shape on
the wet and filthy stone was a boy about his own age or
perhaps a little older, with limp yellow hair that stuck to
his scalp. It did nothing to dampen his jealousy. Without
allowing time to question himself, he set off after Mira,
flinging his wrap aside, feeling sick and light-headed as
he ran.

Her running was deceptive though, faster than he had
thought, and soon he was out of breath. They ran, with
perhaps eighty metres between them, through Portable
Road, then out into the open square above the customs
buildings, and steeply down again. But before they

reached the rolling, dark ships the figure ahead darted left into a way that ran parallel to the waterfront, and by the time he reached the turning himself, cursing his lack of fitness, she had gone from sight.

Kay slowed. He picked his way along the street, looking into all the doorways and up at the black, hollow windows. The buildings were ancient, crooked, leaning on one another, their stone blackened by time. Perhaps she had some lodging here, or a friend who gave her shelter? It didn't seem probable. Mostly these buildings were offices to do with the comings and goings of ships: trading companies, insurance, supplies, permit offices . . . People wouldn't buy living units down this low any more: they'd be mad. The homeless were more likely to be found down in the docks themselves, or along the quays in the ruined, half-flooded buildings further east, where a level of the city had already been surrendered to the flood, before the sea lock was built.

He reached the end of the way and stood at the intersection, wondering whether to descend further and search the docks. He knew that the girl still haunted this quarter but the joy he'd earlier felt in coming through the rain-swept city to look for her had deserted him. The strange scene a few minutes ago, the body on the ground, the jealousy; together they had stolen his good spirits away. The idea of poking about by the waterfront seemed unattractive.

He thought, in self-disgust: Am I to give up so easily? Am I that much of a coward?

Now, of all times, he might be able to help the girl, if he could only find her. She was like him, a victim of circumstance others had fashioned. How could he condemn her? Perhaps the shock of the violent death she had witnessed might even reach through her misty thoughts and bring

some sense back. With this thought, he steeled himself
and turned down to the right, towards the sucking black
water; but had taken no more than a step when something – someone – cannoned hard into him from the side
and brought him smashing down to the wet stone.

It was the spare herself.

She was breathing hard and had her knee down across
his neck. Her eyes flashed though they were still full of
tears, and the look she gave him was a world from the
emptiness he had grown to expect.

'Was it you, then?' she asked bitterly; 'Was it you that
told them where to find me? Was it *you* all along, sending
out the men in grey? Was it *you*, Saint boy, that had poor
Bee killed?'

Her accent was strange, and she might have been a wild
beast, pinning him here to the ground. Kay could feel her
anger and grief. His mind reeled at the change in her. He
could find no voice to answer her questions. Wordlessly
he shook his head. She looked intensely at him, studying
his face, staring into his eyes until he had to shut them to
escape such a look. Finally, abruptly, she rose and freed
him. 'Och, you're not worth it, Kay Saint. You can keep
this city of yours. I'm away from here.' And she turned,
started to walk into the darkness, leaving him lying in the
rain as the body had lain before.

Think! Say something!

He clambered stiffly up to a sitting position and called
after her: 'Please . . . Mira!'

The retreating figure hesitated at the name.

His voice was pleading. He had to make her listen. Why
it was so important he couldn't say, but it was. '*Mira*. No.
It wasn't me. I'm your friend. I *am*. Think of the food, the
other things . . .'

She turned, came back, looked down at him, still

suspicious, angry, hurt. The distrust crackled from her. 'My friend are you? And what do you know of *me*, Kay Saint?'

He took a breath. 'I know who you are. And what you are.'

Her eyes held his, clear and unblinking. He thought of Clarissa's airs and graces and almost laughed.

'. . . And I can help you. I *want* to help you.'

She considered him. He sensed an excitement in her. She *needed* to know. That was why she was here. At last he began dimly to understand. He was every kind of fool.

'Help me how, then?' she asked, and now the voice was a shade softer, not as threatening.

Up in the Portable Road, the security transports had arrived. The sirens were staying still now. No doubt the body had been found and the witnesses, such as they were, questioned. The street cameras swivelled on their stalks, peering into the gloom. On impulse, Kay gestured at the noise, grinning uncertainly up from where he sat in the rain. 'Well, to start with, I can hide you away from all that lot. For a day or two, anyway.'

The man with the ponytail sat alone in his empty, rented room and reflected, wondering what damage had been done.

Events had not turned quite the way he had expected. To be so near to taking her, and then have to turn away, and after his careful work! But then he'd had to make a quick decision and he thought that probably the old goat Tomas would approve of the contact between the boy and Mira being left unhindered. The man had predicted, had he not, that this might be their winning card. Aye, better in that case that Moore had done nothing tonight to suggest to the pair that they had been manipulated.

As for the mess over the boy, Beebop, well, nobody could say why these things happened. The young idiot had wanted to be a hero. In the circumstances there had been no other choice but to put that one beyond telling what he had seen and concentrate on the girl. If in doubt, leave only silence behind: that was the rule of survival and success.

No . . . all in all he had done his work as well as the situation allowed. He tapped out a quick report for Tomas and transmitted it. Then Moore gave a single satisfied nod, and poured himself a whisky. He surely deserved it.

Mira stood in wonder, blinking in the light. 'All this is *yours*? Just a place for you?'

'Yes. Do you like it?'

She moved around the rooms, childlike, touching objects with the tips of her fingers, opening doors, pausing to look at the bathroom for a whole minute. Kay looked on.

Finally she said, shaking her head: 'It's too much for one person, I'm thinking.'

'Yes. You're probably right. I didn't choose it, though.'

She flicked him a glance. 'No, you didn't choose it, right enough. But do you choose it now, then?'

He ignored the question. 'Mira, listen, there's usually a kind of computer – do you know about computers? – well, she's called Jane – she watches me here and does things for me if I need them done. Anyway, I've turned her off for a little while, but security will be suspicious if she's off for long. They might come to check on me, make sure that everything's OK. Or my family: they could turn up, too. Everybody watches everybody else here: it's what they do . . .'

He trailed off. She looked at him, but made no

response. He had no idea whether she understood or not. He was still getting used to the change from the blank eyes and slack, imbecile mouth. Now her face was filled with life. And pain too. She was very beautiful. He felt a bumbling fool next to her.

'So anyway,' he went on, 'there's one room where you'll still be OK, when I turn Jane back on. If you don't mind. And nobody else can get in there, only me: it's got special locks. We can put a mattress there, or something. You'd be safe. Getting into the building was the worst bit. Now we've done *that*, and without Hedge popping up . . .'

'Your big cat,' she murmured.

'Yes,' he said, surprised, 'I suppose he is a little like that; but how do you . . .? Oh never mind, it doesn't matter. Look, just tell me if you understand about the safe room.'

Mira smiled at him, almost mocking, almost like Clarissa now. 'Yes, Kay Saint. I understand about the room. But tell me this; is there time for me to clean myself in your bathroom before I am to be locked in this safe prison?'

'But . . . what about *you*? Don't you want to *know*? Isn't that what you came for?'

'Aye,' she said gently, 'it is what I came for. And I wish to be a little of a human being to hear it.'

While she lay in a bath for the first time in her life, feeling the delicious hot water soothe her body and take off the months of grime, hardly daring even to think about what was to come, Kay took out a copy of the Mira picture that he had left with his sister. He sat with the picture on his knees and tried to imagine how he would feel if he had to learn what this strange-familiar girl in his bathroom must learn. Impossible. He had his identity, he knew who *he* was, was becoming more sure of it every day. It was beyond imagining *not* to know. What would she do, afterwards? Would she try to go back to her old

life and friends? Would she be angry? Would she hate
all Saints, as so many did? Would she storm out of his
rooms, regardless of the danger? Somehow she didn't
seem the storming-out kind. She was so controlled, so
quick. But then, she had made that incredible journey,
alone . . .

While he sat here trying to imagine what it had been
like, coming to this great wind-ravaged city from that
other icy place, there was a sudden banging on the outer
door and Clarissa's voice came distantly through the steel
security shell. 'Kay, you idiot. Why isn't Jane opening this
door for me? Come on, let me in. I know you're there. I
checked entry records. I'm not going to go away.'

He sat in frozen, horrified silence, knowing indeed
that his stubborn sister would *not* go, but unable to think
of what he could say to her to prevent her entrance.
The lie about getting a cold that he had used with Hedge,
perhaps? It was pretty feeble.

'*Kay*. You'd *better* let me in, or I'm going to call security
to get this door opened.'

Mira appeared in the bathroom doorway, wearing his
bathrobe. The crude make-up was gone and somehow
she had washed the scarlet from her hair and combed it
back so that it lay a dark, rich red-brown against her neck.

The streetgirl was no more.

'Is there danger?' she asked, alert to the noise outside
the door.

He shrugged, stupidly. 'My sister.'

Clarissa's voice came again, angrily: 'According to
entrance security records, *I* came in with you, Kay, at
three sixteen am. But *I* know I've been in the building
all evening. Shall I call down and tell them that? Let me
in! This is your last chance, bro.'

Again Kay shrugged, not liking to think what lay

ahead. 'We have to let her in. The corridor cameras . . .
she'll wake the building.'

Mira considered: 'Och, so let her in. I don't mind. If she
is your sister she wouldn't tell, I'm thinking. She must
honour her brother's secrets.'

Oh God, he thought, hopelessly, does it have to be like
this? Does she have to find out like this?

Hardly feeling the ground beneath his feet, he crossed
the room, unlocked the manual door locks, and let
Clarissa in.

TWENTY-THREE

It was a moment caught out of time.

The two girls stood silently facing each other and one might have imagined a mirror between the two. There were differences – Mira was a little leaner, more stretched, exhausted, more used to hardship; Clarissa, more girlish in every way, still had the last of her puppy fat, her skin was oiled and smooth, her hair cut into a tight short teardrop for the Slam competition – but the differences were nothing. They were the same person. The same bright, urgent life shone out from the two pairs of eyes.

Kay thought the silence would never end. They circled each other, slowly, both robbed of any speech. Even Clarissa, who had known before, who had the picture downstairs in her rooms . . . even she was silenced by the reality.

It was Mira who spoke first.

'What does this mean?' she whispered.

That small sign of uncertainty was enough. The mocking light came into Clarissa's eyes and she stepped back slightly, the moment of communion broken. 'You mean big bro hasn't told you?' she breathed. 'You *still* don't know what you are? I'm disappointed. I expected more of myself.'

Mira looked at Kay, said his name, uncertain and questioning, but Clarissa was in control of herself now, and enjoying her advantage.

'Don't worry about *him*. *I'm* the one to tell you. It's only fair. You, darling sister, are a copy of *me*, a *spare*.'

The other girl looked at her, eyes wide and troubled, saying nothing.

Clarissa started again, still inching back, as if to distance herself from the reality of it, and circling Mira as she spoke, making her move to keep eye contact. 'OK. A quick lesson for the unexpectedly dim amongst us. You see, sis, Great Families like mine don't become great and stay great just by accident. They need great people. I mean, imagine what would happen if we just knocked out the occasional baby in the normal, boring old way!' She looked at Kay and smiled sweetly. 'Can you imagine? Then we'd just get boring old regular people. *That* wouldn't be any good now, would it? Not if you wanted to stay great. So, some old crusty relic from our dear departed past decided to remove the uncertainty. *I*, sis, am the best. One of our secret little chocolate box of winners, to keep the Saints on top. And *you* are a spare. A copy of me.'

Kay spoke, hoarsely: 'That's not quite true, is it? You're both copies.' And then, to Mira: 'Clones. Exact copies of another person that lived a long time ago. A very special and wonderful person. There's really no genetic difference between my sister and you. She has no claim to be the original.'

When Mira replied, her face pale, she looked not at him but at Clarissa. 'If we are the same person, why do we not share the same thoughts? Why does your sister fear me when I want only to understand?'

Yes! he thought, she is so right; so beautiful. She sees so clearly. A part of him deep inside, a part that had been gnawed by some unnameable fear, became peaceful. When he heard Clarissa's voice, it seemed harsh compared to Mira's gentle northern lilt.

'Fear? No, sis, I don't fear you. But I am a Saint. You

are not.' Kay saw then, as if waking up, that her circling movement had brought her close to the small, steel control panel for his room systems. Even now, he saw one of the hands by her side twitch gently and start to rise. Surely, he thought wildly, she would not do this? Betray her twin . . .

Yes, she might. Mira was right. Clarissa was *afraid*. Without thinking, he launched himself across the room, grabbed the moving hand, propelled his sister well away from the button that would unleash security and questions and perhaps bloodshed.

That was all he managed to do. With something between a sob and a snarl, Clarissa neatly brought her other hand up, broke his hold, and sent him sprawling painfully over a low table.

'Mira,' he gasped as he fell, 'stop her.'

The two girls' eyes met once more; the one full of anger, pride, fear, danger, the other questioning: Why? Why must you do this?

Silently, sadly, Mira went and stood between Clarissa and the steel panel.

The other girl flushed angry red, snarled 'Errr . . . *not* a good move, sis,' and advanced, stepping lightly in low, fighting stance.

Mira thought: Why can I not just sleep? Who is this person who wishes me harm though I have done nothing? She stood quite still, seeing Clarissa's foot come up high, feeling it punch hard into her ribcage, shunting the breath from her body. With an effort she did not fall, but slowly straightened, looked again at her double, pulling the sweet air back into her lungs.

'Please. Don't,' she said simply.

Clarissa stayed poised before her, a moment's confusion showing on her face from the lack of opposition. Her head shook slightly, almost an apology, and the foot started to rise again. Before it reached its target, she collapsed soundlessly to the carpet and lay in a soft tumble of limbs and white pyjamas. Kay stood shakily behind her, a gleam of dark metal in his hand. He managed half a rueful smile.

'My sister's OK really. When you get to know her.'

Mira bent down, trembling. 'Is she all right? You haven't . . .?'

'No. Don't worry: she'll be fine. I just put her to sleep for a minute or two. Grandfather makes us carry these things when we leave the building. But we'd better get her into the music room. When she wakes up I won't be too popular.' He went to lift the limp shoulders, but paused, laid his hand softly on Mira's arm. 'Please. Don't hate her.'

'No,' she shook her head, 'Sure I do not hate her. How could I?'

Kay was right. When his sister woke in this sound-proofed sanctuary and found that her wrists and ankles were taped, she writhed and fought like a fury.

'Kay! You'd better let me go! You can't do this! You can't! I hate you!'

There were tears of anger on her face and she looked again not at all a self-possessed fighting cat with sharp teeth and claws, but simply a girl of fifteen, rather spoilt and unhappy and uncertain. Looking on, Kay felt a wave of love and pity for her. Again he found himself thanking the fate that had made him different from the rest of his family. An ordinary boy, not even a product of the cheapest Fertility Board screening. The result of a passionate physical union between his mother and some unknown man. A random pot-luck of genes.

And he had spent so long resenting it.

Mira was at his side, wanting his attention. 'I will go,' she said, 'If you would tell me just a little more, so that I may understand, I will go and you and your sister can forget about me and live your lives. There has been too much hurt done already.'

Clarissa laughed from her corner, a hard, unhappy sound. 'Do you think you'll just be allowed to walk out of here, sis? Just leave the building, sail away from the city?'

Mira looked at her twin, then at Kay. 'Why must they hunt me? Why? I want nothing but to be at home, in my bonny country, at peace, with my own people. All *this* . . .' – she gestured at the darkened city visible through the long oval – '. . . it is nothing to me. I am nothing to do with this place.'

Again, it was Clarissa who answered. 'Oh, that's simple, sis. *Cloning. Is. Illegal.* Worldwide. You are the walking evidence. Grandfather will not allow evidence to exist. Not unless it's buried in some godforsaken wasteland where it doesn't know what it is and can't be found. The moment you started to guess or find out any smallest part of what you were was the moment you were no longer a useful spare. Your own death sentence.'

Mira frowned. 'Is this true?' she asked Kay.

'More or less.' He struggled to meet her gaze.

'Then if I am a *spare*, when was I to be used? And for what? To replace your sister?'

'Yes. That could happen. If she had an accident or was very ill. So the people and the Families would not know. To keep stability.'

Clarissa spoke again, quietly, coldly: 'Or simply to replace *parts* of me, if that was needed. You would be a perfect match.'

'Parts . . .' Mira whispered. She sank back against the wall and slid down it, face in hands. Her voice seemed far away. 'I never dreamed that the world could have such a sickness.'

Kay found himself looking at Clarissa. Despite her anger and fear, he could see the deep shame in her and felt it himself. They had never chosen these things, but they had known about them, allowed them to happen. There was understanding in their shared look. Clarissa shrugged slightly as if to say: It is what I am. What I was born to. What could I do?

Mira stirred. 'I will go,' she murmured. 'I wish to be away from here.' And Kay found himself saying: 'I will come with you. If you'll let me.'

She looked up at him. 'Why would you do that, Kay Saint?'

He shrugged. 'I hate it too. You've made me see how much I hate it. I want to learn another way.'

'Very touching! Very lovely,' Clarissa said, sarcastically, 'but still no good. You wouldn't even get out of the city.'

'Yes. Yes, we could. I'll send a message to Sebestova from you, say you're ill, not to be disturbed. I can rig your room system to send the same sort of message every few hours. One for Grandfather too.' He started to pace, excitedly. 'We can find a ship, get smuggled past the sea gates. We could go anywhere. Anywhere at all! I've thought about this so often.'

Mira said: 'I have a friend who told me that not even a ship was safe, if they know you are there.'

Clarissa looked from one to the other, feigning disbelief. 'Have you two gone completely nutty? Of course a ship isn't safe. *Nothing* is safe. But that's beside the point. In . . .' she struggled to see the time readout on the wall above her '. . . in about seven hours, I'm to be present for the final of the Slam League, right downstairs from here. Have you forgotten, bro? You can send all the messages you like: if I don't appear there on cue to wipe the floor with darling Jan, they're going to be swarming around like nobody's business. And even you, Kay, are *supposed* to be there, representing the family. Tomas'll have that door off in a trice if he thinks you're skulking in here with your precious drums.'

Kay looked at Mira, stricken. 'It's true. I had forgotten. There is a competition . . .'

'If you cannot come, I must go alone. It is best, I'm thinking.'

Clarissa shook her head. 'Sorry sis, still only seven hours. Less than that before they look for me.'

'But if you say nothing?'

The other girl, the Saint, looked down. 'I can't do that.'

Mira thought: She is giving me a chance. Even by telling me her thoughts, she is deliberately giving me a chance. Does she hope in her heart that I may escape? Certainly she is not all she seems.

Kay was looking out of the window blankly, idly tapping a finger on the skin of a drum, lost in thought. Mira stood up and went over to him. 'What is this competition? What must your sister do?'

He refocused, came up from the depths. 'Slam? It's a way of fighting. A contest between two people. They're all nuts about it. Haven't you seen it on the street screens? No, sorry, you wouldn't have: they don't show it there, do they? It's Level Three and above. Too much incitement to violence.'

She shook her head. 'Nae, I've never seen it. There will be many people to see this contest?'

'Quite a few, yes. I don't know how many. Loads from the Families and the Fertility Board. At least a hundred in all, with all their staff. Plus anyone watching the broadcast, of course, which will be a million or two.'

'I see. And what does your sister wear when she fights?'

'Oh, they have special clothes too. A sort of black suit. A headguard. Nothing else. No shoes or anything.'

She in her turn gazed out of the window, across the great, sprawling capital and Kay fell silent again, cudgelling his brains for ideas. He felt that if he didn't go with Mira, a part of him would die. It was beyond understanding, but very real. Whatever poor thing he'd become, she could help him to be himself.

Clarissa's voice came clearly, icily, into the silence.

'No, sis, it wouldn't work. Don't even try. You'd get murdered, even if they didn't spot you at once.'

Her brother looked back at her, questioning.

'Poor Kay,' she said sweetly; 'Always a step behind. Your *spare* here is thinking of passing herself off as *me* for the final. What do you think of that?'

He almost laughed. 'Mira? She's not serious.'

'Aye,' she murmured, still looking far into the distance. 'I was thinking of it, right enough. If there is no other way.'

'But she's right! You'd get murdered!'

She sighed. 'Och, perhaps. But by your own account I am also to be murdered if I try to leave this place. What, then, should we do? Free your sister? Harm her? Neither of these are possible, I'm thinking, and I would not have her harmed. But think: no one is truly to be murdered in this contest of yours, I suppose, and so, win or lose, would it matter? Only they must not see who I am, and there must be enough of me left at the end to try to get away. That is all that would matter.'

Clarissa's sulky, petulant voice spoke into the silence: 'Yes. Actually it matters to me! This is *my* day. My day to win. Don't you dare take that away from me! Don't you dare!'

Ignoring her, Mira said: 'Tell me more about this kind of fighting. How long would I have to last on my feet? And if you have scissors and a comb and steady hands, you can cut my hair while you talk. It will do no harm for me to seem as your sister now, will it, whichever way we take? And if you think of another, better plan, for sure I will no argue . . .'

Perhaps if she stayed focused on what was to come, she would not think about Bee. And the man that she had chased into the docks earlier and then lost.

When grey light stole over the silent circle of drums and the first scavenger birds dived and fought away over the docks, shrieking unheard behind the glass, Mira looked at her image in the mirror Kay had brought in, and saw Clarissa. Kay's clever fingers had done a good job with the hair, and he had fetched the black suit, pressed and immaculate for the competition, the face colouring his sister usually wore, and a print-out of her in her Slam costume to work from.

'Don't you *dare* expect to win, Jan Barbieri,' Mira said coldly, scornfully to the reflection in Clarissa's voice.

'Ha, ha,' muttered the real Clarissa, looking pale and troubled, huddled in her corner. 'Now all you need to do is learn to fight like me, ignoring that arm which seems to hurt you so much. Should be easy in four hours.'

'Kay?'

'Yes. I've thought about that. I'll bring in a hand-held monitor. There's bound to be a recording of one of Clarissa's fights somewhere. All we can do for your wound is dose you up on painkillers and tie it up tightly.' He looked worried: 'Mira, it looks horrible. Maybe we can still find another way. You don't have to do this.'

'Aye. I do. The arm will be OK with your medicine.'

The tiny monitor was brought, with two recent taped fights, and Mira sat peacefully in the black suit, chewing fruit supplied by Jane, watching the tapes over and over. Not knowing what he could do to help and unable to rest, Kay said he would go to family breakfast, try to occupy Tomas a little if he was there, make sure that no alarm bells were ringing in the Saint Building. Clarissa slipped finally into a doze, curled up like a foetus.

Left thus alone, high in the Saint tower, up where the light was that she had watched many times, Mira felt curiously light-headed. She knew instinctively that she would need time – a lot of time, spent somewhere safe – to heal the hurts, grieve properly for Beebop and the others, make some sense of what she was . . . *Sweet spirits above, what she was!* But for now she had only to ride the floodtide of events that was sweeping her forward. As she went over what she must do, rehearsing voice and movement and expression in her mind, she felt almost as she did when breaking the new snow, high up on the dawn-bathed ridges. At one time she turned off the monitor, went to stand over her sleeping twin, knelt down beside her and laid a hand on the rich, thick hair. In repose the face that was also hers had lost all anger and fear. And it came into her heart then what she would do, if she did manage to break free of the city. Something so right that she marvelled that she had not seen it before.

'Annie Tallis,' she murmured, 'did you have the same instinct? Were you there to protect and save me when they came and shot you down that day?'

She told Kay when he returned, already dressed in his formal Saint blue and gold. 'There were four on my paper. Four names that Annie Tallis carried when she came through the trees. I want to find the baby. Adeline. That is what is in my heart to do. She is a *spare*, like me?'

'Yes,' he agreed, puzzled; 'the last of your . . . you know, *batch*. But she's in France. All of them get buried in the middle of nowhere.' He took the stack of print-outs and pictures, sorted through them until he found the right one. 'There, that's what she looks like. She's in some village right down near the southern mountains.'

She took the girl's picture, glanced at it strangely, tucked it into her tunic. 'Mountains? Then truly it is perfect.' She smiled at him suddenly, her eyes bright, and he found himself returning the smile.

'Truly it is perfect,' he repeated, trying to copy her accent. And he leaned forward and put his mouth against hers a moment.

Her eyes widened in surprise. 'Now what was that for, Kay Saint?'

He blushed, turned away, feeling a fool. 'Excuse me, it just felt . . . Never mind. I sent messages to my grandfather as if from Clarissa, to get her out of breakfast and other duties. Have you seen enough of the tapes? Do you still think it can be done?'

He knew he was gabbling, but she answered.

'Perhaps. If I may avoid being too close to the people who know your sister well, and if I may wear the head protection throughout.'

'But the fight itself?'

She sighed a little. 'I don't know. I will not be able to fight as your sister fights, and probably I will quickly lose, but that could perhaps be blamed on illness, or her cycle, if she is due. But now you must tell me the rules again. Those watching must not see me make the mistakes of a beginner.'

So they went once more through the rules and the procedure until Mira could repeat all and could name the areas of the body where points could be scored and those, such as the throat, which were forbidden. Clarissa awoke again during this process in a sour temper, not improved by Kay saying to her: 'Look! Mira could really be you. What do you think?'

Mira shook her head soothingly. 'We are each a different person. That cannot change.'

'I should think not, *spare*,' Clarissa snarled. 'I'm a Saint.'

'And I am content not to be. Let us leave it at that and be friends.'

Clarissa said with sarcastic sweetness: 'OK, then, *friend*; take this tape off, please.'

Mira shook her head: 'I cannot.' She asked Kay, 'How long, now?'

'Just over two hours until you should be in the great hall. A little longer until the fight.'

She considered: 'Two hours . . . I'm that tired, I might sleep a wee while. Perhaps I should go now to your sister's room, in case someone should come looking. Surely that would be most normal?'

'Yes . . . most normal, but you know she has a room system like mine: like Jane. I could shut it down for a while, I suppose . . .'

She gave a small wry smile. 'If I cannot pass for Clarissa with a computer, I will not pass with her family and friends.'

'But Sebestova? Her guard, Sebestova. He might be around too.'

She shrugged. 'This is the chance we have decided to take, I'm thinking. So let us take it. Come, you come with me. You'll need to show me the ways of this building: you must also make sure I wake in good time. And then, afterwards, after the contest, you will know best which way we are to take, if all has passed well. To get to . . .'

She paused, glanced at Clarissa: 'To get to the place we talked of. If you still wish to come with me.'

He looked at her neutrally. 'I still wish to come.'

Inside he thrust down the thought of what his mother would feel to have him gone.

He thrust even deeper the thought that this strange, quick, gentle girl that he was to join himself to was a copy not only of his sister, but also of that same mother.

That way lay madness.

TWENTY-FOUR

Madness.

Aye, thought Mira, that was the right word.

She entered the great hall and crossed the wide, polished expanse to sit, alone, in one of the contestant's chairs, a little apart from the square fight area.

The room was thrumming with people and noise. Hard-eyed, black-suited men and women, guards murmuring into wristcoms as they stood watchful at the walls, the splash of colour from the Saints themselves, laughing at some unheard remark as they entered and went easily to take their central places, scattering nods and greetings amongst the guests like bright pieces of candy. But inside the close-fitting straps of the headguard, the world was muffled and hot, unreal.

She studied the great room full of people, making sure that she appeared bored and impatient rather than inquisitive. Only now, after her long weeks in the hateful place, were her eyes becoming used to noticing the differences between the two strangely named sorts of people that filled the city. Bee could always tell instantly: they all could, except the new incomers. But it seemed that these Great Families came from yet another group. It made no sense. Weren't people just people?

The woman was there, she saw with a start, the one from the broadcast who might have been Annie Tallis: the one who was *her* at a later age. This woman glanced across at Mira and smiled slightly. In her mind, Mira saw a body tumbling lifeless across the snow. After that, she

tried to shut out what was around her. 'They will expect
you to be focused,' Kay had said. 'Nobody will try to talk
to you or want to be recognised. Clarissa's always in a
foul mood before a fight, anyway. It's afterwards that
will be more difficult.'

If there was to be an *afterwards*, Mira thought.

Presently a tall, blond-haired boy, also wearing the
Slam clothes, detached himself from two strange, elderly
men all in white and sauntered over to the other central
chair. He had not yet put on his guard and he grinned
at Mira, apparently in high spirits. He said: 'My pretty
little opponent. Have you forgiven me for deserting you
the other day? Can I expect a fair fight?'

'Can *I*?' Mira made herself say in the Clarissa voice
and the boy threw back his head and laughed.

'My prize will be a kiss,' he said, pulling on the head
gear.

This one is very sure of himself. Strangely, Mira found
herself hoping that Clarissa would not choose the arrogant boy as a partner, which Kay had told her was
hoped for by his Family. He would wish to rule you, my
twin. There is nothing gentle behind that laughter, I'm
thinking.

She realised then with a thudding heart that the distant
room noise was dying away and that all were now seated,
except for the guards. A short, grizzled, mild-looking man
in the same green as the square was coming into the
centre. She knew from the tapes that he was to make a
sort of blessing on the fight area and would then become
referee when the contest started.

Cameras watched from their stalks, sending every
move she made out to thousands of eyes.

Madness.

Her wound throbbed despite the medicine Kay had

applied and her hands would not keep still on her lap. The cold blue eyes of the Barbieri boy looked at them and then into her own, widening into a question.

'Ladies and gentlemen,' came a deep, hoarse voice from hidden loudspeakers. 'Ladies and gentlemen. Welcome to our home and to the headquarters of the Saint Network. Welcome especially to what I feel sure will be a truly entertaining spectacle: the final of the Slam League of Great Briton. We're honoured to have you as our guests. And be careful with my granddaughter, young fellow!'

A polite, bored laugh rippled through the seated guests. Mira saw an old man with wild, spouting white hair and an overlarge belly, handing the microphone back to an attendant and sinking into his seat, beside the Tilly-Annie woman. The grandfather, she thought.

Then the referee signalled that she and the boy should rise from their chairs and come to take up positions in the square.

What about the blessing? Is the fight to start?

Sudden panic leaped through her, making her want simply to run. She stood rooted to the spot, halfway to her starting mark on the mat, and the referee whispered: 'Is everything all right, my dear?'

Think of the baby. Think of Adeline and the southern mountains of the land called France.

'Yes. Fine. I'm fine, thank you.'

She went to stand in the proper place, facing the boy, who was looking puzzled now. That would not do. *He* of all of them must believe that he fought Clarissa. She looked at him with as much scorn as she could find and stood in the relaxed pre-fight posture she'd seen on the tapes, bouncing lightly on her toes to warm the muscles.

The referee said something to the audience and then

something to the two fighters – she couldn't say what, merely nodded when the boy nodded – and then, in a dream, the fight began with the bleeping of a device in the referee's left hand.

They must bow to each other as they came out into the main part of the square. She remembered that just in time. After that she must put her hands up loosely as protection, crouch down low, circle the opponent, keep always moving, look for an opening in his defence.

Spirits above . . .

The boy exploded across the square, knocking her hands aside and she saw his foot sweeping viciously at her ankles, while his left hand took a tight, tugging grip on her painful shoulder, making her cry out. She managed to bounce above the sweeping foot and to keep her balance, but could not avoid the hand, which let go of the shoulder and flicked hard off the side of her headguard, making her stagger.

A clock at the side of the square flicked agonisingly through the seconds: 15, 16, 17 . . . Forget fifteen minutes. She would not last one. Already he was launching into another attack, kicking sideways under her guard at the area just above her hip. She felt his toes graze her side as she leaped away backwards, and remembered just in time that she must not step over the white rope, or he would win two whole points.

There was no respite. Again and again he struck forward, through her guard, and she could manage no response apart from to dodge away, watch the hands and feet and try to move before they made too great a contact. Even so, she could feel the bruises. She should counter, put him on the back foot, but she saw no opening.

1.25, 1.26, 1.27 . . .

The crowd were buzzing, some of them calling out,

jeering – she could hear it, even through the guard – and she knew then that it was no good. Her performance was not going to fool them.

As she thought it, the boy finally got a proper grip on her two shoulders and threw her sprawling onto the mat, gaining a whole point for the fall. She lay winded and confused, saw him advance again and knew she must rise, get back to her feet before he came to finish it. If the referee felt that one fighter was in serious danger from the other, or was not defending herself, he would stop the contest, award the win to the other. At least then she could rest . . .

The boy's face was now set in a snarl as he advanced and she sought the strength to roll aside. He knows, she thought, hopelessly. His ugly, angry look, intent on doing her harm, reminded her suddenly of the fight she had seen in the snow between Hopkins and Green. She remembered thinking how alien it had seemed: the deliberate will to harm another, to cause real pain. She was fit and strong and agile, even hampered by the wound to her arm, but still she did not have that will.

Crunch. Another ringing blow off the side of the guard as she tried to rise. The elderly referee hovered close, a finger twitching as he peered at her. He had only to raise his finger and it would all be over.

Perhaps I could borrow this feeling for a time, she thought in a detached, dream-like way, the blood pounding in her ears. Perhaps I could make myself a Green or a Hopkins or an Evan for a short while. Like the children pretending to be beetles over the toolhouse floor. The blood was not just sounding in her ears: she could taste it running over her tongue.

'What's the matter?' the boy hissed, coming in once more, 'Forgotten everything, have we? Not quite able to cut it on the day? Yesterday's model? Or is it women's trouble, perhaps?'

Yes, that was the excuse she'd thought of! 'Women's trouble', he called it. It would not do. Nothing would do but to fight.

'Let's finish this *spectacle* quickly. Then we can have lunch and a nice talk with Tomas,' said the boy.

His foot came stamping down towards her shoulder and she rolled painfully aside.

I will be a Green then. Just for the while.

She made the momentum of the roll take her up to her feet and turned to face the boy once more. There were people on their feet now, calling their derision, voices raised. The quivering finger was almost up. But she saw and heard none of it. Her world drew abruptly inwards to a corridor leading to the person standing opposite her on this mat. An enemy. An animal. A wild dog. An evil to be hurt, exterminated, finished.

'Now it's your turn, boy,' she said in the Clarissa voice.

He grinned and came forward, jabbing with his left hand and she ducked and hooked her foot hard and savagely behind his knee, so that the leg collapsed under him. Even while his head bobbed down, off balance, she made her knee come up to meet it, with a sickening crunch.

There was a gasp from the audience, a few cheers, and for the time being the referee's finger relaxed. Still she was aware of nothing. Just because the beast was down, it did not mean she should not finish it. Growling herself like an animal, she came and grabbed a flailing arm and twisted hard, so that the boy on his knees must turn and bend forward to lessen the pain. With a sudden extra twist and a push, he was sent full length onto his face.

A whole point back to her. And half a point more for the hook and blow. She distantly saw the scoreboard flick up the points and for a moment threatened to resurface and become Mira once more. No good. The Barbieri boy was coming back to his feet, so that she was allowed to advance again. Now he, too, had blood on his mouth and nose. She must make herself love the sight. If she did not, it would be *her* blood. It would be the baby Adeline left to cold fate.

'So . . . game on, then, *spare*,' the boy said indistinctly.

'Yes,' she agreed. 'Game on.'

Had the referee heard what he'd said? She thought not. But what about the cameras? Well, she'd make sure he didn't say it again. The enemy came forward once more, a little more cautiously now, and she set herself to bouncing lightly, moving left and right, changing stance, always moving, as she had seen on the tapes. He came at her with a feinted punch that turned into a kick to the head and she saw it early and laughed at him, grabbed the foot and pushed him hopping backwards towards the edge of the mat. Angrily, he wrenched the foot free just in time, avoiding the rope, but she tripped him once more and put her knee heavily down on the side of his face.

Another point. She was starting to claw back what she had lost. She laughed again, a wild thing now from the ice-bound passes of the North. He came again to his feet, too out of breath to speak further, and looked at her with hatred. He is beaten, she thought, I can truly finish this now.

And yet, even as she thought it, the pretence drained away from her. Truly, she was no Green. She wished no man or woman harm.

'Give up,' she said to him. 'Give up, please.'

Slowly, she watched the comprehension flower in his battered, swollen face, that she could not easily do him more hurt. His eyes narrowed. The room was again quiet as he came forward, guard raised. Mira fought to lose herself in the Green world, to be an animal, but it would not come. She felt tired beyond reasoning. Why could she not just rest?

They were close now, both breathing hard and unsteady on their feet. Barbieri's prideful eyes bored into hers. They said, without words: Forget the competition. We will finish it properly.

His left jab snaked out onto her chin once more and the right foot started to come up to follow. She already recognised the pattern: but could she find the energy to move in time? She doubted it.

She saw the foot lift level with her head and flick inwards.

And then she saw it fall away.

And with a scream the boy dropped back to the mat, with something strange that had appeared at his shoulder. Something that shouldn't be there.

At the same moment she sensed that a large figure was moving in fast behind her, running across the room to the mat, growling terribly, intent on harm itself. There were other shouts, the room was in sudden chaos. Without thinking, she waited until the runner was almost upon them and then threw herself down and sideways, gasping as the body weight struck her full in the back and went tumbling across her.

Painfully she tried to squirm away from the bulk, aware that the attacker was trying also to rise, cursing, roaring at her in anger. Half turning, she saw the face. The big cat. Kay's guard. And in his hand a second knife. With a powerful lunge he brought himself close to the boy's body, lying still on the mat, and raised the weapon to bring it down into the chest.

But it was too late. The surprise had been lost. A second figure was there now. A small, mild-looking man, half the size of the other. Carelessly, he kicked the knife from the big cat's grasp, produced his own weapon, and thrust it powerfully forward and up.

The larger man gurgled and fell.

'Are you OK, miss?' the small man asked. 'That was quick work. Very quick.'

This is someone I should know, she thought vaguely, and smiled as if none of it mattered and she, a Saint, could rise above all. 'Of course. I'm fine. Thank you.'

And then there were doctors for the boy, people crowding around, guards to keep them back . . . and Kay, white-faced, taking her hand, scooping up the soft shoes she had taken from Clarissa's apartment, leading her away from the mat.

'We go *now*,' he muttered; 'the place is going to be a madhouse for ages. But then they'll start asking questions. God . . . *Hedge*. They'll blame it on me. He's *my* guard, after all. They'll blame the Scroat.'

They brushed past the looming faces – Mira caught sight of the Tilly-Annie woman, her features tight as she watched the melee near the mat – and then they were at the exit, going through the long, low corridor that led to the central elevators to take them back to ground level.

Mira felt herself staggering, Kay's arm supporting her. 'You're not hurt?' he asked. 'That fight!'

'No, not hurt. Not really. Just tired and bruised.'

They reached the end of the corridor, the distant noise from the hall fading to almost nothing. But before they could signal for the elevator there were feet running softly behind them. Mira looked back and saw the little man who had congratulated her for her 'quick work'.

'Excuse me, sir, miss,' he said, neutrally. 'Mr Tomas asks you to join him in his study for a few moments. Not for long. Then you can rest, miss.'

Kay said: 'Was this a request or an order, Copper?'

The man appeared to consider, then said: 'I think you should go, sir. It won't be for long.'

The 'study' was higher still than Kay's rooms. It perched right at the top of the building, halfway to the clouds, or so it seemed to Mira. There were windows on three sides and yet, with blinds half down across many of them the place was shadowy.

She stood next to Kay before the great desk and resigned herself to this ending of things. There was nothing left. No card to play. At least now she was caught, she could rest. She swayed and felt Kay's arm supporting her, although he, too, seemed nearly finished. The old man she had seen at the fight came in, breathing heavily, and sat at the desk. He looked up at them, catching his breath, studying their faces. Behind him on the one side stood the man who had fetched them; Copper. And on the other side, further back still, half in shadow, the man they called Moore. Her Gil, returned from death. Either that or his ghost. She would not look at him, though she could feel his eyes resting unblinking on her.

She had known, though. She had already known, God help her . . .

When Tomas Saint spoke, he too seemed tired. 'I'm sorry to have called you up here. You must be exhausted, my dear, after the contest and the unfortunate events which followed. Indeed, I can see that you are.' He paused, gazed down at papers on the desk as if lost in thought, then up again. 'What the results of those events will be is not entirely clear at this stage. It may be that the

Saint family is about to come under some threat. The attempted assassination of our guest, along with all else that has passed, might lead him into precipitate action. The boy is very headstrong: who can judge what he might try? This would seem a good time, therefore, to talk about one or two delicate matters . . . matters which relate especially to *you*, my dear.'

Mira wished that he would call her by a name. He surely knew that she was not Clarissa. And yet he gave no sign that they were meeting for the first time.

Och well, I will play the game a little longer then. It will not be me who helps this Tomas.

'As you are aware – and I think you, too, Kay, though we have never spoken of it to you, the Saint family, like the other Great Families, uses certain *technologies* to . . . shall we say, *enhance* the service we can provide to our fellow countrymen. And, as with all technologies, because nothing can be perfect, we keep parts in reserve. Do you follow me?'

They both nodded. Kay said: 'Yes, Grandfather,' and Mira said it too, using the Clarissa voice.

'Good. Excellent. Well now . . . we store these parts all over the place, but one recently went missing in somewhat peculiar circumstances. In a way, it was, shall we say, inadvertently *switched on*. Since then this part has developed its potential considerably. Indeed, I have had much pleasure in watching just how quickly it developed. And now, it is *here*, with us!'

The watery blue eyes held Mira's own and twinkled.

'No doubt, as I said, *you*, my dear, will feel a particular interest in this turn of events. Now, obviously two parts to do the same job are a waste. And yet . . . and yet it may be that this other part has developed to such a degree that it cannot easily be thrown away. It may *be* that we should seek ways to employ such a useful part. Especially if the family is now to come under the threat I mentioned a few moments ago.'

Tomas stopped and there was silence in the room.

Mira thought. I must ask questions. It would be usual to ask questions.

She said, in the haughty Clarissa voice: 'How did this accident come about, Grandfather? The part getting switched on?' Gil's eyes continued their unblinking scrutiny from across the room.

'Well now, my child. I did not say that there had been an "accident", did I? Many possibilities lie hidden in our blood. But only events can truly shape us. Is that not so? And events can be helped along, given a nudge now and then.'

She fell silent, her mind reeling at his words.

'What about you, my boy? No questions? Ah, but then I think you might know a considerable amount about this already! It might be thanks to *you* that we are able to make a choice now. Am I right? Once more, you see, the events can shape us.'

Kay said sulkily: 'This *part* is a human being. Do you play God, Grandfather?'

'Only when I have to, Kay,' the old man said, gently: 'Only at greatest need. There are others who would go much further than I. If you can only believe it, I wish simply to maintain the fragile balance that keeps us all safe, ready for better times, if they should ever come.'

'The precious Saints! To be saved at all cost.'

Tomas shook his head. 'Not only them. Oh no, not only them. Although perhaps you should not be so hasty to condemn those "precious Saints". You are, after all, one of them yourself, Kay. Perhaps it is time to grow up and fight for your family and what they believe in.'

Kay flushed. He took a step closer to the desk. He could hardly get the bitter words out. 'My *family*? My perfect *family*? The great and the good? Well that's not *me*, is it, old man? *I'm* not the great or the good. Or had you forgotten that you had a Scroat living downstairs all this time, wondering just what he had to do to pass for one of you perfect bloody *freaks*?'

'Please, Kay,' the old man chided, 'learn to control yourself!' He paused in thought, as if debating with himself. 'Yes, all things considered, I think this is the right time for you to know that you are no different from the rest of us. Carried in your mother's body, at her whim, certainly, though you do not share her genes. Allowed also at her wish to grow as a "normal" boy, whatever that may be. But no . . . *Scroat*.' He shuddered at the word. 'Why do you think we have been so keen to employ your talents within the Network? For mere charity? For amusement? You should know us better than that, my boy.'

All colour drained from Kay's face. He seemed transfixed, unable to speak. He made a sound, but no words came.

'Deal with it!' the grandfather said brutally: 'Assimilate it. Grow *up* now, Kay. And if you don't believe what I have said, ask your mother.'

Then he transferred his gaze back to Mira and looked at her long and hard: and there was ice in that gaze. 'So, we have talked. We have played out our scene. Now we move to hard facts. Hard decisions. What am I to do with you? Copper?'

The little man cleared his throat. 'Sir, she *is* good. Excellent. We can all see she is. There would be many possibilities with enough time and sufficient training. But that time will not be allowed us now. The contest was spirited but inauthentic. It made an impression that will stick. Barbieri will certainly not have been fooled, and so he will be that much more careful in future. Then there is the attempted assassination . . . It forces our hand. No, sir, in balance, I cannot advise allowing this one to live.'

Mira heard the words in cold horror, but Kay seemed hardly to notice. Perhaps he didn't understand.

The old man nodded. 'I see. Moore? Anything to add?'

'Aye. Only that if you keep her, you should know that she is wilful beyond belief. I do not think she would ever complete the training.'

There was a sudden beeping from the instruments on the ceiling and a voice said, urgently, 'I'm sorry to disturb you, sir, but there's chaos down here. Mr Barbieri has regained consciousness and is making some very loud accusations concerning the Family. Many other members of the Board and the Great Families have listened to him. Mr Barbieri and some others will be on their way up to see you imminently. They insisted, sir. I didn't think force was advisable, in the circumstances . . .'

'The circumstances being the large Pax contingent here as guests in our building. Very wise. Thank you, Sebestova. I will make ready for Mr Barbieri and his supporters.'

Instantly the one called Copper was bending down to whisper in the old man's ear, but Tomas waved him away: 'No, my friend: we will not make an escape. The Family is to undergo a testing time, but all will be well. We have some allies still. And I flatter myself that I can deal with that boy.' He leaned forward and flicked a switch on his desk. His eyes returned to Mira. He said: 'There; events move along as ever, driving us on. That is the nature of our lives. Reluctantly, I must agree with Copper. Such a waste. I'm so sorry, my dear.'

The door opened and four men entered, clad in the Saint blue and gold.

'Ah, Sergeant, here is the young lady you are to take. I believe you know what to do. Be discreet. Kay! You are to go too. I wish you to learn from this lesson. To wake up, before it's too late. Remember: family comes first. Always.' Then, to the guards once more: 'Look after him. He's had a shock.'

He looked a last time at Kay and Mira. 'Children. You will excuse me. Time is even shorter than I myself imagined. I must work to smooth over these dangerous days; to restore the balance.'

Still Kay said nothing. Mira took his hand, and led him towards the door. The four guards fell in around them. She turned before she left and looked Gil in the eye.

She said: 'I pity you, so I do.'

When they had gone, cool, calm Moore was angry. He said: 'It's madness to send the boy too. He'll help her. I must follow. I must see the deed done. You must allow me that. You *must*.'

But Tomas raised a hand. 'Enough. No, you may *not* go. I need you here, and my men are not babies, to be nursemaided in their work. Besides which, you have made the issue of the girl a personal one, which is a grave mistake, Moore. Even now, she has riled you. I expected better.' A sudden faint hubbub broke out outside the door, a clamour of raised voices, competing to be heard. Sebestova's bass growl was amongst them, protesting. Tomas said: 'Ah, the promised deputation seems to have arrived. Come gentlemen, let us put these accusations to rest, deal with this Barbieri cub. Copper, you may let them in.'

Copper activated the door locks and twenty or so

people surged angrily through, fronted by Jan, flanked by his own guards. They had bound Sebestova's hands and held him roughly amongst them, where he smouldered at the indignity. Behind the guards were members from four or five other Families, mostly from the younger generations. The Board, Tomas noted wryly, was conspicuous by its absence. How typical. How wise. Jan himself was pale, his shoulder bound in bandages, but his voice was loud and aggressive.

'Here he is!' he said; 'The old fox in his lair. Well, Tomas, I have been almost murdered in your own building by a man in your employ. A Saint bodyguard, no less! What do you have to say? And beside that, you have the nerve to put a *clone* into the Slam contest with me. Make no mistake, Tomas, we all know what we saw down there.'

There was an angry chorus of agreement.

The old man smiled politely, gestured wearily to some chairs: 'Please, friends, will you not sit while we talk?'

He wondered now, too late, whether he had not misjudged the situation.

Something was wrong inside the tower. Not this far up: lower down. Even from within the massive service elevator into which the guards had led them, dropping swiftly and silently through the building, Mira could hear faint noises that suggested chaos, perhaps fighting. Sometimes the noise grew a touch louder and then faded again: the passing of the entrances to other floors, she guessed. The four guards had noticed too, and seemed uneasy. They flicked nervous glances each other, and one said: 'Sarge?'

The man in charge shook his head, perplexed. 'I don't know what it is. Trouble of some sort. All I know is we've got our orders. Until I hear different we stick with those.'

Mira was happy to have the men distracted and uncomfortable. It would add to her chances. For sure, she would not surrender her life so easily. She wished Kay would look at her, give some indication that he was alert to the opportunity. She wondered if he still carried the slim weapon he'd used to restrain his sister. Surely if he would only rouse himself, they'd stand some sort of chance.

Yet perhaps he didn't wish to rouse himself. Perhaps he would leave her to her fate. He seemed to have lost all power of thought, staring glassily downwards.

The faint noises were not so faint now. They had become shouts, cries, the crackle of weapons, the sound of thick glass shattering. They were nearing the base of the building and with each floor they passed, a burst of noise erupted through the metal elevator skin. The sergeant now had beads of moisture on his face. He pressed a button and spoke into his wristcom. 'Hawkins? Hawkins? Have you got that transport ready? We'll be with you in two minutes.'

The tiny speaker just crackled emptily in reply.

'Hawkins? Hawkins? Where the devil are you?'

'Sarge,' one of the men said urgently, 'we should go back up. Something's happened to Hawkins. We should find out first . . .'

'That's enough!' The sergeant was taking out a weapon, priming it. 'We take a look, clear? And then if it's no good we'll proceed down: to the garage, or the guard-room. Somebody be ready to close the doors again on my say-so.'

3, 2, 1 . . . The last few numbers slid past. Mira nudged at Kay with her foot, but still he wouldn't look at her. The guard that held her said, nervously, 'Stop that, now.'

She tried to summon some energy, imagining how she would twist free of the man's grip when the chance came. She had to be focused, relaxed. If only she didn't ache so.

Kay! Wake up!

The elevator reached ground level and settled smoothly, a contrast to the chaos around. The doors drew silkily aside and instantly the noise became loud. Mira saw that they were opposite one of the entrances to the building. Not the main one, through which she'd arrived with Kay last night, but a smaller one, facing north. Through the glass she could see a small Saint transport, on fire, and two larger transports parked at an angle nearby. The word *Pax* was stencilled on the nearest of these. Grey figures were pouring out of it and lining up outside, preparing to enter. More grey figures were already in the vestibule. Five or six grim, unmoving shapes had been dragged into a rough line near one wall. The noise of fighting came from somewhere to the left, out of sight.

Already they had been noticed by the Pax contingent. Weapons were being levelled at them. Mira prepared to run. The glass doors were no good, she thought: she would have to go right, back into the building, away from the noise.

'Close up!' yelled the sergeant: *'Close up!'* He opened fire at the figures hurrying towards them, while one of the others stabbed at the buttons to close the elevator door. The man holding Mira pulled her in front of him to use her as a shield, firing over her shoulder while she fought to free herself. Gradually the gap grew smaller. Those inside shrank back to the edges, taking cover, but the smooth metal was only half across when it shuddered and halted, smoking from the blast of a weapon.

The sergeant swore violently. A voice started to speak, both inside the elevator and echoing across the vestibule, coming out of nowhere. The voice was idiotically calm and measured. It said: 'Attention. Attention. There is nothing to fear. This building is temporarily under Pax control, in pursuance of an alleged infringement of one of the international treaties. Repeat. There is nothing to fear. Please simply stay where you are, make yourself as comfortable as possible and you will soon be approached and helped by Pax personnel. Until that time, no one is to leave the building.'

'Bugger that!' the sergeant said; 'Nothing to fear? OK, lads; go for the stairs! We can still make the guardhouse. Somebody bring the prisoner. On my mark: three, two, one, *go*!'

He leaped through the doors, firing his weapon wildly, and the others followed, fanning out as they went. All at once, sparks were flying off the wall and floor and the air was filled with a bitter, burning smell. Within three steps, the sergeant himself had been hit, spinning awkwardly round and back against the blackened elevator door. As she was pushed out, Mira deliberately made herself a deadweight, letting her knees collapse, so that the one that held her would have to carry her or let go. The man brought his weapons round, snarling 'None of that, you! Move it.' And then he too had been hit, sliding silently to the ground beside her.

Frantically, she looked behind her for Kay and realised that he hadn't moved from the elevator. He was standing bewildered, somehow avoiding the volley of fire. 'Come on!' she yelled, but still he did not move.

Their guards were all dead now, save one, and he was wounded, trying hopelessly to pull himself towards the corridor. A grey-suited woman was approaching her, weapon resting in the crook of her arm: 'Miss Clarissa? Miss Clarissa, we do not wish to harm you. Please, just stay there and await further instructions. The lieutenant has been informed. He asked particularly that you be well treated. You must therefore please not resist.'

Ignoring the woman, Mira stepped back into the elevator and slapped Kay hard across the face. 'Your weapon! Where is it?' His eyes wandered to her face and his hand rose to his cheek, touching the reddened patch. Slowly he focused, coming back to the present.

He said, incredulously: 'You *hit* me.'

'Miss Clarissa. Mr Kay. Please stay where you are. The lieutenant is on his way.' The woman was almost upon them now.

'Come *on*!' Mira murmured. '*Think!* Do you have your weapon here?'

It wasn't any good. Kay was still half in his dreams and the woman was there now, pulling her arm. 'Please, Miss Clarissa. Mr Kay. Just follow me over here. You'll be quite safe, I assure you.'

Mira reached for Kay's hand. She spoke in his sister's voice. 'Come on. We'd better do as they say, bro. Jan will sort this out.' But when her hand closed over his, she felt a slim, cold hardness there, nestled in his palm. She glanced a question at him and he nodded slightly. One side of his face was smarting red now. She took the thing from him, feeling the shape of it, trying to remember what Kay had done to make it work. If she had to, she could just bluff . . .

'You over there!' the woman called to one of the security men. 'Fetch two chairs for Miss Clarissa and Mr Kay. Quickly now.' She turned back to say something to them – 'We'll see about bringing in something for you to drink and . . .' – but stopped when she saw the tiny muzzle pointing at her.

'Say nothing,' Mira murmured, hoping the weapon

looked convincing: 'Lead us towards the corridor. On the right.'

The woman paused a moment, and Mira thought that she would call out, but then she simply shrugged and said quietly: 'This is not wise, Miss Clarissa. There's really nowhere for you to go. However . . .' She turned in her stride and started to walk across the face of the other elevators. On the far side of the vestibule, the man sent for chairs reappeared and stood looking perplexed.

'Ma'am?' he called.

At his call the other soldiers looked up from their tasks of clearing away the dead and securing the entrance.

We aren't going to make it, Mira thought. They'll see.

The man called again, more urgently: 'Ma'am? Are the prisoners not waiting for the lieutenant?'

'Answer him!' Mira whispered. 'Tell him something.'

But it was no good. Other figures were approaching them now, reaching for their weapons. One was speaking into his wristcom, perhaps to bring more men from the very corridor they were approaching.

And then, inexplicably, there was a sharp, fizzing *crack* and the whole vestibule was filled with thick choking smoke, impossible to see through. The woman clutched at her throat, wracked with coughing, then collapsed from a silent blow. Mira, too was coughing: she couldn't seem to breathe at all and the tears came running down her cheeks, blinding her. She dropped the slim object she had used to threaten the woman and rubbed at her eyes, without clearing them. Then she felt something being pressed over her mouth and nose.

A voice said: 'Try to hold that there and breathe normally! And don't rub your eyes. We have to move fast, before the smoke disperses. Here, in here.'

An arm guided her towards the wall and into what

Mira thought was another of the elevators, standing open and empty. Kay was bundled in after her, though he didn't seem to be coughing as she was. Then suddenly the door had closed and the chaos outside was distant.

'There,' said the voice, 'that went OK. You should be able to take off the mask now. Your eyes will smart a bit for a while, that's all.'

The voice was right. Mira found that the air in here seemed clean and smoke free: but still she could hardly see a thing. Yet despite that she knew now who their rescuer was: Kay's mother, the woman called Tilly. The blurred outline and the voice were enough. Again there was the sensation of smooth falling. The lights flickered as they went and then disappeared, but the lift still dropped.

'We go down,' Tilly's voice said, 'to the garage level. The elevator will be unaffected by their power cut. There are other systems.'

After a while, the elevator stopped and they stepped out, still in darkness, into what felt like a large, echoing space. Mira started after the woman, feeling her way forward, unsure in the dark if her sight had come back properly yet. Behind her, Kay stumbled, shuffling his way in a dream, and she fought to keep him on his feet.

'What is wrong with my son?' came the voice.

Mira replied quietly: 'I think it is what the old man told him. That he was like you. And I. A made thing. A copy. I understand his shock.'

There was silence after that, only the quietly echoing footsteps. Then Mira sensed that the woman had stopped, and suddenly bright lights shone around them. She saw that they were in a bare concrete cavern, stretching away into shadow. Nearby lay the sleek shapes of three or four transports, painted in the Saint blue and gold.

The woman closed a flap in the wall. 'Come on!' She beckoned them on, impatiently. 'We don't have long.'

Mira said: 'We had thought to take a boat. If we can but get beyond the building we'll be fine.'

'No. A boat will not help you. The sea lock is already closed. Young Barbieri has moved quickly.'

'If not a boat, how then must we go? In one of these?' She gestured at the softly shining transports.

'No.' The woman was leading them to a shadowed area, further under the heart of the building. 'Any of these might do for a while,' she said; 'but they use electricity. They are designed only for the city and their range is limited. And besides that, they are all fitted with trackers, so that security can monitor them. They would take too long to disable.'

Security. Watching, always watching. What a terrible place, a terrible life. Mira looked up at the low dark ceiling and sure enough there were the unblinking camera eyes that lay everywhere. What would they make of this strange little group moving into the shadows, she wondered.

Tilly said 'Lights', and more brightness spread around them.

Mira almost laughed, despite her fatigue. 'And what are these, then? Skidoos with wheels? Do they no fall over?'

Kay's mother smiled back at her faintly, but did not laugh. 'Motobikes. I used to take Kay and his sister outside the city, when he was younger. The stiltways were better kept then, and there were dry fields. But it is not easily forgotten. He was a good pupil. He will remember now.'

Mira doubted that. Kay stood at her elbow, lost in his own uncertain world.

'But first, tell me: where are you headed? Have you thought?'

Silently, Mira took out the picture of the little girl Adeline and showed it, following her instinct to trust this Tilly. The woman took the picture, looked at it. Then she looked long and hard at Mira herself, locking eyes with her.

'This is well done,' she said at last. 'You are truly the best of us. I will do what I can to help you. When you leave here . . .'

She broke off. There was a shout. Feet running down the garage level towards them.

'Quick! We have taken too long. You must go.' She slipped a hand into her tunic, took out a tiny gold square, and gave it to the girl; plastic or metal, Mira couldn't say. 'Take that. Keep it safe. It is precious. Precious information. It belongs to all of us. All Briton, when the right day should come.'

The first figure rounded the corner to their alcove, clad in Pax grey, carrying a weapon. Tilly span and kicked the weapon away neatly, knocked the man sprawling. '*Kay!*' she cried, turning to face the second man. 'The motobike! You must ride! Take the girl to safety. You must go across the old floating bridge. Go to France, Kay!'

Her words were drowned out by shots. Sparks flew from the wall. Tilly had taken the weapon from the second attacker, felled him as neatly as the first, and was firing down the length of the garage.

'Get him moving!' she called to Mira. 'Make him see that all was done through love.'

Then she had disappeared round the corner, gone to face the attackers.

At last Kay seemed to be waking up, looking around him, puzzled, unhappy. 'The *motobike!*' Mira cried in his ear, shaking him roughly, fighting to remember the strange word. 'We are to ride the *motobike* across the old, floating bridge to France. We must go now!'

He made no reply but went slowly to the first machine, unclipped a metal disk in front of the seat and looked inside. Whatever he saw seemed to satisfy him. He turned to Mira, gestured limply at the wall behind her. 'There. Those. Helmets. Jackets.'

She turned and saw the row of black spheres, took two down, handed him one. By the time she had hers on, the garage was filled with a deep, thrilling, roar, the noise of the old machine coming to life. She pushed one of the thick black jackets at Kay, wriggled into one herself.

Spirits above, Mira thought, is he fit to do this?

But there was no choice. She scooped up the second dropped weapon and climbed on behind him. Kay turned the machine around with a screech and a jerk. Ahead, further up the garage, there was thick smoke, people running and shooting, more sparks flying. Kay did something with his hand and they leaped forward, accelerating through the confusion, weaving to avoid the bursts of smoke and figures lying unmoving on the ground. At the end they braked and turned sharply right, going up a short, steep slope. The top of the slope was a steel gate. Even as they accelerated towards it, Tilly was there, opening the way for them, operating the gate release. Behind her a figure on the ground was coming back to its knees groggily. Looking over Kay's shoulder, Mira could see the figure groping for a fallen weapon. She raised her own gun, not knowing even if it would work and fired; again; and again; and again. The figure pitched forward, rolled once and was still.

With a bump that took the machine full off the ground for a second, they reached the exit level and came out into the grey afternoon. A few surprised figures turned towards them, came running, tried to block the way, but Mira hurled the gun at them and with a spurt of glorious speed they were through, tearing down the hill, leaving the Saint Building well behind.

Tilly Saint watched them go.

'That is well done, my darlings,' she whispered, 'on a day when much is badly done for us.'

She sighed, and thrust away the deep weariness within her. She would need to be strong for what lay ahead.

She spoke into her wristcom. 'Christo. This is the time. We need distractions.'

Within seconds there were explosions from several places in the city. Shouts rang out. Smoke could be seen.

'I love you,' she said into the tiny microphone.

'And I you, crazy woman. Good luck. My spirit goes with you.'

But they had already said their real goodbyes. Whilst the guards turned to see the commotion below, she slipped out and past, and by the time they turned back she was lost amongst the lower buildings. She was on her own now.

TWENTY-FIVE

When Moore saw which way the wind was blowing –
when he heard the window-dressing accusations and of
the imminent arrival of the ICSA team, and saw how the
Barbieri boy or those behind him had turned things so
thoroughly against their old allies – then he already knew
where his own way must lie. Moore was not made to be
on the losing side.

When the message was brought of the escape of Mira
and Kay and of Tilly's disappearance, he smiled inwardly
with relief. It was a gift.

'I know the girl,' he said, 'I know her like no other.
I was her watcher. She was even sweet on me. Let me go
after her.'

'You?' The blond-haired cub was furious at the lapse
in his security. Yet his service was stretched. News
had also come of street riots, explosions, fire: even the
Pax Building itself had been attacked, it seemed. The
cub paced angrily, thinking, and Moore watched him
impassively.

For once Tomas truly looked the old man he was.
He looked lost. Moore did not even believe that he had
taken in his own treachery. The same could not be said
for Copper. The man looked at him with cold eyes. Just
let us meet once more, those eyes said. Moore ignored
him. It wouldn't happen: the man was bound tight by
restraining bands, as he himself was.

'OK,' the boy said finally. 'You may go after the spare.

But you will be fitted with a tracker and an enforcer.'

Moore was happy enough with that. He had his own score with Mira. And afterwards, there were ways to remove enforcer rings if one knew the right people. Or simply to neutralise the explosives inside.

All that mattered was that he gain his freedom. He stood while they unshackled him, and blew a kiss to Copper.

But the man was too well trained to let such a small thing get to him. Pity.

The wind buffeted Kay and Mira, making the machine slew back and forth on the road, and fresh rain blew hard through their clothing, trickling uncomfortably down inside. At times they came to great pools of water across the stiltway, where Kay had to slow to walking pace and still a plume of droplets shot up.

As yet, there was no sign of pursuit, though surely it must not be long.

To begin with, Mira had enjoyed the speed, the noise. They had crossed the city in a blur, dodged the astonished people and the Caplink wagons, thundered out of the western city gates, past policemen who had barely got to their feet before they were gone. It was freedom. It was escape, at last.

But as she held onto Kay's waist, exhausted, and the miles sped by, she thought again about all that had passed, about what she was, and especially about what old Tomas Saint had said. She couldn't think clearly. Her mind wouldn't work. Had he planned everything that had happened, from the shooting of Annie Tallis onwards? Surely no one person could control so much. And what had been his aim? To mould her? To make her into a tool he could use? She remembered how she had

been able to become a different, savage person today –
was it still today? – and shuddered. If it was indeed
Tomas' hand that had guided all, still she would not be
the tool he wished. She would save the child Adeline, live
peacefully somewhere . . .

But then a new thought came into her head. Perhaps
this also was intended?

She screwed up her face against the wetness of Kay's
back and thought: I will do it, because I choose to do it.
Because it is the right thing. Because it is what Mira
chooses.

PART THREE

My face in thine eye, thine in mine appears,
And true plaine hearts do in the faces rest,
Where can we finde two better hemispheares
Without sharpe North, without declining West?
What ever dyes, was not mixt equally;
If our two loves be one, or, thou and I
Love so alike, that none doe slacken, none can die.

John Donne (1572–1631),
'The Good Morrow'

TWENTY-SIX

Adeline Beguin knew that there was no more beautiful place than Marie's garden. Not even in the world, wherever that was.

She had fumbled out of her pretty white blouse, draped it round one of the great, fat, earth-brown pots, and was on her belly, following the weaving lines of flat stones set in the earth. Sometimes the smooth, sandy stone under her was hot, hot as the sun; sometimes a stone lying in the shade of the vine creepers was cool as the evening, making her tingle and shiver.

When she'd wormed her way through this paradise after the January monsoon, it had been crowded with surprising colour, a host of sprouting mauves and yellows and pinks. Like closing your eyes and pressing on the lids till the world inside swam, but much better. She'd never be found in that jungle. She'd lain on her back, cradled by the soft stalks towering halfway to heaven.

Now, in the same place, the earth around her stone trail was bare as her arm and smelled of the heat. But still it was paradise because of the many pots, piled over their tops with smaller stones, and with Marie's special plants squeezing out through the gaps. *Sauge* and *coriandre* and *lavande, estragon, romarin* . . . Adeline knew all their names. The perfume was like a drink.

Adeline was so happy here, she thought she'd burst.

Closing her eyes, feeling only with her fingertips and her belly, she set off towards the biggest, most mysterious forest of pots. Passing from sun to dappled shade and back, she curled her body round into the right shapes to slip through the forest, liking the way the curve of the clay would fit her own curve.

Many hours or many seconds later – she knew it was a long time – she came to her secret place at the edge of paradise and peeped over the low wall there. Down below, past the village, the lake stretched away from the fishery, an unbroken tongue of blue glass. Even the peasant boats were too far to see, out where the tongue became an expanse. On the landing beach, the strangers' boat lay on its side, and Marie was down there now, talking to them, holding a paper flat on the ground.

Maybe she had painted one of her pictures and was showing the strangers. Marie made such nice pictures. *'Alors, souriez!'* the little girl murmured. Smile then! If Marie was showing them a picture they must look happy, and not glance about so, as if they feared that the monsoon would come in a minute.

Maman's voice came floating across the garden. *'Ma puce. Ma puce!'* My flea. My flea!

Adeline could hear the soft flap-flap-flap of Maman's rope-soled shoes on the bare earth and stones. She lay flat and small along the base of the wall, half hidden by the great pots, but in the end the inevitable happened and there was Maman's smiling-worried face and her cloud of pale hair. She was hauled out gently, given a cuddle against Maman's breast and a drink of grape juice.

Maman murmured: 'Oh, but you are so dirty, my flea. Look at you! Look at your tummy!'

Adeline looked at her tummy. It looked fine, dark with the sun and dusted red-gold with the earth.

Then Maman said something interesting. She said: 'My poor flea. We will go up into the mountains tomorrow.

Just you and I and perhaps one of those men that came last night.'

Adeline considered. The mountains were hard like dragon's teeth, full of magic. 'Why must the man come? Marie can come.'

'Without doubt, Marie will come later.'

'Why is the man coming, Maman?'

'To keep us safe, my flea.'

TWENTY-SEVEN

'There. Stop it there. No; back a few frames.'

The security film ran slowly backwards in tiny, clear jumps. Mira the spare took her hand out of her clothing and was holding a flash of gold; then Tilly Saint was reaching to take back her gift.

'That's it. Now play that and give me some sound.'

The technician said: 'Not much sound to be had, sir. Too much background noise. They'd been discovered by then.'

'Give me whatever there is, then.' The man was an idiot.

The recording played forward once more, the slip of gold appeared and changed hands, the mouths moved, and all those present strained to make out the words.

'Information . . .'

The rest wasn't clear but Jan was sure of that one word. He had the recording played through four times to be sure, flint-eyed with anger. Then they let the images run on, heard Mira shouting at Kay that they must go to France, saw Tilly clearing the opposition from their way and then escaping herself. The whole sequence, recorded from many different camera points, had been roughly edited together into a fluid whole, seen from a range of angles. For that reason alone, even if there were no other, Clarissa would have been sure that it was being screened this time especially for her.

The fight itself. The meeting in Grandfather's office. Now the escape. She had seen all three, watching in sullen, defeated silence, hands resting in her lap, and the poison was doing its intended work well. Her moment of glory had been stolen from her, her grandfather had hinted at replacing her with the spare in case she could not control an alliance with Jan, her *mother* . . . her mother, who was *her*, had helped Kay and the spare escape and left her daughter to the wolves, humiliatingly trussed up in Kay's drum room. There was no room for doubt in any of these things.

But despite that, clear thought did not leave her. She could see what was happening here; the attempt to manipulate. She knew Jan's ways.

Now he had gone back again to the moment when Tilly handed the comcard to Mira, flaying himself with his failure, allowing his anger to build. Clarissa scorned this self-induced rage: the more so because she could feel a tiny echo of it in herself. Oh yes, she knew Jan. Grandfather was wrong if he'd thought she could not manage this cold-hearted boy.

As he watched the endlessly repeated images, Jan turned casually – as if it had just occurred to him! – and said over his shoulder: 'Miss Clarissa would probably like to return to her quarters now. I'm sure she's tired. Make sure she is very comfortable there. And very secure.'

Yes, she thought as four of them led her up to her rooms, now I am to sit alone and dwell on what I have seen, sink into a blackness of hate and rejection until I am needed. The trouble was, she wasn't sure that clear thought would be enough. The blackness might well win. Even as the doors closed behind her and she sank onto the bed, she could feel it rise up in her throat, worse than when they had bound her, her precious brother and the spare.

She could hardly believe, through her tears, how her

life had changed in a night and a day. She wasn't sure that she wouldn't decide to do what Jan wanted, when he asked.

Why shouldn't she?

In the room Clarissa had left, Pieter was saying, soothingly: 'It is unfortunate, but will come to nothing. Whatever information the Saint woman gave to the girl, both it and she will soon be back here. They all will. The ICSA commissioner will find nothing out of place when he arrives in the morning. No doubt you've located the spare and the young Saint?'

Jan nodded, glad to talk about success. 'Easy, once we knew where they were headed. Punch it up, Hunter.'

The looped security recording froze, faded and was replaced by images of a great waterlogged landscape, bleak and grey in the fading afternoon light. Hunter pressed more buttons and the picture sharpened, magnified. Now a shape could be seen travelling along a black band. Again some adjustments and the shape grew grainily into two-wheeled transport, travelling steadily on the stiltway. The images flickered out and were replaced by a basic, large-scale map, with a bright dot moving towards where the coastline was represented in red.

Hunter said to the control room in general: 'The photos were just a lucky thinning of the cloud cover. This is a heat-generated image from that engine. The satellite's able to pinpoint them to within three metres, even like this. We can't lose them.'

'Nothing on Tilly Saint yet?'

'No. She may even still be in the city, sir.'

They all watched the crawling dot that was Kay and Mira. Silently, Pieter put a frail, ivory hand on Jan's sleeve and led him to the back of the room. The old man no longer appeared reassuring, but instead troubled, compassionate. He spoke hesitantly, looking directly into Jan's eyes as if worried by what reaction his words might have in the boy.

'That woman. Tilly Saint. Has it occurred to you from the recordings that she might be . . . that she might have some . . . *contact* . . . with the Wrecker movement?'

Jan nodded impatiently. 'Of course. The explosions and attacks in the city began on her command. You can hear it quite clearly on the tape. She is a traitor to the Families.'

Pieter seemed relieved, almost shy. 'Quite so. Quite so.'

'Don't worry,' the boy reassured him. 'She'll be caught, even if the Wrecker scum are hiding her. The city is completely sealed.'

'Yes. I see. Well done. Well done.'

'And Clarissa has seen the security films herself. She'll jump at the chance to distance herself from her family, when she's had time to think. Just as you said.'

'Yes. Very well done.' The old man appeared to consider. 'And when will you pick up the boy and the girl? Ideally, we do need at least *her* to open our case with the ICSA commissioner. Living proof is always the most convincing.'

'A chopper team will leave shortly.' Jan smiled coldly. 'Don't worry about them. They're just kids, or *he* is, anyway. They haven't done their homework. The bridge is quite uncrossable. The team would have left earlier, but . . .'

'Quite.' Pieter nodded, understanding. 'All this trouble in the city.'

'Yes.'

'Well, you're doing a fine job, I'm sure. I think I will go to rest a little. Let us know, won't you, of developments?'

'Of course.'

Watching him go, the Executive Lieutenant felt confused. Magnus and Pieter were always so hard to read. Underneath the sympathetic words, had Pieter thought him incompetent for not acting sooner to bring back the spare: or for the chaos in the city? Surely not. The second of those, especially, was hardly his fault, was it? Look at all he'd had to do today! With a knife wound in his shoulder and every part of him aching from Slam! And what was all that stuff about Tilly? Why had the old man been suddenly so shifty about it?

What was he missing here?

Jan felt a fresh surge of anger. His head ached. It was all right for *that* old fart, saying do this or do that and have you done the other and then crawling to his bed. He should stay in his hole in Wales with his experiments and his test tubes. He and Magnus should leave security matters to the experts.

It was always hard to stay angry with the old men, though. They had been kind to him when no one else had. It would have been a vulnerable time for the family without the Board's protection. 'Bring back your dear parents later, using material from the vaults,' they'd said sympathetically. 'Later, when you've dealt with the rebels.'

If only some material could have been saved at Stoneywall . . .

Jan struggled to throw aside his doubts and focus on the matters in hand. First, the two kids on their antique machine. They could bother about the mother later.

'Is the chopper team ready, Hunter?'

'They left five minutes ago, sir.'

Five minutes ago. There. That was efficiency. They wouldn't even need that man Moore. Except perhaps to give evidence to ICSA.

'Good. Let's see the tape one more time then. I want to get a better look at the image the spare shows Tilly Saint in the garage level.'

As Maman fanned herself, and flapped about on the cool stone floor and nervously collected together the few things needed in the mountains, soothed and reassured by Marie's soft voice . . . as little Adeline's remarkable eyes were sheathed peacefully and fearlessly in their lids, to dream of the dragon's teeth, the bright dot on Hunter's screen came finally to the sea.

In her drifting consciousness, lulled by the steady growl of the engine, Mira thought at first that it was just more flooded land ahead. Then she woke up properly and saw the waves, breaking over the stiltway sides. The dark was coming down to end this long, long day, but those were real waves, right enough, green giants crested with white. Kay brought them to a halt. He stopped the engine and climbed stiffly off his seat on the machine. His face was pale, with a faint bluish tinge.

He said dully: 'We should eat something, before we try it.' He felt in his clothes, looked in the carrying box on the motorcycle. But there was nothing, not even water.

Mira stood silently, her eyes fixed on the road that went across the sea. The bare rails at the side of the stiltway seemed to give way to proper walls, as tall as she would be with fingertips raised up, although even then the wind-whipped swell managed to surge over the top from time to time, pouring out again in a foamy cascade from gaps at the wall base. But there was something else not right about this road. It *moved* when the waves struck it.

Following her gaze, Kay said: 'They got it wrong, all those years ago. Just like they did with the roads on land.'

Mira waited a minute for more, then prompted, 'How was it wrong, then?'

He glanced at her, scowling. 'It cost so much that they thought they'd give themselves a safety margin. So it's all in sections. Each section has supports going down fifty metres to air containers, and the containers are tethered to the sea floor. They thought a floating road would be OK – but one that sat well above the surface of the sea. The tethers could be lengthened if the sea rose too much. It would last for ages, they thought. Idiots.'

'A floating road,' she repeated, glad that he was talking again. 'So what happened?'

He shrugged. 'The tethers were let out fully but the sea kept on rising. There was a limit, you see? Every kilometre there's a proper support, going all the way to the bottom. To limit the sideways movement and make it all more secure, hold everything taut. The road can ride up and down those supports on rails, but it reached the top ages ago. So now the road is half in the water. Soon the whole lot will get swept away.' He shrugged again: 'It hasn't been used in my lifetime. It may already be broken.'

Abruptly he was climbing back onto the motobike, pulling on the strange balloon-like helmet, retreating into silence.

She climbed on behind him and shouted in his ear, 'But where does it go, this floating road?' and she caught his faint shouted reply through the helmet:

'To France, of course.'

Then he restarted the engine and further talk was not possible.

Mira felt the bump and lurch as the front wheel, then the back, took them onto the floating road. Although she could not see clearly, she guessed now that there must be some sort of flexible, moving part between each floating section: certainly the bump led sharply upwards, up to where the first section strained at the end of its tether, pushed up by the hidden air containers, yet unable to rise clear of the swell. At the same time, the walls began, shutting out the strong side wind: dark metal barriers, bubbled and blistered with rust under the thick paint, curving slightly inwards at the top. The whole tube-like structure jerked and shuddered nervously under the impact of the waves.

Mira wondered how they would stay on the machine. The water crashed over the tube wall, raining heavily down on their right-hand side, forcing them dangerously close to the other barrier, swilling around the wheels. And then it happened again. And again, without end.

To begin with they did no more than edge forwards, as they had done on the worst of the flooded land sections. The machine slewed drunkenly under the wave impacts, heading from one side of the way to the other and back. But perhaps Kay realised that their balance was lessened at a slower speed, for Mira felt the machine leap forward as he savagely twisted the throttle. From then on, he took them quite fast down a line about four metres from the right-hand barrier. If he strayed any closer the descending water came right over their heads and pushed them right instead of left. He had to *know* which way the water's impact would carry them and to have eight or nine metres of width for correction or he could not hope to keep them upright.

As dark fell, bright light stabbed out from the front of the machine, illuminating the juddering, wet tube that stretched endlessly ahead of them. A continuous arc of water rose up from the wheels on each side of them, like angels' wings against the light. Each time a new wave broke they hurtled in towards the left-hand wall, so that the weaving headlight picked out every mark and blister on the rotting metal before they corrected to the right once more. Turning her head, she strained to see behind, but there was only the sea-stiltway, lit eerily by their red tail light, and again black night beyond. Briton was gone.

As time passed, Mira found herself getting used to the passage. Despite the icy torrents of seawater and the heaving of the road, she felt herself slip towards sleep again, her face nodding forwards against Kay's bony shoulder. Her own aching, exhausted body would not listen to her desire to stay awake. She fought to make herself remember everything that had happened since she last had proper sleep, an age ago. Poor Bee, lying unmoving on the ground; the sudden nausea of knowing that Gil still lived; the time spent with her strange, scornful, frightened twin; the huge, glittering room in which she had had to fight; terrifying, wily old Tomas, controlling everything from his nest at the tower top, ordering her death without the bat of an eyelid . . . But each thing merged meaninglessly into the next, so that the whole made nothing more than a fairy tale.

Every few seconds, she would reawaken with a start in the drenching spray. She held more tightly onto Kay. He seemed so young. So lost. Even more so since he had learned that he, too, was a . . . copy. It was good that he had this task now to concentrate upon.

Bump. Another section. And another. Between sleeping and waking, she quickly lost count. Was it twenty-three, or thirty-three? She had no idea how far they must cross. France might be ten miles or fifty.

May we arrive in the new country soon.

She was aware of thinking this, sometime in one of the shivering, almost-waking moments, and then the next thing was sudden noise and pain and light.

And nothing.

When she could work it out, she found with surprise that she was no longer on the machine. She was lying on the road surface, with the sea foam surging around her body, moving it a little. The light and noise had gone: the pain remained. It was full night and the only sound was from the waves and the creaking of ancient metal.

'Kay?'

There was a pause, then his voice from a few metres away: 'Yes. Yes, I'm here.'

'What happened?'

She heard him groan and soon afterwards a dark shape loomed up before her. 'A big wave. We hit the wall. Are you hurt?'

'Nae. I don't think so. Just bruised. I don't know. What about the machine?'

'I'll have a look.'

The shape retreated again and she heard him struggling with something, then the sound of the engine trying to start, over and over.

'The water's got into it,' he called. And then: 'I can hardly see, though.'

Mira took a deep breath, then rolled over in the surf and struggled up to her hands and knees, then to her feet, in time to meet the next shower of spray, breaking full in her face and making her eyes sting. She rubbed the water away from them and blinked. That was wrong. She could see little lights dancing in the distance. She blinked again, but the lights would not disappear. Instead, they grew perceptibly larger. And now, over the top of the engine-starting noise and the sea, she heard a new deeper note.

She went over to where Kay was bent over the machine. 'Come on, come *on*!' he was saying angrily.

She touched his arm – 'Kay?' – and without looking

up he said, tightly: 'Yes. I know. I've seen. A helicopter.'

An image came to her of an unlikely beast of a machine, something with long spidery-thin arms that was supposed to fly. The lights in the sky were close – the speed of these machines must be tremendous – and she saw that they were bobbing along over the road that led back to Briton. There was little doubt what they were looking for.

'Will it work or no?' she asked Kay.

He had stopped pushing the starting button, and was poking his hands into the greater shadow at the heart of the machine. She saw him bring something out and then he was thrusting the thing at her. 'Here! Dry this if you can. Quickly!' It felt like a metal net, a cylinder slick with the salt water and with oil. She searched for a piece of dry clothing to rub the thing against. Kay was doing the same with other pieces, cursing as one dropped from his fingers onto the drenched stiltway surface so that he had to grope around and begin anew.

The helicopter was almost overhead now. Kay glanced up and muttered the word 'Pax'. Then, impatiently: 'Here, have you got that thing?'

She gave it to him and bright white shone suddenly down on them from above and behind. There was a gale of petrolly wind from above and a deafening roar from the hidden engines, as the beast inched into a position directly overhead. The beam of light, now it had them, held them tight in its glare. Then, as she watched, half blinded and feeling curiously detached, a rope came falling down out of the light, and another, and a third.

A harsh, male voice echoed down, competing with the noise: 'Stay where you are. Do not attempt to move out of the light. I repeat. Stay in the light or we will open fire.'

Kay was pushing the engine pieces back: she could see his hands shaking in the glare, a film of sweat or seawater on his face. Above, there were figures coming quickly down the hanging ropes, six figures in all, gliding towards the ground as smoothly as spiders on a strand of web. Unsurprised, she saw that they wore pale grey.

Mira wondered what she could do, dug inside to see if any reserve of energy still lay there. Kay was back to pressing the button and, faintly against the more powerful noise, she heard the bike's engine trying to start. Without the motobike it would be hopeless, she knew. If necessary, then, she must give him more time.

With this thought, she went slowly to the writhing end of the nearest rope and looked up. Up close, the rope was not a rope at all, but a thin line of twisted steel strands, weighted at the bottom. It was like the cable Evan and his men had used to cross the second loch. The first bulky grey figure was halfway down. She wished she had something to fight with: there was nothing but her hands. Without thinking, her fingers twisted around the cable. She could feel it jerk and twitch with the weight of the two men above. Experimentally, she pulled hard and to the side, but with no effect, except to swing the men a little.

Think.

She looked around for inspiration and saw now that there was a single rail running along the curved metal wall, near the top. A tiny sliver of an idea formed itself. If she could only drag the cable end there against the men's weight . . .

Behind her, the bike engine struggled back to life, first hesitantly, then with its full roar. She glanced round to be sure and saw the twin jets of blue-white coming out in pencil lines from the shiny pipes at the back. Kay, helmetless, was beckoning, shouting at her – at least, she could see his mouth moving – and climbing onto the machine.

Good. Luck was with them. With the bike working her idea might be worth something. Quickly she heaved on the cable end once more, dragging it a metre or two towards the side barrier. When it was close enough, she took the weighted ball at the end of the cable in one hand, and swung it up towards the rail.

The ball hit the barrier a few centimetres below the rail and bounced down, catching her on the shoulder.

A second try. She hauled again on the wire, feeling it tear the skin of her palm with the increasing, wriggling weight of the descending men. More weight because they were now lower down: it would be harder each try. Again she swung the ball, and this time saw it sail up in a smooth arc and drop neatly over the rail, so that when she released the slack, the wire came down against the barrier. Now another loop would be needed, quickly. And a third if possible.

Probably it would do nothing. Probably they could release the cable at the helicopter end. Behind her the motobike engine revved angrily and Kay still shouted unheard: but Mira knew they would not outrun the flying machine. That was sure.

If she could only . . .

Thud.

Even as she was swinging the weight for the third time, the nearest man – perhaps understanding what she wished to do – jumped the last five metres and his boots struck Mira in the back. Then she and he were both flat on the ground, tangled up together, trying feebly to free themselves. If anything, he had fallen more awkwardly than her, coming down from that height, but his weight was half across her, like a great squirming sack of grain, all heavy boots and thick cloth, impossible to move.

And then Kay was above them both, swinging the black

balloon-helmet down in a fast arc, and Mira felt the man
go limp. Kay was rolling him off her. He was helping her
up. Two other men were just reaching the bottom of their
wires, unclipping themselves.

'One more loop,' she cried to Kay, pointing at the wire.
He was trying to pull her back to the bike. Why couldn't
he understand? 'No!' she shouted in his ear. 'I will not go.
Help me!'

He seemed to shrug; went to the hanging cable end and
started to swing it himself.

That left her to face the two men, who were covering
their faces with slim shining masks, taking out weapons.
Casting about for her own weapon, Mira grabbed the
helmet from the ground and flung it at the first, running
forward, shouting at him like the men at home would
shout at the wolves, when there was a pack to be driven
away. At her feet something flashed and then thick,
choking smoke was filling the whole tube of the roadway.
Knowing now that she should hold her breath, she
ran on in the fog, surprising the first man, knocking
him sideways. In his moment of imbalance, she flailed
her fingers across his face and managed to latch onto
the mask, pushing it away from the nose and mouth.
Immediately her victim doubled up with coughing, then
slid unconscious to the ground.

Using up more precious seconds, she looked wildly
about for the second man. He was no longer visible, so
she turned around, to make for the bike and the edge of
the smoke. Her lungs were bursting, her eyes streaming,
and suddenly she was not sure that she faced the right
way. What about Kay, she wondered distantly. Had he
got out of the choking cloud?

A shape which might be the missing second man – or
perhaps another from above? – loomed up like a ghost

and lunged at her, fingers fastening on her forearm, but she shook him off, backed away into the white. Her head was spinning. Soon she must breathe or pass out.

Then, when she least expected it, there was a tear in the cloud. The smoke was starting to clear, blown away by the helicopter blades. Sure enough, as she groped her way forwards, a figure was revealed quite close to her, then another, then another. Three or four of them, surrounding her, closing in. The brightness from above grew as the smoke thinned, leaving her nowhere to hide.

Then, with a savage howl, the motobike was there too, the front wheel forcing the men a pace back as it circled and slipped and skidded on the slick surface, the back wheel throwing up a jet of spray at the masked faces.

As it came round and slowed, she thankfully, weakly, pulled herself up behind Kay. They were moving even before her leg was fully over, so that she had to snatch at his waist to stay on. The back wheel slid left and right with the acceleration as they ripped back out of the last of the smoke. And then they were away, taking in the sweet air in great shuddering gasps, with bright sparks springing from the metal walls, where the men fired after them.

When the world stopped swimming, Mira looked back, blinking. Those on the ground had been left behind, but what of the flying machine? The searchlight slid quickly along the road surface after them, pinning them like butterflies, the voice from above was speaking again, then sure enough the crouching spidery beast leaned forward, began to advance . . .

It was as she'd thought. They had simply released the trapped line from the top. It had been a wasted fight.

Then, before the helicopter had moved five metres, it paused abruptly, tipped further forward, and fell in slow motion onto the road, the steel line stretched taut behind it. As the spinning blades touched the tube walls there was a flurry of golden sparks, a terrible grinding. The blades themselves stopped, jammed and twisted, and the machine at the centre turned instead, hard to the side, slewing round on its skids with its own engine's power so that nose and tail smashed into opposite walls.

Then silence from the beast. And darkness behind once more, save for the red glow from their own tiny light.

'Are you getting this?' Moore asked a little later, playing his camera over the smoking carcass of the helicopter, not quite keeping the grin from his voice.

Damn him.

'Yes. We're getting it. Can you get past?'

'Aye. I expect so. With a little effort.'

'Get on with it then. We want the girl brought back quickly. Before morning, if possible.'

'I understand.'

'And alive, Moore. Do you understand that?'

'Don't worry. Nothing to upset your precious ICSA. Out.'

Jan shut the link. 'The man's a menace. What do you think, Hunter? Can we trust him?'

'No.'

'Even with the enforcer?'

'Even with the enforcer. His feud with the girl is too personal.'

Jan rubbed his eyes. His bound shoulder throbbed. This day should be a glorious one, the first bold step towards a better life in Briton. How had it dissolved so quickly into chaos? Fighting in the streets, fires, Tilly Saint gone and the spare too. Whatever support they had from the other Families would melt rapidly away if he could do no better.

It was difficult to think clearly. Everyone was just waiting for him to make mistakes. Even Hunter, who should be loyal above all else: even he was just sitting there, eyes half closed in his grizzled head, as if he could hardly bear to contemplate the mess.

Jan came to a decision. He said, sharply: 'Send another chopper, then. In case Moore can't get to them.'

'But the fuel! The men!'

'Hunter. The delegation will be here in ten hours at the latest. Don't you think it would be good to have something to show them?'

'Another chopper . . .' the man repeated, sourly.

'Yes. Another chopper. *Now*. Send it to the far end of the bridge, out of trouble, simply as insurance. Then, if Moore succeeds in getting them at the breach, we can use it to bring the prisoners back. And if he fails, our team can take them anyway.'

Hunter tapped out the commands stiffly but without more argument, and the boy-man sat lost in thought, pleased with his decision.

France. Why were they running to France? Answer: seemingly, to rescue or contact another spare. Little more than a baby by the look of that image print-out the one called Mira was carrying. But why in heaven would they bother to do that? It was foolishness. Surely Kay at least would know that the French Families would happily grant permission for the hunt to move there, even if it took a day or two. After all, it was an ICSA matter. If Jan himself had been the runaway, he'd have tried to lose himself inland, amongst the many islands, as Tilly Saint had doubtless done.

Did Moore know what else lay in France to tempt them? he wondered.

It was of no consequence. Even now, Kay and the spare

could not reach that country. Moore would get them, and if he didn't there was the second chopper. After all, they didn't need the baby spare themselves. They could kill it later or leave it alone as they chose. The one called Mira would be enough, with the rest of their evidence. Gods above, the farts from ICSA would be pleased enough to be consulted about *something*. They'd be falling over themselves to ratify the changes that had taken place here, with Mira and the Stoneywall evidence.

'*Sir!*'

Jan shook himself: he must have drifted off. His mouth was dry.

He needed another painkiller for his shoulder.

'Sir. We have a problem. The satellite just went down.'

TWENTY-EIGHT

Tilly dropped her wristcom into the black marsh.

She sat on a soft hummock of moss in the darkness and made a short recording, then her handset followed the wristcom, with a soft splash.

She looked at the water and considered what she had done. She thought of the wise, wild, horse-loving people that she knew had once lived across these sinking lands, watching the stars, raising their open, stone temples, treating life and death with reverence, as a mystery. Did their ghosts watch still, waiting for Briton to wake and find itself?

She, too, would be a ghost soon, singing in the wind. She was tired as never before, but deeply stirred by the simple thing she had done. It left her alone in the night, alone under the iron sky, a heart pumping its hot scarlet blood, a mind reaching out to understand, a cunning animal, a mystery, inconsequentially small in this world that was made for it.

Surely, this was how the horse people had felt?

The wristcom and handset had had to go of course. They would betray friends that she would not want found. The satellites, though . . . that was a much bigger thing. The end of the human contact with space that had seemed exciting and important for less than a century, before the seas rose and ice spread across the north of Europe. No new satellite had been launched in over a hundred years. Who now had the fuel, the resources, the will, the organisation to spend on such matters? From the hundreds of machines that, over time, had been sent to circle the planet, fewer and fewer were working.

Had she the right to destroy that tool? She thought she had.

Just as she was now alone and free with the singing ghosts of the horsemen, this country was thus set free. Free to ... *what*? That was hidden from her. She was a child, feeling her way forward, not even knowing what it was that she hoped for. Except change. An end to the empty lust for control that had saddled her species for so long.

Time to move.

Leaving the door to the communications bunker open to the weather, Tilly set off into the night, running with the ghosts and a smile on her lips. Perhaps it was the gene-memory in her that understood about true freedom.

TWENTY-NINE

There was no new sign of pursuit.

Under the force of the waves the whole bridge rattled and shuddered and leaped beneath the bike wheels.

At one point they stopped and Mira saw that the flexible apron between two sections was partly missing, so that the sea repeatedly surged up through the gap, then drained away again, leaving only a centimetre or two of water on the slick road surface. Kay circled the machine to time the crossing, waiting until the water was retreating before accelerating fast over the piece of road that remained intact. Soon after this, the way changed. The front wheel bumped over another join and then they were climbing, leaving the sea far below. Even better, this section of road was solid and unmoving, so that Kay could make the machine leap forward again. The wind howled up the tube, buffeting them, but the road surface was dry. Beyond the metal tube walls Mira could make out great steel arches, flashing past, marching upwards with them.

Like a true bridge, she thought. A place for all the great ships to pass.

Sure enough, in time the road reached the top of its climb and started to descend once more, following the graceful line of a flattened arc. Kay turned his helmetless head, hair splayed out in the wind, and shouted something quite incomprehensible over the engine roar. His hand came off the handlebars and pointed into the darkness ahead, though Mira could see nothing there.

Then they were down again, off the safe, dry surface, and continuing as before along the perilous, sea-washed road.

Were they close to France? Was that what he meant? Let it come soon, then: let it come soon. Even on the back of the machine, shielded a little by Kay's body, Mira was shivering, colder than she'd ever been in all her life amongst the ice and snow of the North.

If only we could move . . .

As she thought this, she felt the motobike slow alarmingly. Her body weight was thrown forward against Kay, her head knocked sharply against his, and then the wheels were sliding as they locked solid on the treacherous surface. In slow motion, the back wheel twisted round, the bike tipped downwards and they and the machine keeled over into the brine. The two riders rolled across the road, in a sprawling heap of limbs. The bike slid a little further under its greater momentum, the engine still rumbling. Then . . . nothing.

Mira did not need Kay to tell her why they had again landed on the road. She saw why, and felt sick. No more than seven or eight metres ahead, at the place where one floating section should join with the next, there was a long, long gap, filled with boiling white froth. The bike, nowhere to be seen, must have been swallowed by the sea: that was why the noise had cut out so suddenly. A second later and they would have joined it, she thought. But the thing that made her nauseous was *after* the gap: a huge tilting shape, a piece of road standing on its side as it should not. It was like a wall, end on to them, rocking back and forth with the sea's unstoppable power.

Silently they rose and went as close to the gap as they dared.

On one side – the right – the wall ahead was roadway surface, half submerged, flanked at what was now the top by the metal side-barrier: on the other, the left, a complex network of metal struts gave way to huge cylinders, stretching straight out across the waves, heaving up and down, rolling the road section as if it weighed nothing.

'Shit.'

'The tethers must hae broken,' Mira murmured, understanding. 'The air containers came bobbing up to the surface and twisted all else to the side.' She looked at Kay. 'What can we do? Go back?'

He stood undecided, giving no answer. He was shivering and pale, his teeth chattering. He looked near to giving up. She went to him and rubbed hard at his back. 'We should move.'

He said, blankly: 'The helicopter. Pax. They wouldn't let us get back across. And what chance would we stand on foot?'

She went closer still to the black edge where the flexible apron had been ripped away. The sea thundered through the gap with its terrible power, but in amongst the dark waves and the foam she thought she could see . . . something. Lying full length, letting the icy salt water run through her clothing once more, she felt numbly down past the edge, with her hand. The sea fought her, tried to snatch the hand from its purpose; but yes, there was a thick cable, thicker than her wrist – two cables when she explored further – running taut through the water. Maybe there were more, further along, but probably any others would have snapped: these two cables were at the centre, heading for the pivot point of the broken section. They vibrated and sang in the waves.

Spitting out seawater, she went back to where the boy stood, watching. Already he was shaking his head, scornful, hopeless. 'Go through *that*? We'd never make it.'

'Aye, we could.'

He looked at her sharply, still caught unawares by how little she was like the lost soul of Portable Road. 'How then? The water's freezing. And strong enough to break that section of road. What chance would *we* have?'

'More chance than there is in going back, I'm thinking. It's just that first part, ten metres: och, maybe less. After that we'd be climbing through all the metal there, well above the water and out of the wind.'

'And for the first part? Your easy ten metres?'

She touched his sleeve. 'Take that off and I'll show you.'

Unzipping her own soaking jacket, she led the way back to the broken edge. It was strange, she thought. She could hardly move for the deep fatigue within her, yet she had no doubt of their ability to do this thing, and how it must be done. The spray lashed her frozen cheek, cold and sharp and thrilling.

If the helicopters should find us here, it is over.

She slipped out of the stiff leather garment, flexing her limbs to get the blood into them, and lay down once more on the dark surface, her face half in the waves that thundered through the breach. Feeling along under the edge she located the thick, twisted cable, felt it sing with the impact of the water. She gripped it tight and plunged the second hand down, taking the jacket with it. The water caught the leather like wind in a sail, but she fought the pull until the fabric was hard against the cable, and managed with her free hand to drag a piece underneath.

Now the most difficult part. She closed her eyes to concentrate only on what her fingers were doing, and carefully brought the two sides of the material together in the torrent, inching her hands along until they found the zip and where it must fasten. With the cold of the water her arms were losing their feeling. *Wait!* she told them: *work a moment yet.* The two little corners of metal rubbed against each other, deep down in the foam, and then rubbed again. The third time they became joined.

Somewhere next to her Kay was speaking. But she did not hear. All her life was in that little union of the metal and the finger ends that must nurture it. She teased the tag up into her grasp and started to run it away from her, cementing the tiny steel teeth together. And then it was done, and she could withdraw from the edge.

Kay caught her wordlessly and held her close against him. His body was as cold as her own. They must keep moving. It was the law of survival in the cold.

'Your turn, Kay Saint,' she gasped. 'Try there. There's a second cable.'

She watched as he too removed his jacket and lay full length, half smothered by the seawater. Yesterday, she thought inconsequentially, he had been a prince of the world, safe in his palace of rooms in the glass and steel of the Saint Building.

Lost for some moments, she saw that the boy was still lying there. How long?

She bent down next to him and shook his shoulder. Calling his name she started to roll him back, away from the edge. His face was white, the eyes closed. She slapped the cheeks, put him on his side, and at last felt the lifeless body convulse in a spasm of coughing as he spewed up seawater.

When he could speak he said, faintly: 'What next?'

'We get warm. Then we must cross.'

She helped him up and took his hand, pulling him back along the way they had come at a steady jog, back towards the humped bridge section that soared up ahead of them. Kay coughed and gasped for breath but she kept a firm hold of the icy hand and forced him to follow as the road started to climb up through the thin black arches.

'Can't – bloody – do – this,' he said, between breaths.

'Aye. You can,' she gasped back.

Gradually as they toiled upwards, a little life came back, a little warmth. Halfway up the climb Mira felt that her bruised, heavy limbs had begun to move more easily and hauled Kay around to retrace their steps down to the broken section. As she did so, the thing came that she feared; the faint, far-off noise of an engine.

She paused to listen. What would it be? A second helicopter?

Kay showed no sign of having heard, and there was no use spending time waiting to see what would come. Already they were getting cold again.

They set off, running down the dry slope and onto the wet, hand in hand. Kay breathed heavily beside her but said nothing.

At the breach the water seemed to thunder more loudly even than before.

'Right then,' she said matter-of-factly to Kay, summoning the courage for herself as much as for him. 'This must be done *now* without thinking about it, and without getting too cold again. It's simple enough. We each find a jacket sleeve – are you listening to me, then? – find a jacket sleeve, put our arm tight through. Twist it to make it tighter. Then we use the other arm to pull along the cable, or swim if that's easier. It's ten metres. Only ten metres. Count them as you go.'

She squeezed his hand and he echoed faintly, face turned to the thundering, hissing water: 'Only ten metres. Who goes first?'

'You do.'

'You're as bossy as my sister.'

She went with him to the edge, helped him lie down and grope under the water. Then, he heaved himself into the sea and was immediately hidden from her, no matter how she scanned the faint lightness of the foam. Whether he was making progress or had been swept clean away, she did not know. Either way, he was beyond help.

My turn, then . . .

She lay in the cold brine and found the zipped-up jacket easily enough, groped for a sleeve and wormed her hand along inside it, fighting the water as she had before. Then, not giving herself time to feel the fear, she was in the sea, without breath, without strength, pulled and buffeted towards Kay's cable by the surging current. She needn't have worried about gripping hard enough: the sea had twisted her around so fiercely, pressing painfully into her wound, that even if she wished to release herself it would be impossible.

She must do this or drown. An easy choice.

She flailed forwards with her spare hand and struck the metal she sought, then latched on properly, gave a heave, felt the jacket snag behind her as it was pulled flat and shrugged it free. Then again. Then a rest to climb half up on the cable with her face tilted clear of the water so that she could take a new breath. Then down into the water to repeat the progress.

One metre. Two metres. Three?

After three she was no longer sure. The cold was already doing its work, stealing all feeling from the fingers that must locate the wire and pull, clouding the clear intention that she had started with.

Dear fathers . . .

At last, in another lifetime, another reality, she found that she was alive, and hanging on to the first struts of the metal cage that should normally support the road. Kay was there too – his hand had helped her from the water.

'Ready?' he gasped, and she nodded, too spent to speak.

Slowly, they climbed further up into the rocking, shuddering network to where the metal was dry and easier to grip, and then headed onwards, hand over hand, towards France, trusting that the next bridge section would be intact.

In a while, Mira looked back. The breach was still just in sight, lit faintly now by a cloud-smothered moon. She thought she could see a figure standing there, with some dark shape a few metres behind it, large enough to be transport. As she watched, the figure seemed to stoop down at the water's edge, and then disappear.

THIRTY

Early morning in the mountains was fragrant and cool. If one had to travel, this was the time. By nine o'clock the sun would beat at you like an iron bar.

The little procession left Le Porge before the sun was up. Marie was leading, slight and tireless, talking to Maman and helping her with her basket. Behind them came not one but two men, two of the six strangers whose boat lay on the landing beach. Their skins were burnt dark from the days spent in the open and they both wore long moustaches. Little Adeline skipped around them, a bright slash of colour in peasant yellow and red against their faded tunics and broad hats, and asked them a stream of questions.

'What are your names? How do you know Marie? Why are you coming onto the mountain with us? Are you going to do the cooking? Maman does not like to cook! Why won't you answer?'

It was like a tiny bird fluttering around two grizzled donkeys.

'Peace, little one,' laughed Marie over her shoulder. 'You must not always think that others want to talk as you do. Maybe Eric and his brother are happy simply to walk and look around them. You could learn from this yourself.'

'Eric!' Adeline seized upon the information. 'Oh, but it is an *ugly* name. Which of you is Eric? Is it you, Monsieur?' She tugged at one man's trouser leg and he looked slowly down at her, bared his teeth in a mock growl so that she looked uncertain a moment and took a step back.

'My brother over there is Eric. It is he who has this ugly name, little snakelet. I am blessed to be called Serge.'

'Oh, but Monsieur,' the girl said seriously, 'I am so sorry. Serge is much much worse.'

The man called Eric laughed aloud at this, and after a moment, looking perplexed, his brother joined him.

'Listen to her!' Maman said, half proud, half worried that her daughter would offend. 'She could make the mountains themselves speak, she goes on so.'

'Yes,' Marie agreed. 'It is a great gift.'

They climbed steadily, resting often to take fruit and water, choosing the shadowed side of the valley whenever they could, and soon the sweat ran down their bodies and the little girl became silent, carried in turn by the others. When they came in mid-morning to the low, double peak that they must pass through to come to the lodge, the man called Serge was left behind. With the things from his pack he began to make himself a cloth shelter, pegged onto the bare rock, and of the same ancient grey-brown. They left him heating water for coffee, settling down to watch the long, scrub-filled valley that led to this place.

'But why will you not come with us?' Adeline said sadly, resting her tiny hand on his shoulder. 'I have been to the lodge before. It is very cool and there is water also.'

He gave her a craggy smile. 'I am to be the door keeper. I will welcome any guests that come in search of you, little snakelet. Off you go now. Your maman is waiting.'

They set off again, with the child riding high on Eric's shoulders, her fingers clamped around the broad hat. Now the heat made the way three times as hard. You had to concentrate and watch out for the dizziness that could put your foot wrong and send you tumbling down the scree. Maman's dress was wet and lank, sticking to her sides. Even Marie struggled in her shorts and vest. The little girl did not mind so much. She closed her eyes, soaked up the heat, heard it vibrating in the rocks, rustling in the low bushes. It was not usual to be out in the sun at this time, but if one must, then surely it was important to welcome it as a friend. Or so it seemed to her.

And then when they came to the cool, cool lodge, she would smell the earth floor, put her back against the stones, play hide-and-seek in the shadows of the walls.

'Will they really come?' Maman asked Marie, not for the first time. 'Is my little flea so important to them?'

And as before, Marie merely said: 'In the cool season, one fastens the shutters, even if the monsoon might not appear for many nights.'

And in her head, she ran over her slight preparations and hoped that the monsoon would indeed not come.

THIRTY-ONE

Moore looked scornfully at the black wedge of the chopper, sitting at the bridge end, just inside the French border post. Useless! The Pax team were smoking with the two French guards, throwing dice with them under an arc-light, no doubt gambling away their equipment and pay.

He came quite close before they even noticed him, though the first light of day was growing behind the broken cloud cover, showing strips of pale blue. When they did register his presence, they leaped up, reached for weapons: but somebody must have remembered to tell them about him for they paused and did not fire. Then, when he was closer still, they saw his enforcer ring and nudged each other and guffawed. It made him even more pleased that his little Mira had not been stopped by this useless lot.

'I take it that you've seen nothing?' he asked the corporal in charge.

'Not a sausage,' the man said cheerfully. 'They haven't come this way. Got swept off at that smashed-up bit, I reckon. Drove clean into the sea.'

Moore did not smile. He glanced at the helicopter, gestured. 'You carry a dinghy in that, don't you?'

'Course,' said the man. 'In case we've got to ditch.'

'Good. I'll need to take it. And rations for a week. And fuel for the motor.'

'Here, you must be joking, mate! That's our emergency kit, that is!' Moore could see the others listening to the exchange, tapping their temples, laughing at his gall.

He said, unperturbed: 'And then, when you've dropped me off the coast there with that lot, you can go home to your mummies.'

They were on their feet at that, ringing him round. He thought with pleasure how it would feel to dent their heads and their egos a little. But instead he clicked on the comlink to the Barbieri pup.

'Yes, Moore? What have you got?'

Hunter. That was something. Not the boy wonder.

He explained where he was and what he needed. There was a pause while the request was assessed. Moore could easily imagine that Jan had abandoned the decision making for the time being. No satellite, riots in the capital, the runaways probably on French soil, and he doubted they would have caught the Saint woman either. She was class. Tut tut. A nice mess for ICSA to see when they came. The boy was probably skulking somewhere now that his new toys were all getting broken.

'Moore. Are you there?'

'Check. I'm here, Hunter.'

'OK. Permission to proceed as you suggest. But needless to say, if the French catch you messing around on their territory, you're nothing to do with us. Not until we've had their permission, anyway. It's been asked for.'

'Copy that. What about deactivating this piece of crap I'm wearing now, since I'm suddenly all you've got?'

'What about me pushing the button and not having to listen to you any more?'

Moore grinned into the wristcom. 'Point taken, Hunter. Shall I pass you to Corporal Sunshine here?'

'In a minute. First, we think now that Kay Saint and the girl are perhaps going after another spare from the girl's line. Do you have any information on that?'

'Negative, Hunter. There's at least one sleeper community in France, but I don't know where. Watchers never know where the others are: you should know that.'

A pause.

'Copy that. Just thought we'd ask. Nothing else you can tell us, then?'

'Only that it doesn't surprise me. Mira – the spare I was assigned to – is the type. Gets a bee in her bonnet about things.'

'OK. Give me the corporal and I'll make sure you get what you need. Good luck.'

Moore wordlessly unstrapped the com and handed it to the grunt. He enjoyed watching the man's face as he heard the commands Hunter gave him.

Twenty minutes later – far enough for the French guards not to see – he was dropping from the helicopter into fifty metres of freezing salt water, pulling the inflate cord on the dinghy pack, unloading the motor from its floating case. The little craft was tossed around dizzily until he got the motor to click in, but after that, with the nose pointing south-east, it was no more than averagely bad.

Steadily, the line that was the retreating French coast grew solid and distinct, showing rock, seagrass, the occasional tree, a building or two. Fastening the little tiller down with its rubber strap, Moore settled himself in the stern and ripped open one of the ration packs, scowling over the muck inside.

Involuntarily he thought of daymeal in Mira's community. Coming stamping in from the clear cold to find the good beer and bread, and his little Mira lined up with the other women ready to serve the men. How she had blushed when she met his eyes! How she had challenged him with her quick mind!

It was a pity that she had been spoilt by the city. In another existence things might have been different for them. She was worth the picking, that one was!

Mira was warm.

Warm.

There was light all around.

Perfect.

Except that there was a large insect buzzing close somewhere.

The warmth was all over, spreading through her legs and belly and neck and face. The light came pink through her closed eyelids and she could feel her body drink it in. Behind, close against her, there was something comforting and yielding, sending more heat into her spine. The thing was breathing softly, close to her nape. She wriggled closer and the thing let out a sigh in its sleep. A hand that she had not known was flat on her stomach moved slightly and was still.

Mira opened her eyes, squinting against the glare. Before her, a forest of pale, straggly grasses fell gently away towards a barer, grey-yellow piece of land, that in turn became the sea. The ground against her cheek was coarse, grainy. The sun shone over everything. There was barely a wind. Even the green water seemed at peace.

France. This is France.

She smiled to herself and closed her eyes once more, pressed back into Kay's sleeping embrace. There would be a time to act again later. The insect droned on in the background, circling persistently, and then passed away, going south towards the sun.

The next time she awoke everything had again changed.

It was almost dark. Cloud had rolled over, thicker than ever. Two heavy drops struck her cheek and brow.

Reluctantly she sat up and shuffled back to rest against the tumble of fallen stones that had shielded them in their sleep. Her head thudded from too much rest after too little. Kay was not to be seen. The sea was again black and she could hear the heavy waves sucking and breaking on the land. She was hungry and thirsty and her skin and hair itched with the salt that encrusted her.

Vaguely it came to her that there was a stream, a tiny rill with its own miniature valley, winding down to the sea somewhere over to the right. She must have seen it last night: or rather, this morning. *Was* it this morning that they had arrived? Less than a full day?

She got unsteadily to her feet and wandered on stiff, bruised limbs to where the ribbon of fresh water lay. Her feet were bare and she wore only the long top half of the strange, black Slam suit and her underwear. Somewhere the shoes, the thick, uncomfortable motobike jacket and the bottom of the suit had been shed and abandoned. She struggled to remember as she washed in the rill.

Aye. There had been the endless ride. Escaping from the helicopter. The terrible icy passage across to the broken section. And then climbing up, up into the exposed stiltway foundations. But then, much later, at the end of the climbing, there had been another place where the road was torn and Mira had remembered only then that she had meant to bring the jackets to use again, not leave them zipped to the cables. But luck was with them: a small, central part of the tough flexible apron between sections had somehow clung on, twisted though it was, and so they had been able to inch back across to the more solid stiltway, clinging tight when the waves broke over them.

After that, it had been just running. Heavy-footed, slow, hopeless running in their wet things; an endless blundering on into the dark, hand in hand, expecting always to hear the helicopter engines. Her Lomond journey all over again.

'Fuel,' Kay had said. 'They won't be able to keep using fuel to look for us. Not even Pax. It will be all their supply for months . . .'

As the first frail glow started to show in the east, they had at last seen a land mass, low and dark. And ahead of them, far down the heaving road, lights, figures moving . . .

There had been no choice. They had gone as close as they dared to the land, hugging the dark metal wall, and had stripped off the heavier clothes they still wore, fingers slipping and fumbling with the fastenings, climbed over the sidewall and dropped into the waves. And somehow, *somehow* they had made it to the shore. Mira had had to pull Kay the last twenty metres, keeping his face clear of the water.

She shuddered. Having washed away the worst of the salt and sweat from her face and neck, she bent to drink. But Kay's voice came from close by: 'I wouldn't. It's not clean.'

She rose and saw him approaching, walking gingerly, wearing strange, rough, loose-fitting clothes and carrying things in his arms: other similar clothes, an old plastic bottle of water, something that might be cheese.

He said: 'There are animals a bit further up. I think they're goats. I expect they piss in that stream. Here, I got some things to wear. And clean water.'

She took the bottle gratefully and said: 'How?'

'There's an old woman. Pretty crazy too. She knew about us. She must have seen us when we were asleep.

She doesn't stop talking.' He winced as he took the bottle back.

'Your feet are sore. From the bridge.'

He shrugged.

They stood looking at each other in silence. The raindrops were falling more heavily now, puckering the surface of the stream, and the sky was a dim iron grey. Another night was falling upon them fast. Mira found it difficult to think clearly. One step at a time, aye? A wash, a drink, some better clothing, those were enough. At least she was back in the open land.

She felt awkward with Kay and wished she were alone, to clean her body properly, to walk and think a little.

After his terrible lethargy yesterday, the boy now seemed full of nervous energy, limping about, casting her quick glances, rubbing at his nose, eating bits of cheese. He said: 'We can't stay. They won't give up. Not Jan.'

She sighed. 'Nae, I know. Where must we go from here to find the child?'

'It's a village right down in the south. Miles and miles and miles. Almost as far as you came from your home to the city. The village is called Le Porge.'

She considered. 'A boat then? Can we no go by sea? Along the coast?'

'Maybe. If we could find a boat. And if we knew how to make it go where we wanted, which I certainly don't. But maybe we'll do better by road. The stiltways are the same over here as at home. Hardly anyone uses them. The floods will soon make them useless.'

'But your feet.'

He didn't meet her eye. 'Oh, they'll be fine. I'll pad out these shoes the woman gave me.'

Watching him, Mira thought: I would do better and go faster alone. Yet she was half ashamed to think it. He'd given her endless gifts of food in the city, and left that home behind to come with her, though it was not the game he had perhaps imagined. She said: 'Let us ask the woman, then, for the way.'

But when they went up the slope to the pile of rough, mortared stones that made the woman's house, and the tiny creature opened the door, peering bright-eyed round the edge and muttering, Mira could not understand a word.

'*On core! On core!*' the woman tittered: '*Shay la shawnce. Vraymon. La shawnce. Ay la peteet fee oh see. On tray. On tray!*'

The door was held wide for them, letting out a sharp tang of goat. Mira said: 'What did she say? I cannae make it out.'

'It's French. They speak French here. She's pleased to see us and wants us to go in.'

They stood on the earth floor with the goats nosing around them and smoke from the fire making their eyes sting and Kay said: '*Noo dev on allay oh pirin ay. Pour vwah uh nammy.*'

The tiny woman clawed at his wrist and said, eyes wide: '*Lay pirin ay? Lay pirin ay? May say* lwah. *Tray tray lwah deesee.*'

Kay said: '*Wee. Zsh say. May commor ess kon per ee allay?*'

Unable to follow what was being said in this strange tongue, Mira scratched the goats' hummocky heads and looked round the single room. The walls were stained yellow from the smoke. She wondered what it was that was being burnt and why the woman didn't do something to make the fire better. She bent down by the little grate, which had a faded picture of a short, smiling man with a beard hanging next to it, and strained to see up inside.

At once she felt the small, sharp fingers on her own

arm and the voice chattered at her: *'C'est un nid. Là. En haut. Un nid. Les hirondelles. Ils revient chaque printemps.'*

'She says there's a nest. Some bird that comes back every year.'

'That doesn't make any sense. The bird should be here now, then. For the summer.' Perhaps the nest was from long ago. Mira smiled at the old woman, nodded, and the woman nodded back like mad, saying: *'Oh, mais tu es jolie, ma alouette.'*

'She says you're pretty.'

'What about the travel?'

'I can't make that bit out. She seems to be saying we should use the road, but there's also something about a monster. I didn't understand. She goes too fast.'

'Oui. Oui!' cackled the woman: *'Un monstre! Très, très grand, et lent, mais . . .'* She shrugged, seemed to lose interest, went poking around in the corner for something.

They went to the door to let themselves out, with Kay saying: *'Merci. Merci pour tout.'* But the little figure beetled after them and caught Mira once more before they were across the threshold. She poked something under her nose, an old, yellow image of a girl sitting next to a goat. *'Moi!'* she breathed. *'J'étais aussi jolie, n'est-ce pas?'*

Kay whispered: 'It's her. She wants to know if she was as pretty as you. Say *oui* lots of times and *jolie*.' Mira did so, and kissed the old face and felt tears on the cheeks.

Then they went to find the road.

THIRTY-TWO

When the ICSA ship nosed into its berth, a neat, scrubbed, white craft, bearing the ring of clasped hands that was the symbol of the International Crisis Strategy Agreement, it was welcomed by three immaculate files of Pax personnel and by the representatives of six of the twelve Families. Jan himself was as cleanly and impressively turned out as he had been on the night of his acceptance speech. The day was the most pleasant that the city had seen for months, with the suggestion of watery sunshine piercing through a gossamer thin veil of cloud. Unusually, the winds were silent, so that the gentle slap of water against white-painted hull seemed magnified.

Despite the setbacks of the last twenty-four hours, Jan Barbieri had looked out from his quarters this morning and realised in surprise that the city was his. *His!* Old Tomas was in his cell and would stay there no matter what the ICSA delegates said or thought. Kay Saint and the girl had left the country, but they were not important either: they could crawl to whatever hole they wished and rot there. He thrust aside the thought of the information they were carrying: by the time they could use it he would be untouchable. Or perhaps Moore would catch up with them, after all. As for his Clarissa, she would be agreeable and come to see where her future lay, or she would be dispensed with. Not even her mother was a real threat. She had made her puny throw, activated her Wrecker allies, disabled the satellites. Quite futile. Perhaps she had even done him a favour: their loss would give him extra edge over the other European powers. And the broadcasts he had in mind would be only for the ears and eyes of his chosen city dwellers: he would need no satellite for that.

All in all, things felt quite different this morning. He felt alert. He had merely been tired before, he told himself; worried about unimportant details. Not even the persistent throb of his shoulder wound could bother him today.

A heavy rope was thrown ashore from the white craft, a line of spotless sailors appeared at the top of the gangplank and Jan strode easily forward to meet the delegation.

'Welcome, Excellency. Welcome, Madam. Welcome to Briton. Thank you for coming. Welcome, sir. Welcome. Careful on that last step there, sir.'

They filed down, eight crusty old relics in expensive tunics, headed by a white-haired African, looking him over as if he was the tea boy. He shook their hands, bobbed his head respectfully, let them pass on to Magnus and Pieter, standing gravely at his elbow, and beyond them to the other Family heads: old walrus Becker from foodstuffs, George Denny (transport), Julie Walsh (trade and taxation), Angela Steele (power generation) and Gustavo Cooper-Smyth (education and childcare). Everyone present knew that Jan was now the real power here, in this country of Briton. And because they knew that, he could suffer the supercilious looks from the visitors. He could even enjoy them.

When the greetings were over he signalled to his sergeant to bring the men smartly to attention, and led the way past them to the waiting transport. 'This way, if you please. We have refreshments waiting for you. You must be tired from your trip.'

The new dock had been steam-blasted clean just here and cleared of Scroats and Visions alike. Teams had worked through the night to achieve it. The route back to the Pax Building would not take them past any of yesterday's damage: it had been carefully worked out. Nor would any Scroat or troublemaker be allowed at the roadside until they had passed. Since Magnus and Pieter insisted that they play this game – and why not? It couldn't do them harm – they might as well play it convincingly; pretend that the ICSA relics were to be revered.

As for the four or five Families who had finally chosen to send no representatives to this welcome ceremony, seemingly to indicate concern over the rioting and especially the damage to the satellites, they would be punished for their pride in due course. Not that Jan didn't feel pride himself, though: seeing the hundreds of smart, efficient men and women who wore his uniform at the roadside, guarding the route as they crossed the city, he was again surprised at the realisation of what lay in his hands. His parents also would surely have been proud of him. This was his time: their time. The time for the Barbieri family to take its natural position. He, Jan Barbieri, was to begin a new era. It would start with the cleansing of this great city, and the avenging of his parents' death. Then he would look at what new possibilities lay in this technology the Board was hatching.

Regrettably, he would also be the *last* of the original stock. Now that he had taken Magnus and Pieter's advice, there would be no alternative to the promised new technology, unless he was to restart the very process the

ICSA busybodies had been brought here to investigate
. . . or, worse, simply spawn children in the disgusting,
random way of the Scroats. And yet – he smiled faintly to
himself – a child made by him and Clarissa Saint in the
old-fashioned way; *that* might indeed be a child with
promise. He flushed at the thought of Clarissa. All the
times that she had teased him and tied him in knots and
pushed him away when he thought that she was starting
to like his attentions. Yes. When he had a moment he
would visit her quarters, see if she could see sense yet.
She would come to heel. He would make sure of it. She
was indeed a prize worth taming.

The three vehicles passed slowly on, climbing steadily
away from the water, flanked always by troops. The
roadside screens lay silent with the demise of the satellite
feed, and it seemed a relief to Jan not to see them chattering away. The Saints had spread weakness with their
Network. He would bring strength and focus. If he chose
one day to make fresh broadcasts, they would reinforce
these values. The weak would not even exist.

Idly he noticed a snake design – a serpent rising up
from a lake and looking straight at him – newly painted
across a shop window, and wondered how his people had
missed it. Was it vandalism or had the shopkeeper himself
defaced his property thus? He'd send a memo to one of
the captains to look into it. That serpent rubbish! They
were all at it: the unemployed, the drug takers, the weak.
You could sell them any old pack of lies and they'd buy
them in their desperation. All of it would be swept away.

Jan saw that they were arriving. He had been impolite
in his daydreams perhaps. Across the transport floor
Magnus was speaking to the elderly African, Doctor
Amarfio. He (Magnus) looked like a monk or an angel
or a surgeon in his silver-white Board uniform, with

cropped hair of the same shade. He was explaining to the doctor that they were to visit Stoneywall to begin the giving of evidence. They, as custodians of that place, had become aware that the Saint family were using a rented vault to store illegal material.

Amarfio flapped his hand impatiently, spoke in his deep fruity voice. 'Not now, if you please, Mr Stein. The proceedings have not yet begun. You may present your evidence when called upon to do so. At such time others will also be invited to speak. The delegation are here on your invitation and request, but not as a tool to serve your political ambition.'

'Of course. Of course. Forgive me.'

The man in silver lowered his eyes in apology, but Jan could see the irritation in the slight frame. Perhaps inviting ICSA had been unwise or unnecessary, after all. Oh well, it would not harm Magnus and Pieter to be wrong for once.

To prevent any talk of what other evidence they might or might not have to offer to the investigating delegation, Jan said: 'Excellency, we are arriving at the Pax headquarters. Will you and your team take some refreshment with us, when you have been shown your rooms?'

Again that look from the bloodshot old eyes. As if he had crawled from a rock. Amarfio said, stiffly: 'I will consult with my colleagues. For myself, a shower and a little quiet meditation would be better than food.'

It seemed in fact that all eight ICSA visitors felt as the doctor did – they'd probably pigged themselves silly on the crossing, Jan thought – so he saw to their few needs and then went to join the seven others who had been with him on the quay. They, at least, would not refuse the lavish lunch.

It would be a chance to congratulate those of the Families that had chosen the right path.

'Look how the young donkey struts and preens and admires his new kingdom!' Pieter murmured. 'As if this had been about *him*, about *his* destiny.'

'Indeed. He is unwise to revel so openly in this fragile, new-found power. He will antagonise those whom he should count allies.'

'Amarfio can see how little he is needed by this boy. So can the Families.'

'The donkey believes that now the move is made, he is established, untouchable. Today he thinks of all his armed men and women and fears nothing.'

The two were silent for a while. They nodded and smiled at Cooper-Smyth, helping himself to more wine at the serving table nearby. Then Magnus said carefully: 'You have seen the tapes from the girl's escape?'

'I have.'

'And did anything strike you?'

'The image?'

'The image. Yes.'

It was clear, then, that the same vague, cold doubt had infected both of them.

Pieter said, in quiet exasperation: 'I was there when they enhanced it. The donkey blew it up to the size of his wall and still could not see anything there.'

'Quite so.' And then: 'So there *is* something there, my friend? You are sure?'

'You are not?'

Another pause.

'It is not . . . *possible*.'

'No.'

'And yet, the records of this one are now blank, as no

record should be. Not the slightest whisper of a footprint. The girl-child must have at least one powerful believer.'

'The other spare? The woman? The daughter? Or someone else, not from the line?'

'I would say the woman. She has been more active than we guessed in every respect. And I would say also that the woman is our answer. Look! The donkey approaches. Strut, strut, preen. Let us fan the anger in our pet once more. Let him grow to hate that line.'

'Yes,' agreed Pieter; 'But let us also keep him to his task with the inspectors. We must not lose sight of our other goals in this business of the girl-child.'

Jan came over to them, carrying a plate.

'What do you say, my friends?' he grinned; 'Isn't this a good day for us? All your hopes coming to fruition!'

'Yes,' they smiled back. 'Yes indeed. A fine day! Only . . .'

'Only what?'

The smiles faded. Their eyes fell. There was another matter to discuss. Not such a good business. Perhaps . . . yes, perhaps it would be best if he joined them privately after the luncheon?

And so once again the boy was left agitated, uncertain and irritable, kept in doubt by the old men. While *they* . . . they swam in a black pool of fear that they could not even admit to.

THIRTY-THREE

For the first night, Mira and Kay saw none of the goat woman's monsters. They picked their way along the seafront to a place where they could see the joining between floating road and land, but even there, everything was still and empty, the helicopter departed. Only the outdated little border post remained.

Now Kay became wildly optimistic, contradicting everything he had said before. 'Perhaps they've given up. Perhaps now we're in a different country it doesn't matter enough to them. They'd need to apply for permits from the French, after all, to come after us. And look at us: we're not much of a threat to them, are we? Why would they bother?'

Remembering Evan, Mira felt that he was wrong. But she kept her peace, not wishing to break his good mood. He had begun to give her long, searching looks, as if trying to understand something, and soon slipped into a brooding silence.

They joined the stiltway out of sight of the French guards and trudged along the wet surface, sometimes ankle or knee deep. To pass time Mira made Kay tell her French words so that she should have something to say to Adeline, her sister, when they met. In this way, she learned *Oui* and *Non* and *Comment ça va?* and *J'ai faim* and several of the colours. If they could not move faster, she should be a bonny speaker of French by the time they arrived, she thought wryly to herself. In a day or two, after more rest, she would probably be able to run through the night and rest by day, but she did not think that Kay could do so. Already his stride was lagging, thanks to his sore feet. For better or worse, she was tied to his pace now. The journey would take weeks rather than days.

The skies, which had been so clear and blue when Mira awoke in the afternoon, now stayed stubbornly cloudy. There were also frequent bursts of heavy summer rain.

Kay grew nervous and twitchy. He took her hand as they walked, as if doing so were a challenge to her, and she was content enough to let him, if he did not want more.

Eventually, she said with a sigh: 'So. You'd better tell me properly about *clones*. I must know who I am.'

His expression hidden by the night. 'Why bother? What do you want to know?'

'Everything.'

'Everything. OK . . .' He sounded sarcastic and spoke as if to a child. 'Clones are exact copies of people, or animals of course. Just like identical twins. They look the same as each other and have the same genetic information, so that they should grow to the same size, be good at the same sorts of things, be susceptible to the same diseases. They may or may not have the same thoughts or ideas.' He gave a short laugh.

She said: 'Perhaps we're not so different, right enough.'

'You can't be serious!' he said, his temper flaring. 'You two! You think that you're the *tiniest* bit . . .?' He paused, then continued the lesson, speaking coldly. 'Well, anyway, they first started trying to make clones way, way back in the twentieth century.'

'Why?'

'Why? Money! They knew farmers would pay a lot if they could keep having the best animals. The best bulls.

The fattest, tastiest pigs. Whatever. And then there were people who wanted to replace a dead child. Nutters who thought they could have a dead *parent* back, as a son, maybe. People that couldn't have children the normal way, of course. They'd be willing to pay a lot to have one of them cloned. This was before the Fertility Board or anything. Before flooding and the rest. Before population agreements. Even in Briton there were, I don't know, sixty or seventy million or something like that.'

'Sixty or seventy million *people*?' The thought made her feel claustrophobic. Where had they gone for their peace, all those people? Where had they found the singing spirits?

In a while Kay stopped walking and withdrew his hand from hers. 'I want to rest.'

'OK.'

They found a roadside hummock with a stand of half-rotten trees to shelter beneath and shared out some stinking cheese, the gift of the old lady. As Mira ate, she noticed that all the branches on the stiltway side of their shelter had been cut or broken off before they reached their end. She wondered at this but said nothing. Nearby, Kay was muttering, doing something in the darkness, but she still felt his eyes on her, glinting in the shadow.

When he spoke again he sounded so far away that she knew what he'd been doing with his hands. She'd seen and heard it many times in the city. It wasn't what they needed now. He said wretchedly, almost whispering: 'I thought that you were like me, Mira.'

'Aye,' she said with an attempt at a smile; 'It seems we are alike, right enough.'

'No! No, I didn't mean that. Not clones. Not that! Just . . . Oh shit, I don't know.'

'What then, Kay Saint? Two hopeless souls? Two poor wee victims? Two what?'

He let out a great bellow into the night, like a beast in pain, then lumbered at her awkwardly, wrapped his arms around her, tried to kiss her. She could feel the tears on his cheeks. 'Oh Mira. *Mira*. You're so . . .' Feeling smothered, she broke his embrace, stepping back in irritation.

Kay's voice came angry and thick with the drug: 'Why won't you touch me? Little Miss Perfect. Are you too good for me?'

She felt her own temper flaring. 'Nae, you listen to me then! I'm glad to have you with me on this journey. But you need *not* come if you don't wish it. We can part here! And if we *are* to keep company together you must throw your white dust into the water, before it betrays us both.'

There was a long silence. More rain fell, a deluge of swollen drops, so loud on the floods around the road that ordinary speech was no longer possible. Mira saw Kay go to the siderail, bring his arm back and sharply forward again in a throwing motion. It was too dark, though, to say if anything had left that open hand. Love of truth soon went with the drug.

He came back and shouted wildly above the rain: 'There! Are you satisfied?'

'Aye,' she shouted back, giving him the benefit of the doubt: 'Let's go on, then, and forget what passed here.'

She took his wet hand firmly and walked on, pulling him with her, trying to give him some purpose. He didn't resist. 'What else then?' she yelled at him; 'What else about clones? Tell me everything.'

He went on haltingly with the explanation, still shouting to be heard over the rain: 'Cloning was seen as another way to keep power . . . To stay on top. Ahead of the field.'

'How do they decide who to copy?' she shouted back, encouraging him, pulling him faster still.

'It started during all the changes. The floods . . . The end of the government . . . The wars . . . The families that had had power before got together. There was a bank or pool or something of genetic material. All at Stoneywall . . . But it's all a secret . . . it's illegal. Against International Law.'

'And the spares?' she prompted; 'The spares! Like me.'

The squall was dying and his voice became clearer.

'Yes. Spares. All of them . . . believe they're just normal people. They're kept as ignorant as possible. Buried. Hidden.'

'Aye. I see. Why, then, is it not allowed? To make clones.'

'Because . . . it goes wrong. Went wrong. Because . . . because . . . too many were deformed and . . . dead.' His voice was dully fading away. 'The first generation all died as babies. The hundreds and hundreds of tiny bio-switches that follow the genetic instructions don't – didn't – work. In their bodies. Swollen arteries. Unworking hearts . . . They banned it. Everywhere. But the Great Families took over. Somebody must have thought that using clones would be a good way to keep power.' He looked round at here. 'You're the *best*, you see. Almost a perfect human being.'

The new day had begun to steal in from the east, the second dawn since they had run from the city. Swathes of dark, shining water stretched out in all directions, broken by graceful humps and spits of land. They talked no more. Soon, at one of the longer spits, rising up in a finger that pointed east, Mira led Kay from the road and they found a place where they might rest the day.

Before she slept, she thought of what Kay had said and

reached out in her thoughts to all her sisters, living and dead. Annie Tallis, Adeline Beguin, Tilly Saint, Clarissa . . . How I pity and love you all. To be this terrible, made thing and to know it and still to find a way to live! That is courage! How can I ever find such courage? She thought of Clarissa's anger and fear and understood. How she understood.

And in truth, she could understand Kay too. Poor wee boy. His mother had indeed tried to do him a loving kindness, if he could see it.

The goat woman was delighted to have a third visitor in twenty-four hours. Three in a month would have been an event.

Moore sat at her rickety table on the beaten ground before the hovel, looking out on the sea, sipping the warm, fermented milk drink that she had given him to break his fast. He felt his muscles begin to unwind. There was no great hurry. It was pleasant to rest a while and watch the little scarecrow go about her morning tasks.

On and on she chattered. About the goats, about her dead husband, about Mira, who was so pretty. Moore caught only the snatches uttered as she passed him by between tasks, and to those he replied politely in his good French. He guessed, however, that not much of it was really for him. She would have kept up the same stream of nonsense alone.

'Yes,' she had told him excitedly, 'yes, yes! They were here! The pretty girl and the boy with her. I gave them cheese. I showed them my things!'

'That is good!' Moore had replied: 'So good to hear. I was to go with them on their journey but was delayed. Hopefully now I can catch them up.'

'Catch them up. Yes perhaps, perhaps. You also are going to the friends in the Pyrenees?'

'Yes,' agreed Moore, 'we were to go together. Perhaps we will live there now with our friends. Our own farms in Briton have been lost to us.'

He enjoyed his tales.

The goat woman tutted and fluttered and hopped about, remembering when the waters were so much lower, saying how much land her father had owned and then she had lost to the salt waves. Moore nodded gravely, sipped his drink, shared his own false tale of hardship.

'I told them,' the old woman crowed, switching back to the original subject without a breath, 'your friends; I told them. The Pyrenees are far. Very far. I sent them on the road, to find the great monsters that go to the south. Perhaps you may catch them still. Perhaps!'

'Monsters?' Moore smiled. 'You have monsters in this country, do you, Aunty? That would be worth seeing!'

'Oh yes! Yes yes! Monsters. Great machines! I went to ride one once to see my son. But it was too big. I came home. Home to my little house.'

She had shaken her head. 'But in your boat, Monsieur. Without doubt you can catch up with your friends in your boat now the floods touch the old road!'

Moore finished the milk drink, wondered whether to tell the puppy what he had learned. But no, he would leave it a while. The boy could sweat. Perhaps instead he would have a small doze in the pleasant morning air. He was tired from searching the shoreline through the night. A rest could do no harm now.

Little Mira was as good as caught.

Mira and Kay slept away the day, hidden in a fold of slope where the soil smelled sweet and tiny golden flowers on long, lazy stalks performed a fragile dance against the wan sky. The rain came on and off, and late in the afternoon they were woken by thunder, but Mira felt refreshed. Her strength was flooding back. Her sore arm was nearly recovered. Even the rain was warm and cleansing.

They didn't talk much; Kay was lost in his own black thoughts. The last of the cheese and water was shared out and they struck back for the road, turning south once more. As they walked, a string of electric storms passed over, running inland from where the sea must lie. For minutes on end they made their uncertain way in total darkness and then blinding tongues of lightning would come shining off the waters for miles around. If anyone was out looking for them, Mira thought, they would be easy enough to see in these bright moments.

As the hours passed, Kay struggled even more. His right foot, when she looked at it, was badly blistered and bleeding. She bound the foot for him in a strip torn from the Slam suit and they went on, with Kay murmuring and swearing quietly in the darkness. Still they had met nobody on the road. Mira wondered what they could do for food when they grew hungry once more.

She paused yet again for Kay to catch up. Thunder echoed uneasily over her head, and in the distance all around, other storms crackled and rumbled, lighting the floods. Above these sounds there was a whining, a wailing. The wind, chasing between the supports of the stiltway, no doubt.

'A wee while further, if we can,' she called encouragingly to the boy, as he limped towards her. 'Another five miles. Then I'll look at your foot again, aye?'

He grunted at her and she thought idly: Nae, the wind never made that sound.

With a suddenly thudding heart, she imagined pursuit:

helicopters or some other machine. And yet the wail hardly seemed to grow louder. On foot as they were, any pursuit would surely be swift enough to be upon them without warning. This sound was indeed a mystery.

She asked Kay, but he took no interest, claiming to hear nothing until, by the time they stopped for his dressing, the ghostly whine had grown into a high, fluctuating growl, punctuated by deep violent snorts.

Then he muttered: 'The old woman's monster.'

'Aye. At least a dragon, I'd say.'

The thing, whatever it was, was definitely on the road behind them, and slowly drawing closer, despite the earlier impression. Mira turned often and strained to see back along the way, but for now there was no lightning close enough to show the beast.

Kay seemed finally to wake up and said: 'Maybe we should leave the stiltway until we know what it is, anyway.'

Mira wasn't so sure. She hadn't understood what the old woman had said, but there had been no terror or warning in the words. And leaving the road in the darkness would be just as treacherous. The waters were on both sides here, lapping against the road. She said: 'Let's bide a time.'

So they turned and waited, Kay nursing his feet. The whine had grown steadily more mechanical and less ghostly. Under the deep breathy snorts there were metallic clanking and tapping sounds. The distance, or the speed of the thing, was deceptive. They stood long enough for their muscles to grow cold and still the beast had not appeared. Mira imagined they would see it any moment – its size increasing steadily in her mind – and yet, as far as she could tell, it showed no awareness of them. It could be neither monster with nose for smelling, nor pursuers armed with nightsights and tracking machines. Whatever it was, this thing, it was about its own business.

And then, when they least expected it, when the noise had grown to fever pitch, a fresh tongue of crackling white sizzled down into the sea, far out to the west, and – just for that moment – they *saw* the thing outlined clearly and understood. It seemed to be a vast transport, or succession of transports, joined together as the Caplink carriages were joined, but many times larger. Almost the width of the stiltway, and as high as it was wide: square at the bottom, but curving over at the top into a back that seemed lined with huge spines, like some great lizard. And, most surprising of all, a huddle of silent people sitting or lying against these spines: a few even hanging onto the sides.

Some of these riders saw them in the lightning flash, some did not, but there seemed little interest. Blinded again by darkness, they pressed themselves flat against the siderails and the monster slowly advanced; a shadowy hulk, less than a metre from them. Great black wheels turned, checked: the machine snorted, lurched forward again, sighed, clanked on its way. It seemed in no hurry. The speed was no more than a slow run.

'*Montez!*' a thin voice cried from the darkness, floating over the great noise: '*Montez! Vite! Entre les wagons.*'

Kay put his mouth close to Mira's ear and shouted: 'He says we should climb up. *Montez*. Between. *Entre*. There must be a way between these things to get to the roof.'

'Aye, fine. How do we do that in the dark?' she shouted back. 'We'd never get past the wheels. We'd be flattened.'

'I don't know!'

Still the line of transports crawled on. Mira shouted:

'What if we wait until it's past and then follow? There might be more lightning.'

Vast though it was, the machine showed no sign of crushing them. Cautiously Mira stretched out her fingers until the tips brushed one of the slow, black, balloon wheels, then she left it there and felt the others passing, each one exactly the same distance away. She counted twenty-three more wheels before the machine had passed and all the noise came at last from ahead of them.

Mira darted forward and ran her hands over the metal wall that was the back of the beast. 'No good,' she shouted: 'It's smooth. No ladders. Quick! We'll have to run.'

'I can't,' Kay moaned.

She grabbed his hand and pulled sharply. 'Think of sitting up there and not needing to walk! Come on!'

They set off blindly, following the sound of the beast. Every so often there was the clank of the machine checking its progress, then set off again. When this happened they met flooded sections of the stiltway or places where the road surface had decayed and crumbled.

It knows, Mira thought, after a while. It's feeling its way forward somehow, making sure there's nothing in the way. The pace was not demanding but beside her, Kay stumbled over on the broken stiltway surface and cursed and sobbed as she pulled him onwards.

The air was close and heavy with recent rain – the sweat ran down them in rivers – but now they wished it, no lightning shone above.

As the first, hopeful minutes lengthened and became an hour, then two, Kay became leaden and silent. Twice he fell heavily, so that Mira had to grope for his arm in the dark and haul him up, with precious ground lost to the beast.

'Don't give up!' she urged again and again: 'Come on, now. We'll ride on that monster. We'll catch it and ride on it. Think of that, Kay Saint!'

Yet privately she knew that if they didn't catch the beast soon, Kay would be finished anyway. With shredded feet and no food he would be good for nothing.

We could try in the dark, she mused: When the thing pauses before it enters water, we could try to get between the wheels by feel alone. Black balloon wheels as tall as she was, turning slowly, relentlessly, supporting many tons of metal. If they should judge it wrong, if Kay should stumble . . . She shivered at the thought. No they would not try it blind. Better to stop than that.

Or – the other temptation – to leave the boy behind. But even as Mira resigned herself to halting and doing what she could for him, the cloud finally split apart, and the faintest of lights stole over them from above so that at last she could make out the clanking dragon clearly once again. She glanced to her side, at Kay, and saw his pale, empty face, his whole head hanging down as he stumbled on. He seemed not even to have noticed the chance.

'Come on!' she shouted at him: 'It has to be now. *Now!*'

He looked at her blankly, and she pulled him sharply forward, forcing him level with the tail of the trundling beast by brute force.

'Help me! Concentrate!' she screamed at him. They must *not* lose this chance.

She hauled him into the narrow corridor at the side of the machine, then along next to the slow balloon wheels, pressing him against the barrier in case he should fall again. Centimetre by centimetre they gained on the monster. The eyes of those perched on top followed them, those who were not sleeping. One or two pointed and shouted words in their strange tongue, laughed even.

'Help us!' she shouted at them. And then at Kay: 'What's the French for "help"? "Help"? How do I say that? Think, Kay!' but he gave no response, so she screamed the word again in English.

Again someone shouted: '*Montez! Montez! Vite!*'

'I'm trying,' she sobbed. 'I'm trying to "montez". Help us!'

They were level at last with the first gap between the transport wagons. Kay was lolling and lurching like a puppet as she tugged him forward, so that her arm and shoulder ached with the effort. In the dim light, she saw that the gap between wheels was no more than a half metre, just enough to walk through comfortably if the machine was still and the road smooth and it was day.

'I'm going to push you in there!' she cried: 'I think there's a ladder. You have to do that for yourself. Do you understand?'

She did it without waiting for an answer: flung him forward and inwards, through the narrow gap, and followed quickly herself. The light was going again, the cloud tear mending itself. They would surely be squashed like beetles. Yes, she was right, there was a ladder. Kay must have understood a little, for he had a limp hand gripping it, but even as she darted in beside him he tripped and fell and began to be dragged along by that single white hand. Hand and ladder were both fading before her eyes.

'Help us!' she screamed again, trying to pick Kay up bodily and press him onto the ladder as she ran.

And, unbelievably, there was at last a figure descending, and another . . . a hand catching Kay under his armpit. Sobbing with relief, she dimly saw him drawn up the ladder, legs trailing, into the shadow above. '*Montez!*' came the voice. She reached out and felt for the way up herself. Her legs were giving way, turning soft and useless. Her fingers found the spar of metal and held tight: then another one above, then another.

She was off the ground. She was on the back of the beast. Someone had put Kay there, just left him, sprawled unmoving at the top of the ladder. She could tell it was him from the rough feel of the clothes the woman had given them as she dragged herself forward over his body, away from the gap.

'Kay!' she shouted in his ear. He didn't answer.

Feeling her way forward she pulled him a little further from the edge, and then leaned back thankfully against what must be one of the spines that ran down the centre of the dragon's back.

A voice in the dark, perhaps the '*Montez!*' voice, said: '*Plus façile comme ça, n'est-ce pas?*' and laughed.

Not understanding, she said anyway, '*Oui. Oui.* Thank you. *Merci. Merci.*' And then, blissfully, she was asleep.

THIRTY-FOUR

Clarissa was quite prepared to say whatever Jan wished to hear to get out of her quarters.

Yes, Jan. No, Jan. Anything you say, Jan.

Bitterness was expected of her and bitterness she gave. It wasn't hard. She had been left tied up and gagged for long, painful hours before Jan's people had finally blasted off the drum-room door. By that time everything was over, finished. Her mother and Kay and the spare all gone; plumes of smoke rising across the city; Grandfather locked away somewhere. She meant nothing to anybody, it seemed. Her Great Family, first of the Great Families, was scattered and broken. Suddenly she had no future.

Jan visited her in her captivity, flirted, crowed, fed her bitterness, stroked her hair, strutted about with chest puffed out. 'There *is* a way,' he said: 'You were always intended for me, and I will take you.'

The price?

The price for this was threefold: an active hatred of her family and what they had done to her, a sworn statement before the ICSA inspectors that she had not fought in the Slam contest, and a little blood from her arm.

The first meant nothing, the third they would take whether she allowed it or not. The second? She searched her soul and could not see any way in which this would help or hinder what Jan was doing to discredit the Saints. By itself it was circumstantial, proving nothing: if and when they produced more concrete evidence, her testimony would be unimportant.

It was even a balm to think these things through care-fully and precisely, to go over them again and again, lying on her bed looking out at the dreary, restless city. It was like Slam. One didn't become emotionally involved: one only considered the moves possible. There was a kind of hard delight in knowing that she had not lost the power of clear thought. The heavy tangle of emotions she'd felt since Kay had come to her in the night, bringing that image of her twin, were second now to the immediate need to survive, to gain a better hand, to buy time until she could make stronger moves.

It did not escape her, either, that Mira might have gone through the self-same process. A life suddenly swept away; a host of enemies; the need to dig deep and sur-vive. If *she* – the copy – could do it, so could Clarissa. That was sure.

And so she bathed, and went through her exercise routines, and worked on her appearance to keep Jan interested. She must not underestimate him. For all his vanity, and confidence, he would be watching her for treachery. He would not expect total acquiescence, so she did not give it to him.

'Don't touch me!' she said coldly to him, and moved away.

'Why should *I* help your precious inspectors?' she spat.

'You are no friend of mine. I hate you,' she shouted.

She let her old self speak, and listened to it and was faintly ashamed. Yet it had its uses now.

For the cameras, when Jan was not there, she took out an image of her mother, looked long and hard at it, slumped on the bed. She cried softly, grew angry, tore the image and threw it out of the window. A wild frenzy fol-lowed, a fit of throwing things across the room, smashing them. Then when she was exhausted she threw herself on the bed and sobbed until she slept.

The tears and the anger were real enough. And still a tiny calm island at the back of her consciousness watched and helped her use her emotions to show the bitterness that Jan and his friends would wish. And in this way, strangely, she felt a shade closer not only to the spare, but to her mother as well.

With a humility which was quite new to her, she thought: I am being made to grow up. I am being stretched. Now I really will see whether this model is all they say. It was surprising, disturbing even. But not unpleasant.

The third time Jan came to her quarters he asked her about another spare from her line. A baby in France. Did she know where this child was to be found? What did she know about it? Nothing? He didn't believe her!

While he was gone again she racked her brains, trying to picture the images and papers Kay had spread out before her. Had there been a baby there? Yes, she thought there had. The name, she thought, was Adeline. Adeline, somewhere in France, as Jan had said. But she had had eyes only for Mira's image that night. She could remember no details for the others.

The second visit after that, Jan appeared in a foul temper, violent and raving where before he had been cool and superior. She even thought that he might try to harm her and so relaxed into pre-combat preparation while she talked, ready for him. It wasn't clear what had made him like this. He shouted at her about his dead parents, about the ending of his line, about satellites destroyed for ever and Barbieri spares who had been gunned down, unsuspecting. There was much in what he said that she'd have to think about later. Her guess was that someone had deliberately stoked his fury, wound him up about the things he couldn't cope with, as he was hoping to do to her.

And then he came close to her, with angry tears on his hard, handsome face, and whispered: 'Your line will also end, Clarissa Saint. The Barbieri family will have its revenge. *You* will be the last Saint, as *I* am to be the last Barbieri. Is that not fair?'

Still only half clear what he was talking about, Clarissa was happy to nod. To agree again, but with the subtle pretence of fear that instinct told her would be wise: eyes a little wider than usual, mouth slightly open . . . just enough to reassure the boy that he was in control.

He broke off his ranting and his threats and stood looking at her, his eyes becoming hot. Then he bent to kiss her lips, challengingly, hungrily. She could have gagged on that kiss. She found him repulsive. But instinct again whispered that for once she should allow it.

The next time he came, it was to set her free.

THIRTY-FIVE

The Fertility Board facility at Stoneywall was half underground. What showed on the surface, fastened like iron onto the bare Welsh rock, was all heavy white concrete, six metres thick. It might have been built that way for the weather alone – the endless raging storms that poured in from the Atlantic over the bottom corner of the country – but for the lack of any window, the rolls of razor wire, the dogs, the double-gated entrance. Soon, with the hungry sea creeping up the last two valleys, this piece of land would be an island, and the defences would be complete.

Tilly found it an ugly, dreary place. She also found it impossible to believe that any dissident or Wrecker could ever have got into it, whatever the broadcasts and the Board themselves claimed. Not at least without leaving a scarred and bloodstained battlefield.

Watching from above, she ate a little, allowed her body to rest. In truth, she mused, it was not quite the same body of twenty years ago. Whatever unnatural things had been spawned under that white concrete over the long decades, still human cells died, the metabolism slowed, reactions dimmed, and in the end one fed the soil again. Which was as it should be. Every age there had ever been knew and embraced that basic truth, until now.

The Stoneywall helipad, Tilly saw, was satisfactorily empty. No doubt all the chief members of the Fertility Board were in the capital, putting their case to the ICSA delegates. Soon she would be there with them: with her daughter-twin, whom she thought of constantly. This last swift journey, this wild, free flight across her ancient land, beyond price, was now ended. Tilly wondered if she had been self-indulgent to arrange things thus. She alone could do what needed to be done here, at this dreary place, but surely she could have contrived an easier way to come.

And yet: what was harder to track and follow than a lone person, lost amongst the floods and the forests and the empty, mechanised state farmlands.

She shook herself, cleared her head. It was time to act, not to dream. It could not be long before people came to Stoneywall to gather their precious 'evidence'. From her small backpack she carefully took out a formal Saint tunic, soft, clean shoes, a comb, a mirror, some make-up. After her three days of travel she did not present the appearance that would get her into the Board building. As it was, the gate staff here might have been told to forbid her entrance, but she doubted that. The Board were secretive enough not to share their information or movements with their own defenders.

Twenty minutes did it. Twenty minutes and then in the mirror she was Tilly Saint, powerful figure from a feared Family, once again. Tilly Saint, public darling and attractive ambassador for the country of Briton.

She stood up and made her regal way down over the rock-strewn slope to the heavy steel gates. A camera eye latched on to her and swivelled as she approached, zooming in on her features. In the computers inside, her face-print would already be spewing out a matching file. Nevertheless, at the gates an automated voice asked mildly if she would identify herself.

Yes, of course she would. She did so, with a brief, impatient smile for the lens.

'Please wait a few moments,' the voice asked pleasantly.

'Surely.'

The puzzlement no doubt felt by whatever grunt was inside, seeing her appear with neither transport, nor appointment, nor escort, was soon passed on to a slightly senior grunt, and then again to a woman above him. Unfortunate. It was this woman – a top-flight Vision – that finally appeared at the gate and came out to see her, flanked by two guards. A man would have been much easier.

'Mrs Saint! What a surprise. We didn't know that we were to be honoured with a visit at this time.'

Tilly switched on the public darling, but did not gush too much. 'No. I didn't know myself that I would be . . . er . . . calling. I do hope it's not a problem, Captain . . .?'

'Hickory.'

'Quite. Captain Hickory.' She put oceans of subtle respect into the repeated rank title, encouraging the woman to believe that they were almost equals.

'You'll understand . . . ordinarily it's Board policy only to admit with an appointment. A simple security measure.' The captain realised what she had said and went on: 'Not that I mean that *you*, Mrs Saint, would be . . .'

That was good. The captain was now worried that she had been rude to a superior. Tilly encouraged the notion by interrupting: 'Not at all. I quite understand what you meant to say. We must all have our own rules.'

The woman dithered. 'I suppose since it's you, Mrs Saint. Providing we hand-print you in and everything. But may I ask how you came to be here? I mean . . .' She gestured round at the wild, unfriendly landscape.

'Yes. It *is* a bit strange, isn't it? I can't imagine what

your junior staff' (again the veiled compliment, the suggestion of Hickory's superior perception) 'must have thought, seeing me coming strolling out of the blue like that! But with all the troubles in the capital – unrest, fires, those *filthy* Wreckers – I was advised to leave for a few days' recreation. Security is hardly my thing, after all. So I took a single-seat transport into the mountains here, decided to do some walking. Very peaceful; clears the head. And then, since I was close, I thought I might just visit our vault.'

'May I ask why?'

Tilly put a touch of severity into her smile. Time to remind Captain Hickory that an almost-equal had a precarious life. 'No, Captain, you may not ask why.'

A couple more minutes of prevarication by the woman, and then Tilly was inside. After all, she had known almost immediately that they had no orders to detain her: and in that case, it had been inevitable that her will would prevail in the end. The fear of upsetting the great and the good was a powerful antidote to procedure. However bizarrely the great and the good might choose to appear.

The captain took her through the first set of security procedures and the machines serenely identified her as Mathilda Saint, Grade One clearance. How nice. Then into the elevator and down to the vault level.

'How long do you think you might need, Mrs Saint?'

'Oh, not long. Shall we say half an hour? I'll call up on the intercom as usual.'

For Captain Hickory did not have Grade One clearance herself and would have to leave Tilly before the vault gates. Only the Great Families could enter this level.

'Half an hour. I understand.'

Off you trot, little Captain Hickory, thought Tilly; off you trot to check with your superiors in the city that all is well. And you are quite right to do so, for all is far from well. But when I see you again it will be much too late.

She activated the entrance keypad with her private code and presented herself for retina scan.

'Mathilda Saint,' purred the voice, 'please enter. It is good to see you back so soon.'

That didn't surprise her. It made sense, though she hadn't personally been to this terrible place since the material for the egg that was to become Clarissa – and of course that for Mira – had been taken. It had seemed appropriate to take extra interest in the creation of a 'daughter'. Tomas was usually the one who saw to all of it: even for the little girl in France with the impossible serpent's eyes.

No, Magnus and Pieter were clever old ghouls. Somehow they had convinced the security machines that Tilly had visited recently, and no doubt Jan and the Families would latch on to her guilt easily enough.

She entered and was again not surprised to see that of the twelve gleaming bunkers stretching in two lines of six down this otherwise empty space, eleven now stood unaccustomedly open. The only real pity was how long it had taken her to realise, to piece it all together. She had been dreadfully slow. Reported attacks on Stoney-wall, spares disappearing from other Families' sleeper settlements, the communication that Intelligence had reported going out to ICSA from Pax headquarters. And something new taking place at the Board; something that had led to her own carefully placed spies being removed.

Walking slowly down – the sirens were sounding dimly now: the captain had made her call – she saw that each bunker had had its locking mechanism simply cut away, the steel buckled and scorched by the process. Would the Barbieri boy really believe that *Wreckers* could have done this? Come so far into a protected zone and burnt those locks away?

No. He was not meant to. Nor were the other Families.

For one bunker stood whole and closed, still guarding its material. The last of the line. The first that had been filled. The Saint bunker.

'Please present yourself at the vault entrance, Mathilda Saint,' the automated voice was saying with a touch of animation. 'There has been a security anomaly.'

Too late, Captain Hickory.

Calmly, Tilly again went through the correct procedure for opening the bunker. An internal computer manned the defences, quite oblivious to the fuss outside, quite beyond interference. Yes, it was delighted to see Mathilda Saint. Yes, she could enter. Stand clear, please, for the door opening.

She stood clear. She pulled up her tunic and detached the tiny device taped there, in the small of her back. A device undetectable in the entrance screening process. Two harmless compounds, cased in plastic. A thin plastic screen between them. Quite devastating.

She placed the device in the centre of the bunker and pulled the screen out so that the compounds mixed.

She left the bunker and closed the doors.

'Thank you for your visit, Mathilda Saint.'

She heard the faintest of noises through the thick, thick steel. A tiny whiff of acrid smoke escaped from the brief, 10,000-degree furnace inside.

With a sense of peace and loss and fulfilment, Tilly sat on the floor and waited for them to come.

THIRTY-SIX

Clarissa moped and sulked around, a miserable shadow of the self-assured young lady known to all, and could have laughed aloud when she saw what a monumental mess Jan had made of everything.

Her place was apparently with him now, although she had asked about clothes and was told that she would remain in the Saint colours, until they were joined officially. No doubt this was for the inspectors. Jan's attitude towards her, when he was not distracted by the many other things that beset him, seemed to be a mixture of possessiveness, lust and the burning, savage anger from before. These elements together, she reflected with a slight tremor of fear, made him an unstable and explosive package.

The violent anger, she was now sure, was the product of those two doddery old boys from the Board, Magnus and Pieter. Gradually, from Jan's unguarded comments, Clarissa realised that the frail old ghosts had made him believe her own family – specifically her mother – were to blame for his parents' deaths. Why he should believe that, she could not guess.

In fact, her charming, capable mother – who had never seemed to show much interest in anything her daughter achieved – was down in Jan's books as the architect of much of his misery, now and in the past. Not only had she killed his parents, but she had also tried to have *him* killed during the Slam final, she had sent some kind of a shut-down program to the three European satellites from a communications bunker (an elegant little program that simply told the machines to detach from their solar power generators), she had helped the spare to escape with Kay and she had orchestrated the dissident actions of the last twenty years or so.

Quite a list. Clarissa found herself hoping that at least some of it was true.

There were other things, too, that Jan transparently did *not* mention in front of her. Something about the Stoneywall Centre, for one. Nor was she allowed to remain with him when he had his regular meetings with Pieter and Magnus in their lavish guest accommodation.

The net impression she was left with – irrespective of motive – tallied with what he had said in her rooms. Jan Barbieri wanted her line to end. Not just to end, she would say, but actually to be destroyed as quickly as could be arranged. All except her, providing she was his unwilling, but eventually yielding plaything. Where she would have expected the Jan she knew to be glowing with the joy of real power, achieved at a young age, she found him obsessive about her mother, about Mira and even about the girl baby that he had asked about: Adeline whatever-her-name-was, down in France.

He had asked for permission from the French to send forces there. Dr Amarfio and the rest had apparently grudgingly allowed it to be labelled an ICSA matter: the collecting of evidence of cloning in the shape of the clones themselves. Under such circumstances the French permission would be a formality. Especially after destruction of the irreplaceable European satellites by a Saint. If they were delaying by a day or so, it was only to snub the new head of Pax. After all, his destabilising actions had probably sent a tremor through the Great Families of most of Europe.

Amarfio expected any clones collected in this way to be released and returned to their previous existence, once the hearings were done. He had said so, growlingly, in her presence, at the time of her sworn statement about the Slam contest. 'I would remind you, Executive Lieutenant: none of these children – not even Miss Clarissa here – can be held accountable for the actions of the adults involved. To *be* the copy of another human is not a crime under the ICSA charter. We will expect that any such subjects are left in peace at the end of this investigation, whatever the finding.' The old doctor had then banished all others from the room who were not from his own team. He had turned on her a kindly eye and apologised that for the moment her presence was required in this way and asked if she was being treated acceptably.

'It is regrettable,' he had said, pouring her some tea and passing it across the desk, 'that we are unable to come to such hearings with more than a handful of administrative and security staff. But I do assure you that if the boy there or his colleagues are maltreating you, there are certain steps we can take for your protection.'

Unexpectedly, under the gaze of the eight inspectors, her eyes had been suddenly brimming with tears. The moment's kindness pierced her defences in a way that no amount of threats or brutality could have done.

Even more unexpectedly, she found herself turning down this offer of help. 'It is very kind of you, sir. But I assure you I am quite well.'

Amarfio had studied her long and hard. What he had made of the tears she could not have said. 'The offer of help will stand open for as long as we are here, my dear.

After that . . .' He shrugged. They both knew he was powerless to keep her safe for ever.

When she went to rejoin Jan, the tears firmly wiped away, the familiar sulks back in place, he asked impatiently what the doctor had had to say in private.

'Oh, he asked if I was being well treated.'

Jan glared, his knuckles turning white.

'OK, don't wet yourself. I said I was all right.'

But why? Clarissa asked herself. Why should I choose to be with this dangerous maniac who makes my skin crawl every time he touches me, when I have been offered such protection?

The only answer she could find was not a flattering one. Pride, she thought. If all those others, and especially her mother and the girl Mira, were somehow surviving and making Jan's life difficult, and even, in Mira's case, going to help someone else while she did it, then she would do the same. She was as good as them.

Suddenly, to be Clarissa Saint felt very lonely and also very uplifting. It was a weight, always there but never fully felt until now. Vaguely, she thought she could begin even to understand her mother. Her head span with the insight. She was no longer sure that the sulky, attractive girl she had seemed was, in fact, her at all. Maybe she had trodden the same path as Tilly. Maybe she had chosen a role to hide behind and keep her safe when she was too young even to know she needed one.

Jan put his hard hand on her face, pulled it round sharply to inspect it, squeezing the cheeks until they hurt. 'What's wrong?' he asked brusquely. 'What are you thinking? Are you ill? Are you wondering whether to run back to Amarfio?'

She slapped his hand away. Her eyes flashed. 'Show me a little respect or I might,' she said coldly.

It was the right response. He laughed, put his hand back deliberately, caressingly, to assert himself. 'There now. I was afraid my little wild cat was asleep.'

They went on down to the control room, where Hunter had received a report from a man called Moore. He glanced at Jan to make sure that it could be repeated before Clarissa, which apparently it could.

'Moore believes that the two targets are travelling on a drone bulk transport, heading south. He says that their destination is reported to be in the region of the Pyrenees. We've charted the stiltway route and agreed on a point where he could intercept them, unless the French permission comes through first.'

'Good. But you didn't tell him about the French?'

'No. Though he's no fool.'

'Let's let Moore believe he is our only tool for now.'

'I agree.'

Jan glanced back at his future consort. 'And you've started looking at possible sleeper settlements in those mountains?'

Hunter rolled his eyes. 'Yes, of course. But without the satellite it could take *weeks* to find the signs. You must see that. If you're so set on finding the other girl, the baby, it might be easiest just to let Moore track Kay Saint and the older spare. He is talented in such matters. Then, when the French stop dragging their feet, we can go in and get all of them.'

The girl. The spare. The baby.

Clarissa thought of when she had stood face to face with Mira, only a few days ago. She had thought exactly like that. Or at least used those words. But then she had felt so *threatened* by the girl from the North. What if, a tiny voice had suggested, what if this person who is you is simply *better*? What if she has used her talents more wisely? What if *she* deserves to be the Saint and you the spare?

And Mira, inevitably, had been hurt by her rejection. That had been deliberate too.

When the call came in from Stoneywall, Jan was almost hysterical with delight. They had Tilly Saint, trapped in the Family vaults! At last!

His obsession with Tilly and her line was too far advanced now for him to puzzle out why the woman should have chosen to go to that place at all, what she could be doing there, why she might wish to destroy the Saints' own vault. Her *being* there at all was surely a kind of proof that she had been guilty of wrecking the other vaults, as she had wrecked every other part of his life until now. And *of course*, he told himself, she would want to destroy evidence against her own family when she knew of the ICSA investigation.

He did not spend time on the fact that she herself was valuable as living evidence and as the joint-accused of the investigation; and that she had evidently *allowed* herself to be caught. All that mattered was that they had the woman, and she would answer for her crimes.

He came to wake Clarissa – at least he had not demanded that she share his bed yet! – to tell her of the capture. He did not knock. He came in noisily, activating all the lights, his thick Pax tunic buttoned to the throat. His eyes were shining with pleasure. He pulled back the bedclothes and kissed her, a short painful grinding of mouths. Without doubt he wanted his chosen partner to suffer a little from the news.

'My people are bringing Tilly here now,' he fizzed. 'She will be with us by morning. And before long, the other two and your fool of a brother will join the party. Oh . . .

did I tell you? The French have stopped delaying and issued us with a permit to take a limited number of troops onto their territory.'

His wish was granted. Clarissa did suffer. She felt a great wrench at hearing of Tilly's capture, and an unexpected fear for the other three. And still the calm watching voice in her head was there, unaffected. It prompted her to let Jan see a little of her suffering: a few real tears, a moment of genuine hopelessness. And an acknowledgement of Jan's controlling position when she asked:

'*Why* are you doing this? *Why* do you so much want these people to suffer? Can't you just let my mother go?' And she added, in submissive supplication: 'For *me*, Jan?'

Had she overdone it? Apparently not.

'Come,' he said, more gently, gathering her to him. 'This land – this city – has been sick. Surely you know that? It's time for change, Clarissa. *That's* why the inspectors are here. To cure the sickness. There may be some pain in the cure, even for the Families, but it will be worth it. Trust me. And then afterwards, you and I will build a better nation for our people.'

Nothing about murder. Nothing to explain why every last one of her line must be collected and brought here. If they had Tilly, why would they need the rest? She had given her blood sample. The tests would be conclusive.

Yet in his madness, even the baby Adeline was to be kidnapped. Was resentment of Tilly's supposed vendetta enough to explain the need to bring the baby here?

Clarissa dressed herself carefully, choosing clothes she knew Jan liked, and went with him, head bowed, to meet her mother. The inspectors were also there, called from their beds, and so was the ghost called Magnus. She saw him watching her from those mild old eyes and longed to go over and shake him until his bones rattled.

Until he told her what *his* purpose was in all this.

But instead she turned and made some trivial remark to Jan.

Then the slow old transport from Stoneywall rumbled in, and she prepared herself for the reunion.

THIRTY-SEVEN

Magnus watched the clone Clarissa. He studied her as he had never studied another human being. He scanned her face for some sign of difference, something unexpected. Anything. He didn't know what he was looking for, and unsurprisingly he didn't find it.

We are grown into old fools, he thought. We, who are scientists and live by the purity of science, should be immune to whispers of magic and gods and girls with the eyes of a serpent. If indeed the baby in France has these unexpected eyes, then there is a scientific reason. A variable in the process that has not yet shown itself. An exception that proves the rule.

He looked at Jan, standing upright and impressive in the chill morning, and saw how he kept the Saint clone on a leash, like a dog. Not a physical leash. One made of fear and danger and unpredictability, so that she fawned around him and sulked and looked for his approval. There was no dignity in it, but it was good that this one, at least, had been broken. For Magnus doubted now that Jan would dispose of her. The attraction was too evident.

We are doubly fools, he told himself sternly. In our ridiculous fear of the impossible, we have pushed our tool too far. Now it may be that he is set on a course that not even we can stop. Everything could be lost if he won't keep his head.

Somehow, they would have to make sure that Jan satisfied the inspectors *before* he satisfied his bloodlust. And if possible, whatever was done should look like an accident. Yes, that was the way they must go. They must teach Jan to be a little patient and a little careful.

Seeing the new hardness in Jan Barbieri's jaw, the glint in his eyes, Magnus thought that what they should fear most, as scientists, was the creature they had helped to mould. Yet in his old man's heart he still feared the child more.

Marie left the low stone lodge when mother and daughter were both peacefully asleep. She shared a word with Eric, dozing in the doorway, and then set off down the mountain paths once more, glad to be alone in the cool night.

She walked carefully and lightly, hardly clicking one stone against another, but still Serge loomed up from her blind side when she neared his post, and had a blade pressed into the small of her back. She could tell from the sound of his breath that it was him and so did not break the arm that held the knife.

'Good,' she said. 'You were not sleeping?'

'I was. But you make the noise of three goats.'

They laughed. He gave her coffee, brewed thick and black as treacle on his field stove. Then she continued her descent. As first light showed behind the peaks she came again to Le Porge. She looked at her adopted village with love and sadness. It clung on to the baked roots of the mountains, its toes lapped by the lake, and seemed to her to be everything a man or woman might want. Like Moore, she had grown up in a city, and like him also she had been a little bewitched by the place she had been sent to as watcher. If she was allowed, she would marry here and work at the fishery and tend her garden and die here too.

But if – when – the storm came, baying for dear little Adeline, she would turn it aside if she could. If.

Pierre, the one of the six who had stayed here, was sitting at the waterfront. His great bulk certainly looked like it could turn aside any storm.

'*Salut!*' he called cheerfully. 'It is done? The girl is safe in her refuge?'

'*Oui*, Pierre. It is done. We have set our game. Now we can only wait and hope.' She sat down beside him, took off her shoes and bathed her feet in the warm flood water.

'Oh, little Marie! You must not be gloomy. In all probability the other girl will arrive soon. Perhaps today . . . it is going to be a fine day! Then she will take the child and your job will be done.'

Marie smiled doubtfully. 'Certainly. That would be neat, my friend. Is life ever so neat, I wonder? I don't think even Tilly had a clear idea of what this Mira would do when she arrived. I asked her, and what was her answer? Only that a great game was being played out and we should not fear to play for lack of seeing the other hands.'

Pierre rubbed his hands together, thoughtfully. 'I see.' He brightened: 'Then, little Marie, let us play!'

THIRTY-EIGHT

For three days and nights Kay and Mira rode the back of the dragon as it crawled on its slow, blind path towards the south.

Kay lay in a fever for much of this time, but the man who had helped them, whose skin was as dark and rich as wee Joan's eyes at home, and whose clothes were pure white sheets wound about him many times, gave her a little water, and salt to rub into the terrible blisters, and helped her move the boy when it was time to dismount. This happened three or four times a day, whenever there was a change in the beast's routine. The first such time was only an hour or two after they had climbed up in the dark. Mira was woken by the dark man shaking her shoulder, grinning at her with his white teeth, saying: '*Descendez! Descendez!*' It was obvious enough what he meant, even if the word had not been so like English. All around, the riders from the top were hastily jumping and climbing to the ground, passing down bags and bottles, dodging out between the huge wheels. There were orange lights flicking on and off at the corners of the wagons and a thin siren.

'*Descendez! Descendez!*' The man went to take Kay's shoulders and looked at her expectantly. '*Vite! Vite!*'

Blearily, she crawled across to help him. She couldn't make her brain work. They've found us then, she thought vaguely. They're stopping the transport to take us back to the city. But the transport was not stopping, and the siren came from the wagons themselves. Besides, she could see nobody except for the straggly line of people running alongside and behind the dragon, clutching their possessions to them in the first light of day.

Between them, with little help from Kay himself, Mira and the stranger managed to ease the boy down the ladder and she guided him back out through the wheels, where a running woman cursed angrily in the strange tongue and thrust him against the rails out of her way. Slipping through, Mira shielded Kay with her own body until runners and wagons were passed. Again, she thought, hopelessly, fully awake at last, we must run again! For how long? We cannot do it. It was a disaster. Kay was white and slick with sweat and would hardly put one foot in front of the other: they would soon be left behind.

On top of the beast, the lights and sirens stopped, and then she saw the dark man skipping quickly along the back of the last wagon and leaping, in a flurry of white clothing, down to the ground. He saw her and grinned his broad grin and pointed up at the machine, now empty of all riders. *'Electricité! Ça pique!'* he called.

The man came back to where they struggled and again took Kay's shoulder and helped him along at a slow run. He seemed to have great strength hidden beneath his sheets. Up above, something almost beautiful was happening to the wagons: the huge, vertical spines were growing skywards, splitting open, flowering into a series of graceful, curving dishes pointing at the heavens. *'Soleil, soleil!'* panted the man, and he gestured upwards with his hand. The sun, she thought, understanding: Solar dishes to give the beast power.

'Maintenant, c'est bon. On peut remonter.'

Monter. We can get up again. Relief flooded through her.

Sure enough, the running line of people began to flit back in between the wheels and swarm up the ladders to the roof once more, where they spread out their things and sat in the low, shaded space under the dishes. They would not have managed with the semi-conscious Kay, but the dark man called sharply to others to help, and this time he was passed up over the smooth tail of the last wagon. When Mira had gone up the ladder herself and went to make him as comfortable as she could, he was shivering and mumbling. He looked up at her, eyes flickering half open, and said faintly, 'Rissa?'

'No. Not Clarissa. Mira. The spare, remember?'

'Mira,' he murmured, puzzled. 'Mira.' Then he slept again.

This was the pattern for their journey. Heavy, lifeless hours, lying or sitting amongst the rabble of silent passengers, drifting in and out of consciousness. Then the sudden lights and sirens and the bustle of people hastening to reach the ground before the 'électricité' ran through the skin of the beast. Whether it was to let the machinery of the dishes work unhindered or more like a dog ridding itself of fleas from time to time, Mira could not tell. The whole thing seemed to be automatic, driverless, guided only by a memory of the route and the power to detect obstacles ahead. What would happen, Mira wondered, if the road was blocked? On the second day she had a chance to find out. A great branch had tumbled across the way from an overhanging tree. Reaching it, the dragon lurched to a clanking halt . . . and then snorted forward again. One inch. Another. In tiny, powerful movements, the beast snorted its way over the broken wood, splintering it into a thousand pieces. It would take a massive obstacle to stop such power. At other times the water rose to as much as a metre above the road surface: again the machine checked, then snorted forward, the black wheels churning through the flood. Mira hoped that the beast would not choose to electrify itself at such a time; for sure, they could jump down, but how would they ever keep up with the wagons to remount?

As the hours ground on, the wan countryside of lakes and scrub-covered ridges, dotted with the occasional dwelling and yellow pocket of cereals, gave way to a more continuous, rolling, green upland on the left, with almost unbroken sheets of shallow, shimmering water stretching out west, to the right. At the same time the shifting bank of clouds finally gave way completely, broke apart, and turned eventually into soft white tufts, floating in a deep blue sky. Between these tufts, a sun such as Mira had never known beat down on the land and water and turned the chilly space under the dishes into an oven.

'*Soleil!*' grinned the dark man, delightedly. '*Mon ami le soleil!*'

'*Oui. Oui. Bon. Soleil!*'

Gradually, Mira picked up more words from the dark man and from other travellers, until she could say enough to ask for food or water or help when they must dismount or climb up again. Some ignored her completely, one even spat angrily at her – '*Chienne anglaise!*' – but their new friend seemed to radiate good humour in their little section of wagon roof, so that many gave a bite or a mouthful of water for the sick boy: '*Mon ami: le garçon malade*'. Kay himself lay in a deep slumber, muttering and twisting about from time to time, but his colour slowly returned to normal, and the swelling in his feet started to subside, so that Mira felt able to leave him while she jumped down to wash hurriedly in the flood waters, racing after the dragon when she had finished. Back on the wagon roof she took off the rough, goaty clothes and made do with only the grubby Slam suit top, cutting off the sleeves with the *'couteau'* that the dark man – Yusef – lent her.

Yusef laughed and said: *'Pas chaud. Pas encore,'* but ten minutes after her delicious cool wash she was once more running in sweat.

From the late afternoon of the second day, there were people to be seen in the surrounding country. Not many – a man rowing a boat out on the water, two girls waving down from a steep slope where they were tending plants, a woman washing her clothes in the flood – but enough to make the bright landscape seem populated and friendly. At the same time the dragon started to make occasional halts. They would have the siren-and-light warning as before, to give them time to scuttle free, but then, surprisingly, the whole lumbering convoy of transports, eight in all, clanked to a stop.

'Électricité!' Yusef said cheerfully. *'Touche pas! Livraison! Livraison! Regarde.'*

'Regarde' meant to look at something. Mira helped Kay sit down on the ground, propped against the rails and watched with all the other riders while an old grizzled man and two wiry teenage boys who had been leaning on the stiltway barrier, waiting, came forward and walked along the wagons, to the fourth in the line. Then the man brought out something from a pocket, a slip of paper or card perhaps, and pushed it into the side of the wagon. With a hiss, a section of the wagon side-wall split open and some heavy, complicated piece of machinery, painted red, was swung out on a tiny crane and placed gently at the feet of the man and the two boys.

'Montez! Montez!'

Already the door was closing and the dragon moving,

lurching back into life, growling and whining. Helpful arms pulled Kay back to his perch, the others went up the ladders, and things returned to normal. Behind them, on the hot road, free here of the waters, the man and his sons started to wrestle the red-painted thing over the stiltway rails: Mira saw now that a flat, square boat was waiting there, bobbing gently. She wondered how it would possibly float with such a weight inside and the three people too.

Six more times on the journey, there were 'livraisons', which seemed to mean a drop-off, although each time the objects were vastly different: a great roll of metal wire, a wooden crate of something, a stack of plastic sacks, and – the last time – the graceful, white folded sails for a wind generator. For the sails, seven people waited, and two shabby horses stood ready with a rusty metal wagon, but even then the seven had not managed to lever the heavy sails up onto the wagon floor by the time they grew too far behind to see.

Kay finally woke, free of the fever, free of the drug.

'How long?' he asked. 'How long have we been on this thing?'

'This is the end of the third day.' She gazed out to where the sun had started to sink into the waters, enjoying the respite from the heat, scenting the fragrant countryside to their left. The dishes above had already folded into their spines, and the sky lay open to them, a rich, bottomless deep blue between day and night. 'It's a bonny land, is it not? But hot, mind.'

'Yes,' he said vaguely. 'The third day.' And then, more urgently: 'So where are we? Have you asked?'

She shrugged. They had passed a few places where the stiltway had divided, with other smaller routes heading off east, but the dragon had unhesitatingly kept to its

path. 'Nae. I've no asked. We're heading south, that's all
I know. And resting a while, which we needed, you and I
both.'

He gave her a searching look and slowly shook his
head. She saw anger settle back onto him.

'Ask Yusef here,' she suggested. 'He might know where
we are. And thank him too. He has helped you many
times in your fever.'

He didn't answer her, but turned to the black man,
and began a vigorous conversation, with much nodding
and pointing, up at the sky and forward, towards the
south. Eventually, with the dark almost upon them – a
pleasant, starlit dark, not the total blackness of three
nights ago – he turned back and said: 'It's lucky I'm
back to normal. The stiltway turns east sometime early
tomorrow. Apparently this transport is bringing machinery down from the capital to the second French city,
Ma-Seul, right down at the foot of the central uplands,
near the southern ocean. We'll have to get off in the
morning and find another way to cut back to the mountains. It's all flooded there, Yusef says: a huge inland lake.
We'll either have to go around it or find a boat.'

'A boat then,' she replied. 'Your feet are no ready for
another long march.'

He rolled his eyes at her, but she cast herself down full
length on the metal roof to sleep: a deep sleep at last, with
no need to watch for both of them. She should be grateful
that the boy could finally look after himself.

She nudged Kay with her toe: 'Wake me if the sirens
start, aye?'

Out in the dark, on the water, Moore looked at his
compass and his watch. Yes, unless he had made a mess
of his calculations, it was time. He pushed on the little

folding tiller and brought the nose of his craft around to face the land, increased the power of the tiny engine.

In twenty minutes he was at the mouth of what had once been a great river. Now there wasn't much to choose between river and sea. The floods had taken this whole coast for hundreds of miles. The only difference as he crossed the line was in the depth of the water, but in a dinghy that was irrelevant.

A few more hours, chugging slowly over the lost lands beneath a sky studded with brilliant stars. Then Moore idled the engine and slipped the boat's nightsight from its pouch. Scanning the gloom ahead, he laughed softly. There was the thin line of the stiltway, exactly where he had expected it. Slowly he ran the glass up and down the road in both directions. Nothing yet. He still had time to find a suitable place.

Little Mira, here I come.

In the dawn of this fourth day, the fifth since they had left Briton, the stiltway turned sharply east, as Yusef had predicted, but on the other side – to their right – the waters spread out flatter and wider than ever, unstirred by any wind. Mira had not known such silence in the landscape since she had fled from her home. It was like the silence between the red cloud pines when the mist wound in, and yet it was an open, echoing silence instead of a closed, mysterious one. Only a stray bird called intermittently across the shimmering blue, darting down from above to plunge for a fish or an insect.

Kay and most others were asleep but Mira saw Yusef's eyes shining, his face turned south, his mouth murmuring a low song or a chant. She understood at once: it was a time to thank the spirits, to call out to the land in love. She wished she had such a song.

When he had finished, she smiled and nodded at him and he smiled back. They sat in companionable silence a while, content, but eventually the strange, dark-skinned man said, a little sadly: '*Bientôt. L'électricité. Le jour commence.*' He shrugged.

She said: '*Oui. Je comprends,*' and mimed the mad scuttling about and noise there would be when the sirens went for the dishes to be opened. The mystery broken for a while. She mimed tears for that and waved an arm to indicate the world, the peace violated.

Yusef nodded some more and grinned and copied her action.

Pointing to the south-west, to a smudge of brown and green that shimmered over the water like a dream, she asked in her faltering few words of French: '*C'est là? Les Pyrénées? Les montagnes? Là?*'

'*Oui,*' he agreed: '*Les Pyrénées. Il faut traverser les eaux.*'

She bent to wake Kay. 'We must go soon. Yusef says this is nearly the place.'

He sat up, blinking, sleepy and tousled for a moment, smiling at her, and then the guarded look crept swiftly back. 'I could do with some breakfast first, if we have to go charging across the country again.'

She shrugged. 'There is no food. Not unless someone will give you some, further down the wagons.' But soon they heard a great cheer, and then a hullabaloo of shouting and musical notes. Further along the water, strung out by the roadside, lay a cluster of small boats. The boatmen were standing up, calling out to the approaching travellers, waving bright flags and sounding horns.

'*Une boutique!*' Yusef called, over the racket. '*Une boutique sur les eaux!*'

Even before the dragon drew level with the first boats, many of the riders started to shout down to the boatmen, single words repeated many times, the name of the thing they wished. When one or other of the 'shopkeepers' shouted back – '*Oui. Oui. Ici, Monsieur!*' – the rider would descend quickly, take the thing he wanted to buy, pay for it, and race to catch the transport wagons again, clutching the new pie or bottle or hat. It was a noisy, confused process. People bumped into one another, or tripped, or dropped their fresh food as they climbed back up the ladders. Some boats were swarmed around, so that there was not time to serve all if the riders wished not to be left behind. Tempers became short and there was much pushing and jostling. In the middle of it all the sirens went for the solar dishes to be extended and those half-way back had to turn quickly and descend to make room for the exodus from the roofs.

In the noisy crush between the lumbering wagons – the strange, beautiful flowers growing on their tops – and the shop-boats, Mira became separated from Kay. Looking around, she thought she saw his head bobbing amongst others a little further back. Still, his feet were almost healed. He would be able to get back to the transport roof unaided. When the last wagon had passed, she thought, she would come slowly after the bee-like swarm and then, if he had fallen back for any reason she would find him and make sure they did not miss one another. In the meantime, she had a few moments to herself to look around. Even with no money, the little fragile boats full of things for sale were fascinating, full of colour and pungent smells.

Near her, she spotted Yusef. He was grinning away as ever, trying to buy a bag of little cakes, offering less than the boatmen wanted. Even as she watched she saw him gesture to the transport: the last wagon was level with them now and clearly the man would have to give in on his price or lose the sale. In a moment, Yusef had his cakes and was turning to follow the stream of riders clambering back onto their perches. Taking her time, Mira turned too, waiting until the dragon had rumbled on and she was the last to follow. Kay could not be seen. He must already be back aboard. On her right the line of boatmen and women were starting to pack their things away, some rowing slowly back out onto the glassy blue water, the odd few calling out to Mira as the last possible customer.

'Mademoiselle, Mademoiselle! Du pain? Du vin? Un chapeau?'

She smiled, shook her head, held out her empty hands, saw the shrugs.

One young man, baked a dark bronze by the sun and with black, curly hair, grinned shyly up at her from his little boat. He didn't seem to have much for sale but he held out half a pie, globules of thick gravy dripping to the ground.

'Ici, Mademoiselle. C'est un cadeau. Tu as faim.'

The pie looked good. He pushed it towards her with one hand and mimed eating with the other. She smiled back at him, touched by his kindness, and their fingers brushed as she took the food. Mmm, truly it smelled delicious: fresh and savoury. The last wagon was twenty-five metres down the stiltway now: she could still catch it easily. Just one bite, and then she'd run on, share the rest with Kay. The young man watched eagerly as she bit into the pastry, laughing as the juice ran over her chin: 'C'est bon ça? Ça te plait?' And then for some reason the pie was on the ground, split open in the dirt and she was beside it with her senses reeling.

And Gil stood there on the road.

He opened his mouth to speak, but no words came, for

the young man who had offered the pie had scrambled ashore and now flung himself at Mira's attacker, taking him by surprise, knocking him sideways, off balance, and heavily against the rails at the far side of the stiltway. From there, they staggered back again, locked together, and then collapsed, in slow motion, and became a writhing, snarling jumble of limbs on the hard road surface.

Mira climbed dizzily to her feet. She could see already that it would not go well with the brave pie man. He had blood on his face and Gil was starting to extricate himself, delivering hard, telling blows as he did so. For sure she must help him. And yet . . . the pie man was not alone. When they saw one of their fellows thus assaulted, the other boat people began to climb on shore themselves. Ten, fifteen, twenty of them, all ages and shapes and sizes, they advanced on Gil where he stood over his attacker, breathing heavily, and they reached for him, grabbed at his clothing and arms and legs, muttering angrily.

The first few were felled easily by his blows. After that, Mira could see nothing except a close angry knot of people on the road, shouting and heaving. Somewhere in their midst, Gil himself was swearing loud defiance.

She shook herself, trying to clear her head. The dragon was far, far down the road now, just a dark shape in the distance, yet still possible to catch if she ran like the wind. Kay would be searching for her amongst the riders, wondering where she had gone. But then, perhaps it would be best to stay and deal with Gil? Surely he would cause them more trouble if he was not stopped here.

It was difficult. For sure, she had no appetite for murder, no more now than she had the night she sent him into the frozen stream. She felt almost reassured to know this. Perhaps she was not so changed.

She would leave Gil to the boat people. If she ran now, she could still catch the transport, leaving him far behind.

'*Mademoiselle.*' A quiet voice spoke beside her. She turned and saw the young pie man. He had blood on his mouth and running from his nose, and his clothing was torn, but he seemed unconcerned. '*Mademoiselle. Tu viens maintenant. Viens avec moi. Dans le bateau.*'

He gestured at his little craft, went towards it, beckoning her to follow. '*Viens. Viens! Marie m'a envoyé. Marie? Adeline? Tu viens!*'

She was amazed. He spoke the child's name! And that of the watcher: Marie Coutures. She turned to look at him, into the dark eyes, and knew that she must decide at once. Kay and the transport, or this unknown person and his little boat. The fight on the roadway would not last for ever.

She took a breath, then stepped down into the boat after the wiry young man and immediately he was casting off, taking them expertly out from amongst the other craft. When they were twenty metres out, he turned the nose of the boat and bent his back to long, powerful, steady strokes with the oars, following the dotted craft that had already headed out onto the expanse of water.

After a minute, he paused to wipe the blood from his face. '*Couche-toi!*' he said to Mira: '*Couche-toi là.*' He mimed lying down, pointed to the space on the boat floor, a mess of sailcloth and old bits and pieces and a wooden box with three pies in the bottom, such as the one he had offered her. Mira did as he wished, realising as she did so that if she were invisible, they would be only one of ten or twelve little boats for anyone scanning from the shore.

She smiled at the man. '*Je comprends.*'

'*Oui. Oui. C'est mieux.*'

She wondered what was happening to Gil. She

wondered if Kay was still on the dragon's back or if he had dismounted to look for her. She watched the regular tightening of muscles in the young man's brown back as he rowed. She smelled the salt and the pies and the water and the sun on the tarred wood. She closed her eyes.

It was good to let someone else decide for once.

When the boat people had finished with him, Moore lay on the road for a while, assessing the damage. Peasants! They had not known how to hurt him badly, but still he ached. More than that, he was furious that once again the girl had slipped away. She seemed to have the luck of the devil.

When he was convinced that there was nothing a night's rest wouldn't cure, he got to his feet and looked around.

The last boats were already moving away from their stiltway moorings. The occupants shook their fists at him and shouted abuse as they went. Casually he returned the compliment, using words that some of them did not even know. He took out his field glasses and swept them over the water, studying each craft. Nothing. If she was there, she was hidden. Still, he had his own boat and a little fuel left. If the fuel lasted out, he could go and search amongst them.

He thought then of the speed with which that young idiot had hurled himself into the attack. He'd watched him offering the food to Mira and how she'd batted her eyelashes at him, little bitch. It had made him angry enough to strike immediately, but perhaps that had been a mistake. Thinking about it now, Moore wondered if the young gallant had even been *waiting* for the girl. Certainly they were getting near the mountains. Could it be that Mira was expected?

He shrugged. The pie seller had been no soldier, for all his bravery. If little Mira had defenders awaiting her like that one, there would be no problem.

So, the boat. He turned and walked slowly northwards, towards the stiltway's east-facing elbow. After eighty or so metres, he lowered himself down over the side of the road, into the shallow water, and swam under the supports. The little dinghy was tied where he had left it. He clambered up over the side and sat in the rear, looking at the gagged, bound figure lying in the bottom.

Kay looked back at him, defiant but scared.

Perhaps, Moore thought, he would not have to search through all the sellers' boats, after all. He took out his radio to make his report to Hunter.

THIRTY-NINE

Even the Families who had snubbed Jan by their absence at the arrival of the ICSA team had sent one or two members to the first open report of the inspectors' findings. The boy-man saw this and knew with cold satisfaction that the changes he had made had been accepted, willingly or not. The city was restored to good order; a curfew had been imposed. Tilly Saint had been caught red-handed at Stoneywall. It was well known that he now had his permission to pick up the others in France. Yes, all the loose ends that had troubled the anxious old fools were being tidied away.

And today that goat Amarfio would ice the cake, though he might not want to.

When the remaining Saints met with their accidents, Jan thought, that would be accepted too. He gave Clarissa's limp, submissive hand a squeeze. Even *she* would accept the new order. It had taken only a few days for her to buckle to his will, for all her cockiness before. When the last ends were tidy, he would arrange a public ceremony to join her to him. The people would like that.

What a couple they'd make! They'd purify this polluted city and be the envy of every civilised nation state. And soon the Board would have their new screening process completed. They would people this new state with hard-working, obedient, perfect human beings. History would see his time in power as the start of a golden age.

Dr Amarfio, immaculate in formal white ICSA robes, rapped his gavel and raised his hand for silence. On his left, under Pax guard, were those accused of breaking the international agreement. Tomas, sitting hunched and shrunken, a shadow of the man he had been a week ago, hardly seeming to take an interest in the proceedings; and Tilly, tall, calm, dignified, smiling benignly at her peers. With them were the remaining Saint bodyguards: Copper and Sebestova, both wearing restrainers, both looking murderous.

'Representatives of Briton,' Amarfio said into the expectant silence, 'we have called this hearing to declare our findings to date. We are here, as you know, in response to an allegation of creation of illegal human copies, by one of the Great Families of your nation. However, before I give you our preliminary verdict on this matter, I would like the record to show the following observations. They may not change what happens from here on, nor can they change our own legal rulings, by which we are bound, but those are not reasons not to speak the truth as we see it.

'The first observation, then. The allegation and the invitation to investigate came in this case jointly from your Fertility Board and from Jan Barbieri. This followed Mr Barbieri's own very recent ascent to a position of power. We have also observed that certain decisions that may concern Briton's present and future as a whole, seem at present to be taken exclusively by, again, the Fertility Board and Mr Barbieri. I leave you to draw your own conclusions as to whether these various elements are connected in any way.'

Jan got to his feet: 'Your Excellency! We protest at this *outrageous*—' but Amarfio held up a solemn hand: 'Please. Be seated. Be seated. We *will* speak on these matters, and our records – as always – will be available to all other ICSA signatories. If necessary, the room will be cleared and the observations and findings made and officially recorded in private. Interruption will serve no end.' He waited until Jan had sunk slowly back to his place, the boy's face flushed with anger. 'Thank you. Now, the second observation. This concerns the evidence that was presented to us on our arrival.

'We were told that, uniquely amongst the Great Families of Briton, the Saint family had used a programme of systematic cloning in order to ensure retention of their privileged position and especially the contracts that they held from the state that was. I may as well say that the first reaction of all eight of us in this inspection team was identical. We believe cloning for such reasons as those I mentioned to be not rare, but *widespread* amongst the ruling classes: both of Briton and of countries elsewhere. It *is*, however, painfully rare for ICSA to be approached to investigate the practice, and in every case to date – they number four – the inspecting teams have concluded that allegations have been made as a result of one ruling body wishing to disadvantage another ruling body.' The doctor looked dryly around the room, his gaze stopping at Jan's face.

'Do I make myself clear, I wonder? I think so. So . . . in this particular case my seven colleagues and I were interested in the background situation as well as the hard evidence for the alleged offence.' He paused, straightened the papers before him. 'When we arrived, ladies and gentlemen, we found a city in some degree of chaos. One Great Family had used force to remove another. Anarchists or protesters had apparently taken to the streets in great numbers. Two members of the deposed Great Family were on the run, one even leaving his home country to escape. Soon afterwards, all three of the European-controlled satellites were disabled. In short, although efforts were made to insulate us or to hide the signs, there were all the hallmarks of considerable political upheaval: which is exactly what we expected.

'"So," we said to our hosts, "we are here. Where is the evidence for your allegation?" "In Wales", we were told. In Wales, at Stoneywall, there was apparently considerable technical evidence of a cloning programme in an underground vault used by the Saint family. This would be brought to us soon. *Living* evidence would also be provided in the shape of Mathilda Saint and her daughter Clarissa, plus one or two other clones: just as soon as they could be traced!

'Unfortunately, before we could see the technical evidence, it was apparently destroyed. This was done by Mathilda Saint herself, who then allowed her own capture. So, one piece of evidence lost, another regained. But *why*, we asked ourselves, would Mrs Saint bother with destroying evidence if she knew our case could still be proved through her?'

Murmurs across the chamber but Tilly herself sat unmoving. Once, briefly, those eyes sent their glance across the room to her daughter, and found their gaze returned. A single slow wink passed from mother to daughter, making the latter smile involuntarily. Clarissa looked quickly away, fighting to retain the bitter, sulky look. She didn't know what she had expected from her mother, but it had not been that. Something inside her, something without name, became joyful.

Amarfio's voice continued: 'We were interested enough in this puzzling question to wish to see the famous vault for ourselves. We had not been invited to do so, however, and we did not wish our hosts and their friends to be aware of our desire. Thus we approached another Great Family – one that we had reason to believe might help us – to see if they could perhaps bring us some record of the vault. Early this morning they delivered the following pictures, taken last night and transmitted by radio signal.'

Lights were dimmed and on the screen behind the inspectors, a series of images began, starting with the entrance to Stoneywall's restricted Level One. Slowly, steadily, the camera operator took the audience around the whole length of the vault chamber, showing each burnt-open bunker in detail, including the bare insides. The final image was of the Saint bunker, now also standing open. Inside, this one was scorched and blistered throughout and the floor was thickly coated with fine, pure-white ash.

Into the silence Amarfio spoke dryly.

'Again, I remind you, our observations have no legal weight; but they *may* be of interest both to yourselves and to other ICSA nations. We conclude from these images that eleven of the twelve bunkers were opened in an identical manner, and their unknown contents cleared by a person or persons with unrestricted access to the Fertility Board's Stoneywall Centre. Dissident operations were suggested to us, but we find this *very* improbable. The twelfth bunker, which Mrs Saint opened herself and destroyed, had deliberately been left whole by whoever emptied the others. Why? For us, the inspectors, to see. As to what the other bunkers had contained, I doubt you here today need any suggestion on that. Lights, please.'

Now, whatever the doctor might desire, the murmurs became uproar. Voices were raised, accusing fingers started to be pointed at Jan, clenched fists banged table tops. The Pax guards overseeing the line of prisoners looked around uneasily. Three other guards, hearing the noise, came running in from the corridor, looking to Jan for instructions. Furiously, he waved them back to their posts. He certainly didn't need protection from *this* rabble. If necessary he'd shoot them all himself.

Who, he wondered, scanning along the rows of faces, *who* had been that Great Family member who had supplied the pictures? Why hadn't Pieter or Magnus warned him? He looked across to where they sat, mild and unthreatening as ever. Pieter, he thought, gave the faintest of shrugs and then shook his head slightly, willing him to be calm, to weather the storm.

Eventually, after some minutes, the audience settled once again into tense silence, waiting to see what else the inspectors might produce. Again, Amarfio rapped his gavel.

'I see that I have given you some cause for thought. I hope that that may prove to be a positive thing. Let us then move on to our findings in the matter of Saint family violation of the anti-cloning agreement. Here, having already made my previous background comments, I will endeavour to be concise.' He took one of the papers up from the table, scanned it briefly as if to confirm its contents, and looked up. 'Ladies and gentlemen of the Great Families of Briton, members of the Fertility Board . . . having taken DNA samples from both Clarissa and Mathilda Saint – both given freely and with their consent – we have concluded that the former is a clone of the latter, or – more likely perhaps – that both are clones of some other person. Without further evidence we cannot be sure. The matter of responsibility is unproven, but . . .' he raised a warning finger for silence, '. . . *but* my colleagues and myself have found it fair to conclude that the cloning process has, indeed, been used deliberately, and that this is unlikely to have been without at least the knowledge – probably the co-operation or desire – of the two adults here accused.' He gestured at Tilly and Tomas. 'On behalf of the International Crisis Strategy Agreement, we therefore have no option other than to sanction their removal from power. What else may happen to them is beyond our legal control, but we would recommend a maximum sentence of five years' incarceration, should they be tried by any civil British court. That recommendation will also be recorded.'

Again, a break for the reaction to fade.

Tomas, hearing the sentence, put his head in his hands, but Jan felt his previous fury drain away.

Amarfio had indeed iced the cake. The rest – what had gone before – was irrelevant bleating. *This* was what the old farts had been invited here to do. The country was securely his.

'However,' the doctor intoned, 'there rests the matter of the other alleged clones, both of whom are reported to be in France. We were asked to lend our authority to a request to the French powers to allow an expeditionary force there, with the object of bringing these two people – two *children* I should say – back to Briton to be used as evidence. Indeed, as we had not at that stage been presented with *any* concrete evidence, we complied with this request, rather against our better judgement. *Now*, the case being sufficiently proved, I have spoken with my fellows and we are all agreed that no such force should be sent. Not, at any rate, upon our authority. We consider that neither of the two subjects in France, *nor* Clarissa Saint, none of whom are legally adult, can be held responsible for any misuse of cloning technology. To punish them or disrupt their lives in any way hereon would, in our view, be inexcusable: the cause of needless suffering. We therefore intend this day to send a message to the French, *removing* our endorsement of Mr Barbieri's request.

'Do I make myself clear?'

FORTY

Pieter sighed. He went to the window and spoke with his back turned. 'We have been careless. We have lost support from some of the other Families. We have allowed question marks to arise over our actions. Things that were acceptable whilst unspoken, are no longer so. It would be unwise now to antagonise our allies or the inspectors further.'

Jan kicked at the carpet. 'We *need* to retrieve the information that the spare is carrying,' he said tightly. 'Did you see Tilly Saint's expression? She believes she's won. Whatever's on that card could harm us far more with the ICSA or the Families than those Stoneywall pictures or any of the other rubbish. And besides, I want that line of the Saints *ended*. I will do to their family what they did to mine.'

'But you'll keep Clarissa? She's to be an exception?'

The boy said carefully, looking down: 'I am to be the last Barbieri. She will be the last Saint. It's a balance. And it's what you *wanted*, isn't it? What you *told* me to do; to please the precious Families!'

Magnus put his thin hand on Jan's shoulder, placatingly. 'My dear boy. We've never *told* you to do anything, I hope. We've only advised, always in your interests, and in the interests of our great nation. We all want the same things for Briton, do we not?' The old man looked searchingly up at him: 'If we have done anything to upset or anger you, I am truly sorry. We both are. Perhaps after all we should not have told you the truth about your parents and the other, more recent attacks. I believe now that we should not. It would have been kinder. And yet, you are now adult. A grown man with responsibilities. You had a right to know; or so we thought.'

Jan looked down at the curious little figure and for the first time felt the ghost of a suspicion that he was being played for a fool. He said to them: 'All that business about the vault. Amarfio suggesting it was a different person who'd emptied the others. Was that true?'

Pieter turned back to face the other two. He seemed unusually restless and irritable today. He snapped: 'Amarfio? What does *he* know about anything? Is he a policeman? A detective? Obviously not! For what could be more likely than the Saint woman destroying the cloning potential of rival Families, taking her time to do so, planning it to the letter, using her Wrecker contacts to help . . . and then returning hastily with a thermal bomb to destroy evidence against *her* when she knew the inspectors were here? Hmm? Amarfio! His type just enjoy making mischief.'

'Yes,' Jan agreed: 'I see that. But why then did she allow herself to be captured afterwards?'

'Why? *Why?* Do you think she *knew* she would be detained after her quiet little arson? Do you think she *wanted* to be captured?'

Yes, Jan thought involuntarily: yes, he would say that that was indeed what she had wanted. Again the ghost of doubt flitted through his mind, quickly and uneasily suppressed.

Magnus was saying to Pieter: 'Calm yourself, my friend. Calm yourself! It does no good to get so upset. We cannot change things that are past. We need only decide now what actions should follow.'

Jan said stubbornly: 'My man is very close to the targets. I say we go anyway. In and out overnight, pick up the spares or eliminate them there. Get back that comcard. The French won't even know we've been.'

'And if they *do* know you've been? If they lodge a complaint?'

'If they complain, we say that the mission was sent to get evidence for the ICSA team *before* today's report hearing. Amarfio might not even send out his message to the French authorities until tomorrow.'

There was silence between the three of them. Stalemate.

Eventually Magnus said soothingly: 'So be it. Prepare your mission. Go and get the spares and the stolen information. Go now, today, before the French permission is rescinded. I will tell Dr Amarfio that you are ill and send your respects for his safe voyage home. But, Jan, my boy: if you are set on bloodshed, let it be an accident, obvious as such to all. And not on French territory. I think . . . um . . . perhaps something at sea?'

Pieter was nodding. 'Yes. If it must be done, the sea is best. Too expensive to investigate. Too dangerous.'

Jan gave each a curt bow, the ghost forgotten. 'I will go and prepare,' he said.

When he had gone, Pieter gave his colleague a thin smile: 'I think that went rather well, don't you?'

'Yes indeed. *You*, my friend, were inspired. Getting so angry with the donkey like that. It quite made him forget his doubts.'

'It was not hard, my brother. I *do* get angry with him. He's such a *stubborn* donkey.'

'And what about his mission?'

Pieter shrugged. 'He was set on going. He has to have some outlet for his anger, I think. And for us, after all, it will solve the question of that unfortunate baby.'

'Yes. That is true. But are we not then two paranoid old men, who should know better?'

'No, brother. We are two *careful* old men who *do* know better than to allow the more dubious and gullible elements of our population any kind of talisman, however false.'

Thus reassured, the two smiled, clasped frail hands, embraced.

'It is a pity,' Magnus said, 'that we will not have the body, afterwards. We could get the truth about those eyes, perhaps.'

FORTY-ONE

Whilst Mira dozed, sprawled out on the old baked timbers in the shadow of the thick, brown sail the young man had set, her rescuer sent a short message back to Le Porge in the agreed code.

When she had the message, Marie went down to the water, to where Pierre was himself dozing under a solitary tree. She said: 'The girl is coming. Aziz has her in his boat. But he says there was a pursuit. The hounds may know that we are here. He is not sure.'

The fat man growled sleepily: 'Let them come! We will give them a welcome.' And then: 'What else does Aziz say?'

Marie grinned. 'Only that she is beautiful and very hungry. She ate two of his pies.'

They both laughed at that.

'Trust Aziz. Ferrying a beautiful girl in his boat, all alone. Feeding her his pies.'

Clarissa hurried down the corridor, thankful for the oasis of freedom while Jan had his meeting with the skeletons. She knew that it was freedom of the building only – she would not yet be allowed outside – but then her mother must still be somewhere in this building too. If only Jan would take his time with his plots, she might manage to find her. It suddenly seemed more important than anything, though she did not know what she would find to say. Deep down she felt a cold fear that it would not be a cell that waited for her mother, but something more final.

Rounding the corner that led back to the hearing room, in case the prisoners had not yet been removed, she almost ran into three of the ICSA inspectors. They were sauntering along, chatting, sharing a joke about something. Two women and a man. Seeing her, one of the women, very pale and blonde, with a strong accent to her English, said: 'My dear, I am good to see you. I like to tell you, we are very sorry to have brought you so much . . . *problem* in our coming. With the law, it is like that! The law is kept and still persons are hurt. The little persons.'

Clarissa said: 'Please. Don't worry. It's not your fault.' She tried to get past – time was precious – but still the woman stood in her way.

'Please. I want to say more. I know Dr Amarfio offer you help. A little love. And you said no, you don't need help. Maybe you are being *strong* girl, brave, I don't know. I still think you need help. And so I say to you, I have a daughter also. In my house, in Switzerland. She has sixteen years, about like you. We have nice house, but she is lonely there. Father is dead. If you wish, you come and live here with us. There is room. Far away from Mr *Barbieri* and all this things. No one hurt you. All safe there. I see well the way Mr Barbieri behave with you. Why not come?'

Again the unexpected kindness was almost too much for Clarissa. This woman she didn't know was offering her everything she could want! A home, safety, normality, love. She had a great desire to say: *Yes, oh yes, take me with you*. She was left trembling with it. She dared not even meet the woman's eyes, for fear that the treacherous words would slip out.

She thought of the cameras above them, recording all this, considered how she might use it.

'You are very kind,' she said clearly to the woman, 'really, I am grateful. But there is no need. I am to be Jan's partner. I will have a very good home here. I'm sure he will look after me. Now, I was just on my way to try and see my mother.'

The second woman said something in a tongue that Clarissa could not understand. Her colleagues listened and nodded agreement. The first woman said: 'Come. We go with you. It is good if you can see your mother. Maybe she persuade you: to come to Switzerland. At least we can be sure no one stop you to see her.' She turned back the way she had come. 'Come! Come! They keep your mother on the upper basement level. We all go.'

Wordlessly, Clarissa followed the three inspectors. Jan and his spies could make of it what they wanted: this was one kindness she could not refuse. Together, the four of them went to the central elevators and down below ground level. Why must they keep her down here? she thought bitterly. She could easily be up in one of the top floors. She loves to be up high.

The Swiss inspector led the way from the elevator along a dim passage to a door with four giant guards. The cameras swivelled as they went, recording their progress. The inspector said to the guards: 'We come to see your prisoner. Please to open the door.'

The men eyed Clarissa doubtfully. One of them said: 'Excuse me, ma'am, but we should call in: check it's OK.'

'Then please do so,' the Swiss woman said sharply.

The man pushed a button on his wristcom. 'Mr Hunter, sir. It's Private Jacks. Sir, three of the ICSA people are here. They want to see Mrs Saint. Clarissa Saint is also with them.'

There was an inaudible reply and the man unclipped his wristcom and passed it across. 'Ma'am, Mr Hunter would like to speak with you.'

She took the device. Clarissa watched her jawline harden in determination. 'Good day to you, Mr Hunter. Here is Frau Kästener of the International Crisis Strategy Agreement team. I wish access to this prisoner. Please do not delay. Our report to our superiors will be made today. I do not wish to add your name with the problems we have in this inspection. ICSA have unlimited access. Here and every place. That is the rule.'

Another inaudible reply.

'Yes? Well, Mr Hunter, I want to tell you that ICSA also has code on treatment of prisoners and their dependents. *All* in report. And if evidence for obstruction is strong enough, we send new team. Bigger, more power. Turn your little city upside down, looking for worms.'

Again the reply, much quieter this time.

Frau Kästener smiled and the muscles in the pale jawline relaxed. 'Thank you Mr Hunter. You are very good man.' She handed the com back to the guard, who listened a moment, said 'Yes, sir!' and punched the keycode into the door panel.

'There you are, ma'am. Take as long as you want.'

Frau Kästener bowed a little bow, waved Clarissa towards the door. 'You hear this man, my dear. As long as you want. We stay here outside a while, in case you need us.'

She started asking the guards about where one might dine out, for the last night in Briton. Clarissa didn't hear the guard's reply. She was already pushing the heavy door open, walking through, closing it behind her.

Inside the room was bare and very bright. Two cameras leered at each other from opposite corners. There was

neither window nor furniture. Her mother sat against the
wall on the left, eyes closed, face relaxed. Without those
eyes opening, a smile crept round the corners of her mouth.

'Darling. You came.'

'Yes.'

Now she was here, Clarissa couldn't think what she
wanted to say. Suddenly a few minutes in this empty
room did not seem enough to show all her feelings. It was
too much.

And then Tilly was up from the floor and holding
her close, fiercely, squeezing the breath from her lungs.
And Clarissa was holding on just as tight.

'My poor love,' her mother murmured at last. 'You
were left all alone.'

Yes! Why? Why did you leave me alone? She stayed
silent. She had to stay silent or the dam would burst.

They broke apart but stood facing one another, hands
linked. Tilly studied her, looked carefully into her eyes.
She nodded, as if reassured by what she saw there. 'My
Clarissa,' she said gently. 'You are grown into a woman,
and I hadn't noticed.'

'Your skiing. Your Wreckers. Your love life!' Clarissa
tried to make it sound like a joke. She choked on the
laugh. *Remember the cameras!* 'I didn't really know you
at all.'

'Yes. A terrible mother. I didn't trust myself. How could
I? What right had I? You see . . . you – were – *me*.'
The last word was no more than breathed. Clarissa's head
was spinning.

Tilly caught hold of her again. It seemed after all that
not many words were needed. They rocked gently in their
embrace. Silent streams of tears came from both. Noises
were coming from the corridor. Running footsteps. Raised
voices.

'I'll come again,' Clarissa whispered miserably.

'There, there ... don't fret, my love, my daughter, my sister. I am content with how things are. And I am proud.'

Jan was in the room now, pulling Clarissa away from her mother. *'Out!'* he said furiously to her. She went in a dream and he followed. The heavy door closed, the electronic locks activated. Their quiet click sounded like the end of the world to Clarissa. Jan took her arm and escorted her back to her rooms. At the doorway he said, more calmly: 'That was not such a good idea. You are upset. She doesn't deserve it, my love. When did she ever have time for you?'

She made herself nod. 'I know. I know. It was foolish.' She held onto him, reached up to kiss his cheek. He watched her doubtfully.

'Sleep now,' he said, and pushed her into the room, shut the door. With the greatest of efforts she did not kick it down again, or smash the glass table in the middle of the room. She went instead to the toilet. There, at least, the cameras would not watch her. She sat down, feeling her heart thud, and felt under her tunic collar for the little hardness that had appeared there, teased it out. The tiny external earpiece from a handset, with one recording stored in it, according to the single red dot on the read-out.

She screwed it into her ear and listened. It was her mother's voice, singing softly:

> *Blessed children,*
> *You are given this sleeping serpent;*
> *Stretched across the years,*
> *Its strong, bright coils buried deep*
> *In the marshes and the flood waters;*
> *Its mouth closed on its tail.*

And when the serpent wakes,
And it is full grown and nourished,
And the beautiful, sleek, knowing head is lifted up,
And the two eyes open, one brown, one green;
Then, blessed children, you may ride its back
To freedom and love.

For this serpent is no tempter:
She is your truest friend.

There was a pause at the end of the song.

Then: 'Have you heard them singing this, my love? Many of our people are singing these words, or saying them, or writing them. Ordinary people. Not like us or the Visions. I don't know where the words come from or what they mean, but still they touch something inside me. I feel . . . a great hope, for all of us. For all Briton. That may seem strange to you.'

Clarissa thought the recording was ended, so long was the silence in her ear. She sat trying to work out what Tilly meant by what she had said. Somehow, she had expected words of love, or at least something solid that might be used against Jan. She thrust down the disappointment, reached out to flush the toilet for the microphones.

And then the voice started again.

'Now I have muddled you with all this strange talk. My poor Clarissa. Let me just say two more things then. One is that I love you and have always loved you. The other is that it strikes me that this strange thing that we are, you and I and the others . . . maybe this is like the "bright coils" of that serpent in the song. Don't you think so? I don't know why I should think this. Is it the unbroken line we form? The coiled strands of our genes? And there is something stranger still. The newest of our sisters, the one Mira and Kay have gone to find. *Her eyes are brown . . . and green.* Now I must go. Live well, my sister. Live proudly and with my love.'

With her head reeling, Clarissa cast the little nodule of plastic into the toilet, sending it out to the rising sea.

In the night, Jan came to wake her, as he had done only a few nights before. Again he came in like a flurry of snow, activating bright lights, stripping back her bed things. Again he brought news.

'Come,' he said. 'Get dressed. We leave in fifteen minutes. Don't bother with prettying yourself up.'

She squinted in the light. 'Leave? Where?'

'To southern France. By chopper.'

'France! Are you mad? It's the middle of the night. Why now?'

He gave a tight cold smile. 'We have to collect one or two people, my love. And anyway, it will put all thoughts of running to *Switzerland* out of your mind, won't it?'

She reached for her dressing gown, careful not to show elation. She had pitched her actions correctly, between trust and mistrust. The idiot was keeping her close to him, just in case. He could not be sure that she would not choose to go to Switzerland, or to see her mother again.

'OK,' she said. 'If I could have a few minutes to dress?'

He looked at her with his hunger, then turned smartly about. 'I'll be just outside. Don't be too long, my love.'

Half an hour later they were airborne, flying fast and low over the wave tops. Jan watched Clarissa broodingly. He met her eyes and deliberately pressed a few buttons on his wristcom.

'There,' he said, with a small mirthless smile. 'Another problem ironed out, my love.'

And back in the Pax Building they came for Tilly, as he had ordered.

FORTY-TWO

It was first light, the time of transition. The chill air was singing, rich, other. Mira was lying in the clean snow. She scooped handfuls of it over her legs, starting to cover them. As she did so, she felt them grow warm. When her legs were buried and snug, she moved on to her tummy. She was lying flat now, looking up through the snow-heavy branches at the pale, low sky. The scent of the branches and the snow was rich in her nose. The warmth came up to her tummy. Still she heaped up the white, handful by handful, up over her breasts and as far as her neck. Then her hands and arms and shoulders wriggled themselves into the soft down.

She was protected, warm as toast. Only her face lay uncovered, hearing the snowy songs weaving between the trees.

'*Mademoiselle! Mademoiselle!*'

Her eyes flicked open. The young pie seller was there, above her, rowing away, grinning down. The old oak under her body was hot with the sun and humid from the leaks. She felt drowsy, happy, sad, moved by her dream.

'*Mademoiselle*,' the young man said again, '*Le Porge. Nous arrivons. Un quart d'heure.*' He let go of the oars a moment and held up ten fingers, then five again. '*Quinze minutes. Quinze. Un quart d'heure.*' Fifteen minutes. Quarter of an hour.

She nodded, wondering vaguely how long they had been on the water. It was still impossibly hot, even with the faint breeze that came in off the sea, but the sun was

starting to dip low in the west. She must have slept away
most of the day, on and off. Perhaps it was for the best.
There was still the final effort to come. A child to meet
and help, if she could. Somehow she would soon have to
dig deep for energy and the power to move events once
more. It was a blessing that she had been given this
golden day: to eat, to sleep, to be soothed by the young
man's oars and the slap of water on the hull. A day to be a
child once more herself.

She smiled up at the pie man, shading her eyes, and he
smiled back from his thin, strong face. He must have been
rowing for hours with barely a break, but he didn't seem
tired. Surprisingly she found herself imagining running
a finger over those brown, muscly ribs; perhaps kissing
them. How lovely it would be just to spend a few days
with a boy – with this boy – and to do only what ordinary
people did. What every boy and girl did. She felt herself
blushing.

She shook herself, trying to clear her head of such
dreams. She sat up, pushing the sailcloth shelter aside,
making the boat wobble.

'*Voilà!*' the young man said: '*Le Porge.*'

They were moving away from the wide, open expanse
of blue, Mira saw: onto a narrower tongue of water. On
their left and right great shoulders of baked land climbed
out of the water like the shoulders of a sleeping dragon:
red-brown soil peppered with patches of scrub and grass-
land and low, twisted trees glinting with dusty silver bark.
Further on, half lost in sun-haze, the shoulders grew into
the largest mountains Mira had ever seen. Marching in a
line, east to west, as far as she could see, they climbed up
in raw, sharp splendour.

She felt her heart soar at the sight. *Mountains. Home.*

The tongue of lake wound in between the first few hills,

finding its way into a drowned valley cradled at the foot of the larger slopes. '*Là,*' the pie boy said, and pointed to a cluster of buildings at the far end of the water. She looked where he pointed and saw the village. Adeline's village.

Like Mira's own village, the houses of Le Porge were mostly low and wooden, except for one or two older, tumble-down stone houses near the water. Here, though, the planks had been stained brightly white, against the heat of a sun that beat down upon the place so savagely, drawing any moisture from the soil, turning the ground to fine red dust. The wooden buildings were all set well away from the waterline, allowing for further rise in the floods, with the furthest ones some height up the first slopes. The whole of the end of this tongue-shaped inlet, when they reached it, was closed off with a black barrier, lying like a snake across the water.

'*Pour les poissons,*' the pie boy said. For the fish. On the other side of the barrier, there were smaller enclosures, perhaps for the different sorts of fish that were being farmed there.

At the first barrier the boat could go no further. The young man rattled his oars up through the rowlocks and let the prow nudge gently into the bank. He stepped into the shallows and offered Mira his hand, steadying the boat with a thin bare foot. '*Voila. Le Porge. Il faut marcher un peu.*' You'll have to walk a little.

She took the hand and stepped after him. As she did so she saw that his face was marked and bruised where he had fought with Gil. She indicated with her fingers, stopping short of actually touching and he shrugged, grinned his carefree grin. '*Ça, ce n'est rien.*' The water was cool between her toes. They splashed up to the bank, to the hard dusty path that ran there, and then the boy went back to catch the rope from his boat and heave it up after them, the wet wood of the hull shining and dripping like a fish. *'On y va,'* the boy said, and they turned left to head for the buildings, passing other boats that lay drawn up above high water.

Mira went as if still in her dream. She saw now that there were people around the end of the inlet, some sitting in the dust doing something with barrels and metal pipes, two edging carefully, balanced on the dividing barriers that went across the water, carrying long nets. As they drew near, a man came heavily out from the shadows of the first, tumble-down stone building and blocked their way, feet astride. Like her pie boy, he was bare to the waist, but where the boy was lean as a rope, this man had a mound of bronzed stomach hanging over his trousers, and great, knotted arms. Behind him, three children ran laughing between the houses, all too old to be the child Mira sought.

The man scowled at them for a split second as if in anger, then his face broke into a broad smile. *'Aziz!'* he roared. *'Aziz, petit chiot, elle est vraiment belle, hein?'* and he clapped a massive hand on the boy's shoulder. To Mira he said: *'Bienvenue, Mademoiselle! Bienvenue!'* Welcome! He kissed her on both cheeks, embraced her as if they had met many times, almost lifting her off her feet. *'Viens! Marie t'attend. Elle devait dormir un peu, mais elle t'attend.'* Come! Marie is waiting for you. She had to sleep a little, but she's waiting.

Mira said: *'Merci. Merci, Monsieur.'*

Still there seemed nothing for her to do or think about. These kind people who somehow knew of her arrival were in charge. She couldn't even properly speak to them in their tongue.

Together the three walked up to one of the old stone houses, a tiny, leaning building with the dry mortar

crumbling out from between uneven stones and wooden
shutters half across the windows, twisted and warped
from the heat of many summers.

'*Marie!*' the giant bellowed, as they got close. '*Marie! Elle
est là!*'

A thin, musical voice came back from inside. '*Oui,
d'accord. J'arrive. Attends-moi dans le jardin, Pierre.*'

The big man – Pierre – gestured onwards with his
head. '*Le jardin,*' he said gruffly. They walked on past the
house and Mira saw that behind it there was a large, level
space, surrounded by a low wall. Inside there were many
red-brown pots of herbs and flowers and a straggling,
climbing thing that clung on to a framework overhead.
From this there hung clusters of swollen fruit: deep-red
globes that Mira did not recognise.

It was a fragrant, peaceful place, half shaded, and from
one side the beach below could be seen, and the tongue
of water, which wound out, cool and inviting, towards
the open expanse of lake.

'*Bienvenue! Bienvenue*, Mira.'

She turned and saw that a young woman had come up
the stone steps from the house. The woman was slim
and not tall, but moved with cat-like grace. Pale brown
hair hung in a simple, short plait down her back.

'Welcome, Mira.' The woman held out a small hand,
studying her face.

Mira took the hand. 'Thank you. You speak English!'

'*Oui.* A little. I am Marie Coutures. A watcher. You
know this already, I think. And you are Mira. Another
from the same series as the girl I keep safe. You have
already met Aziz,' she gestured at the young pie man,
'. . . and Pierre, who was watching by the water there for
your arrival.'

Feeling slightly unreal, Mira nodded and smiled at

each of the men again and said '*Bonjour*' and shook their hands. Aziz grinned with amusement. The skin of his palm was hard with rowing. She said: 'You are all very kind. And Aziz saved me on the stiltway.'

Marie nodded. '*Oui*, I know this already. It was fortunate. Come, sit down, and tell me a little of your journey. Tell me especially, what was this man who attacked you? Do you know him?'

Mira sat as she was invited, on a stone bench in the shade. 'Aye, I know him, right enough. He was *my* watcher. His name's Gil. He's hunted me since the day I ran from my home.'

The woman nodded again. She spoke quickly to Aziz and listened intently to his reply. 'This boy you came with, this Kay . . . is he strong? In his mind, I mean.'

Mira was surprised. 'Kay? Why? I don't know. Och, strong enough, I guess. But he was on the dragon – that big transport – and I lost him. He must be away to the south now. And cursing me.'

Marie shook her head. 'No. Aziz tells me that your watcher, your *Gil*, took the boy. I wish only to know how long he may give us. He knows where you were going, I suppose?'

Dazed, Mira whispered, 'Yes. Aye, he knows.' Poor Kay. Caught by Gil! And she had not known, had not helped him!

'Please,' Marie said gently, reading her thoughts. 'Do not be regretful. It was not to be helped. Probably, if you had aided the boy, neither of you would be coming here.'

Mira shook her head, almost angrily. 'I hardly know why I *have* come, now I'm here. Such a long journey it's been. But I wanted to save the baby, to keep her safe.' She looked down at her hands, resting in her lap. 'Instead, I've brought the danger with me, perhaps.'

'*Non, pas du tout*. Not at all. Don't think this way, please. Tilly was very pleased by it; by you coming here. She told me so. And probably you are after all the best one; to keep Adeline safe, and to teach her, too, as she grows.' She put her hand on Mira's. 'Your instinct was right. There are many, many things at work here, I think, Mira. You must not worry.'

The man called Pierre said something in his growling voice, sounding like a question. Marie nodded. Again there was a conversation in rapid French, all three of them speaking in turn, gesturing up at the mountain, turning to study Mira – she heard them say her name, and Adeline's – and eventually all nodding agreement. Pierre stood up, bowed a little bow to Mira – '*Mademoiselle, excuse-moi*' – clapped Aziz on the shoulder once more – '*Chiot!*' – and stepped over the low wall, starting back down the slope.

Marie said in English: 'Please. Excuse me. My friends do not speak your tongue. But we were speaking of what must be done. What best chances we have. And we have decided a plan, but if you agree, only. So, Pierre now goes to watch a little more while we talk, and I will get something for us to drink, if you have a thirst.'

Without waiting for an answer, she disappeared into the house, returning with three tall glasses.

'So,' she said again, 'we are like this. Adeline, the child, is hidden in the mountains. She is with her mother. Because of what has happened in your country, I have told this woman about her daughter, and about you. She knows who you are and why you have come here. The child, of course, knows nothing.

'We think now that it is certain that someone will come. If your *Gil* is here, then others will be here too. Perhaps even now they watch us. For this reason, we decided to wait until dark. That is three hours or more. At that time, Pierre will take all others from this village along the path beside the water. They will go to another village, a few hours' walk. There they will be safe. It is not their problem, I think, though many would give their lives for the girl. At that time, I will take you into the mountains. It is better to walk at night in any case. The air is cool, and those who come after you will not so easily see.'

She smiled shyly at Mira. '*Tu es d'accord?* You agree with this plan?'

'*Oui.* Aye. I am happy with whatever you think best. You're very kind.'

They don't need me, she thought: I was foolish to think that they might need me. This Marie, she is a hundred times more capable of looking after Adeline than I would be.

Marie said: 'I will prepare the things we will need. I will also warn those on the mountain to be looking for us and for trouble. If you wish you may sleep, inside in my bed. Or you may eat. Or Aziz can show you the village and the fish farm. It is not much.'

Mira replied: 'If those are my choices, I will go with Aziz, if he doesn't mind. I slept in his boat. I'd like to see the place where my . . . sister has been living.'

The woman smiled, said something to Aziz, bringing the boy's flashing grin out once more. 'There,' she said. 'Look: I do not think he minds too much!'

And that was that. Aziz stood and waited for Mira to follow him – '*Viens, viens!*' – except, before she could go, Marie caught her hand and looked into her eyes. 'It is good that you have come,' she said. 'Really. Thank you.'

'*Viens!*' said Aziz, rolling his eyes.

Gil cursed with irritation when he saw Kay had managed somehow to leave the boat. He hadn't thought the boy was even conscious, certainly not capable of pitching himself out of the dinghy and getting to safety. But then perhaps he hadn't got to safety. The chances were not high, in his condition, with hands and feet bound, in twenty metres of warm water.

Gil scanned the lake all around, but there was no break that he could see in the glassy surface, no soft splash of a swimmer, nor the rolling, bobbing log of a body. No, the boy was definitely dead. Perhaps it had even been deliberate. One thing was for sure: Barbieri would not be pleased, not even having *proof* of death. Still, Gil had handed him the others on a plate: what more did he want, arrogant young sod?

Actually, Gil had had to admit to grudging respect for the Saint lad. He had worked on him for upwards of an hour without a word coming out. Nothing polite, anyway. Then, even when Gil had found the tube of powder – Green Starlight; expensive stuff! – and forced some of that down the prisoner's throat, Kay had still not given him anything important, despite his eyes and mind wandering. With time wasting and the last drops of his fuel gone in midwater, Gil had had to resort to a call to Hunter. They'd got the boy's mother, stuck her on the other end of the vidlink, threatened to start cutting her. *That* had got pretty quick results.

Then he'd had to get close enough to the shore with the oars. They were a bloody joke on these service dinghies; it had taken ages. He'd waited till evening was closing in, and swum to the bank for a little reconnaissance, leaving the dinghy on its mud weight. Sure enough, after he'd watched for a couple of hours, training the nightsight down the inlet, he'd seen his little Mira, *still* with that irritating peasant pie seller, walking by the water.

It was enough. Confirmation of target. He sent the

information to Hunter and swam softly back to his dinghy, already planning the beating he'd give the pie boy for getting too familiar with his Mira.

And then the boat had been empty.

Oh well. The Saint kid had served his purpose. Gil chewed on some bullet-hard rations and settled to wait for the chopper. Much though he'd like to go in alone, Hunter had told him to sit tight, on pain of having his head blown off by the enforcer ring.

The sooner he got rid of *that* thing the better.

Despite what she had said, Mira did eventually sleep. She slept nestled close against Aziz, in the tickly, scented scrub on the slopes above the village. She slept with a smile on her face and a hand thrown loosely over him. She had had her wish and spent a few hours doing nothing more than talk – as far as talking had been possible – and wander about and flirt a little with a boy. She had felt normal.

Watching her sleep, Aziz thought that she was the most beautiful girl he had ever known, strong and sad. Her kisses had been as sweet as honey. He stroked her hair and waited for Marie's signal. When it came – soon, so soon – he reluctantly awakened Mira as he had done in the boat earlier, but using her name now. *'Mira. Ma belle Mira. C'est l'heure. On y va.'*

'Oui, oui,' she murmured sleepily, stretching, *'on y va. Je comprends, Aziz.'*

She felt warm and happy and whole.

Together they went down to the stone house, through the now silent and empty village, to where Marie had three backpacks ready, and mountain shoes for her. *'Ça va?'* Marie asked with a small smile: 'Aziz has taken care of you?'

'*Oui. Ça va très bien.*'

'Ah, soon you will speak French beautifully, I think.'

They shouldered their packs and left the house. It was a fine night for walking, the black sky bright with stars, the air no more than warm. The mountains beckoned Mira, stronger than ever. She reached for Aziz's hand in the shadow.

But Marie signalled them to silence. '*Attend!* Wait! There is something . . .' Her face began to crinkle into fear and despair.

Something. Mira heard it too. *Something.* She knew what kind of something: she'd heard it before. It came rushing low across the water, faster than a mountain eagle and swooped down on its prey, its stark lights blinding them. And there were no lines or wires this time because the thing was settling, there, right in front of them, and spilling out its grey figures.

They were running. Everyone was running and shouting.

Marie had beckoned and screamed at them to follow and was past the chopper, making for the mountain path. She had shrugged off her pack and had opened fire with a weapon of some kind. As Mira ran after her, she saw two of the grey figures fall. But then, next to her, Aziz was knocked down too. She turned to help him up and saw Gil, punching and kicking at the boy like a maniac, grinning as he did it.

With a cry of rage she knocked him aside, sent him sprawling in the dirt like a puppet, reached out to pull Aziz back to his feet. But too late: there were figures all around now. The great grey monsters that had dogged her from the day Annie Tallis had been shot down. She crouched low, putting Aziz behind her, watched the men advance. Even as they came, closing their circle, she thought again with gratitude to all the spirits of how she had been normal this day. A golden day indeed.

The first man was felled by a kick without a sound. Then the second, the third. Mira was like a thing possessed, yet she had never felt so clear-headed.

'Aye. Come on then!' she called to them.

And they did. And when six of them had been knocked down, she felt a stinging pain in her leg, and the world faded to nothing.

She lay in the dirt herself and did not see Jan come to stand over her, holding the stun weapon that she had felt. She did not hear him curse his men and Moore for their incompetence and send three of them, including Moore, after Marie, to try and find where she had hidden the child.

She did not see either, the look of pure compassion that her twin gave her from behind Jan's shoulder.

But then, neither did he.

FORTY-THREE

The next time Mira awoke was very different to the last. Her mouth was dry and felt choked with dust; her head was ringing; there was a continuous pain in her leg. She was in some dark, stuffy place, a building. Her hands were bound tight behind her. There was a figure bending over her, barely visible. The figure said her name, once. Then a tiny light snapped on, and she was looking at her own face.

She tried to make sense of it.

'Wait. Don't try to move,' whispered the face; 'I'll give you another shot. Jan used such a high setting. Wait. You'll be better soon.'

A hand reached out to her arm. There was a tiny pain. Then a thing she didn't know was there was taken off her mouth, stinging her. A piece of tape, perhaps. A bottle was thrust between her lips: beautiful cool water that she could hardly swallow. She gagged, choked, coughed.

'Shhh!' said the face.

In a little time she felt better, as her face had promised. The heaviness left her limbs. She could think more clearly. She was able to put a name to the face.

She whispered it. 'Clarissa.'

'Yes,' said the face, 'Clarissa.'

'But . . . But you hate me.'

The face moved from side to side in a negative. 'No. How could I hate myself, sis?' The face smiled and Mira smiled back.

She said: 'Where are we? Where's Aziz? Marie? Where's the child?'

'We're still in that village: Le Porge. You've been out for two hours. Aziz is the boy you were with? He's in another building, the next one up, pretty beaten up but he'll be OK. Marie is up in the mountains. Moore and a couple of others have gone after her and the little one.'

Mira struggled to move, flexed her limbs. 'Then I must go to help them!'

Clarissa's face smiled: 'Why do you think I'm here, sis? That's the idea.'

Mira said hoarsely: 'We can both go!'

The smile disappeared. ''Fraid not. Jan's still on the prowl. He'll probably check in here again soon. He'll have to see someone or he'll send more men up after you. He's pretty furious already with how his mission is going.' She reached behind Mira and the binding cords were abruptly parted. 'Now. When you feel well enough to move, we'll change clothes. The guard knows I came in here – he thinks it was on Jan's order – and so he'll expect to see me leave. It's a piece of cake. Only . . . don't go storming right off in full view or someone will see and realise. There are guards on each side of the village, including the path to the mountains. Have you got all that?'

Dumbly, Mira nodded. 'But what will he do to you, when he knows?'

Clarissa shrugged. 'Don't worry, he wants to marry me. He'll calm down soon enough.' Mira didn't think that rang true, but the other girl went on: 'Oh yes, the com-card my mother gave you. They took it back when they went through your stuff, but I've stolen it again. I left another in its place. Now, can you stand? Quietly! OK, let's change clothes.'

Mira stood and then they were two halves of a perfect whole. She said: 'My sister.'

'My sister.'

They embraced.

The moment Jan realised that the little bitch was gone from the field tent they'd rigged under the chopper, he knew where she'd be. In a flash, he realised how he must have been fooled, how the little *slut* had used and manipulated him and taken advantage of his unusual mercy over the last few days.

The bitch!

The fury burnt white hot in him. He would make no more mistakes, leave nothing to chance in his desire to appease the Great Families, or the French, or any of them. The girl would be broken, properly broken over weeks or months, as long as it took – he wasn't going to be beaten by such as her – and would then become his obedient wife. As for the other one, the one that had humiliated him in front of the Families . . .

He reached inside the chopper for a weapon. Not a stun gun: something more permanent. Then he ran softly to the building the spare was being kept in.

The guard, seeing his expression, was a babbling flood of excuses. '. . . on your orders . . . assumed you had okayed it . . . member of the Families . . .' Just what he'd grown to expect, since coming to power. Useless. He struck the man down, sent him from his post.

Then he kicked open the door, flicked on his torch.

Yes, they were both there. Rats in his trap. His wife-to-be he struck savagely across the mouth so that she hit the wall hard. The other one, who had already been freed by that *bitch*; for her he did nothing more than raise the gun and fire. And again. And again.

Almost noiselessly, the body slipped to the ground. There was silence except for the soft sobbing coming from his traitorous little viper. Well, there was Lesson One in her re-education.

'Now,' he said, the fury spent, 'there is no point in trying to set free a dead person, is there? I suggest you return to the tent and sleep. And I will be watching for any more tricks. Clear?'

He waited until the girl had stumbled out ahead of him, followed her up the slope to the chopper, saw her lie down inside, her head in her hands, still sobbing. He was glad that he had finally managed to reach her, to make her feel something, through all the little tricks and schemes she used to mock him and the world. He gave a satisfied nod, and went out to contact Moore, find out what the hell was happening up there.

He got no further than lifting his hand to activate the wristcom. A blow from behind, and he was stretched out, unknowing. The girl stood over him, her face smeared with tears. Almost, she took the weapon from his belt and ended it. Gods above, it was what he deserved! She was shaking. She imagined pulling the trigger: the relief.

And yet she was no murderess.

She looked carefully round for the guards' positions, then went to the house where Aziz was sleeping, bound and bruised, and cut his bonds. He would not wake and she could not afford much time, so with difficulty she pulled him out of the house and dragged him into some bushes, until he was well hidden. As an afterthought, she ran back to the chopper and managed to find some water, and took Jan's gun: both of these she lay beside the sleeping pie boy. There, he would have a good chance now. The best she could manage.

Finally, the sorrow and pain of it almost an agony, she

went back into the house where she had been five minutes ago. There, on the floor, she found the golden comcard, overlooked by Jan in his fury.

With this in her tunic, she planted a soft kiss on the cheek of her dead twin, left the house and ran up still further. The guard at the top saw her. She smiled at him, masking the grief. 'I've a message from Lieutenant Barbieri.'

'Yes?' said the guard.

She delivered the message and left him sleeping too.

Then she was away.

FORTY-FOUR

She was the wind.

She was a young deer.

She was free.

The path was parched bare by the baking sun, day after day, and by the feet that had trodden and fashioned it. Even in the dark, it was not hard to follow, or not at first. For half an hour she climbed steadily, breathing more freely with every step, welcoming the mountains that cradled her and kept her hidden from those below.

As for what had happened this night, she thrust it fiercely away from her. There would be time to mourn soon. At that time the grief would engulf her, so strong could she feel it. For now, she must just run, keep her head clear to help the child, if it were not too late. Somewhere . . . *somewhere* up amongst these hard, beautiful, merciless peaks, little Adeline and her defenders were being hunted by three men. She didn't even know *where* . . . yet she would find the way. She would help.

The first obstacle came after forty minutes or so: a division of the ways before a great broken rock, a shadowy hump split into two parts as if by a giant fist, each part many times her own height. Here, the path seemed to circle the rock and become almost a stairway, snaking up the bare cliff ahead. If one turned left, there was another wider way, large enough for three or four to walk abreast, but this seemed to be heading away from the higher peaks again, as if it wanted to dip back down to the water. To the right lay the least promising path of all, more like an old, pebble-strewn streambed than a true path. It meandered across a short open patch of ground, almost flat, and then clung to the bottom of an impossibly steep ascent, dotted with low, twisted trees.

The girl placed her hand on the broken rock. It was still warm from yesterday's sun. She leaned there, taking a moment, looking for any sign on the ground of which way others might have gone. The path to the left seemed too obvious, too large. Could the child have managed the steepest way, the staircase, she wondered. Could she have been carried? Perhaps. Yes, perhaps so.

She tried listening – breath held – for any sound from above or to one side or the other. Nothing was to be seen. Nothing could be heard.

Finally, instinct took her to the right, to the dry stream. She ran that way, over the smooth, clicking pebbles, and then almost at once abandoned the choice, caught in terrible indecision. Yet even now Jan and the men below might be stirring, coming up in fury after her, or calling for reinforcements. She had to go *up*, to become lost high amongst the mountain tops, where they would not find her. So she swallowed down the doubt and ran on, tireless, light-footed, thinking only of freedom and of her purpose in being here.

And as she ran she came suddenly level with a hidden cleft in the steep slope to her right: a narrow, concealed gully that seemed to bear out the idea of an old stream, cutting its way through the rock over millions of years. Again nothing was clear: again she must choose, and she chose the gully, going slowly over the shadowy, loose ground.

At the far end she emerged between two mountain shoulders like sentinels, and discovered that she was at the base of a long, climbing valley, wide and open. Here, whether from the shelter afforded by the slopes, or the slightly colder, higher altitude, or from the moisture the stream had once provided – perhaps did still provide when it rained – there were many more plants. It was a low, thorny scrubland, cupped and shielded by the outer barrier of lesser peaks to the right and the onward march upwards towards the high centre of the chain to the left. Even a rabbit or two moved amongst the bushes, searching out the more succulent leaves, skittering away into the darkness as she sprang past.

And here, she had at last a sign that she had chosen the right way: the lifeless shape of a man in Pax grey, lying across the streambed. Encouraged, but also doubly fearful lest she were too late – spurring herself on with visions of little Adeline falling into the hands of the hunters – she ran as she had never run.

Do this now, this little thing, she thought, or regret the lack of doing for ever.

At the top of the valley, there was a steeper climb, leading up to another narrow way, this time between two low peaks. Her breath felt like knives as she forced one foot in front of the other and made the leg muscles straighten again and again, bearing her slight weight ever upwards. Perhaps it was the altitude, starting to take its toll. She could *hear* the breath being sucked into her lungs; hear it inside her skull even, as a terrible roaring. Then, when she paused for a moment to scramble on all fours over a smooth boulder, shredding the skin from her knees, the roaring carried on.

She stopped and listened. Yes, it was coming from ahead of her: a man growling or calling in pain.

There was soon another body: another man in pale grey, but the noise was further still. She climbed and climbed and came to the remains of some sort of shelter made of cloth, seeming to be attached to the wall of rock on the left. And it was in front of this that the noise was being made. A man sat there in the shadow, leaning backwards, a darker patch staining the clothing all down his right side. He was making a continual anguished growl, and in his lap he cradled the head of the woman, Marie. She had not managed to reach the child before she was overtaken. She lay still, eyes closed.

'Monsieur, Monsieur!' the girl gasped, struggling to get the words out, fighting for breath: 'Où est Adeline? Où est l'enfant?'

He did not answer and she shook him, repeated the question, shouting it in his face. Slowly the eyes swivelled up and seemed to take her in. He raised a languid hand, gestured behind him. 'Adeline? La petite coquine? Descendez un peu. Allez à gauche. Remontez. Il y a un bâtiment là. Un cabin.' The hand waved vaguely, describing the route. Then he seemed to lose interest and slumped forward again, his hand stroking Marie's brow.

On she went, forcing her feet to work, on up between the twin peaks, then sliding and skidding down the loose scree on the other side, tumbling painfully for twenty metres or more when she lost her footing. When she stopped rolling, she stood and turned to look back to the north, to a wide gap that had opened in the wall to her right: to where the dark waters lapped the feet of the mountains.

There was nothing to see, no indication of what might be happening below. But there was, she fancied, the tiniest hint of day growing in the east. Maybe she imagined it: the stars were still as clear as ever above her in a velvet-black sky. As for the air, it was clear and warm even at such a height. How good it would be simply to sit and watch the dawn arrive and breathe that good air.

Move . . . Rest later . . .

She turned back with renewed concentration to the sharp descent in front, sliding and leaping and skipping down, sending little avalanches of dirt and stones bouncing ahead of her. Then there was another, steeper climb, up to the left, as the injured man had told her. A climb and then a cabin . . .

She strained to see any building, but could not. There was only a fingernail of moon tonight: twenty or thirty metres beyond her the mountainside was a uniform dark grey and would most probably stay that way until the sun sent its help. She started up this new climb, once more straining for any sound ahead, going more carefully now that she might be close. Yet a new calmness descended on her. There was no use in imagining horrors. She had seen horrors enough, and made her own choices where she was able: trying to save Adeline was surely the best of all of them. If she was too late, she would think again, find new choices.

The ageless mountains embraced her and cared nothing for her plans or hopes. She ran silently, steadily, picking a careful way across the slope under the stars. In an hour or more she saw the stone building, a farmer's bothy, no more than a vague pale square, above her to the left. She cut across and up, slowing to a careful walk, listening.

In the doorway sprawled an inhuman shape, a man who might even be the brother of the injured man she had seen before. So much blood shed: so much effort to find and to protect a child. The building was dark and quiet, the interior beyond the doorless entrance hidden in shadow. To make certain she went in and felt around the earth floor with her feet, whispering, *'Je suis une amie . . . une amie'*. There was no reply, but her foot caught on something lying near the entrance. She took it outside and saw in the faint light there, a piece of patterned material; a long triangle, something that might have been used to wrap a child or tie a person's hair, perhaps.

At the same moment she heard finally a faint cry, echoing down from somewhere higher up the mountain. A woman's voice, she thought, raised in defiance and terror. She let the strip of cloth fall back to the ground and set off once more, sprinting up the dark rock, trusting her feet to find their own way. Her breath came fast, her body felt light, hard, strong. The muscles in the backs of her legs, flooded by adrenalin, drove her unfalteringly up, up towards where the sound had been. To the right now, a great, dark chasm had opened, a blackness amongst the grey. To the left she came to a place where the rock wall twisted round to become almost vertical. Between these, a narrow path climbed, and on the path, movement, more shouts, confusion . . .

She slowed to a walk and came stealthily upon the scene. There was a man there, ahead, angry, shouting now. Above him, in a cleft in the rock wall where she had climbed, exhausted, a woman was crying, screaming, picking pieces of loose rock from around her and hurling them down at the attacker, not seeming to care that her perch was so precarious. Soon she would run out of stones and the man, who was shielding his head with his hand as he tried to come up towards the woman using feet alone, would be able to advance unopposed.

It was at once apparent that the man had no weapon. Perhaps it had been knocked from his hand by the rain of stones. Perhaps in his arrogance he saw no need for a weapon. No matter. She also had chosen to come unarmed: she was sick of destruction. Her mission was mercy, rescue, not death.

She could see no sign of a child. *Too late*, her senses

screamed. Her stomach lurched with nausea, thinking of the drop that was there. And yet, reason told her that if the child had been dead, the man would not be trying to climb. The woman would surely mean nothing to him. She turned her head, trying to see up above, running her eyes over the rock wall. Sure enough, she heard a tiny, thin voice; the sobbing of a child far above: 'Maman . . . Maman . . . J'ai peur, Maman!'

Unseen by the shouting man, the girl started to climb, trying to work her way up to the level of the voice before she traversed. There were many hand- and footholds, but the rock was loose in places, giving way as she gripped it, so that her body slid back down towards the black chasm below and she had to snatch wildly at other holds to stop her descent. The edges of rock were sharp, cutting into her palms and knees. The third time she slipped, a larger piece of debris bounced noisly away, clicking down over the craggy surface, taking others with it. She hung there unmoving, praying that she hadn't been heard. Further along, and above her, the woman and child were still crying, but the shouting had stopped. The moments passed. Where was he? Was it safe to move?

And then craning down, she saw his head coming along the narrow path, and he was there, ten or more metres below, perfectly still, staring up at where she clung. A patch of dark stained his face – blood from the mother's stones perhaps – but he was still arrogant, smiling, sure of himself.

'Aye,' he called. 'It's well met indeed, Mira. You've done well to get up here like this. What *must* that poor fool Barbieri be up to? Can't seem to get anything right, can he? Never mind. It seems that we must have another drama under the bonny stars. And this time, little Mira, it's your turn to take the fall. Fair's fair.'

He started to climb.

'Go back!' she shouted down. 'Leave me alone. Leave us all. What is that child to you?! It is over. Hadn't you heard? The Saints are finished! Turn back. Let me take the child.'

'I will not.'

She twisted back to the rock and climbed away from him, hearing his heavy breath below her, trying to make her way up and across to where the child still snivelled.

'Go back!' she called again, and again he replied: 'I will not.'

She glanced down. He had not gained; the distance between them remained unchanged as they climbed, and now she saw that the rock wall ahead was becoming less steep again, although still loose and perilous.

'*Maman,*' came the child's tired, tearful voice.

'*Oui. Oui, ma puce. Je monte, j'arrive,*' the woman sobbed.

The girl could see the mother, now, over to her right, making her way up with shaky, feeble movements, looking as if she might give up and slide off the mountain at any moment. And above, between the two of them, she picked out a small shape. Adeline. Her twin.

Her hands were wet with sweat now. It was in her eyes, stinging, half blinding her. Angrily she wiped it aside with her arm. She could *do* this. She needed only courage, patience. As fast as she dared, she made for the child. Behind, the stones rattled as her pursuer tried to close the gap.

'Go back!' she called. 'It is the last warning.'

He laughed from below. 'Little Mira. So you are *warning* me now? How you have changed! You used just to ask: "Please Gil, tell me about cities, tell me about life in other places, tell me who those terrible men were who came to our community." But now you think you know it all. So *sure* that your genes will save you! So *sure* that your line is invincible! And what of me? Do you think I am a plain, dull, talentless Scroat, then? Think again!'

She might have made further reply but that she needed her strength for climbing. Let him think what he wanted. She was almost there. Ten metres, eight, six. To her right, the mother was still trying to scramble up, exhausted, her movements weaker than ever. The child sat in the moonlight, hair dark and shining, eyes large, surprised, watching her.

'*Qui es tu?*' she asked. Who are you?

'*Je suis ta soeur.*' I'm your sister.

'*Ma soeur?*' the little girl said scornfully, as if talking to a child herself: '*Mais je n'ai pas une soeur!*' But I do not have a sister!

The mother, who had heard, stopped trying to climb up and said: '*Si. Si, ma puce. Tu as une soeur! C'est bon. Il ne faut pas avoir peur!*' Yes, my little one, my flea. You have a sister! All is well. You need not be afraid!

With a last lunge, she reached the tiny, bright-eyed child. She was sitting in what was almost a natural chair in the rock, her legs swinging over the edge. The huge eyes dominated her face. The girl wanted to hug the child, look at her, hold her close, keep her safe, but Gil was now coming to the easier part of the slope. He would be no more than two or three minutes.

'How are we to move you, then?' she said gently. She put her arms under the girl's shoulders and lifted. She was not heavy, and yet heavy enough to make escape uncertain.

'The end, Mira,' Gil called up, scrambling crablike over the grey rock. 'A pity. There might have been much between us!'

The girl bent, with her back to Adeline and pulled the

small hands over her shoulders. The child did not resist, so she straightened up, taking the weight on her back, testing it.

'*S'il vous plaît*,' whimpered the woman, who had stopped moving below and simply hung wretchedly onto the rock. '*Sauvez l'enfant! S'il vous plaît!*'

'Too late,' Gil snarled.

The girl turned to the rock face and started to climb once more – 'Hold tight, little one, I'll need my hands.' She did not know where she was climbing to, only that the danger was at their heels, and that if she should turn to face it, a life would be lost; perhaps more than one. With strength she did not know was there, she pulled them both up, the girl murmuring some nursery song to herself and clinging tightly to her neck with sharp little fingers so that her rescuer could hardly breathe.

How long it went on, she did not know. Gradually they made their way up towards what looked like the top of the climb, a place where the mountainside had been broken or split, and steadily, centimetre by centimetre, Gil came closer to them. Twice, his reaching hand grabbed at her foot. Twice she kicked it away and climbed on faster. She was sobbing herself now, the child still strangely calm and trusting on her back.

It was no good. She wouldn't be able to stay ahead. She couldn't hold the child all the way to the top of the mountain. The decision was made. It was to be Adeline's life, or Gil's.

'*Assis. Assis*,' she whispered to the girl. Sit. Sit. At the same time she turned and lowered the little body towards the ground. Obediently the child sat down, still humming, and began to suck her thumb.

Thus unburdened, and taking in a great gasp of air,

Clarissa made her muscles relax. She stood, feet apart, braced on the slope as she would be for Slam, and looked at the figure approaching. She should give the salute, the bow of the head, she thought, curiously detached: she should wait until he was up and ready, but then this was not Slam.

'Will you not turn back?' she asked, softly.

'I will not then, Mira,' he answered, his eyes locked on to hers.

'I am not Mira. And you have not the right to speak her name.'

He was there now, scrambling up, half running, half climbing, rushing at her, confusion and anger on his face at her words.

She came down to meet him. It was such a simple thing. So small. She saw him come, measured his size and strength, the anger in him, saw the moment when he was not quite balanced . . . and nudged almost gently at the front foot, so that the ankle turned as he put it down. Then, as he fell to one knee, cursing, she stepped lightly behind him, took his shoulders, twisted sharply to the left, and let go.

A full point at least.

The body rolled and bounced down the slope. There was hardly a noise, save for that; the sound of a soft, heavy thing on rock and the skittering of the scree. She thought he would stop himself with the spread limbs that grasped for a hold. She started down the slope to finish it. Yet there was no need. At the lip of the steeper section the shape that was Gil hung briefly, then disappeared.

She went down there to see. He would not resurrect himself again to haunt their days. The shape of him lay sprawled and twisted on the path far below.

*

When the mother came upon them, Clarissa and the child were both hugged together, asleep on the grey rock, softened by the sliver of moon. She reached out and touched them, stroked the two heads of dark hair. Two children where she had had one.

She would let them sleep while she watched. Then, when day came, she would have to wake them. Others would be coming, Marie had said. Others who wished to harm the younger girl and the one who was almost a woman. There would be goodbyes. At least for now.

FORTY-FIVE

When she saw the parachutes, far away, Clarissa laughed aloud.

All across the northern flanks of the mountains, dropping from a sleek silver shape in the sky like a curtain of white flowers, swaying softly in their descent against the deep blue. As many as thirty of them. A last roll of the dice. Jan, or the old skeletons, must be desperate, or consumed with anger. Yes, that was more likely. Or perhaps, after all, he had got the French families to help him.

'*Belle!*' said little Adeline, pointing with delight.

'*Oui. Belle!*' she agreed. The schoolroom French she had learned with Kay would soon come back. When it did, she would tell the child about her other sister, who had given freedom to both of them. About all her sisters.

'Come on!' Clarissa said brightly: '*On y va*. Let's show these poor souls that we were born to the mountains.'

They stood at the highest point. All around, the great raw, twisted shapes marched away, blue and green and brown in the sun. The two girls turned away from the white flowers and looked down at the next wooded valley and the peaks rising beyond.

Clarissa took Adeline up on her back, and ran on, the girl bouncing and giggling, her impossible eyes alive with the excitement of a strange new day.

As for the men in grey: they were not important. For this day, they were nothing.

AUTHOR NOTE

A word about climate change, cloning and the background to Sharp North.

How did Mira's world become as it is in this story?

Well, it is widely known that rapid climate change is taking place right now. It has probably been known for twenty or thirty years, yet this is one of the many life-changing issues that governments really don't want to tell the truth about. It is, after all, much easier to have a good wrangle about fox hunting, about house prices, or about quarter per cent interest rate increases, than to tell people that they need to change the way they travel, consume or work.

The way in which climate change will affect Britain is not clear. One scenario, the one that I have chosen to adopt for this story, is that the warm ocean current coming across the Atlantic from Central America will fail. This current keeps us temperate (i.e. comfortable and warm) even though our country is as far north as the snowy wastes of Canada or the frozen forests of northern Russia. Its failure might well be brought about by melting arctic ice because the added fresh water would change the percentage of salt content of the cold currents that in turn become our benign North Atlantic Drift. (High salinity is vital to the working of the transatlantic current system.) So, while global warming widens desert areas and causes average temperatures in many parts of the world to rise dramatically, we could expect that northern Europe will experience a sharp *drop* in temperatures, bringing constant ice and snow to our shores for a long time.

In *Sharp North*, a couple of centuries or more from now, this process is almost complete. In other words, Britain has been through its deep-freeze years and is warming up again, finally thawed out by the vastly changed temperatures worldwide. Only in Mira's Scotland is there the remains of the ice. Further south there is a band of constantly turbulent weather where warm air meets cold, lying across much of England, including the windswept capital. Obviously rising ocean levels (from those melting ice caps) will also have taken their toll, flooding many lowland areas and causing whole cities to disappear.

Some scientists estimate that changes such as these could occur extremely quickly. The deep freeze, for example, might click in in the next twenty years, almost overnight. (As soon as the North Atlantic Drift fails, our temperature falls!)

By Mira's time, the climate change scenario has had profound effects. I envisage that populations have had to decrease sharply to meet available resources, travel is difficult and uncommon, fossil fuels are very scarce, and huge industrial economies are a thing of the past. Technological development has frozen as the world warmed up, thanks to the flooding, the displacement of whole populations, the collapse of infrastructure and so forth: so much of what is available to those future Britons is what we would find now. However, genetic technologies are still available – kept so by the Families – and cloning and genetic screening have been used as an elitist tool to retain power.

Human cloning may or may not have already occurred by the time you read this, but if it hasn't, then it will be along very shortly. The vested interests are such that governments get ever closer to it, eroding the safeguards with each round of legislation, especially when they worry that someone else might get there first. Why is it going to happen? Is it for humanitarian reasons? Well, I doubt it. Couples are already asking to choose the sex of their children, when that is possible. Who can doubt that they will in future be asking about hair colour, sportiness, intelligence, good looks, life expectancy . . .? Here, then, is the root of the kind of elitism we see in *Sharp North*. Mira and her sisters are ostensibly the best there is: sharp, agile and beautiful. But what must they feel like themselves? What kind of a mess does being a clone make of their lives?

Ultimately, Mira's answer to all those who seek to mould or control her is simple, powerful and loving; and spreads outwards in ripples, bringing light to many other lives.

Patrick Cave
February 2004